GARDEN OF THE 8TH CIRCLE

AN INFINITES NOVEL

ELLEN CURTIS
MATTHEW LEDREW

GARDEN OF THE 8TH CIRCLE

AN INFINITES NOVEL

ELLEN CURTIS
MATTHEW LEDREW

ENGEN BOOKS

Published in Canada by Engen Books, St. John's, NL.

Library and Archives Canada Cataloguing in Publication

Title: Garden of the 8th circle : an infinites novel / Ellen Curtis, Matthew LeDrew.
Other titles: Garden of the eighth circle
Names: Curtis, Ellen, 1993- author. | LeDrew, Matthew, 1984- author.
Description: Series statement: Infinity ; 4
Identifiers: Canadiana (print) 20200296744 | Canadiana (ebook) 20200297201 | ISBN 9781989473658
  (softcover) | ISBN 9781989473665 (PDF)
Classification: LCC PS8605.U78 G37 2020 | DDC C813/.6—dc23

Distributed by:
Engen Books
www.engenbooks.com
submissions@engenbooks.com

First mass market paperback printing: August 2020

Cover Image: Ellen Curtis

For our friend,
Paul Carberry
and his daughter,
Dana Carberry.

PROLOGUE

Payson, Arizona

Before it all went very, very wrong -- we wanted to let you know that things *could* be good. There is lightness in this world, no matter how much the darkness tries to suffer it out. Madison Williams knew that, even as she stretched bracing tape over her knee and tried to stop the blood that was oozing forth from it.

"Get back in there!" someone yelled from the huddle of players on the bench, as someone scooped the soccer ball out from under their captain's deft feet. The cleats scraped against each other, passing like ships in the night, and all at once the progress they'd made in corralling the ball toward the southern goalpost was lost. The crowd that had been cheering for Madison now groaned, and the crowd that had been groaning cheered.

Madison cursed and slapped her knee in frustration as she got up, sending sharp shoots of pain up her thigh that she regretted, but used to her advantage. She used it like energy, gritting her teeth and transforming it into fuel. She stepped back toward the ball, limped three times, then found her footing and broke into a jog, then a run. As her pace increased so did the din of the crowd around her, starting with applause and ending in hoots and hollers, yells and horns as she reached her full speed. She was the fastest in her league and within seconds was just behind the player who had stolen the ball away from their team.

She was sixteen, with long blonde hair that moved as one solid wave back and forth as she ran for the ball. She was five-five, one-hundred and twenty pounds, with that sort of clear complexion that most people had to pay obscene amounts of money -- or master Photoshop -- to achieve. She came by it naturally, her sun-kissed cheeks and forehead all the evidence of their authenticity needed. People were naturally drawn to watch her, with that sort of expected, asexual attraction that infants had to some faces. Eyes were drawn to her, and she made sure that while they were on her she did something to impress.

She poured on the speed and dove in front of the opposition's lead runner, extending her leg and scooping the ball out from under him and rolling out of the way. He continued forward several steps, as if taking a moment for his momentum to realize what had happened. The ball had gone sideways, into the waiting steady foot of Madison's best kicker, who was now bolting his way up to the southern edge of the field.

Though she'd tried to protect her knee, the skid that resulted from her dodge caught the edge of her wrap and ripped it clean again, the bandages fluttering in the breeze like a mummy's wrap. She cursed again as blood found its way to air, no longer held at bay by the tightly wound cloth and flowing freely down the calve of her leg. She hissed as the air stung at the gash, crimson somehow getting onto her green jersey and making a red sash across her number, 42. She shot her head up and looked downfield to see Tim Grimes -- and his shimmering vinyl number 88 -- kick the winning goal into the blue team's net. Their goalie dove, both hands outstretched, and for one glorious, slow-motion moment all involved hung in midair, breaths caught in chests and hands clamped tight. The ball slid between the reach of her deft fingers, continued forward, then crashed into the back of the net, shoving it backward.

The crowd was on their feet instantly, their roar deafening, as Madison's team surrounded her. Fans of her team yelled for her, while fans of the opposing team yelled at the upset -- but as Madison's teammates gathered around her and her smile grew until her cheeks hurt, she gazed out onto the crowd and almost everyone was yelling and whooping cheering.

Except, she noticed, a group of three blonde girls that stood just to the left of the bleachers. They stood silently; their faces as devoid of emotion as if they were watching numbers on an excel spreadsheet scroll by. They stood, each of them with their arms crossed behind their backs, in descending order of height. The tallest's arm was intersected with the leg of the bleachers, wearing a black-and-white horizontal-striped shirt with a leather jacket. The girl next to her wore a pink dress shirt with a cat's face knitted into the torso of it. The smallest -- no more than ten -- was wearing a yellow sun dress. They all had eyes of a deep blue, thin noses that expanded out at the nostrils, and a plump, well-defined jawline that came down to a squared chin.

Madison stared at them for a long moment, her smile fading only slightly as her teammates circled around her. She tore her gaze away several times as her team swarmed her, but each time some unknown itch in the back of her eye made her vision sink back down, away from the adoring crowds and to these three -- these specters, standing like statues, with the glow of the afternoon sun caught in their golden hair and making it shine like halos.

She turned back to the bleachers, where she saw her father, Cliven, shaking both his fists in cheer, a broad smile over his lips. He was balding except for wild patches of gray behind his ears and was waving a green felt triangular flag on a long plastic stick. In any other circumstance he would have looked like a madman, but here he was simply the loudest of a large crowd of supporters.

"She did it, Lindsay!" Cliven yelled, shaking his fists with the excess energy and adrenaline of the match. "Madison, she did it! Did you see that!"

"Yes!" Lindsay yelled, turning to Cliven and kissing him full and forceful on the cheek.

"You her folks?" a man sitting in the row in front of them asked, turning and smiling. He was waving his own green felt flag, but with slightly less enthusiasm than when he had started.

"Yes," Cliven said, smiling. He turned to the man, who extended a hand to him, and Cliven took it and shook it.

"You must be proud. Co-Ed Leagues are hard; she stood her own."

Lindsay Williams beamed with pride as her husband clasped the hand he was shaking with his other hand.

"Thank you, yes," he said, his cheeks pushing up against the edges of his eyes. "Yes, we're very proud of her. Good grades, too. She's great, she's --"

He turned back to the crowd of green jerseys that had dominated the corner of the field a moment ago and had now made its way up the centre field. It was hard to tell with the mix of blonds and redheads and brunettes... but he didn't see his daughter's straight curtain of blonde bobbing from side to side as they made their way up the field. None of the crowd was meeting his eye either, as she so often did, their faces always finding each other in a crowd.

For reasons he couldn't have known at that exact moment, his smile began to falter and sidle back down his face. His grip on the man's hand eased and he let his other hand fall aside, dropping the hard, plastic straw that held her team flag. His head scanned left as if on a dolly, lolling over the rest of the field: the only green it found was the grass itself.

"Lindsay," he said, his voice wet and hoarse all at the same time. "Where's Madison?"

Lindsay turned to where her daughter had last been and found that there was now only vacant field. She tracked the course of the team huddle and scanned each face, moving from person to person with increasing anxiety, before standing in her seat and turning around to look out over the bleachers. "Madison?" she said. Then louder again: "Madison?!"

Cliven got up and started to push his way past the crowd, making his way down towards the team.

"Madison!" Lindsay screamed again, though too

many others were still doing the same, cheering her name with delight. Only those closest to her noticed that her tone was not the same as theirs -- it was bereft of cheer, and with each utterance more and more anxiety crept in, like a cancer.

She spun, trying to see around the edges of the bleachers to see if her daughter had disappeared beneath them to see a friend or teammate away from the crowd.

In the distance, just beyond the edge of the parking lot and stepping out into the expanse of the vacant field beyond, were four blonde girls, walking away in unison. They walked in a straight line, in order of descending height.

The second from the right had a long curtain of hair that bobbed back and forth when she walked, and beneath her arm was a bundle of green fabric.

CHAPTER 01

The Payson Mall was hot and humid from population: bodies filtering in and pushing about, and a wide glass ceiling that let in sunlight but kept in heat. It was chilled outside but inside it was too warm to keep a coat on, and the air conditioners worked overtime to battle against it. The Food Court was the worst of it: thirty or more mini-kitchens packed into a tight, cramped space, each one frying and searing and boiling their own dishes, made to order for the masses. The heat fought to leave people as they moved from the cashier to their seat and then away to another cashier, radiating out of their pores in waves that could be felt and seen in the mist above each stovetop.

It was the way Victor liked it, cramped and hot. It reminded him of home.

He was a broad man, with shoulders that seems to stretch out forever and long, blond hair that was smeared unevenly over his chin in ragged, unshaven scruff. He wore black shirts, almost exclusively, and the sort of big belt buckles that one associated with men from Texas -- though as far as anyone knew, he was not. His chest was wide but tapered in quickly. He looked like a Viking, dressed like a cowboy, but moved through the busy masses of the mall like a ballet dancer.

He lifted his tray to avoid some small children that were running past him, smiled as he watched them go, then took his place at his table with four others.

Chad Matthews looked up from his phone as Victor sat down, doing a double take as he noticed the dish that the older man had sat down with. It was a mess of gray-green chunky sludge topped with alternating swirls of bright red and a viscous, textured brown. To Chad's eyes it looked more like the aftermath of food than food itself, and he felt his gag reflex urge. "What the heck is that?" he asked, dropping his knees from the edge of the table to lean closer. Chad had blond hair much like Victor's, except more the tone of hay than Victor's gold. He was lanky, and his hair bobbed out in front of him when he moved forward, so he pushed it back.

"It's Peanut Green Stew," Abby said, taking a bite of one of her fish cakes. She was short and slight, her auburn hair back in a ponytail. She was wearing a t-shirt with the happy face from Nirvana's *Nevermind* album on it. It had ripped sleeves and she'd bought it that way. It had been a favorite of hers for the last month, in constant rotation. She'd been surprised to learn that Nirvana had been a band. "He gets it at the Vietnamese place, they're the only place in town that'll make it for him."

Chad curled his lip. There was a flat crepe beneath the jiggling mess of brown and green and red, as though it were meant to be served as a wrap, even though there was far too much of it to have wrapped. It was also far too…

liquid-y.

Theo watched this exchange but did not enter it. There was a thin layer of sweat over his brow, but not from the heat. He was swallowing often, his gaunt, rough cheeks a pale shade of green. He took a deep breath, exhaled, then took a bite of his gyro. Tiny curds of goat cheese tumbled out from between wisps of shredded spinach and black olive. He picked them off his plate and ate them as well.

Theo watched as Victor took a large forkful of his meal, which somehow was solid enough to stay on his utensil, and shoveled it into his mouth. He chewed out one side of his cheek, swallowed, then motioned to Chad: "You can have some, if you want."

Chad shook his head emphatically. "No actually, I'm good."

Theo grinned slightly as he watched it, then turned across the table to Alice, who was chewing her chicken-corn soup and watching the exchange with the same sort of resigned acceptance that he did. She turned to him as well, and when neither said anything they shrugged in near simultaneous precision and went back to their meals.

Chad opened his can of Dr. Pepper, wiped the lip with his sleeve, then took a short sip. He placed the can back down on his orange tray, where it stood alone, looking more like an art display than a meal. An odd modern update of Warhol's Campbell's Soup Cans.

Abby was in mid-bite of her second fish cake when she noticed, finally, that the only thing on Chad's plate was a can of sugary cola. Her hand fell and her head fell forward slightly, hanging as if she were a puppet whose strings had been cut. "Please don't tell me that's all you have to eat?"

Chad shrugged.

Abby ran her fingernails through her hair. "You can't just... you're going to get scurvy."

"He's too lucky to get scurvy," Victor said calmly, between bites.

"You know what he ate yesterday? Potato chips. Nothing else. Just... potato chips."

Victor paused, then nodded. "He *may* get scurvy."

Abby huffed, looked back at her paper plate of food, then slid the extra plate she'd taken to guard against the heat of it out from underneath.

Theo watched as she started to assemble several cakes of fried fish from her plate onto the second, then he turned to Chad, focusing his gaze just past the blond man's head and lingering there for a moment. "Don't," he said after a moment, waving at Abby without looking at her.

She paused.

"This was his plan from the start. He knew you'd take pity on him."

Abby stopped, narrowed her eyes across the table at Chad, then dumped the food back onto her own plate.

Chad furrowed his brow and raised both hands to Theo. "What the hell, man."

Theo shrugged and took another bite of his gyro.

"Offer still stands for some of mine," Victor said.

"I'll pass, thanks. It looks like tomato paste and peanut butter."

"It actually *is* tomato paste and peanut butter," Victor chuckled, chewing.

"Lucky guess," Chad mumbled, as several people brushed past him to make their way through the hall between tables. The halls between the table were moderately wide, but then, so were the majority of the people who frequented the mall. "This place is packed today," he continued, turning around. "What gives."

"Flea market," Victor replied. "Second Tuesday of every month the shops close early and the hall space is used for tables. It's popular, it gets crowded."

Alice looked from Chad to Victor, and then back again. She pushed her dark hair out of her face to keep it out of her soup, then took another spoonful of it. It was thick, with large chunks of chicken that you could tell were hand-separated. No machine-made chunks of chicken that large or unwieldy. They were big enough that the meal may have represented a legitimate choking hazard for anyone under the age of ten.

Theo looked up and around at the crowd that orbited around them again, fresh drips of sweat squeezing from his pores.

To everyone else the main source of light in the grand dining area was the open skylight above. There were streetlamp-like poles stationed at intervals throughout the area, but they were off during the day and turned on automatically when the light from the sky got dim enough. To Theo, there were more lights in the room -- a light for almost every person in attendance. Every man, woman, non-binary and child had their own screen behind them. It was a billboard that displayed their thoughts: a representation of whatever was on their mind. There were album covers playing pop songs that were stuck in people's heads, memories of gleeful children, and sexual fantasies. There was everything a human was thinking on, each on a large hi-def screen that yelled for attention and couldn't be turned off.

There was a child screaming on his left, and to his right was an obese man sitting alone who couldn't help but focus on the shrill sound. His screen was the screaming child again, and it continued until the penetrating yell was in surround sound on either side of him. Theo grimaced, a shudder running down his spine as he tried to block it out, then forced himself to take another bite of his gyro. Sauce squeezed its way out through the loose seams of its breaded pouch, draining and dripping into a pinkish pool on his tray.

Victor watched him as he chewed the boiled spinach leaves of his meal, slurping the green leaves coated with brown and red. He picked up his complimentary paper napkin and wiped his mouth, then stood. "Come with me," he said, motioning to Theo.

Theo cocked an eyebrow at him. He was still chewing his gyro.

"What's going on?" Abby asked.

"Field training," Victor smiled. He picked up the remainder of his Peanut and Greens Stew and placed it onto Chad's tray.

Chad recoiled slightly as the sweetness of the nuts and the tartness of the spinach and tomato reached his nostrils.

Theo squinted, then took the last bite of his gyro and stood, wiping the last of the sauce from his lips. The two of them turned and walked away from the table and into the deep of the mall, away from the bright of the skylight and into the artificial din of the halls of shops and kiosks that were already preparing to close up for the market.

Abby watched them go, her eyebrows knitted together in something approaching apprehension.

Chad inched the plate of multicoloured food away from him until it was in almost the exact centre of the table between the three of them, and then took a sip of his soda.

Abby frowned, then scooped a large portion of the Peanut Greens off her plate and slopped it down onto her own, revealing the soft tortilla shell underneath. She cut off a chunk of it with her fork and scooped it onto her plate as well, then replaced them with three fish cakes and fries.

Alice rolled her eyes and then did the same, taking the remainder of the Peanut Greens from the centre plate and replacing them with a small plate of her chicken corn soup. It was chunky to stay on the paper plate, leaving most of the broth in her bowl. She took a tentative bite of the Peanut Greens, paused, shrugged, and then put a large forkful into her mouth.

"Gee thanks guys," Chad said, smiling with bathos sincerity as he pulled the plate back toward himself, moving his half-empty can of cola out of the way to make room for it. "You really didn't have to --"

"Oh, shut up," Abby smirked, taking a heaping bite of her greens. They were surprisingly good.

In a coffee shop named Birch Dozens that was nestled

on the lower floor of the mall, two people sat at the booth nearest the archway that led back out into the market proper, one male and one female. He was tall and lanky, and she was less so of each. She had deep blonde hair and wore horn-rimmed glasses that glinted purple in the light. The names printed on the sides of their paper cups with smiley faces were 'Marcus' and 'Carla.'

They sat and watched the patrons of the mall walk back and forth, even as the other customers of the cafe changed and moved from their seats, cognizant of the fact that it would soon be closing. Marcus looked out upon those masses hawk-like, finding a person, studying them, then turning away to the next once he'd reached some internal quota.

Carla also looked out upon the crowd, but with less interest. Her straw played against the edges of her mouth and between her fingers. For a long moment, her eyes lingered on a small redheaded child whose plumped fingers were outstretched towards a man who looked very much like her. She was mouthing gibberish, yet the father understood, and a moment later she was on his shoulders and laughing.

Marcus found someone off in the distance, too far away to have seen them, and trained his eye on them. He followed her, a woman trailing two children in her wake, until Carla's oscillation with the straw caught his eye. "Are you okay?" he asked, shifting his attention to her.

She did not respond, not hearing him at first over the drone of the crowd, so focused was she on the abyss that lay just beyond her vision. After a moment, her gaze snapped to him, and she forced a smile that was devoid of emotion. "I'm fine." Her nose twitched twice and she sniffed back only once, then sighed and forced herself to focus on the crowd in front of them.

He hesitated, unsure of himself in a way that was only socially acceptable in boys of a certain age that he'd already outgrown. He reached out suddenly and touched her hand with his own, working his thumb into the cavern of her palm. "Think about how close we are. That promised land... it's almost here. We're almost there. We are breathing air of its trees, even now."

She winced, her gaze falling back to the child with red hair and her father for only a minute, before she scoffed and arose from her chair. "Let's go," she said. "There's no one here and we have supplies to get."

Marcus looked at her with some small amount of surprise. "If you're not up to it, I can --"

"Move," she said. Her tone would have been harsh if there were emotion in it at all. She stared at him in a way that implied she would not say it again.

After a moment, Marcus got up and followed her out of the coffee shop.

The main hall of the Payson Mall took several branches and corridors away from the food court, making room for as many shops and businesses as it possibly could within the same limited space. All of them converged back at the escalators, though. An aerial view of the mall would have looked yonic, with the food court at the base spreading out into arches of hallways, each of which came back to meet at its peak. The escalators were as far as the top floor went, the area beyond stretching out to the jewelry stores and fashion accessory shops. The lower floor continued back beneath them as well, stretching back to the food court itself and housing coffee shops, cell phone providers, gadget shops, and bookstores. The area below the escalators was wide and open, the most void-of-sell-space area of the entire mall. It was used to house Christmas villages and Easter huts, and other seasonal events, but today it was full of people setting up foldable tables as they prepared their goods for the Tuesday Market.

The space was fuller than Theo had ever seen it, filled with patrons and sellers and friends of each, workers closing up the traditional shops, and security. There were several long tables of used comic books being set up, and a gaggle of eager teens waited along the side for the market to open so that they could rifle through them for a hidden gem or collectable.

Theo and Victor looked down upon it all from the glass railing that marked where the upper floor stopped short. There was an ascending escalator on their left, and a descending one on their right. People travelled up to the top floor and down to the bottom in seemingly equal numbers, and thus the sea of the gathered masses below them remained a steady swarm of talking and moving and yelps and odors.

And each and every one of them had their own screen behind them that only Theo could see. Everyone was yelling out a Technicolour scream to be heard, to be seen, to be paid attention to: except Victor. Victor had no screen behind him; he never had.

Theo winced as the brightness of the screens grew so

collectively bright that it would have blinded him had it not been chiefly visible in his mind's eye. "What are we doing?" he asked. He tried to block the screens with his hand, but it was in vain. They were thoughts. He could see their glow through his palm, diminished barely at all by his perception of their placement.

Victor leaned out onto the glass railing, putting his weight on its stainless-steel edge. He arched his feet, leaning forward until his nose dangled over the steep drop to the concrete tiled floor below, closed his eyes, and took a deep, calming breath. It was as though he were trying to breathe in the masses, to take the scent of their perfume and cologne and body odor and take it all in as one whole, the way strawberry and ice cream mixed together to form the memory of the ice cream parlor next to his grandmother's house.

"Victor?"

"We're hunting," Victor replied, opening his eyes even as he fished his phone out of his pocket and turned it on. There were three separate text notifications that he dismissed, then he opened the camera app and aimed it down at the crowd. He held it out and away from him, almost as someone did when they were about to take a selfie, except he had the device in landscape mode. Theo wasn't sure if the selfie-similarity was an intentional effort to disguise the action, or if Victor perhaps had legitimate issues seeing the screen if not. Victor cocked his head out toward the null space beyond the camera's focal point: "What do you see?"

Wincing, Theo turned and stared down at the horde of screens stepping slowly from one space to another.

There were forty-two different songs playing, none of them with the same beat, tempo, or cadence. Several were in different languages. Some were perfect recreations of the songs performed by the original artists: those people had ear buds in and their screens were just rebroadcasting the signal. Others were songs stuck in people's heads, and he'd learned over the years that *nobody* ever remembered a song exactly right. The brain jumbled the lyrics, sped up the tempo, mistook the chorus. There was a blonde girl wearing a long-sleeved white jumper who was mentally singing along to Taylor Swift's *Style* but changing the lyrics from "out of style" to "out for a while" with no hint of irony. She was gone in an instant though, hidden behind four other screens. A dozen or more screens were X-rated in the extreme: sometimes with fantasy, sometimes with memory, sometimes with the preoccupation of picturing the people in their lines-of-sight in the buff. Several others also featured adult-content but took their subjects to an extreme place: beyond sex, and far into violence. The people with those screens behind them seemed calm, they didn't appear sinister, and yet there were acts so depraved on their screens that Theo wasn't even comfortable classifying it as sex.

There were budgets being balanced, children being thought of. There were anxieties and fears and joys and sorrows, all on display and all the most important thing there was, to that person, at that time. Each of those importances infested Theo's mindscape. He couldn't just see and hear those thoughts... that was the practical effect, the way his brain sorted the information into something he could process. In truth, they were becoming his thoughts:

he was absorbing them, each wanting priority, until there were so many voices in his head, he found it hard to hear his own.

"Unn," he said, forcing his eyes shut tight and looking down towards the ground between his feet -- like someone fighting carsickness. He shook his head, trying to force the last remnants of the songs he'd had implanted into his skull out. "There's too much, too many."

Victor nodded. He lowered his phone, which Theo only now realized had been in video mode. "It must feel like being in Black Springs."

Theo turned to him apprehensively, then nodded.

In his youth, when his ability to see the thoughts of others had first begun to manifest, Theo Flaherty had been incarcerated in a mental health facility called Black Springs. There, his powers had grown, and at night he'd been able to 'see' into the minds of his fellow patients -- murderers, schizophrenics, and the disturbed. Their thoughts had travelled across the void of space between them and entered him, and without any knowledge of what they were, he'd thought they were his own. It had taken him years to develop the boundaries and the visualization tools needed to process the stimuli as external: as video screens that were wheeled behind people, the projections on them flapping out the back of their heads, full of sound and HD 1080p. Sometimes they were 3D. But no matter how far he'd come, the mention of Black Springs still had the ability to send cold shocks down his spine.

Victor's face was expressionless, the perfect definition of a poker face. He turned back to the crowd, watching them mill about with an odd chaotic regularity. They moved randomly, but somehow still formed rough lines as they passed around each other. It was something he found unique to Western culture: people forming themselves into lines.

In some of the countries he'd visited, men only walked themselves into lines when they were stepping before a firing squad.

"Try again... focus on just one of them."

Theo frowned, took a deep breath, then raised his head again. Again, the screens assaulted him, like several hundred televisions blaring, most on different channels. He started to squint. "I'm can't, I -- why are we --"

"How do you see them?" Victor interrupted. "Is it little pools of light, is it colour, is it --"

"It's screens. Everyone has a screen behind them, and it displays what they think. It shows me what they're thinking... right now. As though I'm watching it on a television, or a billboard. With sound."

Victor nodded. He looked out at the crowd, as though in describing it Theo had suddenly made it visible to him. "Turn back again."

Theo did, wincing from the effort of it.

"Where are they plugged in, the TVs?"

"They're not... they're not plugged in. They're not real. They're just screens that kind of... float there. There are no cords."

"Make them," Victor said, bluntly. "The screens aren't there. Your mind made the screens, so make the cords. Make them stick out of the back like thick, black tendons, and they all run into power bars, and all the power bars drag behind people. Then group them together, maybe.

A Mom and Dad and Baby might each have their own screen, but they share a power bar. They're a unit."

As skeptical as he'd been, Theo was starting to see it. The cords came out from behind the screens, just as Victor said. They fell straight down, without the hindrance of a shelving unit or entertainment station to obstruct them. They looked like the thickened, twisted strings of helium balloons, which in turn made the screens' weightlessness noticeable for the first time.

"Got it," Theo nodded. "Yes."

"Start pulling plugs," Victor said. "Pick someone -- one person -- you want to focus in on, and leave his power bar. Everyone else: start yanking. Power bars, they have those big, red buttons. Picture them, and start stepping on them."

In Theo's mind's eye, screens started going dark. They didn't disappear though: they remained hovering behind each person, like rectangular black obelisks, just waiting to be reactivated. Some kept the glow of the last image that had been on on them, the way CRT screens had up until the late 90s. "It's... working," he said slowly, unsure of himself.

Several screens he'd turned off flickered back to life.

"I can't keep them off."

"That'll come," Victor said. "Or it won't. You don't need them off forever... if I could show you that, you could just turn your powers off completely. That's not how this works. It's like a sense: you can't just turn off your sense of smell, but you can will yourself to ignore a pungent odor, as long as it's not too unwieldy."

Theo nodded, continuing to flip switches. Despite the

fact that they came back on, it was like a game almost: how many can you make go dark before they shutter back to life, with that fake electronic hum that his mind added for affect? He was sweating from the strain of it, garlic-flavored salt-water rolling into his ocular orbit and narrowly avoiding stinging his eye.

"Pick someone to keep light. Get as many others dark as you can, then focus in on one."

Theo squinted, finding a heavy-set male with no facial hair who was standing in front of a long white box filled with comic books, flipping through them with the same speed that card sharks shuffled cards. The screen behind him was a still image, not a video. It was a mostly purple image with two cartoon characters entangled in each other on it, their limbs stretched and contorting as they fought. The lower of the two he recognized instantly as Spider-Man, the dominant character a flaming skull clad in leather with pinprick red eyes. The sound that accompanied it was humming, but it was nothing to do with the image. The youth was humming to himself, the theme to The Great Escape.

"Do you have something?" Victor asked.

Theo nodded. "The kid in the red, by the comic-book tables. He's thinking of the comic he's looking for, it's a Spider-Man comic. It's not a video, it's just a still image."

"Who's on the cover?" he asked, without emotion. He asked as though the question were on a sheet in front of him, like a queue card.

"Spider-Man. And another guy, he's a skeleton. He's scary looking, flaming."

"What's his name?"

"I don't -- Ah, Ghost Rider. It's Ghost Rider."

Victor nodded and stepped forward until he was in Theo's field of view. He was staring at the male in the too-tight red shirt now as well. "Tell me what he wants to do once he leaves here."

Theo scrunched his nose, then turned away from the crowd. "That's not how it works. My powers, they don't... I can only see the surface-level thought. Like a radio feed."

"You knew the name of that character. You didn't, at first. Where did you get that from?"

Theo paused. "I don't... I don't know."

"You told me once at Black Springs you saw that a man had abused his sister when they were younger."

Theo winced, but nodded.

"How did you know it was the sister, and not just a girl? It could have been any girl."

Again, Theo scrunched his nose, the way he did when he was confused. His slight freckles were caught in the crease of it, becoming pressed white lines. "I'm not sure."

Victor gestured forward, placing one heavy hand on Theo's shoulder and pointing at the red-shirt comic-fan with the hand that held his phone. "You're not just getting the image. It looks like a television, but it's not one. You also get *context*, when it's needed. But you don't visualize that, it just... comes. The way you recognize characters you haven't seen in years when you're flipping through old channels. It's effortless. So effortless you don't notice."

Theo nodded, moving from the Spectacular Spider-Fan on to his friend, a girl with purple hair and a large piercing that weighed down her lip. She was worried about her mother: her screen was her bed in the chemotherapy ward of Palo Verde. But there was nothing in the image itself that told him it was the girl's mother, nor that it was a chemo ward... nor where the ward was, he realized. He'd gleaned the information without realizing it. "Yeah. I didn't... I never thought of it."

"It's a sense, like sound. Like smell." Victor cleared his throat. "It comes so naturally we don't think to examine it. Seriously: when was the last time you dissected *how* you smelled things? You just: do." He paused. "Go back to the kid. That information you got from him, the name of the character. Try and focus on that if you can. Use it like a gateway to get more."

Theo swallowed. "How do I do that?"

"Question it. Interrogate it. Work that muscle." He gripped Theo's shoulder, like a coach encouraging a player's throwing arm. "What issue is it?"

Theo's nose scrunched again. "Spider-Man number seven."

"Who wrote it?"

"Todd McFarlane."

"Who drew it?"

"... Todd McFarlane."

"Who else is in that issue?"

"... someone named Hobogoblin. Mary Jane."

"What's he want to do when he leaves here?"

"He wants to take that purple haired girl home and have her," Theo answered, the words coming before he had time to think about them. He gasped when he realized what he'd said, and before his eyes the image changed. The comic cover faded away, transitioning into a dark room lit with only hints of blue. Most of the screen was taken up by the male's bed, and he knew it was his bed without any clue where the information came from, he now realized. The duvet was white and looked fluffy, like something a caring older relative would have picked out for a gift. The girl with the piercing was laying on her back, her scant weight barely disrupting the position of the sheets. She was moving along with his motion, the image a point-of-view shot from the youth's mind's eye. Her shirt had been pulled up, revealing further piercings. He couldn't see her in the dim light of the basement room, all he could see of her breasts were the sparkle of those metal piercings moving.

How had he known it was a basement? He wondered.

"Jesus," Theo gasped, turning away from the crowd. He pressed his mouth into the crook of his arm as though he were about to vomit. People stepped away from him, but nobody helped.

Victor remained at the rail, glowering down at the red-shirt as he held up a comic in a mylar bag to the light, trying to see cracks in its spine.

Theo coughed, then turned back. He stayed back from the rail and the view of the crowds, but he could still see the glow of their screens flickering back on even through the floor. "That's... that's fucked up. I've never done that before."

"You have, without realizing it," Victor said in a dismissive, clipped tone. "Was it consensual?"

Theo's head snapped towards him. "Pardon?"

"The sex he's planning on having," Victor repeated, his eyes locked on those vibrant red rolls. "Is it consensual?"

Theo thought. "Yea... yes. She's his girlfriend." He paused. "How do I know that?"

"How *do* you know that?" Victor stressed, turning. "You're getting this from him remember. He might think she's his girlfriend, that doesn't make it so. What does *she* think?"

Theo swallowed hard, then stepped back up to the rail. He pulled the power bars again, making screens go dark until enough were black that he could focus on hers. Her mother was still there, sitting in a pool of anxious thought. *What room is she in?* 315. *What days are her treatment?* Wednesdays and Fridays. *Who is your boyfriend?* An image of the red shirt, slightly trimmer in her mind's eye, faded into view. His name was Chris, he now knew without knowing how he knew. "They're together."

Victor nodded, then turned away from the pair as though he'd never even seen them. He picked up his phone, engaged the video recorder, and aimed it down until its view held most of the crowd again. He cocked his chin forward. "Turn them on again. Not all of them, do it in batches. Get beneath the surface... find out what they've done. Find out what they're *hiding*." He pressed record. "We're hunting for assholes."

CHAPTER 02

The crowd moved freely in and around each other. It felt wrong to compare them to a colony of ants -- disrespectful in premise if not in meaning. He compared them instead to a bottle of Orbitz soda poured over a steep incline of hot concrete: the spheres moving this way and that as dictated by random, unseen forces like heat pockets and uneven spread. The people moved like that. Calculating the motion of any one of them was next to impossible, but Theo could still track them in a crowd: the images on the screens behind them made them identifiable. Nobody thought exactly the same, nobody pictured things exactly the same, nobody even perceived the same stimuli exactly the same.

Once you'd seen the man that was humming along to an Alanis Morissette song but picturing Taylor Swift in his mind as if they were one and the same, you could find that man's screen in a crowd with a quick glance over the assembled masses: he was the one who thought the video for *Ironic* looked like the video for *22*.

Theo had always been good at Search-and-Find books

as a child.

Victor scanned the crowd, looking from one person to the next with a sort of clinical detachment. His phone was extended out in front of him, doing sweeping passes of the crowd, but he wasn't looking through the screen; he was looking over it at all of the Orbitz bobbles as they moved to and fro over the hot concrete of the floor. His eyes fluttered over them all, finally landing on one of them.

"Thin guy, red jacket with the black cap." Victor said, turning his camera slightly to follow the man he was talking about. He was indeed thin, almost ghostly, and his cheeks were pockmarked in a checkerboard pattern that looked almost too uniform to be coincidental.

Theo found him and narrowed in. The screen behind him was large and glowed purple, shimmering behind him like a halo. It was an image akin to a lava lamp, with inky black swirls coming in and out of the frame. Theo narrowed his eyes and focused in, and soon the perspective of the image changed. He was seeing the image through the man's eyes, like twin cameras, and when his head turned away from the psychedelic lamp and toward his television, he saw legs sticking out from under a bean-bag chair. There was a retro game on the screen in front of him, the pixels as big as grapes and portrayed as wobbly chunks of gelatin on the screen too advanced for them.

"He's worried he'll be kicked out of his apartment. The rent is due, and his unemployment is running out."

Victor moved the camera away from the man in the red jacket without a word of acknowledgement, moving the lens and his gaze back over the crowd. He found two people, one a middle-aged woman in a sun-shirt and jeans, the other a young brunette girl of no more than seventeen. "Woman in the yellow shirt, four o'clock. With the girl. Get the girl, too."

Theo took a second to find them; they were at his five o'clock by the time that he did, and he watched both screens flutter to life. The woman's image was that of a bathroom stall, the younger partner's of tiny balloons being corroded away by stomach acid. The latter was imaginary, he realized quickly, an image of what the girl thought was happening inside her own body at that exact moment. In real life she had one arm clutching her stomach tight, he realized now, the other being hauled by the woman.

"She's a drug mule, the younger one. They're posing as mother and daughter, but they're not. She's bringing something -- cocaine? -- across state lines. They're from out of town."

"Where?" Victor asked, following the two with his camera. "Give me an address."

Theo squinted. "Her name is Dawn Hall; they live across the border in Texas. 871 Mable Drive, I can't get the town, sorry. She doesn't know it half the time, she's strung out." Theo frowned, his forehead furrowing. "She's a runaway, I think. I'm trying to get the address, but it keeps getting garbled up with her home address."

Victor nodded. "That's a start, move on." He scanned the phone over the crowd again, following his line of sight with it before narrowing in on an older man with balding hair that stood out in ruffles of gray behind his ears. He had a deep scowl that cut lines down either side of his face, and tiny eyes that watched everyone who walked past him -- but he smiled pleasantly when anyone made contact with them. "The old man on the bench. Looks like Robert Redford if he lost sixty pounds."

"Who?" Theo asked, breaking his concentration for a moment. All the screens in the hall flickered on again momentarily, and he winced from it before he found the man on the bench. "Never mind." He focused in, and for a moment the picture on the screen was so dark Theo wondered if he'd accidentally turned it off. It flickered and fluttered, with spastic white tracking lines appearing across the top and bottom of the screen, like an aged VHS recording. The light on the screen was dim, but before his eyes, shapes started to take form in the dim glow of the moonlight.

"Ugh," Theo grimaced, turning away from the crowd below once again.

"What?" Victor asked, keeping the camera focused on the target man.

"His name is Hugo Lightner. He's -- he was with his granddaughter. When she was eleven." He coughed, as if trying to get up something sick in his throat. "He spent six years in state lockup for it. He's out now, but he's not supposed to be around kids."

As if on cue, Lightner waved at a young girl that passed by with a used action figure she'd purchased. She smiled back.

"If he did time, I can find him in the federal database." Victor frowned, catching the moment between Hugo and the child in HD quality. "I'll send this to whoever is supposed to be watching to make sure he doesn't do this crap."

Theo nodded, then turned back to the crowd, keeping

his gaze steadily away from Lightner. He started to scan, managing the screens that were on and spending a few moments on each internal narrative before turning to the next one, waiting for Victor's next instruction.

After a moment, none had come. He turned. Victor had lowered his phone, which was now recording his jeans in picture-perfect quality. He was staring at the escalator, his head slowly rising to keep one person centered in his gaze. Theo followed his line of sight, eventually finding a blonde woman of medium height and build. She was halfway up the escalator, letting the motors carry her up as people walked up around her. Her hair was dark at the roots, and she had wide, horn-rimmed glasses on. There was a coffee cup in her hand, still billowing steam.

As Victor watched her, Theo watched the colour drain from his face until it became as pale as jellyfish flesh. For a moment -- only a moment -- there was a flicker of light behind Victor's head. It was like a glowing rectangle, snow-crash white, as though the fixture of a fluorescent bulb had shimmered to life behind him. Before Theo had a chance to acknowledge it, it was gone.

The woman turned right at the top of the escalator, becoming part of the crowd of the theatre.

Victor started walking, following her without saying a word. He stepped in time with her, the two of them synchronized without missing a beat.

"Victor?" Theo called, stepping after them with only a moment's hesitation.

Victor kept moving, winding in and out of the growing, bustling crowd as they went deeper and deeper into the theatre, past the ticket kiosks and concession stands.

People walked in and out, the traffic dense as one show ended, and another began.

The woman with the blonde hair moved throughout the crowd with ease, shifting from one foot to the next, finding gaps in the personage and slipping through them.

Ten feet into the darkened hall Victor ceased stepping around people and started bumping past them, his broad shoulders connecting with people not quick enough to get out of his way as he brushed past them. Several curses followed in his wake. He kept his eyes trained forward, ignoring those behind him as though they had ceased to exist.

"Sorry," Theo said to one woman he passed, whose screen had become tinted red after Victor had roughly rubbed elbows with her. "Victor!" The rectangle of light flashed behind Victor again, like a bulb trying to flare on after a power surge. It wasn't white this time; there was an image on it. It was a dark room, and he could only see highlights -- but there was a man standing in the centre, and the light played off the greasy heads of children standing away from him in the distance.

Before he could focus on any one of them, the image shimmered away again, as though this new projector Victor had grown out the back of his head were on the fritz.

"Victor!" Theo hissed, reaching him as they turned a steep corner into the main concession area that led to the actual hall of screens. He cupped the taut flesh of Victor's arm. He pulled away suddenly and Theo grabbed at it again, more forcefully this time.

"Where did she go?" Victor asked suddenly, turning

back to Theo with urgency. He grabbed Theo by the arms when he did not answer immediately. "Could you read her?"

Theo narrowed his eyes, only realizing now that he hadn't been able to see any screen -- any thoughts -- displayed behind her head as he had everyone else in the crowd. He'd been too distracted by the sudden *appearance* of Victor's screen to notice the absence of another. "...No," he said, after a moment's hesitation.

Victor cursed, loudly and with vulgarity, drawing the ireful glances of many parents taking their children to animated matinees. He turned away from Theo and scanned the crowd again, his eyes moving feverishly from one patron to another.

"What is it? What's going on?" Theo asked, stepping around to be in his view again.

Victor's eyes fell on a door, hidden behind the last manned kiosk at the theatre. It was stainless steel but dull, its design doing everything it could to hide its presence, except for the glowing red EXIT sign that screamed it. He cursed again, under his breath this time, then pushed past Theo and made his way towards it.

He shoved it open and stepped out into the rear parking lot of the Payson Mall, which was lined with beaten cars that each had the same employee-only parking validation sticker on them. There was one car between the rows with its engine running, a blue two-door with deep scrapes that ran alongside wood paneling. When he looked, Victor saw the blonde woman with the dark roots disappear inside, her hair caught in the hinge of the open window.

The car started to pull forward, its engine revving to life.

"Damn," Victor snarled. He dug deep into his pocket and produced his phone -- which was still recording -- and aimed it at the escaping vehicle. He zoomed in on the license plate as much as he could as it weaved around the zigging, zagging lanes of the parking lot, then disappeared around the corner into the ether of the rest of the town. Only then did Victor lower the camera and press the stop button. He watched the screen to make sure the lengthy video saved properly.

The light flickered behind Victor's head again, this time an image of a small girl with the kind of white-blonde hair that many children have but few adults do. She looked scared, and for a moment the image on the screen was Victor himself, as though his mind's eye were outside his own body. He looked scared too. Theo stepped back from him a pace, turned to see where the car had vanished, then turned back. The image was gone without a trace, as though some block had been reset. "What was that?" Theo asked, exhaustion in his tone.

Victor opened his messaging app and texted the video to two recipients, one labeled X and the other labeled Y. Only when the whoop sound of the message sending went through did he put the phone away.

"Who was she?" Theo asked again, rephrasing the question.

Victor's gaze became long and vacant, one eye always on the corner where the car had vanished, as though expecting it to reappear. He breathed, deep. The colour had not yet returned to his cheeks.

CHAPTER 03

Payson, The Past

There had been a coin in Hungary, and there had been three men trying to get it. It had seemed an insignificant thing at first, but three men -- and Tash -- had all but ended themselves either trying to get it or trying to keep it from the others. It had had hollow notches in it along one side, and three parallel rectangular holes in its body. It had been large and weighty, and when held in the palm of one's hand it comfortably covered up all the user's first knuckles.

In the end Victor had melted it in a forge that he'd made using two buckets, some concrete, and a reversible vacuum-cleaner he'd stolen from a utility closet. Tash had kept watch as the disk had melted, and just as the last of its odd symbology had sputtered into nothingness, one of the men -- a man named Ramsey Hinge -- had appeared and made for them. Victor had backed away and Tash had kicked over the hastily made forge, spilling the glowing orange alloy out onto the grass. The grass caught flame from the heat of it, the moisture of its life erupting into steam. They had run, quickly, but not so quickly that Victor hadn't turned back at the last moment to see Ramsey -- scream-

ing in agony -- clawing at the molten metal to try and gain purchase on the last of the coin. He had melted his own fingers down to cauterized nubs, but he was still going.

They had gotten the first available plane to Britain, and from there to Payson, Arizona. It was one of those small towns that had the amenities of a city: an airport had been needed in the region, and a town had sprung up around it. There were more hotels and coffee shops than the population could have reasonably maintained, powered by the tourist dollars of those forced to stay overnight during a long layover.

One such cafe was Penningtons, the sort of small tea and coffee establishments frequented by hipsters who had no money for rent but were willing to pay $8.95 for a sandwich once a day. The venue itself was tiny, no more than seven feet from the back wall to the glass windows, but the area out front was vast and always full of sun. It was squared off from the rest of Callahan Street by an iron fence, the kind with ornate spears on the top of each spire. Inside the courtyard were over a dozen circular glass tables, each with black iron legs that came out like letter C's and came together at their backs.

Victor and Tash sat at one such table to one side, the afternoon sun shimmering off the table and lighting their whole faces with warmth. Tash had tea in a delicate cup and saucer of china. Victor had the same, along with a large paper bowl of roasted red pepper soup that he tasted from gingerly, careful not to lose any in the scruff of his moustache.

The china had been on display along the back wall of the serving area in an antique cabinet. Tash had been forced to put down a security deposit on both pieces before she was allowed to use them, and when they were taken out, the old woman behind the counter had eyed the paper card that read "display only" *several times and huffed at each one of them.*

Victor swallowed his latest mouthful of soup, paused, then took his first helping of tea. He paused and then stopped, tilting the cup towards him, and eyeing the purple-hued liquid inside. "Rosemary?" he asked, his eyes flitting up to meet Tash's.

She nodded. "For the burns."

There were a series of thin, snake-like burns that worked their way from Victor's left wrist to his elbow, each taking their own path and puffing out like varicose veins. They were red still, and those closer to the crook of his arm had gauze strips taped to protect them.

He smiled and lifted the damaged arm, wriggling the fingers and watching them dance. "This? Nothing. Better than what happened to Ramsey at any rate."

She grinned at him, her mouth a tiny thing that was barely visible over the curvature of her teacup. "Did you know he'd go for the coin, even after it had started to melt?"

He raised an eyebrow to her, wriggling his seared digits. "What? No. Of course not... I don't think anyone could predict that someone would do something that stupid."

"Really? You didn't 'do the math' on him, or something of the sort?"

He paused, then sipped his tea.

Her smile receded slightly. "You should try and solve things without violence, you know."

"I know," he hummed. "But sometimes that's all there is. And it's not like I made him try to pick up molten gold. But... sometimes, like I say, that's all there is."

She squinted, her smile slowly perking along the sides of her lips again, then nodded.

Behind her there were people gathering in a small crest

alongside the street, around an enclave where the sidewalk dipped out to make room for benches and a small copper memorial. They were gathering, quietly, in a semi-circle around one man, who was holding a large stack of papers. He was standing on one of the benches, making him appear a good foot taller than the nearest-sized man.

"Where did you get to at the height of it?" Victor smiled. He picked up his paper bowl, squeezed its edges together until it started to funnel, then took a long drink of the soup with one hand. When he was done, he wiped his mouth, and she still hadn't answered him. She had one eyebrow raised to its highest arch. He lowered the bowl. "You know, in Budapest, when Ramsey and Jona were on my tail... where were you?"

She smiled, opened her mouth to respond, then caught herself in a laugh instead and put down her tea to stop herself from spilling it. She worked her tongue around her mouth and looked everywhere except to meet his gaze, then started again. "Ahem. There was a, ah... someone was in trouble. It couldn't be avoided."

Victor narrowed his eyes but couldn't help but smile. "You found someone in trouble at three a.m. on a Thursday night in the middle of Budapest?"

She licked her lips unconsciously, then smiled.

"How cute?" he asked dryly.

"Oh, ten out of ten to be sure. You'd have been proud."

"Somehow I doubt that," he smiled, then raised his damaged arm and wriggled the fingers again. "Explains why you're guilty over this, though."

"One has nothing to do with the other, I assure you."

He rolled his eyes, finished his soup then placed the used bowl to one side. He pulled the tea closer, its aroma wafting up *in the windless afternoon to his nostrils.*

The crowd behind Tash's head had grown quickly to nearly double its original size. People who were walking past, enjoying the unseasonably warm weather, diverted their paths when they got within earshot of the man with the papers. Some listened for a moment and then pressed on, but most abandoned whatever task they'd been on to stand, hands on hips, and shake their heads with each point the paper-wielder made.

Victor's brow furrowed, the one small crease arching up from the left eyebrow when he did. It happened when he was his most thoughtful, and Tash had twice warned him that if he didn't stop soon, the crease would become a permanent fixture of his features. He craned his head to see the parts of the crowd obscured by Tash's shoulder.

Tash narrowed her eyes, then turned around in her chair to see for herself.

The men and women assembled should not have been assembled together: not here, not in this part of the country and not at this time. There were men and women, but minorities both visible and non-visible were stopped as well (the only non-visible male couple made visible by the coloured handkerchiefs sticking out of their back pockets). There were young men wearing black tees and breathable shorts that had been out for an afternoon run, and old men in sunglasses and broad-brimmed hats with splotches of sunblock smeared on their noses. Three black men stood together, and a fourth off to himself. There were two women in hijabs standing right next to three white thirty-somethings in wife beaters and red tans -- the type who would typically have something to say to women wearing hijabs -- and yet they ignored one another peaceably, their attention too focused ahead.

"*Colourful crowd,*" Tash remarked, not turning to face Victor when she spoke. Several other patrons of the restaurant had turned in their chairs to watch as well. "*Can you hear them?*"

"*No,*" Victor admitted after a moment's pause. "*There's anxiety in that crowd, though. Dread. This isn't some Sunday sermon.*"

"*Sunday sermon wouldn't have such a diverse group,*" Tash said, nodding towards two people of vastly different cultural faiths standing next to each other, each paying equal attention.

"*Some of them are hard to read,*" he said. "*But it's not street magic, that's for sure.*"

Tash turned back around to face him. "*Do you see what's missing?*"

He craned over her shoulder again. A woman walked by with a stroller, paused, then continued on. "*No,*" he admitted, looking from one face to the next but not seeing much of anything -- they were all turned away from him.

"*There aren't any children there,*" she said matter-of-factly.

He looked again and saw that she was right.

"*Nobody with children stayed in that group... whatever it is, it's too hard to deal with with children. So dollars to donuts it is a missing child.*" She turned back to the crowd. Just as she spoke, as if on cue, the man standing before the crowd raised one of the sheets of paper. It wasn't legible from where they sat, but there was a large square photo in the centre in the style of every Missing Persons flyer ever printed. "*Sad,*" she commented, her voice faraway.

Victor clasped his lips and turned to her for the first time since the crowd had gotten his attention. She was still looking away, and so she didn't bother to mask the way her eyebrows *curled up... that pitied, mournful look that she only ever had when she thought he wasn't looking.*

"Do you want to help?" he asked, wiping his mouth once more to assure he got everything.

"I do," she said, in a voice nowhere near them.

Victor got up and Tash followed suit. When she did, one of her slender hips knocked the table and her cup -- tiny purple flowers and all -- tilted from its perch and toppled over the side of the table. It hit the stone tiled ground with a shattering snow-crash staccato smash, sending the willowy handle flying towards the road.

"Ugh," came a grunt, loud and annunciated, from within the cafe. And old woman snapped a dishtowel aggressively, then placed both hands on her hips and glared out at Tash with a knowing, I-just-knew-it sort of look.

The cup had shattered so wholly and completely, it was unrecognizable from what it had been before.

CHAPTER 04

Payson, The Present

Chad stood in front of a large half-circle building that looked like an oil barrel tipped onto its side and buried up to its middle. It was massive but never looked it in pictures, seeming out-of-scale with everything around it. Chad stood at the edge of the property along the cracked sidewalk of Prescott Street, just outside of metal gates that slid closed on rusted wheels at night. He held a small stack of paper in his left hand, scant enough that it struggled to stay rigid in his grip.

In faded red font across the front of the building read the words PAYSON MUSEUM OF FLIGHT.

"What are we doing here?" Alice asked, looking up from her phone and taking in the whole of the building. It glistened in a way she did not like, the light of the mid-afternoon sun reflecting off the segmented metal siding that went all the way down either side of the thing.

"I wasn't going to ask it," Abby said. She smirked as she looked from Alice to the building, and then finally back to Chad.

"It looks like a government building," Alice said. She shifted from foot to foot, bringing her left hand up to hug her right arm. She was wearing a loose plaid shirt she'd found in the spare room closet, the type that was stereotypical in lumberjacks. It was big enough on her that she could wear it like a jacket, and she wore it like one.

"It's not," Chad replied. "I mean, I guess it was, at some point. But it's not now." He frowned, then stepped forward. "Come on, you have to see this."

The three of them entered the Flight Museum, Chad ahead of the others and Abby convincing Alice to continue at several junctions. The area inside was one large room except for an office at the back, which had been created not via construction but by simply wheeling in an aged mobile home and arranging the red letters to spell OFFICE on its side. There was a young man standing in its doorway with slick-backed brown hair. He looked like Sebastian Stan and was eating tuna directly out of a can with a pocketknife. He was the only employee in sight.

The hanger was divided with pipe and drape that went up to just above eyelevel in some areas, and just below in others. Each section was made to be disguised from the next, so that you walked through it and that each new exhibit took you through time: the first planes were older, used in World War II. They got more advanced as time wore on, a stand-up plaque providing a picture of each in their prime, the years it was in use, and a small blurb of relevant information.

Alice stopped at one plaque, looked at it, then took out her phone and snapped a picture of the plane. A buffering animation appeared in the centre of the screen, and after a moment a wall of text and a black and white photo appeared. "I can find ten times the information presented here on my phone. In seconds." She scrolled briefly, lost interest, then minimized the app.

"That's not why we're here," Chad said, finally coming to a stop in front of a jet that was near the back of the building, a dozen feet from the man scraping the last bit of meat out of a tuna can.

Abby raised an eyebrow, staying back in the null space between he and Alice. "Why *are* we here?" she asked.

He turned to her, then motioned back towards the jet. "You don't see it?"

She looked past him to it, for the first time. The jet was large and modern, built in the last thirty years. It was that sandy beige colour that most military vehicles of the time were, the colour that would make it blend in when parked in the desert. Its nose had a silver tip and its wings came out with metal winces that looked like claws every few feet. They looked like talons, but at one point they'd carried payloads. The cockpit was a glass oval that peeked up from the nose of the craft, its window the gray tint of sunglasses.

The word *freedom* had been stenciled across it in black calligraphy.

Abby stopped when she saw the word, freezing when she saw the distinct, loopy letter *e*'s and the way they stubbornly refused to connect with the *d* and the rest of the word beyond. Her brow furrowed slightly as she regained the use of her legs and stepped up beside Chad, awestruck.

"What?" Alice asked, looking up from the plaque she

was reading.

"Is that what I think it is?" Abby asked, still staring at the round, cursive letters. They looked to have been translated directly from someone's hand, blown up and amplified until they dominated one side of the plane.

Chad flipped past the first two pages he'd printed out, then came to a full-page photograph. He folded back the two extraneous pages, then handed the entire pad to Abby without a word.

The picture was of Victor, standing in front of a large sandy-coloured fighter jet, much like the one they were in front of now. He was wearing a checkered red shirt... the same shirt that Alice had coincidentally pulled out of the back closet and was now wearing, she noticed. He was smiling so wide that he was barely recognizable as the stern, serious man they'd eaten with the day before. His hair was pulled back in a ponytail and looked short, though it may well have been the same length it was now. His cheeks were high and scorched with sunburn.

His partner, Tash, stood next to him. She had more visible freckles here and was dressed in a black tee and jeans that looked as though they'd never had a crease in them. A leather jacket that couldn't possibly have been hers was slung over her right shoulder, and she was smiling sweetly into the camera in a way Abby thought the Tash she knew was definitely capable of, but had never seen with her own eyes.

In the picture, Victor's bust obscured the penmanship along the jet. The only part of the word visible in the photo was *free*.

Abby looked from the photo to the jet and then back

again. It was not the same photo she'd held in her hands months ago. It was a printed copy, the pixilation clear around the edges of Victor's smile, missing some of the differing shades in skin tone and getting the image confused.

"How did you find this?" she asked, handing him back the pages and taking a step towards the plane.

"Luck," Chad said. He handed the pages back to Alice without explanation. "I was trying to find the class of jet on Google and this came up. Location tracking, I guess."

Abby shot him a wry look.

Alice looked up from the photo. "He looks so young."

Abby nodded. She was now close enough that she could reach out and touch the jet, so she did, feeling the solid, dense weight of it beneath her palm. She swallowed.

"That's an F-16, Block 50," the man from the back of the room -- who looked like Sebastian Stan -- said, striding up to the three of them. "They used to refuel in Payson before heading out to Iraq and overseas during the war."

"Which Iraq?" Chad asked.

Stan shrugged. His hands were deep in the pockets of his one-piece grease-jumper, bulging them out on the tops of his legs like extra knees when he leaned forward. He clacked his tongue against the roof of his mouth as though he were working it around his teeth, a large meaty toothpick.

Alice held up the picture and pointed to the plane, tapping it twice. "Is this the same jet?"

Stan stepped forward with a quizzical expression on

his face. He produced a thin pair of glasses from his pocket and slid them on with a practiced motion, transforming from grease-monkey to hipster in one fluid movement. He took the page gently between his thumb and forefinger, squinted at it, then looked back at the craft he stood in the shadow of. "Without serial numbers there's no way to be sure, but yeah. Yeah, that's it."

Chad stepped back from the jet, backing up until Abby was fully in his field of vision. She was wearing jeans that were tight and clung to her upper legs, which he tried and failed not to take notice of. Tearing his gaze away, he looked at the backdrop around the jet: that gray, dull metal sheen that every airport hangar had. He could see the photo in Alice's hand from where he stood, dangling in his peripheral vision. The sky behind Victor and Tash was a bright, clear blue that brought out the yellow of his hair and made it glow like sunbeams.

"It wasn't taken here," Chad said, matter-of-factly.

"No, definitely not," Stan concurred. He released the photo and Alice brought them back closer to herself as he stepped away and looked to the actual jet. "She's been here ten years. She was decommissioned and stripped and given to the Town of Payson; been here ever since."

Abby reached out and touched the plane again, pressing against it with both palms. They were moist from sweat but she clung onto the same spot, each on either side of a camouflage splotch. She pressed her weight against it, feeling its resistance, the density of it pushing back against her and making her real.

Chad watched her. He smiled at first, but it slowly faded the longer she communed with it, and by the time she turned around it was gone completely.

"Where was it before it was mothballed?" she asked, sniffing and composing herself.

Stan shrugged. "Overseas for the early nineties, I'm guessing. Back and forth between here and there, fighting Sand -- fighting Iraqis."

Chad winced, catching that he'd caught himself.

"She was sitting out at Payson airfield for ten years of so before they officially decommissioned her. They took her up every now and again on the town's birthday and the Fourth, but for better part of a decade she sat out there."

Chad nodded, looked at each of the women, then turned and stepped away from the jet.

Abby lingered, taking a moment to pull herself away from the sight of it. "That was it," she said, speaking as though she were giving them information they didn't have themselves. She spoke with a hushed tone.

"Yeah," Chad agreed.

She leaned forward and took his face in both her hands and kissed him, passionately but briefly, taking his upper lip between her own. "It was taken here, right here in Payson."

Alice furrowed her brow. "What's the big deal?"

"If we assume it was taken at the airstrip, we have a rough timeline of when it was taken. Super rough. But it's something," Chad said.

Abby took the picture from Alice, looked at it, then turned back to the actual aircraft, getting one last glimpse of it before it vanished between the pipe and drape completely. She turned to Chad and kissed him again.

∞

"Is there anything yet?" Victor said, his voice near the level of a growl. He was hunched over his desk in a position that would lead to a stiff neck in any man his age if maintained for more than forty minutes. He'd been sitting like that for well over an hour. There were two screens opened to him, one from his laptop and the other from a tablet he'd propped up into landscape mode. He was facing the laptop, and in his peripheral vision, Tash moved into the frame on the tablet.

"Would you like to switch jobs? Because the DMV has become *shockingly* better at warding off motherfuckers since the last time you got me to do this," she said, the cheap speakers cracking at the K sounds as she spoke.

"You calling yourself a motherfucker?"

She shot him a droll look which didn't quite land, looking at where he was on her monitor and not where he was in his space. "I'm the queen motherfucker."

He almost smiled, but something in the act made him tense and he looked back to the moleskin journal sitting next to his keyboard. It was propped over with a diamond-shaped paperweight. He repositioned himself on his chair, small with comfortable cushions patterned to look like leaves and a bamboo back. He rested his elbows on his knees and clutched at his hair with both his fingers, the light from outside still slicing him right down the middle. On the moleskin page held open were six numbers, preceded by the colour 'blue' and the phrase 'Ford?'.

"You got that in as an eight, not a zero, right?" Victor asked. He stared at the plate number he'd scribbled down from the video he'd filmed, the blue ink from his pen bleeding out into the thick paper of the notebook.

Tash shot him an annoyed look, light from the phone she was calling from shimmering in her brown eyes. "The day I mistake an eight for a zero on a plate is the day I hang this up."

"You have an eight though?"

"Yes, Victor. I have an eight."

He frowned, tore his gaze away from the notebook, and turned back to his computer. He grabbed the mouse -- a wireless bulb the size of a small shot-glass with a red light at the tip -- and switched tabs on his computer from *The Daily Courier* to *The Arizona Republic* and began scrolling through the archived web articles. He'd limited the search to several keywords and was scrolling through months of headlines.

"Arizona Child wins Tri-State Championship"

"Child Actor to appear in Hollywood Blockbuster"

"Child and Safety regulation updates impact Arizona District Schools"

There was a sound from the phone, a clattering of something long hitting something solid, impacting over the course of several strikes before settling into a position of rest. Victor recognized it; it was also the sound his keyboard made when he found himself awash in frustration.

"That doesn't sound good," he said with a smirk, his tone approaching one of levity.

"The plates are fake, Vic. They're fake as fuck."

He turned to her, the scant smile disappearing from his face. "Pardon?"

She sighed. Her face was full of tension, deep lines cut along either side of her nose that bisected the patches of freckles that rested there. Her cheeks were thin and long, like the rest of her, and it made the mop of pixie-cut dark hair on her head look fuller than it was, her brown eyes larger than they were. She stared at him through the screen and many miles now, the lines under them showing her age. Their age.

"Tasha?" he repeated.

"That combination of the three in the middle, the two and the eight and the --"

"Yes."

"That doesn't go together. Ever. It's sanctioned off for movie studios and stuff like that so that they can use real-looking plate numbers without accidentally copying something someone owns in real life. And there, the tags," she reached for something off screen, fiddling with a computer of her own, "the tags are up to date but they're the wrong colours for the wrong year. I can't get anything from them."

"They were used in a movie then? Local production maybe? That one with the comedian was shot here, wasn't it? Horrible film."

"I don't know," she huffed, her face aglow from the second screen again. "There's no... there's no database of stuff like that easily accessed."

"I didn't ask if it was easy."

She ignored him. "It could be anything. It could be plates the owner just made up themselves, knowing that number set would confuse the system. It could be, I'm saying, literally anything. Unless you were a cop running the plates at the time you saw it, you probably wouldn't even notice the difference."

He huffed again and turned back to his computer. He scrolled through another page of headlines and links, then clicked to load the next page and waited for it to do so.

She frowned at him, the motion exaggerated on in the sixteen by nine aspect ratio she was presented in. "Are you... sure you saw what you think you saw?"

He raised a thick blond eyebrow and slowly turned it towards her.

"I'm just... you were training Theo. The place was crowded. Things happen. Happens to me all the time, you see a face in the crowd you think you recognize, and when you catch up to them, it's totally different. I thought I saw you in Lenox Square the other day, but it was just some kid."

He turned away from her as the page loaded.

"I'm just saying, our brains do weird thing with facial recognition. It's weird. Our brains are *programmed* to recognize faces well, but it works too well. We'll see things where there's nothing to see sometimes."

"Oh?" he said, turning his laptop screen toward the phone so that Tash could see it.

Displayed prominently across the width of the screen was a headline that read: "Local Teen Missing after Big game Win." Below it was a school photo of a blonde girl in a soccer jersey, and a caption that identified it as having been provided by the family. She was smiling brightly.

He turned the screen back around so that he could see it and started to scroll through the article, which had been printed in *The Payson Sun*. He started to scribble notes into his moleskin opposite the faux vehicle information.

"One missing girl is very sad, but it does not a plot

make," Tash said, her voice coaxing and empathetic. "Sometimes a cigar is just a cigar, and sometimes a missing child -- while sad -- is just a missing child."

"Not in Payson."

CHAPTER 05

Payson, The Past

The sun was hot against the land, blazing down from a cloudless sky and turning the wheat field a bright, luminous yellow. It glowed like the sun as Victor and Tash stepped through it, each blade and kernel perfectly lit and visible. The smell, like the stale barns of his youth, came to Victor's nostrils and tickled them lightly.

"Step," yelled a man a few hundred meters ahead. He was wearing a blue polo shirt and baseball cap, and a large brown mustache of the sort that went out of style in the 70s. 'Porno 'Stashes,' they were called now, as they had been in style at the early rise of the pornographic film industry and had gained longevity in the popular culture as such. There was a silver whistle dangling from his neck by a nylon string. He picked it up and gave two sharp toots that made nearly one hundred adults -- Victor and Tash included -- step forward.

Victor gently pushed several stalks of wheat aside with a gentle motion of his arm, wincing as the sharp points of several blades agitated his burned forearm. His head moved back and forth across the gaps he'd made to examine the ground for any-

thing that appeared out-of-place. There was another man -- one in his late fifties with bushy eyebrows and the balding remains of a bowl cut -- six feet to Victor's left. He made the same sweeping motion as Victor did with his arm, forcing over stalks without breaking them and examining the ground underneath the way a mother with a comb parted a child's hair to search for lice.

Six feet to that man's left a woman did the same. To her left, a man in his mid-twenties did so, but with slightly more vigor, leaving abrasions and cracks in the stems as he searched each section.

To Victor's right, Tash scanned the ground she'd exposed for any sign of disruption: a toy, an article of clothing, a lock of hair, anything. Her arms were long and lanky, and they spread out in wide arcs that took great swaths of the wheat with them and gently pried them back to reveal the bleached undergrowth between.

A large, pear-shaped man with suntanned skin that was dark around the eyes stepped up next to the Caller, spoke something to him covertly, then motioned to the side where three men searched the wheat field. The upper rim of a badge stuck out from the front of his jeans. The Caller nodded.

"Step," the Porn 'Stash said, followed by two sharp toots on his whistle. Victor and Tash stepped forward as one, careful to only step into a patch that they'd visually cleared. They spread their arms again, revealing a new section of ground.

Tash looked up at Victor from her hunched-over position, a wry smile playing across her lips as she watched his head travel back and forth, blond hair moving like curtains in the wind.

On one of his turns to examine the foliage he caught a glimpse of that smile, so familiar to him, but did not let it distract him from his pattern of looking left, then right, then left again until *he either found an artifact or was told to step forward.*

"What?" he asked when he caught the edges of her smile again on his next pass.

"Nothing, just... I thought you were done following orders, is all." She winked at him, even though she knew by the placement of his head that he couldn't have seen it.

He stood a little straighter and frowned at her.

"Step," Porn Stash yelled, tooting twice. The man next to him nodded, tipping back his hat and revealing a starkly receding hairline.

Everyone stepped forward except Victor. He watched Tash step forward, push aside her wheat blades, and begin to examine. After a moment he stepped forward into his place in line and pushed his lot aside, sighing as he scanned the newly revealed plot.

"This isn't In-Country. This isn't remotely the same," he said.

She stuck out her tongue without looking at him. "Don't be sensitive. It wasn't a criticism. You look bored when you're driven. You look so... serious."

"I am serious."

"I know, but now you look it." She shot him a wry glance, only for an instant, then moved in to examine a blade of discoloured grass.

"I want to find the man that took a child; can you explain to me why that's so wrong?"

"It's not," she said, raising her hands in defense. "Although, I'd have said I'm more interested in finding the child."

He shot her a serious look.

"Priorities, and all."

Victor stood up and turned, his gaze falling over the assem-

bled hundred men who all stood in a line, each six feet apart, to search a hayfield a child went missing near nearly a mile wide.

There was a young woman -- no older than twenty -- standing at the far end of what Victor could see clearly with a milky, bland expression pasted on her sallow, sagging jowls. She was too young to have jowls, yet her cheeks sagged and moved in the scant breeze like a person half her age, and she canvassed her six-foot area with a thousand-yard stare, not seeming to focus on any one thing before her.

Victor stared at her for a long moment, her forehead large and so creamy white that if it hadn't been for the sweat rolling down it, Victor would have mistaken it for a mannequin.

Tash stopped her head swivel and turned up to Victor, standing to meet him and follow his line of sight. "What's with that girl?" she asked, cocking her head toward the pale youth.

"Step." Two toots.

"Nothing," Victor replied, his voice almost a whisper. "Literally, nothing. It's just... well, look at her. Look at her face."

Tash looked at her, tilting to one side. Her cheeks looked hollow, devoid of colour to the point of being ashen. She had a far-off stare, the sort of unfocused gape that one got when their minds shut off in the middle of a tedious trek or a long exam. Waking sleep, an old partner of hers had once called it, a step removed from meditation, and unintentional.

"I don't see anything," she said, almost under her breath. "Except that she shouldn't be one of the people looking for evidence."

Victor nodded.

Tash looked out among the assembled masses. "I think you get this many people together, you're bound to get one or two non-thinkers in the group. Law of averages, annat."

He frowned. "Look at her again. That's not lack of thought, that's lack of feeling. That's lack of... that's just numb. All over, head to toe, numb." He sighed, then let his gaze fall over the assembled search party just as Tash's had. He lingered first on a woman with curly blonde hair who was using a metal tool to push her wheat aside, rather than her arm. Her mouth hung loose too, and when he followed her eyeline he found that she, too, was staring off into the void of the golden stalks.

There was a third, far off into the distance. A twenty-year-old in a red baseball cap. He'd stopped investigating the patch of growth in front of him and was staring off into the horizon line... but something in his posture made it clear that he wasn't admiring the blueness of the sky.

"You seeing this?" Victor asked, cocking his head.

Tash noted the two others Victor had noticed. "There are space cadets. What do you want? There's probably lead in the wate--"

Without warning, the balding man with the bushy eyebrows next to Victor burst into tears and fell to his knees as though they couldn't hold him anymore. It happened so suddenly and the sound of the emotion as it bubbled up and splayed forth snapped both Victor and Tash out of their examinations of the faraway and back to the here and the now.

The man stuttered and stopped like an engine in the cold of winter, each breath escaping through a chest wracked with sobs. There were tears, so many tears that it seemed impossible that he'd only just started, and when Victor got closer, he realized that the man must have been crying silently for some time. There were small round moisture marks all along the collar of his red cardigan.

"Step." Two toots.

Victor raised his fist high, his arm at a ninety-degree angle. Tash saw it and quickly did the same, and then got three sharp blasts on the whistle in acknowledgement. He knelt down next to the man, both of their knees sinking with the weight of them into the soft soil of the field. He reached out a steady hand, veiny and calloused from use, and laid it firmly on the man's shoulder. "What's wrong, old timer?"

The man sniffed back hard, a wet sound, trying to compose himself. His lip, trembling to the point that it made his cheeks vibrate, was steadied and he forced a smile. He looked up to make eye contact with Victor, then immediately lost control again, tears running down his cheeks.

"Should we call someone?" Tash asked.

"No," Victor said with certainty. He rubbed the shoulder with a gentle, firm pressure.

"I'm sorry," the man said, his shaking jaw having trouble forming the words with cohesion. "I just... I'm sorry."

"Nothing to be sorry for," Victor said, his tone matter of fact. He let the man cry a minute longer, massaging his shoulder all the while with a gentle, firm pressure. When it had gone on long enough that he could hear Tash move from foot to foot, he spoke again: "What's your name, sir?"

"Garrard," the man said, sniffing back. "Garrard Clements. I'm sorry, again, I'm so --"

"It's alright," Tash said, her voice smoother than Victor's.

"It's my girl, my girl and I just... I'm sorry, I just, all this, it just brought it all back and..."

A woman in her fifties with a shock of bright purple hair stepped up next to Garrard, appearing through the tufts of wheat. She put her hand on the man's free shoulder and leaned close to him, a mirror image of Victor. But instead of resist-

ing and fighting back, Garrard fell to the side into the woman's arms and started to sob violently.

After a moment the two stood, and the woman led him away from the search party. Victor stood and watched them go, and when they were far enough away he let his gaze fall over those amassed again, ignoring those with blank expressions and looking instead at the rest: there were many others with tear-filled eyes and reddened cheeks, and with shirts dotted with the dribblings of tears.

"I haven't heard a man cry like that since I was in country," Victor said, his voice low and hoarse.

"What was he saying? Did his daughter go missing, or-"

"You don't break down like that when your daughter goes missing," Victor snapped. "You break down like that when your daughter goes missing and they never find her."

He continued to watch the crowd as they turned away from the sight of Garrard Clements being escorted off the field. One wiped his eyes and one, far enough away that she wasn't quite clear to Victor, fell to the ground with her hands over her face just as Garrard had, attracting the attention of those around her. She was far enough away that it took a moment for the sound of her wails to reach him.

Victor turned to face Tash, his eyes bloodshot. "There's something very wrong in this place."

CHAPTER 06

Payson, Present Day

Carla sat on the corner of her single bed that was too small for her, which itself was in the corner of a room that was almost too small for it. The room was dark, lit only by the blue light of the moon that filtered in through the small, rectangular window. It outlined everything with a teal tint, as though someone had sketched the scene in a rough outline and forgotten to go back and finish the lines or add colours.

The room was so small that if she extended her legs, she would have touched the opposing wall. The room had once been larger, she knew, but walls had been added to further divide and segment the space more and more. She could tell which wall was original and which had been added; the plasters were different shades of off-white.

There was a quilt covering the small bed of the sort a grandmother might make, although she knew no grandmother had. There was one pillow at the head of the bed, but it was large and firm enough that it felt like three lesser pillows. She felt the diverse topography of the quilt beneath her palms, the way the pattern rose and fell in diamond and square shapes.

There were sounds starting. The creaking, moving, hushed voices that came through the walls as muffled warbles. The new wall to her right was not as insulated as well as the others, and the sounds came from it more freely. There was giggling and hushed whispers, and the sound of old springs.

Carla ran short fingernails through her bottle-blonde hair, working them down to the darkened roots and scratching at her head with such vigor that the flesh of her brow moved back and forth. The action brought a tingly sensation to her scalp and she smiled, briefly, before a startled thump in an adjacent room brought her back to reality. It was followed by laughter, and then low tones that were not quite the cadence of speech: just vocalizations.

She fell on her side like a chopped tree, crashing onto her bed as her pillow bent up around her and to either side of her. She brought her knees up to her chest and held them there with clammy hands. Her thumbs traversed the smooth flesh of her kneecaps, the left one finding resistance against the mangled remnants of a very old scar, the sort one got during the careless jaunts of childhood.

The sounds from the walls continued, coming from every part of every floor until it was hard to tell one from the other.

She woke up at three am with a moist, salty pillow beneath her. She didn't remember why.

CHAPTER 07

Chad sat at the desk at the end of his room, hunched over a small moleskin notebook he could barely see. The lights were out, with the only illumination the blue sheen that came in through the window and bathed everything with its glow.

The picture of Victor and Tash in front of the jet sat propped against his window. On the notebook he'd written the rough estimate of the dates he'd gotten at the air museum: over a decade but less than fifteen, end to end. It was a wide margin, though not as wide as he'd thought given the lack of puff and crow's feet under Victor's eyes. Something since the picture had aged him, and dreadfully.

He took out his phone and held it under the desk when he turned it on, containing the glow and making sure it was on the soft orange light of night-mode. He brought up a web browser, closed his eyes, and took a deep breath. When he opened them again, his thumbs punched in the date range he'd marked in the notebook, Arizona, and the word 'news.'

It worked better when he had steady breath, he'd been finding.

The first article that came up was about a fire that had torn through the low-income housing sector of downtown, roughly eight years prior. Three men had died, and a child. There was a photo of the blaze, but none of the victims.

Chad's gaze flickered from the screen and back to the photo. Victor's skin was the same perma-tanned it typically was, the underside of his arms and palms milk-toast white. There was no soot or ash anywhere, no hints of it hiding behind his ears or other hard to wash places.

He frowned, then clicked the article nonetheless and waited for it to load.

"Nnnm," came a soft coo from behind him. It was followed by the sound of rustling sheets.

Chad turned the screen off on his phone and laid it face down on his desk, then turned his chair around ninety degrees.

Abby was laying in his bed, his ragged purple comforter covering the swell of her bare bosom as she stretched, barely awake, and in the same motion switched on the dim evening light he kept on his bedside table. A warm glow came from the small plastic circle she pressed on, illuminating the room with the sort of pleasant glow that would allow one to see but not wake one up.

She rubbed her eyes and propped herself up until her back was against his headboard. "Why are you awake?"

"Couldn't sleep."

"I'd assumed that much," she hummed, smiling as she leaned forward, stretching her hands the length of her covered leg. "What time is it?"

"Late," he said. His tone was neutral. "You should go back to bed."

She shot him a knowing look, her eyes smiling at him. He did not see the irony of what he had said, and it was in those moments when she'd caught him in a moment of minor and indulgent hypocrisy that she liked him best, she was finding.

She brought herself up to hug her knees, pinning his blanket to her torso in a way that kept her covered only by quirk of gravity, and he felt himself stirring when he watched her do it. He was no longer able to sit comfortably and lowered his left leg to the floor. It was numb now, blood rushing back to it from the place where he'd had it pinned.

"What are you working on?" Abby asked. Her hair fell forward onto her bare shoulder in wispy strands as she brought her hand up, squeezing a tense muscle she found there.

He glanced back at his desk, saw the phone lying face down next to the notebook, then forced a smile and turned it back on her. "Nothing."

"You have a shit poker face."

He grinned roguishly. "Then to what do you attribute my poker-playing acumen?"

"Blind luck," she drawled, stretching out the K sound and leaning her neck forward comically. She craned her neck up to see what he was hiding on his desk but saw only the closed notebook and a ball-point pen he'd gotten from the Payson Trust. Her mouth moved into something not unlike disappointment and she lowered herself back down, only then catching a glimpse of the photograph of Victor and Tash that was nestled neatly against his windowsill.

Whatever portion of the odd expression she'd been wearing that had been a smile quickly faded. She sighed. "Is there a reason you're ruminating on that?"

He winced. "You were excited today."

"Yester*day*. Day being operative part of the word, here. Holding on to that and keeping it long into the night is... it's unhealthy."

"If it was unhealthy, I'd have lucked into falling asleep," he said, forcing a grin.

"Be serious, please." She paused, then moved the hand that had been gently kneading her own neck up to the roots of her scalp, shaking loose some of the frustration that found itself nested there. She turned her attention to the pile of her clothes that sat in a neat pile on the top of his dresser, stacked in the order she'd need to put them on in. The room was wide, and there were at least ten feet between her and the clothes, a distance which hadn't seemed long in the heat of late night.

She turned back to the picture, its corners flicking minutely from a minor updraft, then back to him. "Did you find anything?"

A smile perked along one corner of his mouth. "I'd tried looking through the date-range that the picture was taken in the local papers, but couldn't really find anything." He spun the ninety degrees back to face his table, plucked his phone off of its perch, then spun back. "The problem is local papers. Their archives are bad, the websites never work the way they're supposed to. They also get most of their *news* news from bigger papers. The hard-er-hitting stuff, you know?"

She nodded.

"So I mean, what's left when you take all that away? Fluff. Bridges opening and mayoral appearances and some local baker trying to bake the world's largest oat-meal-raisin cookie that had nutmeg in it, because she can't come close to the actual world record so she changes the recipe enough that they give her her own category."

"That happens?"

"That happened." He turned the phone on and upped the brightness so that it could compete for his attention in the now-brighter room. "So, I figure, gotta go wider. Anything big enough that it'd be what we're looking for would make national news, right? So, I'm plugging in the date range when the picture of the jet could have been taken, and I'm cross-checking stories from Arizona."

"For a decade."

"For that specific decade, yeah."

She frowned, glancing back toward his dresser. "What are you looking for?"

"I'm not sure," he admitted, opening the web browser, and thumbing through the articles his search had brought up. "It has to be *something*. Something big enough that I don't think it could escape the public eye, but maybe not so big that it's... obvious? He couldn't have had a big part in it, otherwise the search would have --"

"No," Abby stressed, raising her hand to stop him. "I mean: *why* are you looking?"

He stiffened. "He's hiding something."

She rolled her eyes.

"No, he is. I know it. Know it the same way I know when a flush is coming on the river, or that my seven-deuce will be enough to win the day, this one time." He tapped the centre of his chest with all five fingers of his right hand. "I *know* it. Here."

She worked her tongue around the back of her teeth, again throwing a sidelong glance at the top of his dresser. "And if he is? Hiding something, I mean. We all are. We all *do*. What's that going to prove?"

Chad winced. His attention wavered from her pale face for the first time since she'd woken, darting to a framed photo on his dresser, next to her clothes. It was of them: he, Abby, Theo, and Jaycee. Jaycee was holding his little sister Koy on his shoulders, her chubby hands having flopped down over his eyes and making them all laugh just as the picture was taken.

"He expects too much of us," he said, his voice distant. He was still staring at the picture when he spoke. "More than he can be. I *know* that. He just... I need to see that. I need him to see it, and I need him to see that I see it. I need him --"

"Exposed?" Abby finished, her voice a soft thing in the back of her throat.

The word caught on his tongue at first, then he nodded.

She shook her head. "Why do you need to prod at things? Why can't a good man just be that: a good man?"

Chad frowned, looked away from the picture, then shook his head. "There are no good men."

She sighed and got up, holding his blanket around her like a dress with no straps, and made her way across the room to his dresser. The remainder of the blanket trailed along the ground like a gown, billowing when it met obstructions.

"Where are you going?" he asked.

"Back to my room," she said. She picked her underwear up off the top of the pile and maneuvered it around her left foot without dropping the blanket. "I still need sleep tonight."

"Hey. Hey, stop." He got up from his chair and stepped over to her. She looked away as he rested his hands on her hips, careening his head around her until they made eye contact. "I'm sorry, okay? I'll come to bed. I'll stop. Just... just stay."

She frowned and sighed, looking at the pile of her clothes right next to them.

He leaned his head down and kissed her, lightly, on the lips. He pulled his head back enough that he could see her, and she finally met his gaze, those soulful brown eyes twinkling in the first light of early morning that was finding its way in through the window. "I am sorry," he said again, quietly. He leaned his forehead against hers and rocked back and forth, his arms at her waist carrying the motion into her, until they were both dancing to some unheard rhythm. He leaned forward and kissed her again, longer this time, her hand making its way up to rest along the short hairs at the back of his head.

"Please stay?" he asked when they parted.

She nodded, and both of them stepped back across the room towards his bed. Halfway there, the blanket fell away, and suddenly the only thing covering her was the glow of dawn's first light. She smiled, and where the blanket had gone the kiss remained.

They got less sleep than she'd hoped.

Abby lay next to him on his bed, the light over the trees catching the touch of sweat that covered her and making her glow Her face was slack and calm, the angelic face of a loved one in a dreamless, peaceful sleep.

Chad stared at her for a long moment, gently brushing her hair back out of her mouth, and smiled warmly.

He laid back on his bed next to her, the covers somewhere in the no man's land between the bed and the dresser, and took out his phone. He turned down the glow, opened his browser, and began to scroll through his search results.

CHAPTER 08

Laramie, Wyoming

"Math is everything," said Professor March at the front of the class, his large glasses magnifying his eyes to comedic proportions. The words 'Statistics and Anthropology' were behind him in big, black letters on the board, though the H was missing from Anthropology. "That's why Math Nerds are Math Nerds. It's not that we like the numbers – well we do, but that's not the point – we like ordering the world around us. Math can tell us just about anything about the world we live in, and the universe we exist in. It's how we can measure the declination of words like 'succumb' in the English language over the last thirty years, or calculate the death tolls from attacks that haven't happened yet, or extrapolate the number of times one must shuffle a deck of cards before they are 'truly mixed.' Math is everything, from the most mundane statistic to the most grandiose and life-altering equation, like measuring the distance between stars or the point of origin of the Big Bang. Math is everything."

Sig Kincaid sat at the back of the amphitheater, listening to Professor March's lecture with half-hearted enthusiasm. He had heard this particular speech before, as this was his second time taking the course. There was a certain rhythm to it, a practiced tempo that his ears could not ignore. More than that though, he couldn't ignore the floppy ear lobes and large Coke-bottle glasses that had earned the Professor the nickname "March Hare" among the student body at UWYO.

The March Hare turned toward the whiteboard behind him and scrawled a large number sixty-three in purple dry-erase marker. Kincaid remembered, absently, that the last time he had taken this course it had been a red marker. He had liked this next part at the time, but found it tedious upon repetition. Despite the path his life had taken, he wasn't the sort of man who liked doing the same thing twice.

"Kennedy was shot in 1963," the March Hare said, circling the number haphazardly.

This was a good bit and enough to make the cackles of anyone with a conspiracy-theorist hiding inside them stand on end. Using math and statistics, the March Hare would find the number sixty-three in books, poems, random stimuli, and universal constants that all spelled out to make a paranoid person believe that this awful – but seemingly random – event was actually, at best, a part of a universal constant... and at worst a conspiracy of galactic proportions.

He would then go on to undercut the whole speech, and segue into an explanation about how numbers and statistics could be made to lie about anything, how 75% lean and 25% fat were the same number but one was used to make the product sell better, and the ethics of data skewing. But all of that was minutes away. At this moment the March Hare had barely finished explaining the trajectory of Oswald's bullet, and was doing so at such a tired pace that implied that he was in no way late for a very important date.

Kincaid made a note in his notebook of the date next to the same note he'd made the previous year, starring it. The blue lines of his book had begun to bleed into one another, distorted from repeated trips in the rain to and from his dorm. He sighed, his eyes falling onto a pink slip of paper edging its way out of his binder. It was his eviction notice from his dorm, advising him that his student loans had been retroactively withheld and -- as a result -- he was behind on his room and board.

There were several sheets poking out of from behind the crumpled pink paper. Want-Ads for Roommate Wanted. Boarder Wanted. Tennant Wanted. Each had pull-off tabs sliced into their ends. For the first few he'd tried, he'd taken a tab, but after a few responses of "we've already filled our vacancy" he altered his approach to taking the entire sheet. Why leave room for the competition? Still, even those with rooms still free needed money he didn't yet have. First month down. First month plus security deposit. First and last month, plus security deposit. None of which he had. If he did, he wouldn't have to move at all.

One brightly coloured flyer stuck out from behind them all, black ink printed on bright green paper. There was a cartoon image of a girl in a bikini along one side, and across from her hip a grainy photo of a large multi-dwelling house. The text along the top of the sheet read

"Pledge at Epsilon Gamma Nu." It was followed by information about the history of the fraternity, written from a biased point of view. Along the bottom, in bold Helvetica font, it read: "Successful Pledges Room Free."

Kincaid frowned. He lingered on the message a long time, the March Hare's lecture having become background noise. His eyes began to wander from the page, eventually finding their way to the nape of the neck of the blonde girl just ahead and to the right of him. She was wearing dangling gold earrings, the sort that caught the sunlight in such a way that let you know they were gold, read gold, not the cheap imitation stuff.

She turned slightly, the hairs on the back of her neck raising in the sort of way that happens when you realize, for no reason at all, that someone is watching you. The sort of feeling that eyes were upon you that must have given rise to the theories of the EPR Paradox. Her eyes were bright blue. They met his and he smiled honestly and apologetically, nodding and brushing the air with his hand.

She did not return his smile, turning back towards the March Hare with what he thought were the beginnings of an eye roll before she was out of place, fixing her hair and flashing a stylish gold bracelet as she did so.

He frowned and turned back to his notes. Was she just trying to pay attention to the lecture? It was possible, he didn't know her. But something in the twitch of those perfectly pink lips and the way her eyes had started to roll gave him the impression that she wouldn't have given such passing response to him had he been white.

He wondered, briefly, if Professor March had ever

done the statistics on that to try and get the numbers on racist tendencies in sexual coupling. What was it that attracted black men to white women that also rarely attracted white men to black women? What were the numbers on each gender being attracted to the opposite gender of a different race, or the *same* gender of the opposite race, for that matter? He entertained those thoughts briefly, and started to summarize that those open enough to be in a same-sex relationship were also open and inclusive enough not to be tied down by the binaries of race, then thought better of it. He shook the thought away. <<

She turned slightly, the hairs on the back of her neck raising in the sort of way that happens when you realize that someone is watching you. Her bright blue eyes scanned the row behind her, found nothing amiss, then turned back towards the front of the class. She chided herself on her paranoia and blamed it on the lecture.

"Sixty-Three is the exact number of chromosomes found in the offspring of a donkey and a horse," the March Hare said. That factoid was new, and didn't sit well within the rest of the lecture.

The theatre was large, with a capacity of at least two-hundred seats, roughly 125 of which were filled at the moment. Kincaid sat in the back row, and from here the March Hare seemed like a small figurine that could fit between his thumb and forefinger, like the Mighty Max toys of his youth. He moved like a toy with poor articulation too, only bending at the waist and the elbows as he moved to animate his points. When he moved his hips, the lobes of his ears giggled.

Of the 125 students sitting in this second-year statistics

lecture, almost every head and back-of-neck he looked out upon was Caucasian. This wasn't something he was often aware of, and it rarely came up, but something about statistics brought it out in him. He remembered having similar thoughts in this class the first time he'd taken it, though not during the same lecture. The last time had been his first time hearing the lecture, and the only spare thought he could remember having experienced was to wonder if Marilyn Monroe and JFK had done it exactly sixty-three times before they both ended up dead.

This time, his mind wandering, he became acutely aware of his status of a minority within a minority within a minority. Percentage of African Americans, thirteen. Percentage of African Americans that went on to a post-secondary institution, six. Percentage of African Americans in Numeracy-Centric programs of study, one. Percentage of African Americans in this class, 0.8. With every number he felt his world get smaller and smaller. He wondered, from his place at the back, how many people in this class would have rolled their eyes if they'd turned around and caught him looking at them? A small number to be sure, this far north of the Mason-Dixon... but not none. Was this blonde girl with the penchant for gold the only one? Even if her gesture had been racially motivated and she was the only racist in the room, that put the number of racists and the number of Africans in the room on equal footing. It would only take one more racist for them to outnumber him by double... a sobering statistic.

He was just about to push this thought out of his mind and try to regain his focus, when he realized he was wrong: the percentage of people of African descent in this classroom had doubled now, up to 1.6 percent. Still not enough if it was time for the revolution, but still more than he had thought.

It had been easy to miss the 'new addition' on his initial pass through the rest of the theatre. The man he'd miscounted sat in the very front row, as close to the March Hare as he could. He was large and broad, looking as though he should have had a hard time in the confining, flip-desk seats of the classroom. His size hadn't made it hard to notice him though; if anything, it should have made him stand out more. What had made Kincaid miss him on his initial count through the classroom was that his skin wasn't black or brown or deeply tanned or whatever the politically-correct way to describe the African hue was nowadays: it was gray. His skin was patchy and gray and looked dusty with white flecks, as though someone had gently patted him behind the ears with chalk-dust.

He was an albino.

For a moment the statistician-in-training within him began to calculate the odds on that subset of a subset, but he stopped himself, because he was sure that this man had never been in this classroom before. It was hard to keep track of all the students – especially in a class this size, with people adding and dropping and sitting in, but this large bald albino was definitely new. He wore a blazer that had definitely been a part of a large tailored suit. Suits that large had to be tailored. There were bumps along his scalp, hard to make out from this angle.

There was a man sitting next to the albino in a row that was almost otherwise vacant. He was bald as well, but other than that was the large man's opposite number. He was sickly slender, the sort of figure that friends would call "a stick" and "skinny" in jest while actually being concerned. His skin was pale white with just enough pigmentation that he couldn't be mistaken for a different hue of albino. He was wearing a short-sleeved tee-shirt that looked to be the type that bore a band name, and although Kincaid couldn't have guessed which one, he laid odds that it was Nirvana.

The second man's head turned slightly, the same way the blonde girl's had. It turned so that he should have been able to see his nose in profile, yet didn't, but did catch a glimpse of dandelion-yellow sclera before the head turned back around to the front.

Professor March motioned to the albino man and smiled. "But you don't have to take my word for it," he said, capping off some point that Kincaid had faded out for. "We have a special guest lecturer with us all week, Dr. Fnu Jona, an expert on cultural and spiritual anthropology." He raised his hands and started to clap, and maybe all of the student body did the same.

Kincaid craned his neck up from the back of his chair, trying to see the ashen man the March Hare had introduced.

Jona stiffened his blazer with a pull at the bottom of it, then took up the pen he'd been working with in his large gray fingers. He leaned in close to the man he sat next to, whispering: "Did you catch that?"

The young man next to him didn't say anything, still looking at the number sixty-three on the board in purple marker.

"Maximus?"

Jaycee turned and smiled, then nodded politely. "You're sure it's him?"

Jona flipped his book closed. He got up, then threw a rueful smirk toward Jaycee. "Despite what Professor March would have you believe, Maximus, numbers do not lie." He said this even as he straightened his blazer once more, pumped it twice from its bottom, and made his way over to the professor with mock joviality.

They exchanged kind words, then Professor March sat down next to Jaycee, in the seat Jona had vacated.

Jona stood at the head of the lecture theatre with all the UWYO students staring back at him expectantly.

He had brought two items with him, and they now sat on the table beside the water bottles the university had provided. One was a thick paperback book with a well-worn spine. The other was a single unlit cigarette. It sat there, its dry leaves almost falling from its thin paper sleeve, just shy of the book's spine.

Jona had never smoked a day in his life. The cigarette, which he'd brought in behind his ear and laid perpendicular to the uppermost edge of the book, had been something he'd adopted after seeing a novelty item in a college's home: an 'emergency last cigarette' sealed behind a seamless tube of glass. He'd found it amusing, and the next time that same college was going out for a smoke, he'd asked to borrow one.

"You don't smoke, Jona."

"I'm aware."

The man – Herbert Whineguard – had produced the

cigarette from a fresh pack and handed it to him. That same cigarette had been brought to every first lecture or guest lecture he'd attended in the decade since... just in case it went bad enough to necessitate an emergency smoke.

A young girl in the second row from the front began to shuffle uncomfortably. It was like a yawn, that kind of shuffle – it spread from person to person, as soon as it was seen. Before too long the majority of the crowd was fidgeting in Jona's peripheral vision, looking like a disinterested audience at a sports event trying unsuccessfully to start The Wave. He repressed the urge to smile at the thought as the minute hand on the clock behind him snapped to seven past the hour.

"With respect to Professor March," Jona began, smiling politely. It fell away quickly. "I couldn't disagree more."

Most of the class listened, but in the back, Kincaid's eyebrows rose to their highest peak.

"Anthropology isn't math. Anthropology isn't about mathematical truth; it is about human truth. That is the difference between the etic and emic approaches, and do not ever let anyone tell you that one is not better than the other." He paused, regarded Jaycee and March each for a moment, then gripped either side of his podium and continued. "I could prove it to you. I could bring you some work by Stoller or Robinson or Erikson or Douglas. We could go back to the beginning, with Marx and Freud. I could read to you from *I, Rigoberta Menchu* or *The Diary of Anne Frank*... but it all falls short. It all gives some small part of what anthropology is and yet still reduces it, doesn't show it for all that it is. In truth, Anthropology is less defined by what it *is*, than what it is *not*. And then I remembered this." He laid his hand on the thick book on the desk, his massive palm landing with a heavy thud. "This book is the basis of all anthropological thought. It was the starting point from which all our branches – sociology, archeology, cultural and social anthropology – stem. It is, ironically, our genesis."

He eyed the crowd and waiting, then allowed himself a smile. "You'll see why that's funny in a moment."

He picked up the book, cupping the spine in one hand despite its girth, and carried it over to the student on the far left of the front row. "Take a moment and look at that, then pass it along. Everyone touch it but be careful with it; it's a relic."

The thick book on the student's lap was a large green paperback edition of the Good Word Bible. The pages were wafer thin and translucent, yet the book was still incredibly thick. The student – a woman with long brunette hair – looked from the book to Jona, then back again, then passed it to the next student to her left.

"That book," Jona said, wagging his finger as he turned and walked back to his chair, but did not sit down in it, "that book is the originator of all anthropological thought. All scholarly thought actually. Back in the day, to be a 'scholar' meant literally to study the Bible... as though we were going to find something new in it after reading it for the thousandth time."

He picked up a black marker and wrote August 3, 1492 on the dry-erase board behind him, then capped the marker and put it back down. He walked to the desk, picked up the bottle farthest to his left, unscrewed the cap, and then drank half the bottle before stopping for air. "Who can tell me why that date is important to anthropology?"

There was silence in the class. The book was still being passed from student to student, some of whom took genuine interest, thinking there was some clue hidden on or in the text. Two seemed appalled when it came to them, unsure of why it was being used as a prop. It had made it through only ten sets of hands.

In the front row, a man with thick brown glasses raised a single finger. Jona nodded at him, and he answered: "Was that when Columbus first set sail looking for India?"

Jona nodded. "It was, yes. That was when everything – *everything* – changed--"

Kincaid hiked himself forward on his chair, paying attention closely to what this man -- one of the only men he'd met in months that sounded like him -- was saying. <<

Kincaid raised his hand. Jona nodded at him, and he answered: "That when Columbus first set sail looking for India."

Jaycee turned around in his seat to meet Kincaid's eye. His own were large, and jaundiced.

Jona smiled. "Correct. That was when everything – *everything* – changed because as we all know, he went looking for India and found—" He paused and held up his hand to the class.

"America," enough of them said in unison as to make it sound like a chorus.

"Nice to see you're all here," he smiled. "But they

didn't find America... what they found, was something that *wasn't* in that book." He pointed at the Bible, which had made its way to a twentieth student. He took the last of the first bottle of water then threw it over his back and into a trash bin under the dry-board. "There was this existential crisis in the intellectual world: this book was supposed to have the answers to everything, and yet here was this huge thing – an entire continent – that wasn't in it! How could the book tell everything and leave such a big thing out? Thus was born," he pushed his forefinger into the air with a flourish, "the first anthropologist."

He paused. The book was still making its rounds, but no eyes were on it: all were on him. "We didn't call them anthropologists at the time of course, we just called them scholars. Hundreds of them – thousands over the years – tasked with studying that book and trying to find where in it it could be interpreted to be talking about the New World. Some studied from home, others branched out, missionaries and the like, to those new places to spread the word but also try to uncover the word within those new places... and some came back with a very specific answer: the New World isn't in the book."

He opened a new bottle of water, but didn't take a drink from it yet.

"They said the New World isn't in the book. This book, the book that's supposed to have the answer to everything in it. So one of the two must be false, and since we can go to this New World and see it and touch it and know that it's real... then it must be the book that's false." He drank, taking all the liquid as far as the label. "They broke from the church – over time, of course – but they were still scholars, only now they didn't study the text for the answers, they studied reality for the answers. They looked to ourselves, to humanity: our past, our society, our cultures, the differences between our cultures, the similarities between our cultures... they became students of mankind itself, the first anthropologists."

Jona pointed to a scruffy man in his late twenties in the middle of the hall. He was wearing thick-rimmed glasses and a saggy coat. "Why study other cultures? What were we looking for?"

Kincaid raised an eyebrow.

Jaycee turned around again, to watch him.

The scruffy youth stopped for a moment, mouth agape. Finally he said, with confidence: "To see if every-one is the same."

"No," Jona said sharply, then took a drink from his bottle. "To see if people are different."

The youth rolled his eyes.

"There's a difference," Jona said, pointing to him. "Believe me. Intent matters. *Placement* matters. Dirt is just matter, out of place."

<< The scruffy youth stopped for a moment, mouth agape. Behind him, in the far back row, Kincaid raised his hand again.

Jona cocked his head toward him.

"To see if people are different," Kincaid said, with confidence.

Jona smiled, then nodded gratifyingly. When he turned back toward Jaycee, the latter's eyes were filled with shock, and somehow, fear. Jona nodded at him, once.

The crowd was silent. The textbook had stopped its

rotation around the room.

Jona drank from his bottle. "From the very start, from that first Lacanian, Mirror-Stage moment, Anthropology had a task. It was defined, as we all are, by what birthed it. It was to look at things dispassionately, the whole thing: all of it, and decide from it, what was true. Emic from etic. Cultural norm from original truth. Religion, from cult."

At the last, the crowd's attention, which had begun to waver, snapped back to attention.

After the lecture, Jona sat back on his stool. Many students had left, but fifty or so had stayed past the allotted time. They were huddled around the stool now as Jona nursed his final bottle of water, most of them standing with their bags slung over their shoulders and moving from one foot to the other, stuck in a dance between staying and going. It was late. The lecture had gone on longer than it has been scheduled, and even after Jona had concluded several students came up to him with questions... the answers to which had gotten the attention of some of the other students, who followed up with questions of their own. They filtered out slowly and unwillingly, each faced with the duel desires for the lecture to end and to not miss anything.

"... well, White could be a bit of reductive in all his thinking, if we're being quite honest," Jona said, before the student had even finished asking the question. "I mean I get what he was going for, bringing that sort of 'evolutionary' methodology to anthropology... but the problem with bringing evolution into anthropology is that

the second you start using it, you start classifying different cultures on scales of advancement, and calling lower
entrants 'primitive' and the like. It's all well and good to
call animals primitive, but human cultures? And his way
around it... coming up with a mathematical equation to
determine the worth of a society... well. Judging a society
as evolutionarily inferior, or superior, by any standard
of measurement, no matter how well intentioned, seems
wrong to me. It seems like the nature of the question is
ethnocentric. That is asking a question you guarantee an
ethnocentric response, and yet it seems to be a question
many anthropologists do endeavor to ask. My problem
with "rating" societies based on even something so seemingly scientific and quantifiable as "energy" and its effect,
judges the goals of the society as well. Has a society that
"produces less energy" failed in some way? If it is not
meeting its own goals then maybe, but if a society is meeting its goals -- reproduction, nourishment, safety -- then
I'm not sure how we can judge in based on any measurement of energy."

The student nodded empathically.

There was a blonde woman sitting in the first row of
chairs that hadn't been there while he was giving his lecture. She was drifting in and out of view, the only person
sitting while so many others crowded around, as though
she were fading in and out of existence. Her eyes were on
him, he could tell that much – the flashes of eye contact
that came between legs and from around thighs unmis-
takable. Her eyes were blue. Her lips the sort of soft pink
usually reserved for roses in inspirational watercolours.

"Sir?"

Jona turned to the student, a portly young man with freckles at the corner of each eye. He realized he'd been asked a question, but had no idea what it had been. "I..." He felt his gaze returning to the blonde woman with the bright pink lips, but found that she was gone. He shut his mouth, finding it agape. "...I'm afraid you'll have to pick up my book if you want any more on that subject," he said distractedly, with an air of forced joviality to his tone.

The portly student cocked his head to one side, as though that answer hadn't quite made sense to the question asked. In all likelihood it hadn't.

Jona got up, leaving what remained of his bottle of water, and the Good News Bible behind on the desk. "You should also try *Why Nations Fail*. Robinson has some interesting points... repetitive, but... interesting..." He moved out into the hallway even as he finished his sentence, among the specimen samples and faux-tribal art that sat in glass cases along each wall between the entrances to each lecture hall.

The hall was empty, save for him.

CHAPTER 09

Payson, The Past

Tash laid on her stomach, her feet kicked up to the peak of her legs and the soft, unsupportive mattress of the Motel 83 curling up around even her scant weight. Her laptop was open in front of her, balanced precariously on the edge of the bed. Her hand moved, scrolling through the articles her search had brought up -- and her hair moved, twitching in the hot air that came in through the window they'd opened.

Victor lay on the opposing bed, propped up against the head-board in such a way that his neck would make him regret it in the morning. He was watching the television -- a tiny rectangle with dead pixels -- and every few minutes he would raise the remote control like a gun and stab at the Next Channel button with the sharp nail of his thumb. The picture would flicker, as if finding the next signal were somehow difficult, then change. The new picture flickered into view with distorted, over-saturated colours for a moment, then normalized. Victor's lip curled when he saw the picture fade-in on a talk-show pundit wearing a blue suit and blood red tie, and he changed the channel again quickly.

"Can't find local stations," he said. His lip was starting to curl.

Tash turned to look at him over her shoulder. They laid end to end on separate beds, her head occupying the same place as his thick-booted feet. She tried to meet his eye, but he would not turn his attention from the screen, and her gaze fell over the rest of him. "How's your burn?" she asked, her eyes falling to the puffy tendrils that still poked out of his arm.

He held it up without turning to her, the arm glistening with aloe in the light from the television. "Healing."

She watched him and it, studying them both for signs that he was hiding something. After a moment she went back to her work.

The Motel 83 was the only motel in Payson that was in operation this far out of season, they had been told, after calling two others only to have the calls redirected to the owner's personal cells. There was one hotel within the town limits that they could find, a multi-floor chain location with exorbitant rates that were set by head office, not reflective of the relative vacancy of the location. They'd found Motel 83 at the bottom of a list of possible accommodations and had almost missed it: it had no picture, no price, no number, and no reviews. It read like a badly phrased text ad at the end of the search history, and for a moment Tash's eyes had confused it with an ad for diet pills.

It was a long, one floor building that snaked this way and that, forming an S along the grounds behind the main office, which was separate. The connective tissue between the three main long sections of the building were just metal awning, but the affect was still there. All the rooms were on ground level, and they all had a doorway on either side of the rooms: one that led out to the parking lot, and another that connected to a long *shared highway filled with vending machines and ice makers.*

Each of the rooms were dark, with no overhead lighting: only bedside lamps, and any light that came in from the bathroom. The paint was gray, the floor a deep, earthy brown.

Victor changed the channel again, and suddenly there was a full-frame image of a white man behind a desk on the screen. There was space along the wall to the left of the screen, and occupying it was a photo of Briana Redding, the same school photo that had been on the Missing Persons posters they'd seen being erected. This photo was in colour though, the blonde of Briana's hair a bright sun shining down on the newscaster's shoulders. The photo was enlarged to the point of pixilation, the tears in the reality of the image starting to show: teeth were not individual actors, but one long strip of white that protruded below the girl's upper lip.

No matter how it appeared in the image though, the teeth still smiled, as did the clear cheeks and bright blue eyes. The whole of this girl, Victor realized, was smiling.

He sat up in his bed and brought his legs up under himself until he was cross-legged, getting closer to the screen.

Tash looked at the image on the screen, then at him. His boots now had the covers wrapped around them and entangled with them. "There's going to be sand in that bed for days."

He smirked. "I'm sleeping in the other bed."

She scoffed, laughed, and turned back toward her screen as the newscaster began to speak. He had a pale complexion and hair that swept back. His teeth, like Briana's, were a perfect line across his lower lip. Teeth and hair, Victor had called the average television reporter, once. Teeth and hair.

Tash scrolled down the mostly gray screen. There were white boxes with text in them at regular intervals, each one paired with two borderless photos: one of a child, one of an adult. Some didn't have any adult pictures. Most of the children's pictures were school photos... but not all. Some children, she noted with apprehension, were too young to have had school photos. "I'm not getting any closer to --"

"Shh," Victor hushed, raising a finger to her and not taking his eyes off the screen.

She turned to the screen, watched the man in the suit talk for a moment, then turned back to her laptop. She sighed, then moved the curser down to the lower-right hand corner of the screen and hovered over a small flower-shaped icon. When the curser touched it, it glowed green and she right-clicked, bringing up a list of three names, each with their own circle-headed bust of a human next to it.

The last on the list was named 'Spoiler.' She hovered over it, hesitating a moment, then turned back to Victor. His eyes were still glued to the man behind the desk. She clicked the name and a small rectangle appeared on the screen, covering part of the gray-hued files she'd been scanning through.

"Need help," she typed into the rectangle, then hit enter.

For a moment there was nothing, then a circle of dots in the centre of the screen started to spin. They stopped, started again, then stopped again. Finally, the response came, contrasted by a pink speech balloon: "There are twelve ducks in New Amsterdam."

She smirked, then typed. "But only five in St. Louis. Deforestation. Fight the power."

After a moment of the spinning icon again, the reply came: "What do you need?"

She copied the web address she'd been working within and pasted it into the window, then hit enter. "I'm looking for missing children in Payson. We're hunting one, but Victor thinks there's more."

The eye-roll emoji returned.

She laughed.

"What's happening?" Victor asked, barely turning his head in her direction.

"Nothing," Tash responded. She turned back to the television long enough to catch the end of the broadcast, which declared that the Payson PD had no further leads at this time before switching to a story on a flooded bridge. She frowned. "You sure about this?"

He nodded. His chin was rested on his clasped hands, his thumbs running down the line of his Adam's apple and making it bulge. "You didn't see them. Not like I did."

She nodded, absently.

Her computer chimed.

"You talking to him?" Victor asked.

"Yes," she said as she turned back to grab at the mouse. "I couldn't find anything."

"Delete that account, when you're done."

She shot him a droll look. "Don't act like I'm not the one who taught you that, please."

In the chat window a long URL link had appeared against a pin window. She clicked it and it opened up a new browser, which brought her to a page she did not recognize. It also had a gray, utilitarian background, but this one was a slightly darker shade. Like the page she'd been on, there were white textboxes accompanied by photos of children... but none of adults alongside them.

There were four on the main page, each smiling out at her from school photos on blue backgrounds. Some were older than others, some were missing teeth. Some had light hair while others were full albino blonde. One girl who smiled out at her caught Tash's eye: she was wearing a bright red bow with beveled edges, of the sort that was displayed proudly and took time and effort to get in. There were no hidden plastic clips: it was tied in, weaved throughout the bright blonde strips of hair meticulously. The girl looked out of the camera, through the pixilated screen, and directly into Tash's soul.

She swallowed. There were four of them on the screen, but as she scrolled down, there were more. First eight, then twelve. Each had a caption under their name in bright, red font:

MISSING FROM RUMSEY PARK

MISSSING FROM STAR VALLEY

MISSING FROM PAYSON

MISSING FROM PAYSON

MISSING FROM MESA DEL CABALLO

MISSING FROM PAYSON

"Victor," she said, and was surprised when her own voice was wet.

He turned to her and she turned the screen toward him. "Star Valley, that's near here... right?"

Victor narrowed his eyes, then nodded.

She turned back to the girl with the red ribbon. It brought out the green in her eyes and made them sparkle like gemstones, shimmering in the focal point of Tash's field of view.

"Do you see it now?" he asked, somewhere behind her.

Tash nodded. She took a deep breath and felt something swell within her that had never been there before that moment: something primal, maternal. It started in her centre and ebbed out, like anxiety but different, more focused. She clenched her jaw when the feeling reached it and squared her shoulders, then got her notepad and started to write down the names of the children and where they'd vanished from.

In that moment she knew: she was going to help these children.

CHAPTER 10

Payson, The Present

"Nine ball, side pocket," Theo said, just as he snapped his pool stick forward. The impact of it hitting the cue was as sharp as a lightning strike, and in the blink of an eye it had travelled the length of the table. It cracked against the Nine, sending it hurtling toward the pocket where it was swallowed whole.

Alice looked up from her phone as it went in, smiled, then pushed off the wall she'd been leaning on. Theo had sunken four balls in a row, culminating with the sinking of the nine that ended the game. After the first two, she'd taken out her phone and started to check her social media notifications.

"Rack them back up?" she asked, bringing herself forward until both her hands were rested on the table.

He nodded curtly, fishing the rack off of the hook it hung on and tossing it to her with a slight spin on the throw. It was a throw he'd learned in school, but it hadn't been taught to him for throwing Nine-Ball racks. It had been taught for throwing knives, in such a way that they always landed with accuracy.

The rack spun like a frisbee, tapping against Alice's solar plexus. She caught it between clapped hands, spun it on her finger like a basketball, then snapped it down into position at the down-end of the table.

The rec room was on the first floor of the house they all shared, a few scant miles outside of the Payson city limits. It lacked the large, magnificent windows of the rest of the floor. The ground sloped up around it, giving it the look and feel of an above-ground basement, right down to porthole windows that edged the wall close to the ceiling.

There was an actual basement, but Victor kept that door locked at all times. Chad had attempted to jimmy the lock once when they'd been living together a little over a month, but it had been to no avail: the seals around the door were so tight that not even a draft or a beam of light leaked through.

The rec area was long, taking up at least three quarters of the length of the house. It was sectioned into areas by furniture: the back of a couch creating the illusion of a barrier in otherwise open space. This faux wall separated the part of the room with the pool table, card table, and dart board from the part of the room with the television and seats, which was itself separated by a well-stocked bookshelf to make a reading nook.

Alice arranged the balls within the plastic diamond: the bright yellow One in front, and all the solid colours circling its perimeter. The blue Two was on the left, the red Three on the right, and so on. The only striped ball - the titular Nine - was snug between them all.

When she was done arranging them, she leaned back and looked at what she had made, the mix-matched colour wheel squished into a diamond-shape. "They all protect the one in the middle," she motioned to it, gliding her hand through the air above it.

"That's one way to look at it," Theo said, dusting the top of his stick with chalk.

She looked at him, the smile she'd had tested around the edges. "I assume there's another?"

He smirked, walked to the other end of the table with the cue-ball in hand, and began to line up the shot. "The one goes in front because you're supposed to hit them in order -- you're supposed to go through all the steps -- but that's not the real goal. The goal is that Nine, but you can't get to it."

He cracked the stick forward again, so fast that Alice jumped. The balls scattered wild behind the pressure of Theo's arm, ricocheting and tumbling this way and that before coming to a rest. The result was a solar system that had been conceived by a mad god, and no balls scored. The Nine, for all the chaos that had surrounded it, remained in the exact position it had started in.

Theo waved to the pattern of balls. "All these, these are bullshit. The Artifice. These are the lies we tell, the lies we're told, the lies we believe ourselves. All this bullshit, all these tiny goals we let people see, all surrounding the one truth," he motioned to the Nine. "All of them insulating against the truth, until you can't even get at it. That's the real joke, is that we want to get at the truth, but we can't even make the effort, not right away. We have to chip away at all this... this bullshit first."

"It's, like, pretty early in the day for this," Alice drawled, rolling her eyes as she stepped around the table with her stick, looking for an angle from which to strike. When she had walked fully around it, she found the One, nestled comfortably along the edge of the upper corner pocket, with only the Three between them. Her mouth warbled as she examined the angle, then she leaned forward and started to line up her shot, making several tentative pushes forward.

As Theo watched her, a large screen behind her faded into view, as if crosscut on some film-student's mixing board. For a moment both the screen and the loveseat behind her were visible, as if the student were playing with the juxtaposition of the two for a thesis he'd hastily cobbled together. On the screen was the shot from her point-of-view, the stick hitting the cue perfectly and dead centre, the cue rocketing forward and slamming into the One at a perfect angle to just allow it to skate past the Three.

"One Ball, corner pocket," she said under her breath. She pushed the stick forward like a cobra, but in reality, the stick glanced off the top of the cue. The ball still moved forward at a more-or-less straight purchase though, connecting with the One with a soft -plink- and not with the thunderclap it had in her imagination. The One rolled forward gingerly, then fell into the corner pocket where the soft leather caressed it.

Alice stood up proudly, as though she'd performed the task just as she'd meant to, her small mouth brimming with pride. She looked at Theo, whose eyes were focused somewhere in the void behind her. "What are you looking at?" she asked.

"Nothing," he said, unable to keep the smug smile off his lips. "Nothing at all. Good shot."

She shot him a weather eye, then moved around the table to the corner that now nestled the One Ball. The cue was now roughly in line with the Two Ball, and a straight shot would have sent it hurtling into the corner pocket with ease... but on the billboard screen behind her, a different scenario played out. In it, the Two ricocheted off a position just down from the side-pocket, instead hitting the Nine Ball and sending it rolling into the bottom left pocket opposite the One, and ending the game.

She thought about this for a long moment, several arcs, angles, pressures, and possibilities coming to her. She looked at Theo once, but the screen had telegraphed that she was going to do that as well, and he'd turned away to one of the prints on the wall, an aerial shot of a racked 8-Ball set.

She frowned again, leaned down, and fired at the Two without saying a word. The cue moved wide, hitting the solid blue orb and send it hurtling into the side pocket. "Yes," she said, then moved to make her way to line up with the Three.

"Nah ah, nope," Theo laughed, walking around to the side pocket and fishing the Two out of it. He gripped it as though he were going to try and slide it across home plate, then moved it next to the Nine at the starting mark of the table and placed it down with enough force that it stayed there. "Scratch."

She furrowed her brow in her best approximation of surprise. "What? How was that a scratch?"

"You never called it."

"So I forgot to call it, I mean --"

"And you were going for the Nine."

She stopped, pursed her lips, then let herself fall back to lean against the wall adjacent to the table. Her eyelids lowered until there was very little left to them. "Fine. Cheater."

He shot her an ironic glare with one eyebrow raised, then moved toward the outer edge of the table and moved the cue into the position he wanted to fire from.

Behind Alice, her billboard had changed to a split screen: one side showing her hitting the balls around the table, the other the single cover of Limp Bizkit's *Break Stuff*, which was playing over the fantasy tantrum. The cover wasn't quite right, the details and colours were off... but Theo still recognized the album for what it was, he realized. Just as he recognized the tantrum of hitting the balls as fantasy, not as a plotted plan. These things came to him through osmosis: he saw the image and knew.

He thought back to Victor, and the flickering image that had appeared behind him. There was a man in it with arms outstretched, only there briefly, like a ghost burned into the picture of an old tube television set.

"I've been lied to a lot," he said finally, even as he made his attempt at the Two. "Corner pocket."

He hit the cue, struck the Two, but missed the pocket.

"Sorry," Alice said. She pushed her rear off the wall and bounced back into standing position.

He smiled at her and didn't need to look at her billboard, because he knew it to be true.

CHAPTER 11

Alice sat on the porch behind Victor's house as dusk fell, a book in her hand that she was only nominally reading. It was *Watership Down* by Richard Adams, and she'd picked it up upon recommendation from Victor roughly a month ago. Since then she had read it in starts and fits, starting over at least three times (but skipping parts she found familiar), and had yet to make it to the end.

Once, Abby had commented that the book scared her -- as the animated film had an entire generation of children -- but Alice had assured her that reality couldn't have been further from the truth: it wasn't fear that led her to put down the book over and over again, but indifference. No matter what she did, she could not find it in herself to care about rabbits trying to accomplish the monumental task of crossing the road.

She found her eyes lolling in the void between the lines on the page, and let the book fall forward onto her chest again, as it had many evenings before. She looked over it and up the walkway that led back to the house, taking in its shape as the last of the evening light cascaded off it.

The house was large, fit easily to be called a mansion in certain circles. It looked to have started as a small, square home of brick that had been added onto again and again: first a north wing, then an east one. Then multiple floors were added, some unevenly, rising like peaks into bedrooms and private areas. The five of them -- she, Theo, Chad, Victor, and Abby -- fit into it easily, each with their own space and space enough for more again. There were rooms that she still had not been in.

She twisted her tongue around her dry mouth as she stared at it. Suddenly, the thought of that house -- and the untouched rooms within it -- intrigued her more than the careful and inoffensive prose of Richard Adams. The house seemed to glow as the light faded. The brick of it was a shade of red she'd never seen before -- a sort of bright pomegranate red -- that retained the light from the day and kept its colour, even in shadow, holding it against her green shutters.

There was a clock face that was stopped near the back, facing north. Both hands were stuck, forever facing the number eight in such a way that the hour hand was all but invisible. Victor had pointed it out to her once, the first day she'd arrived, and had said that, "Time stood still here. It's the Infinity House." His tone had been of the sort that only Dad Jokes were delivered in, and he'd laughed honestly afterward, then gotten quiet.

She clicked her tongue against the roof of her mouth several times, put her book down on the glass table next to her, then started back towards the house.

∞

The first three doors Alice had tried had been bedrooms, or at least, rooms that could have functioned as bedrooms if desired. They had closets, and the space where beds could go. One had been filled with books; another had been completely vacant.

The fourth door had been toward the rear of the first floor and had been locked. She tried it, came up solid against it when she'd expected to step through, then frowned. It was under the stairs that led up towards the second level and was small. She'd thought it was a closet again, but when she'd come up solid against it, it had produced a long echo.

She frowned, stopped, and stepped back. The door was perfectly white but yellowed from sun bleach in uneven patterns from the adjacent windows. There was a rectangle of gray drywall colour at eyelevel, where at one point there had been a label or name that had since been removed.

She moved her mouth back and forth, sighed, then stepped forward and ran her hand along the top of the doorframe until her finger finally found purchase on something hard and cold. She slid the rippled pads of her fingers over it, slipped it loose, and then caught it as it fell in a cloud of thick dust.

It was a key.

She smiled to herself, then slid the key into the door's knob. It went it with some effort, making a pained sound as she twisted it, but did unlock and open the door. It swung open as though of its own power once the knob was fully turned, revealing a long, narrow staircase that made its way down to a dark cellar, or basement.

"Yeah, nope. I've seen this movie," she said to herself,

taking a step back from the door and turning to head back up the stairs. All at once she stopped, as if coming up short. She ran her tongue along the front of her teeth again, remembering the book about rabbits that still rested in the hot desert air out on the porch and the cool lemonade in the fridge, just five rooms away. She sighed, turned back, and stood at the mouth of the long, dark stairway.

Despite her own reservations, she found herself reaching out and fumbling along the edge of the wall for a lightswitch, eventually finding one and flipping it into the on position. A light flickered to life at the bottom of the stairs, showing their end and providing a dull glow to the space between.

Swallowing hard, Alice made her way down the stairs, the light becoming brighter and brighter as she went. At the bottom of the stairs was a large room with a dust floor, the sort of unfinished basement that was common in coastal homes, but some would consider unmanageable in Arizona sand. The floor was hot, keeping the heat from the sun and bringing it in from below.

The light cast a circle onto the floor, and all around it was blackness. It was a cellar devoid of belongings, a pantry bereft of food.

The only item, placed squarely in the middle of the circle, was a small box. It was matte black and seemed to absorb the light, a void in the space the was somehow deeper than the shadows around it. With the same unconscious trepidation with which she'd stepped down the stairs, she approached the box.

She took a deep breath, knelt down, then opened the box with both thumbs.

Her eyebrows raised.

CHAPTER 12

Victor affixed a picture of a young blonde to his peg-board, which itself was propped between two wooden chairs. He held his thumb down with undue force, his calloused digit pressing until it indented the airy material. He stepped back from it, his hand finding its way into the briar patch that was his unshaven chin.

Below the photo was a map reference, with Payson in its centre.

Behind him, the rest of the team sat -- save Chad -- at the dining room table. Chad was walking to and from the coffee pot delivering drinks, which he got exactly right to the drinker's specifications without having asked. He handed a solid black mug to Abby, steam barreling out of it, then turned and caught Victor's eye. "Correcto?"

Victor's nostril twitched. "No. Thank you."

Chad turned to the girl. In it she was wearing a jersey and holding a soccer ball. It was the type of photo that parents would get a large sheet of back from the school, picking out the exact one that they wanted before ordering their own large sheet of that one: two large pictures, four medium, and two dozen wallet-sized photographs. The studio lights washed out her features, but even so he could tell she had sun-kissed cheeks -- and that she was pretty. She looked, in many ways, the way he thought his sister might have when she got older. "She's pretty," he said, motioning to the photo with his mug.

"She's missing," Victor snapped. He said it as though it were a correction or amendment to what Chad had said. After a moment, his voice softened, and he added: "They're always pretty when they're missing."

Abby raised her eyebrow at that but said nothing.

Theo leaned forward.

"Her name is Madison Williams," Victor said, rapping his white knuckle against the photo. He'd printed it out on his computer, and it had perpendicular scan lines from top to bottom every inch or so. It struggled with the green of her jersey and made it look striped, though it was not. "She's sixteen years old. She was taken from a soccer game, out from under the nose of parents, friends, teammates, and coaches. Gone -- like nothing. Like she wasn't even there."

"That's... not easy," Chad said. He looked from Victor to the picture, and then back again.

"Not as hard as you'd think," Abby corrected. Her hands were clasped together at her chin, her index fingers forming a steeple against her lips. "There's nothing like plain daylight to hide someone in."

Chad raised an eyebrow.

"How many times have you walked past a screaming kid at the mall in the middle of the day? Ever question it, even a little?"

Chad's face lost some of its colour, and he took a sip of his coffee.

Theo sat up straight and crossed his legs, his arm dangling over the side of his chair. Alice was next to him, still eating the eggs he'd made for lunch. "Missing girls is a little outside our purview, don't you think?"

"There are going to be more," Victor said, his voice a harsh kind of whisper. "A lot more."

Theo narrowed his eyes. "You can't know that."

For a moment -- not even a second, really -- a billboard flashed on behind Victor's head again. It looked black and white but wasn't. There was a light behind a man, so bright that it made the hair around his head shimmer and glow. There were similar affects all around him, and his hands were outstretched -- and then it was gone again, the image a ghost on the retina of Theo's mind's eye.

Theo blinked twice and then squinted, trying to make the image return, but it would not be beckoned.

Victor noticed the attention he was getting, and ignored it. He took out a sharpie and marked a large green area on the outskirts of Payson's mapped area with a red X. He stepped back, twitched his left eye, then moved back in and drew a large circle around the region surrounding Payson, with the X in its centre. He left Payson out of the sphere, the lines avoiding the town at right angles until the circle looked more like a crude attempt at drawing Pac Man.

"This is where the girl was taken from: Payson Field," he said, pressing against the X with his thumb. He then brought it wider, spiraling out until he'd reached the edges of the circle from his point of view. "And somewhere in this area, is where her kidnappers are."

Alice looked up from her eggs, scrunching her nose at the semi-circle. "How's that?"

"Most kidnappers hunt within twenty miles of where they're based, but never within the exact three-mile radius of their home. It makes this... donut shape... of a danger zone." He brought the sharpie closer to the map again, discolouring the area immediately around the field to illustrate his point.

"Is there a reason that radius doesn't extend into the city?" Theo asked, furrowing his brow.

The image of the shadowed man with the halo of light flickered into view behind Victor once again, then skittered back to wherever it went before Theo could pull any information from it. He winced, coughed into his knee, then turned away.

"Yes," Victor said. He did not elaborate.

Alice put her hand on Theo's shoulder, noticing that he was shifting uncomfortably.

"They're going to be in a large house," Victor said. He wrote the word 'large' alongside the circle to illustrate. "A big, multi-bedroom thing. It'll probably have been renovated recently, and not professionally. Makeshift sleeping arrangements, made by dividing one room into two, or three, or more. That kind of thing."

Chad squinted. He gripped his mug by the brim and placed it down on the table beside Abby.

"There'll be debris outside from it, maybe lumber. They haven't been there long, so these materials will be new."

"How do you know that?" Abby asked.

"Because there aren't more *kids* missing," Victor snapped, turning and making eye contact with her. He turned back to the map and wrote the word 'RENO' in capital letters. "A lot of them will be blond, like her -- not all of them, but most. Blond hair, blue or green eyes... and it'll be secluded. They need room to branch out, a lot of property. But it won't all be bedrooms, there'll be game rooms and lounge areas... it'll be nice. Enticing." He thought for a moment. "They're probably squatting somewhere."

"Like Gavin was," Chad said, staring intently at the X, a splash of red among the sea of green.

Abby turned to look at him with horror.

Victor nodded. "Yes. Yes, like Gavin. There will be a large mix of ages... oldest will maybe be thirty, maybe a little older. But they're there." He tapped the semi-circle twice.

"How can you know that?" Theo asked.

Victor pointed to him with the sharpie, opened his mouth as if a snapped retort were on the tip of his tongue, then stopped himself. He sighed, took a deep breath, then finally said, "Because I did the math."

Theo stepped from the narrow hallway and into Victor's office, moving a stack of blank paper out of the way as he did so. Victor was hunched over his desk making a note in a small green moleskin, a colour that Theo had never seen him use before. They'd always been beige, always. Victor's computer was open in front of him, and an RSS feed of missing people was self-scrolling along on it. A file would cascade up from the bottom, like a late 90s screen saver, remain for a moment, then continue up past the top.

"You're pretty sure there are more kids missing?" Theo asked. He leaned against the doorframe with his arms folded, watching as profiles slid by on the screen.

Victor nodded. "I am."

On his cot behind him was the pegboard he'd affixed the picture of Madison Williams to, and the associated map reference. There hadn't been any more X's added to the map, yet the sharpie lingered near it, poised and ready for when that action was needed.

Theo looked at it, the felt tip of the marker exposed and becoming dryer by the moment, and realized it had been a very long time since he'd painted. He wasn't sure why or what had happened, but his brushes were in his room with base-white dried into their bristles, gluing them together into a molded, misshapen phallus.

"You've got them pretty freaked out, I think," Theo said, after a long moment looking from one artifact in the room to another. The bookcase behind Victor was filled with books, most of them hardcover, and most of them without any indication of what was within them on the spine. He'd watched Victor pull books from there without even sparing a glance at the shelf before.

"They probably should be," Victor said under his breath. He typed something into his computer, waited for it to load, then scribbled a circle followed by two triangles into his moleskin.

"Are you writing in code?"

Victor closed the notebook and slid it to one side, then turned his chair to address Theo for the first time since he'd come in.

"Sorry, I --"

"Is there something I can help you with?"

"Sorry. Right, sorry. You, ah... you said earlier we were hunting for assholes."

"Yes," he said, his fingers lowering to dance over the cover of the moleskin. "And we definitely found one."

"Yeah," Theo nodded, sparing a glance at that picture-perfect class photo of Madison Williams. "No yeah, for sure. But when we were getting that, training -- when we were *hunting* -- I saw you."

Victor stood up a little straighter. It was almost imperceptible, but it was there. "You saw me in her mind's eye?"

"No... no. No, she didn't have one. It was weird, it was like she was just... blank."

Victor nodded, knowingly.

"What I mean was I saw *you*."

He stiffened again.

"Your billboard. Your... the representation of what was going on in your head, that flickered on for me, just for a second. That's... that's never happened before. You've always just been blank."

Victor shifted in his chair, then took the green moleskin and moved it into his desk drawer. "That's interesting," he said, without looking at Theo.

"I thought I might have been mistaken, but it flashed up again downstairs... just for a second, really. It was a still image, but it was so quick it might have had motion and only had time to show me one frame. It came up... it came up just as you were talking about the missing girl--"

"Is there something I can help you with?" Victor asked suddenly, turning his steely gaze up towards Theo.

Theo stepped back, startled. "Sorry. It was just... it was weird. Is there a reason I can't see you? And... is it the same reason I can't see her?"

Victor pursed his lips. "No."

Theo squinted. "No there's no reason, or no it's not the same reason?"

"Take your pick, honestly," he said. His mouth barely moved when he spoke, a thin slit in the lower portion of his head, and yet his voice seemed heavy and weighty with the command of it.

Theo turned as if the leave the room, stopped himself on the doorframe, then turned back. "It was a guy."

Victor looked up. He'd fished a normal, beige note-book out from under a stack of papers. "Pardon?"

"What I saw on your billboard. It was this guy, standing with a light behind him... made him look like he was made of shadows and glowing all at the same time. His arms were stretched out, and there were people--"

"We've had trouble in L.A," Victor said curtly, cutting him off.

Theo stopped. He stepped back into the room fully. "Pardon?"

"There've been reports coming in from my contacts." He turned in his chair and reached into a short stack of paper that were so neatly arranged Theo had thought they were blank, but only the top one was. He withdrew an article that had been printed in the *L.A. Times* about a sink-hole that had collapsed an emerging suburb. "Something bad went down out there, I need eyes on to see what's happening."

Theo's brow furrowed as he read through the article.

"Someone I can trust."

He looked back at Victor, and almost laughed.

"I'm serious." He motioned forward with his fingers. "Give me your phone."

Theo narrowed his eyes, then produced the phone as requested and put it into Victor's waiting hand.

Victor immediately started adjusting the device settings. "Turning on the phone tracker. In case something happens."

Theo thought he saw the beginning flickers of a screen coming to life behind Victor again, but it was gone before he could even be sure if it was there. He squinted, looked back at the article, and finished skimming it. "It's a sinkhole."

Victor's eyebrows went up and he smiled as he shook his head. "Not according to my sources. According to, there was a wholly different reason for the cave in."

"Black Springs?"

"I don't think so, no. But worth checking into."

"Any reason your source can't do it?"

Victor paused. He fixed his shirt by tugging on its edges. "Deep cover. If I knew just how big this was, I might risk it... depending on. But without knowing, they're better where they are."

Theo paused, thought about that for a moment, then nodded. He looked back at the article, turned the page to see if there were more, then handed it back. "I'm not supposed to go back to L.A. Part of a deal I made to get me and Alice out."

Victor nodded. "We'd give you cover. And L.A.'s a big city, I'd like you to remember. Believe me, that's a place you can hide forever and nobody would find you if you didn't want to be found."

"I remember. I hid there."

"There you go," Victor smiled, pointing at him with an extended hand. He let his hand fall, and then his manufactured smile slowly did the same. "I need you to do this. I'd send the whole team, but..." he looked away from Theo's eye contact, to the still image of Madison Williams.

Theo looked at the girl, with the sun-kissed cheeks and the toothy smile. He took in a deep breath, let it out as a sigh, then nodded.

"Thank you," Victor said, honestly. There was a spark of snow crash behind his ears, but was once again gone before Theo could make anything of it.

Theo turned to leave the room, stopped himself on the doorframe again, then turned back. "Keep Alice safe."

Victor met his gaze, paused for a moment, then nodded once.

Theo left to pack his bag.

CHAPTER 13

Payson, The Past

Victor and Tash sat in the tiny office tucked in the very back of the Payson Police Department, their elbows wedged together in the space where the two chairs met. The chairs were positioned as far apart as they could reasonably be, and still the both of them sitting blocked the entrance to the room from the public-end. There were two entrances, the second behind the desk. The desk -- a large, single piece of mahogany -- took up nearly the entire width of the room. Anyone who sat behind it and wanted to get at the files on the opposite side of the desk would have to stand, exit the room through the staff door, walk around the hallway, enter from the public door, get the files, then return.

The room, already small even by small office standards, was made smaller by bank boxes stacked high. They teetered and swayed in a breeze that was not felt but must have existed, ventilating up from some unseen corner of the room. The office had no window.

When the bank boxes leaned forward towards the pair they did so in unison, closing in from either side as the air conditioning kicked in. It gave the vertigo-inducing impression that walls were literally closing in. The third time it happened, Victor felt his chest tighten with a claustrophobic clutch -- icy hot fingers he hadn't felt around his heart in years.

"Are you alright?" Tash asked, not looking at him. She was scanning the papers pinned to the bulletin board on the other side of the desk. The words 'Have You Seen This Child' appeared on most in stern, black Impact font. They weren't the standard police flyer, she noted. They were made to look like them, as if someone had had an official Amber Alert flyer on their desk as a template and had tried to recreate it, but had gotten the fonts and the kerning and the justification not quite right.

Victor looked down at their arms touching on the armrests, then shifted his arms tighter into his body until they weren't touching. It was hard to do in the tiny space. "I'm fine."

She frowned, then rolled her eyes slightly as she looked away from him. The gesture was for herself and no one else, a momentary and unconscious expression of everything Victor.

Slowly he unfurled himself, until his arm was again on the hard, wooden armrest between them. He looked, as she did, at the posts on the cork board opposite their seats. Unlike Tash, his gaze darted from the scan-line laden sheets to the bank boxes that towered over them, linking the names printed on the sheets to those scrawled on the boxes in black sharpie. McWebber. Stahl. Suitor. Grande. The names on the board corresponded with the boxes, at least one box per name but sometimes as many as three.

"There are a lot of missing kids," Tash said under her breath, words jumping off the pages at her at random. Nouns like place names, family names, suspect names.

"There were," Victor corrected, motioning to the brown boxes with the faux wood-grain pattern on them.

She furrowed her brow at the statement for a moment as her attention shifted, then saw what he was referring to.

There was dust on the boxes, thick patches of it. Some of it was in layers: dust that had settled, been moved when a more recent casefile had been accessed, and then settled again. Most of it though was quite old, the only movement it got was the towers of cardboard swaying in the conditioned air.

Victor looked back to the children that stared back at him from badly printed photos pinned to the board. The more he stared, the more he began to see similarities... not to one another -- though some features crossed over -- but to people he'd seen before. There was a boy who looked the same across the T-intersection of his nose and eyes as his father, Garrard Clements. The name in bold font beneath him confirmed the connection, but there were more. Faces he'd seen in the field that had been stricken with grief, reflected and mutated here in school photographs too old to still be relevant but kept in use all the same.

The more he looked, the more he saw many of the then-assembled crowd in the photos that lines the far wall of the office.

"So they were grieving?" Tash asked, still noting the names on the bank boxes. "All of them?"

"Most of them. More than fifty percent." He paused. "I could see it on their faces, when I thought to look. Posture, cadence, everything... it screamed grief. Sorrow."

She nodded.

"They weren't working out of altruism; it was a need. It was a hope, that if they find this one... then maybe. But it's not the hope that borders goodwill, it's the hope that borders despair. The kind of hope that makes someone spend their last dollar on a lotto ticket instead of food. The type of hope that can break a man if its tested... even prodded."

Tash pursed her lips.

"I don't have a word for that kind of thing."

"I don't think one exists."

He crossed his arms. "It's everywhere here, whatever it is. The more I look, the more I find --"

The door behind the desk opened, and a tanned pear-shaped man with a receding hairline appeared in it. He looked around the room with his mouth open, as if there were any room for someone to be except directly in front of the desk, then extended a hand to Victor and Tash.

"Detective Gordon Melquist," he said, in that practiced way that people who had to say their named often did. "Sorry for the long wait."

"It's alright," Tash smiled. They shook briefly.

"Really isn't," Victor added. He also shook the hand, giving it two solid, forceful pumps.

Melquist smiled out one side of his mouth, in the way that only people practiced in taking lip from others could do effectively, then pulled out his chair until it hit the board behind it. "I hear you two have been helping look for Briana Redding?"

Victor leaned back onto his chair, which creaked and moaned under his substantial weight. His eyes narrowed.

"Yes," Tash said. She gave Victor an annoyed glance over her shoulder as she moved forward onto the edge of her seat. "We were flying through; we saw the posters being put up."

Melquist raised an eyebrow. "You folks don't have lives to get back to?"

"Ex-military," Victor said under his breath.

"Conscientious objector," Tash added, raising her hand when she did as though it were a learned response.

Melquist looked from one to the other, then chuckled a little.

"Our tax dollars at work, hnn?" He picked up several sheets of paper off of his desk, tapped them against their edge until they were uniform, then put them in the bin for outgoing mail at the far edge of his desk. "Well, we appreciate the help. Missing child, as many eyes as you can muster helps."

"You seem like you're old hat at this," Victor said, nodding toward the corkboard filled with pinned flyers. He reached forward and plunked a blank sheet of paper off of Melquist's desk, then held it up as if to ask if he could use it. Melquist nodded, and Victor produced a pen from his breast pocket. He braced the sheet against the arm of his chair and started to write, glancing up at the board between scribbled lines.

Melquist watched this, looking from Victor's scribbling to Tash with a flicker of his pupils several times. He wetted his lips, smacked them, then eventually shrugged and leaned back in his chair. "Every town's got some, yes. Sad fact of the times we find ourselves in, I suppose." He turned his chair awkwardly in his small space, craning his neck so that he could see up towards the board. The papers moved and fluttered in the breeze from the invisible air conditioner. "Society is what I blame, honestly."

Tash raised an eyebrow at that. "Not sure I follow."

Melquist licked his lips again. He put his hands on the desk in front of him, resting them on the side with his pinky fingers until they were two columns. Between them, in the vague expanse of air, was his point. "We make all these rules. How to act, how to be, what to expect. We make them and we write them down, so everybody starts playing by the same playbook. But once the rules are known, someone will come and figure out how to mess with those rules. It's like a program: if it exists, someone will figure out how to hack it. It's what happens when you have defined rules."

Tash opened her mouth to object, paused, then closed it. She frowned. "Strange stance for a detective."

He motioned to the cork board wall. "Missing Person's Detective. You do this particular part of the job, you've got to be more a pragmatist. Your goal isn't meting out justice, it's finding the kid alive. Whatever line of thinking gets that job done is the correct one, honestly."

She nodded reluctantly.

"I've been the lead on over a dozen missing children's cases in this town," he said, motioning to the wall behind him without turning to look at it. "Few dozen more in the few town's surrounding. Sometimes it's the cousin, sometimes it's the weird neighbor you never thought too hard on before... but someone's got each kid. For every kid on that wall, there's some messed up person who saw the cracks in the system and wriggled through them."

"Or one person," Victor said under his breath. He held up the sheet of paper he'd been writing on, already wrinkled from the way he'd been writing on it. He'd written not the names of the children, but the places around town they'd all been abducted from, from their posted sheets.

Melquist furrowed his brow. "Pardon?"

"You have a town map?"

Melquist squinted, then reached into his desk and withdrew a cheaply produced town map, of the sort sold in gas stations for the express purpose of getting newcomers lost near tourist traps. He handed it to Victor, who spread it out to its fullest, its corners edging into Tash's territory.

"You're familiar with the ten-mile rule?" Victor asked, taking the tip off his pen again. He looked at the first place name on his list, found it on the map, marked it with an X, then drew

a large circle around with the X at its rough centre. He checked the name off the list, then moved on to the next and repeated the process.

Melquist watched, standing up off his chair slightly to see. "I am," he said.

Tash watched the both of them with interest.

"Most kidnappers, rapists... non-murder assaulters, they like to stay within ten miles of their place of residence." He spoke as if Melquist hadn't said he knew the rule. He drew a third circle, around his third X. The circles were beginning to intersect. There had been a large area that had crossed over the first two, and a small area that was germane to all three. "It's just the Catch 22 of it. Hunters hunt where they're familiar. Where they're comfortable."

"Not always the case," Melquist added.

"Often the case," Victor said. He drew a circle that was apart from all the others, on the far side of the Payson map. When he drew his fifth, it was up with the cluster of the others though, and narrowed the area in common even more.

Of the dozen places he'd circled, ten were clustered together like a bunch of grapes. They had one shared area: the upper tip of Payson, and the long strip of wilderness that made its way up from it, a no-man's-land between it and the next town. Victor outlined the shared area to make the lines thicker and bolder. What was left was an oval with sharp peaks, slightly yonic in nature. A womb that took children in, rather than expelled them.

Victor turned it around to show Melquist, who had been watching the entire time. "Have you checked this region?"

"We have, actually." Melquist frowned. His voice had taken on a gravelly texture it hadn't had before. "This might shock

you, but we've checked it extensively."

Victor shrugged. "Check it again. There's a reason everyone in this town feels like the weight of the world is on them, and I think that feeling stems from right here." He tapped the middle of the oval he'd made.

"Victor," Tash said cautiously.

"That's great and all, but you're ignoring these two," Melquist gestured to the two circles that did not fit into the Bunch-of-Grapes pattern.

"Unrelated. A weird uncle or neighbor, like you said."

Air escaped from Melquist's mouth in a dismissive pout. "That, sir, is called a Confirmation Bias. You're only looking at data that confirms your theory and dismissing the things that go against it. That's bad math."

Victor frowned, looked at the map, then stood up. "You mind if I keep this?" he asked.

"That map you marked up on me with information I already had? Yeah sure, take it." He fiddled with the papers on his desk again, stacking them. "And while you're picking through the kids we haven't found yet, I'd like to remind you that there's a list twice as long of kids I have found. Thanks."

Victor folded the map the wrong way, bunching it, then shoved it into his jeans pocket.

"We didn't mean to offend," Tash said, smiling her best customer-service wide smile.

"Speak for yourself," Victor smirked.

She elbowed him.

He reached into his pocket, produced a card, and handed it to Melquist. "If you need us for anything, no matter how pedantic. We'll hand out lemonade at the searches, if it'll help."

Melquist took the card, flipped it between his fingers, then *nodded curtly to Victor.*

Victor and Tash made their way around the confined seats and the bank boxes that stood above them even when they were standing and then all the way to the public exit of the office. The Payson Police Department itself was small, a mirror of the tininess of the Missing Person's Office. They had to move and push themselves against the walls as they stepped past people going to and from their desks.

"Do you ever think to yourself: this time. This time, I'll get along with people?" Tash asked, as they opened the doors back out into the passably fresh air of Main Street.

"It's occurred to me once or twice, but it never feels right." He smiled at her. It was the same sort of smile he'd worn on the day he'd met her, albeit changed slightly at its edges by age.

He took the badly folded map out of his pocket and waved it in the space between them, his feet firmly planted. "This is it. Whether he sees it or not: This. Is. It."

She eyed the map as it fluttered about close to her, then nodded. "I think you're right."

Victor paused. His shoulders deflated slightly.

He turned to the street, the same one they'd been on while drinking coffee, days before. It was as equally filled with people as it had been, though now he saw them differently. Their faces were weighed down by gravity, as though being closer to the equator than much of the rest of the country increased its pull on them. They looked sad... even children, he noted. They walked with purpose, following the paths laid out by their parents: like no group of children he'd ever seen before. They walked without imagination, without the spring in the step that heightened emotions brought with them.

Some walked without any emotion at all, he noted. Child

and adult alike, stepping to and from the events of the day like zombies.

"Bad math, my ass," he breathed, shoving the map back into his back pocket.

Payson, The Present

Victor sat at his desk with his laptop to one side of him and a tablet to the other, a notepad that had been scribbled on to the point of no longer being legible between the two.

Alice peeked through the crack in the door at him. Beyond his hunched shoulders was the bulletin board he'd had down in the kitchen, the face of the young girl still clipped to it. Beyond that on the wall was a Van Gough painting. Not an original, just a mounted print.

It was one of his wheat fields. The blue of the sky seemed to have been scraped on, leaving uneven trails of paint that started thick and then thinned out to near transparency the further they went to the left. It seemed like wind, like the wind was blowing in great blusterous gusts. She'd never seen something so still convey so much movement before.

The wheat field was mounted high on the wall -- not at eye height where it ought to have been, but so that its edge grazed the ceiling. There were holes in its frame where it had been bolted to a wall at some point, but not this wall. The bolt holes were now merely that: holes.

Below the frame but still above the desk was a second pegboard, this one secured to the wall. On it were pictures he'd had printed on photo paper -- not because he'd wanted them to look pretty, but so he could write on them with a dry erase marker. Each one had a number on it, from one to five.

Abby was in the centre, with a #1 scrawled in the corner of the print. Chad was to her right, his marked with a less decisive 2-4 and a question mark. To Abby's left was her herself, Alice, a number 2 stamped on her prominently. Theo was below that with a number 4, equally as firm. There was a man she'd never met before but recognized instantly as Jean-Claude Maximus below that, with a 5+? printed on it.

There were several more there that she did not recognize, lower.

She held the box in her hand, looked down at it wearily, then held it up to chest height. She cleared her throat.

He did not notice.

"Why is this here?" Alice asked, cutting through the silence he'd cultivated in the room.

He turned sharply, not seeing her step into his doorway. She was holding the black box open and pointed at him, revealing a service revolver and bullets, displayed in lush red felt. The box was made for the gun, notches carved in the shape of the fabric to fit the metal.

His face sank. "Where did you find that?"

"In the basement," she said, without shame. "Why is it here?"

"It was mine." He reached out and took the box, closing it. There was a latch on it and had had no lock before, and he reached into his desk drawer and produced a key lock. He locked the latch, placed the key into his pocket, then put the box in the desk drawer that he'd gotten the key out of. "It is mine."

Alice winced, then nodded. "Sorry?" she ventured.

"Don't be," he said with little emotion. He turned back toward the screen and away from her.

CHAPTER 14

Payson, the Present

Alice stepped into the living room of Cliven and Lindsay Williams with great trepidation. The air inside was still and stale, and the two figures therein sat on the couch like statues. They weighed it down with the grief of themselves, the pressure of their forms creating asymmetrical U's in the weak springs.

Abby stepped into the room first, without Alice's hesitation. She walked through an archway that was narrower at its base than at its peak, continuing up straight and then blossoming out with swirls and curls of wood. Like a sprout of cauliflower. Or a mushroom cloud. The association, however brief, made Alice's feet stutter at the entrance to a room that was painted a dusty rose and tried hard to be inviting.

There was a coffee table in front of the couch, barely a foot in front of Cliven Williams' left knee. Abby was in front of it when she turned around and saw Alice still hesitating at the door, prostrate in front of the wall of stale air. Abby raised her eyebrows in an exaggerated fashion and cocked her head back towards the room, and without a word Alice entered and stepped up beside her.

There were two disembodied shadows stretching into the room. Alice knew they were police officers that had been stationed to stand watch over the Williams' -- both women had walked past them when they'd come in -- but that seemed an eternity ago, and now they were just human-shaped collections of darkness. They moved along the floor, tapping each other and motioning to something beyond their field of vision, and whispering things too low for Alice to hear. It was like watching a mime do a shadow dance, but after the show, the curtain was pulled away to reveal there had been nobody casting them at all.

Lindsay Williams was holding a doll that was too old to have belonged to her daughter. It was the sort with felt stuffing in the torso and limbs, but with hands and a face made of hard porcelain. A hairline fracture ran from the base of its bonnet to its chin along one cheek, the fracture catching the light from the window across from them. Lindsay rubbed her thumbs along the doll's torso in a steady rolling pattern.

It had been hers, Alice realized with a sudden clarity. The truth had come like a bolt from the blue, sudden knowledge that just *was*. The doll had belonged to Lindsay when she'd been a child. It had provided comfort and solace against troubled times... and slowly, as she'd aged, she'd put it away. But now, in a moment of extreme stress, the doll had made its return. As Alice watched this woman of nearly twice her age rub a doll's chest as if to try and resuscitate it, she wondered if she were even aware of the act.

"So, you're here to try and help?" Cliven said, a heavy hand on his wife's knee as he lifted his gaze to first Abby, then Alice. "Help find Maddie?"

"Yes," Alice said suddenly, finding her voice even though her throat was dried and swollen.

Abby turned to her, surprised she'd chosen to speak first.

"Yes, absolutely. We're here to help."

∞

Madison's room was the sort of pale pink that befitted the room of a girl half her age, a remnant of a more innocent time in the young life. As Alice looked around the room, she could see the timeline of her interests -- from My Little Pony to Barbie, from Barbie to Lego, from Lego to a sudden shift to the male physique in blockbuster films. Shifts seemed sudden when glancing across cluttered shelves, but Alice knew they happened gradually. She'd lived through them.

Alice picked up a music box off the dresser and moved it in her hand, watching the way the light reflected off the alternating octagonal sides: red, then white, then red again. It was painted the colour of a circus tent and roughly shaped like one. It was handcrafted, with all the imperfections and quirks that came with being handcrafted. It left an oddly shaped patch clear of dust on the dresser when she plucked it from its perch. As she looked from one group of toys to the other, you could gauge the length of time since she'd lost interest by the collection of dust on it.

She opened it. Along the inner cap was a mirror that

reflected her eye back at her, and standing via a spring motion was a small ballet dancer. Her paint was chipped and her left foot -- risen in an artful pirouette -- was missing, but she still swirled when a slow Russian waltz began to play, quietly filling the room with somber tones.

"That was painful," Abby said, stepping in from the hall and leaning against the doorframe.

"Did they share anything useful after I came upstairs?"

Abby shook her head which Alice only saw in the reflection of the music-box mirror. "Same thing they said to the police -- one minute there, next minute gone. Not that that's their fault mind, just --"

"It's just not useful," Alice finished.

She nodded. She paused a long moment, watching as Alice watched the box use the last of its kinetic energy. She swallowed, glanced at the closed window spreading its light on her, then shifted her weight from foot to foot. "You shouldn't have been so enthusiastic, you know."

Alice paused, closed the mute music box, then turned to face her from her spot on the floor. "What do you mean?"

"You told them we'd help."

"We are here to help."

"But you told them we *would*. There's a Grand Canyon worth of difference between trying to do something and actually *doing* it, don't pretend you don't know that."

Alice's mouth warbled at the corners and she stood up, dusting dirt from her knees. "Have you ever been without hope?"

Abby had opened her mouth to answer before the

question had been fully posed. When she heard it in full, she stopped herself, a shimmer of images playing across her mind's eye like cards fanned from a magician's deck. Dead boyfriends, mostly, but also friends, and a street she didn't know the name of yet called home. "Yes," she said after recovering.

"Then you know how draining it can be. False hope is bad, but it's better than none." She walked to the window and looked out. The silhouettes of the police had been replaced by two actual policemen again, each standing relaxed but ready on either side of the Williams' front stoop. Their squad car was parked on the side of the road, roughly perpendicular to the house, and shone brightly in the afternoon sun. "We are going to find her, though."

Abby frowned. "Maybe you're the one who has false hope."

Alice looked around to the floor, along the long stretch of uninterrupted baseboard that ran from Madison's bookshelf to her dresser. There was dust on it as well, except for a clear patch in the centre. "We're going to win because at the end of the day, policemen are still just men; and well-intentioned parents are still just parents. We're women, we're looking for one of our own, and we will find her."

She reached down and pressed her nails against the section of baseboard without dust and was almost as shocked as Abby was when it tilted away from them, revealing a thin rectangular arch cut into the wood.

Abby's eyebrows went up.

Alice reached into the newly discovered portal and withdrew a small notebook. It was bright purple with ink stains along the edges of the pages. It had very little dust on it, and one of those locks that was just for show. She felt the weight of it in her hand for a long moment, considered opening it, then clasped it between her thumb and forefinger. "I'll ask the parents if I can borrow this," she said, almost to herself. She made her way back to the window, paused at the sound of almost inaudible speech, then opened it. The police, standing on either side of the porch, were talking in hushed tone.

"Theo calls us the 'Death Twins,' you know," Abby said, crossing her arms. She was watching the journal clasped between Alice's fingers as though she expected it to sprout spider-legs and scurry over to her. "I'm sure he means it well. But it... makes sense... right? I mean, you can't die. My powers freak out around death. You're the only one who *can't* freak me out... makes sense that I'd be comfortable around you, right?" She shifted uncomfortably.

"Shh," Alice said, bringing a finger to her lips.

Abby frowned and finally entered the room, pushing off the doorframe and stepping over to stand by Alice, the police coming fully into view and their conversation now heard, barely, over the wisps of wind that flew across the air.

"Shame," one of them said, turning and motioning back towards the house.

"Real shame," the other reciprocated. "Don't think they'll be able to help?"

"Didn't much help last time," the officer shrugged, moving an acorn off the stoop with his foot. "Part of me doesn't even think they'll find her alive, if I'm honest. Because we know it's not him again."

Alice furrowed her brow.

"What's that mean?" Abby asked, stepping so close to the window that the trails of her sleeves touched the screen. "What's 'last time' mean?"

"Let's find out," Alice said with bite. She turned swiftly and made her way down the hall with the floral wallpaper that she'd come up minutes before, down the staircase that was too tight for two people to walk side-by-side on, and was birthed back out into the hall that led to the Williams' living room. They were on the couch still, a red rabid rage having grown in Cliven's cheeks, while Lindsay had been reduced to tears.

She held up the notebook, breaking stride only momentarily. "I found this, can I read it? I swear I'll get it back to you."

Cliven looked ready to object, but Lindsay nodded.

"Thank you," she said, continuing past the room and out towards the front door.

"I'm so sorry," Abby said, stepping into the frame of the door behind her. "We'll try everything we can to help, I swear."

Alice pushed the front door open, appearing between the two police officers and placing both hands on her hips, brash and without fear of consequence. "What did you mean by last time?" she said as the screen door slammed shut behind her. She turned to the cop who had spoken it and made eye contact which took him aback.

"Sorry," Abby said, following through the door that had been all but closed in her path. "Sorry, she's --"

"Last time," Alice said, cutting off Abby before the officer could turn his attention toward her. "You were talking about the last time this happened, what did you mean?"

The two exchanged a look, and the cop she was addressing straightened his shirt in a way she'd seen doctors do before: the way that prepared them to make a prepared statement.

"There were kidnappings before here, years back," the other officer said.

Alice turned to him, slowly.

"If you'd lived here, you'd have known. It's not a secret."

"So when was this? This non-secret thing?" she asked, raising one eyebrow.

Abby stopped and watched the exchange.

"Ten?" He looked at the other officer. "Ten years ago? No, my daughter was five at the time, I remember because my wife didn't want to send her to school. Must have been thirteen years ago."

Abby straightened.

Alice nodded and started to walk back towards their car. When she was halfway to the street and Abby was behind her, she turned on her heel once more. "And you're wrong, by the way. We're *going* to find her."

She got in the car and slammed the door behind her.

A moment later Abby got in and sat beside her. "That was intense," she said, her tone somewhere between awe and respect.

"We're going to find her," Alice reiterated.

Abby nodded curtly, then started the car.

CHAPTER 15

Outside Payson, The Present

Chad and Victor sat at the kitchen table, which had been voided of all food and utensils save for a cup of coffee each. Chad's was nearly white with cream and had just as much sugar. Victor's was only slightly discoloured, the result of a small amount of liquid from the bottle he kept in the cupboard.

Apart from the two mugs, the table was tight with stacks of paper. Some were in manila envelopes, others kept together in neatly pressed stacks with staples or paper clips. There were children on the front page of each -- some young, some old. They stared back from the kitchen table, the same way children must have from the backs of milk cartons in the late 80s.

There was a laptop open on the chair to Victor's right. A web browser was displayed on it, open and set to Google, waiting.

The black-and-white faces of missing children looked back at Chad from beyond the veil of time. He got caught in it for a long moment, then shuddered. "The laptop, please," he said, motioning to the chair.

Victor picked it up without a word and laid it atop the pile of papers in front of him.

Chad leaned the screen up so that he could see it. He did not want to sit. His fingers hovered over the keys for a long moment, like an author contemplating how to attack their first scene of the day, the blinking curser in the middle of the screen haunting him. "I don't know what to search for," he said finally, exhaling emphatically.

"Search for anything, try and get lucky," Victor said. He took a long glug of his drink. It smelled of almonds. "We've done this before. With Gavin."

Chad squinted, sighed, then looked back at the screen. The curser was an axe; each time it appeared it chopped and chipped away at his sanity, daring him to put something -- anything -- into the search bar. And with every passing second, he proved unable to match its bluff.

In his right pants pocket, he was aware of a rectangular piece of glossy paper. He shouldn't have been able to feel it, but he could. He could feel where its edges stopped, the slight differences in texture and consistency when running his hand along the outside of his jeans. He could especially feel the crease that ran down its middle, the fibers bulging and folding from multiple foldings.

He felt it in his pockets the same way he had been able to feel a single, crisp one-hundred-dollar bill carried in the zippered pocket of his jacket. Those bills, though scant in design, had seemed to weigh heavy when he was walking the streets of Salt Lake City, marching home from a poker game he shouldn't have been at. On those walks, he felt that thin slip of paper with every stranger that passed him too close, with every storekeeper that leered at him too long, and with every stiff bite of breeze that meandered past him. The bill was always there, always heavy, and always a stray thought away from his fingertips. Now as Victor shifted uncomfortably in his seat, Chad found his fingers were in his pocket once more, examining the edges of the photograph they found there.

Chad typed the word 'Payson,' and then the word 'Armstrong,' then backspaced the second word.

"Why did you delete that?" Victor asked.

"Didn't feel right."

"Try it anyway."

Chad frowned deep out of the corners of his mouth, then retyped the word and pressed enter. The first several hits were people -- social media profiles, 411 pages, directories. Several more were in reference to the astronaut, an article written, or a detail mentioned somewhere in the myriad of text in the article that made it also associate with Payson. What followed then were a long list of businesses in the town Payson who had proprietors with last name of Armstrong. Office supplies and firewood, used cars and boat repair services. There was a listing for someone who worked at the town office.

"I don't see anything probative," Chad said, deleting the entire phrase from the search bar.

"You never know," Victor said. He scribbled some of the links that had been on the screen into his moleskin.

"Don't," Chad tisked. "Those aren't... they didn't feel right."

"Have you been noticing a feeling that goes along with what you do?"

Chad paused. "... no. But that wasn't... it wasn't anything."

Victor nodded, then continued to make the notes anyway.

Chad frowned, then turned back to the blinking curser. He brought his hands to the keyboard and rested them tentatively along its edge, the thumb of his right hand hovering over the letter J with nervous intent. He hit the key once, then the H, then backed the both of them until the curser blinked with triumph again. "I can't stand being behind a desk."

"We can move to the couch if you'd --"

"That's not..." he paused, then took a mouthful of coffee. "It's not the location, it's the act. Can you imagine this, all day, every day?"

"Honestly? No."

Chad almost smiled, then felt the weight in his pocket again and didn't. He cleared his throat and turned his eyes back to that menacing, oppressive curser.

"You know who would have been good at this," Chad said, as he pushed back his hay-coloured hair.

Victor looked at him with one eyebrow raised, his expression neutral and unknowable, any tweak of his mouth in the positive or the negative hidden behind the strands of scruff that hid the corners of his lips.

"Jaycee," he finished, bobbing his head to one side as if the name itself would make his point.

He thought he saw Victor's mouth ebb downward slightly. The deep ditches that connected his nostrils to the sides of his mouth blackened.

Chad typed the word 'albatross' and hit enter. There

were links to a local zoo that had had the bird, once, nearly a decade ago; and a hotel that had borne the name also returned hits. It had been closed since the late 80s.

Victor did not comment on the results or write them down, his pen hovering over the moleskin the same way Chad's had over the keyboard. He didn't look at the screen so much as past it, staring at some secret position on the wall behind the laptop. "He couldn't have stayed."

Chad backed up the word 'albatross,' paused, and frowned. "I get that you think that, but it's bullshit."

"There's an ideal to what we do, here. There is meaning to it, even if it's not always apparent. When we're done, the world will be a better place. Infinitely better. But for it to work, we've got to be better than the people we go after. Not just at our best, all the time." He turned to look at Chad, whose mouth had the deep recesses of someone trying to understand but whose nature was fighting it. "At our worst, we have to be better than they were at their best, you know? I can't have you here if you take a life."

Chad's mouth opened in a scoff at that. "That wasn't his fault. That couldn't be--"

"At his *worst*," Victor reiterated, pausing for emphasis, "we still have to be better. We have to hold up to that ideal, otherwise all this," he waved at the house around them, "all this isn't worth anything."

"Then maybe it's not worth anything," Chad shrugged apathetically. He turned back toward the keyboard, paused for a long moment, then sighed in a final way. He reached into his pocket, leaning forward against the table to gain purchase, and fished out the glossy rectangle of paper that had been weighing it down.

It was the picture of Tash and Victor, with the word *'free'* behind it stenciled across a plane and a bright blue backdrop. He pointed it toward Victor faceup, as if securing him in the photo's crosshairs. "What's the story behind this?"

Victor's eye's flitted to the photo, then remained there for a long moment. His face was still and statuesque, yet somehow Chad still saw a change in it. "Where did you find that?"

"Upstairs. Abby found it, I think. It was taken here, right? Here in Payson, I mean? About ten years ago?"

Victor reached out and took the picture, pressing it between his fingers so tightly that it bent. He turned it around to face him awkwardly, rotating his arm instead of the photo. "It was a long time ago," he said with a low voice, staring at the younger version of himself. Tash was looking at the younger version of him too, one of the rare times when they both saw the same thing in the same way.

"You look happy there," Chad commented.

"I'm not," he corrected, finally turning the photograph around and pinching its corners with both thumbs.

Chad furrowed his brow. "What's the significance of --"

Before he could finish, Victor took the picture tight in both hands and twisted them in opposing directions, the gloss of the page ripping along its bright edge of sky.

"No!" Chad yelled, gesturing both hands toward it. He stood for emphasis, knocking the laptop back onto the desk as he reached for the photo. Victor pulled his arms away, still tugging the two halves of the picture in opposite directions... but he made no more headway than the slight tear he'd made at the apex of its fold.

He tugged again, but his fingers slipped on the gloss. Again, and the picture stubbornly refused to come apart. His hand slipped on the third and his left hand lost its purchase, sending his elbow back into the arm of the chair and sending green lightning bolts of pain rocketing up into his torso. "Dammit," he cursed.

Chad snapped the picture away from him. He cradled it for a moment, then examined it. The tear at the top was only superficial, creating a mesh triangle of white cloud where before there had only been blue sky. Chad folded it quickly along that mark and pushed it back into his pocket.

Victor breathed heavily from the exertion of simply trying to separate the two halves of the image.

Chad shook his head, moved the laptop toward Victor without a word, then stepped out of the kitchen.

CHAPTER 16

Laramie, Wyoming

Kincaid took the offer to pledge for Epsilon Gamma Nu, and so Maximus did as well. The application process was easier than either had thought it would be for such an organization.

Five of them stood in a row at attention, like 4F teens before a draft board. They were in the living room of the Epsilon Gamma Nu Chapter House, which looked, to Kincaid, to be in a constant state of disrepair. He had, on occasion, been in houses and rooms where it was too dirty to sit, but this was the first he had ever been in in where there was too much clutter to even stand. Someone had cleared a strip, ten feet by two feet, in the centre of the room where the five of them stood. It looked like it had not been cleaned so much as a coffee table had been quickly removed, creating a void in the space.

Across from the five, just below a large television that hung from the wall at a downward tilt, was a large and comfortable looking chair. It was clean and looked and smelled like leather and had gold etching along hardwood arms. The seal of The House, two lions in opposition to one another, had been embroidered in thick gold thread into the headrest. A boy of no more than twenty-two sat on the chair slanted to one side, one leg cocked in the air with his knee at a pointed, high angle that showed how sharp and slender it was. He was wearing a suit that fit him impeccably, seeming to move with his body as he shifted positions, looking from one pledge to the next. The strap of a holster ran from his left shoulder to his right hip, where it vanished from view. His hair was blond and stuck up in the front, its length defying gravity. It was the sort of blond that was almost white and would have appeared fluffy if not for the product in it. His sharp jaw and chin rested between the thumb-and-forefinger of his right hand. His left dangled over the edge of the chair, showing off the thick gold ring that adorned it, also featuring two lions.

On the arm of the chair to his left sat a woman. She had long black hair that flowed all the way down to her hips and wore a t-shirt and cut-off jeans that displayed her legs and midriff. She was slender, the sort of slender that men were supposed to say they found unappealing in this politically correct, enlightened age, and yet could not keep their eyes off of when they found it. Her eyes seemed large and their lashes long and thick. She was wearing a jacket that was far too big for her and was looking at her phone, oblivious to the five men across from her or even the man she was ostensibly on the arm of.

Kincaid felt his vision move back and forth like a ping pong ball, from the smooth midriff of the girl to the hidden area of the holster strap at the man's hip. He was conscious of his gaze but couldn't stop it, the energy to tear his gaze from one item just forcing it onto the next, his pupils the victims of a war between his two most primal instincts: that to survive, and that to reproduce.

There were more people in The House but not in this room. The room was open to two separate hallways on either end and at both exits, and men and women treated the archways as though there were a bubble containing it. They came, usually holding a beer bottle or a red solo cup, looked through the doorway into the hall at the five men standing ramrod straight for a moment, then left again without a word. Men seemed to do this more than women and with different looks. Men looked appraisingly and expressionlessly, as if in a staring contest in which the combatant would not turn to stare back at them. Women stumbled into the frame of the doorway with a smile and a laugh, turned when one of the five caught their eye, gave them the elevator with their gaze, then left the frame again with laughter like water boiling over.

"Pledges," the boy in the suit said finally, not looking up at either of them, but rather at some spot on the floor at their feet. Kincaid wondered at first, privately, if he were even speaking to them. His fingertips danced gingerly along the leg of the girl next to him. Suddenly he stood up, placing his hands on his knees and getting to his feet with mock effort. "My name is Bernard, I'm your Chapter President. You're here because you want to be among the best. Epi Gamma Nu only takes the best." He leaned over and kissed the girl on the arm of the couch. She tilted her head up to meet his mouth with hers without even having been looking away from her phone when he'd leaned in, as though she'd known to do it on that cue. "In nearly seventy years we have only ever taken the best. Our chapter's alumni includes senators, fortune 500 members, statesmen, and world leaders." He turned and smiled at them from one side of his mouth, meeting their gazes for the first time. He looked at them each in turn, pausing only briefly at Kincaid, then moving on down the line. Without turning back to her, he pointed at the girl. "This is Denise; she heads our sister sorority. Their membership has gone on to be senators and first ladies. They head financial institutions and educational institutions." He turned back to her again, smiling. "...And they fuck impeccably."

Denise looked up from her phone and smirked devilishly, but did not say a word to encourage or refute.

Bernard spun back around and found himself facing the first man in line, a tall blond boy who looked almost like a fun-house reflection of Bernard himself: taller and lankier, but Arian of the type that only decades of breeding within Western-European circles could accomplish. "You're here because you want to be the best too," Bernard continued, clasping his hands behind his back and stepping forward past his distorted mirror-image. The next in line was a scruffy boy with closely shaved dark hair. He stiffened as Bernard passed. "You want to be a part of that proud tradition, to transition from the family of your blood to your family that goes beyond blood, beyond brotherhood." He passed Kincaid, turned to look up at him, then continued. The fourth in line was a large fat man, but the sort of fat that lent itself to football scholarships, beer drinking contests, and, paradoxically, slender women. The large man stood at a stiffer attention as

Bernard walked by. "You want to be leaders, and to have the full force of the chapter behind you, and some of you will. Some of you are here because you're the best..." He reached the last man in line and did not regard him. He stepped past and stared out into the hall. "...And some of you are here because someone pulled some strings."

While Bernard's back was turned, Kincaid leaned forward slightly to see around the fat man's protruding form.

The man of the end of the line was tall and thin, his limbs looking too long, as though they'd been stretched out. His skin was sallow and yellow, the flesh under his eyes tinted pink in addition to that. He was bald and his nose looked short and stubbed from this angle, as though it ended as the base of the skull and left the pledge's nostrils open to the air.

It was the man who had been in his class, Kincaid realized, with the albino professor. Jona.

"Sound off when I get to you," Bernard yelled loudly, removing something long and black from the holster at his hip.

Kincaid snapped back to attention before the man turned around, and he felt his heartbeat double as Bernard stepped back to the start of the line, having circled around behind them. Then there was the click of a switch and the low, abrasive buzzing of a motor, and he realized what Bernard had had holstered: an electric razor.

He stood behind the blond youth for a moment, then hit him against the back of his shoulders: hard. "I said sound off."

The blond rubbed the back of his neck. "Rutterson,

Daniel."

Bernard grabbed his head in the palm of one hand, fiercely holding on by one ear. He brought the razor forward and made a straight line up the back of the boy's head, blond locks flittering to the carpet floor and making a trail of stubble from the base of his skull to the tip of his crown. "You're not Daniel Rutterson, not until we say you are again. As of right now names are too good for you. Until you've been accepted by your brothers, you are merely: Pledge."

Daniel reached up and touched the rough scalp where his hair had been, feeling along the previously cushioned valleys of his skull.

"Is that clear, Daniel?"

Daniel did not respond.

"Is that clear, Pledge?"

"Yes."

"Pardon?"

"Yes, Chapter President."

Bernard nodded, then the razor back to the head and took away strip after strip of shaggy blond hair. The clippers sputtered only once, becoming knotted by Daniel's left ear. Bernard had yanked it free with an audible tearing sound, and Daniel had ground his teeth so as not to scream, but the rest of the hair had come off without a problem. When all the other hair was gone, Bernard took his eyebrows too, leaving him to resemble a shaved monkey. He then reached into his pocket and produced a dollar-store disposable razor and handed it to Daniel. "Keep it this way until you get through. This is kinda the opposite of the normal rule." He palmed Daniel's bald scalp one last time, chuckling. "If there's grass on this field, you can't play ball."

The process was repeated with the next in line, a dark-haired youth named Craig. His hair had already been close-cropped and hadn't needed much attention, but Bernard went over it once for affect and then scraped away the hair below his lower lip and, of course, his eyebrows. He was handed a blade in turn as well.

Kincaid watched this out of the corner of his eye. It was amazing how much removing the eyebrows could change someone... It's not clear upon first glance exactly what's wrong. Eyebrows are used by so many people to emote, so a face without them seems strange, the smiles and frowns both not quite right.

Bernard reached Kincaid and sighed, then moved a plastic chair around to stand on so that he could reach the top of his head.

At the end of the line, the man with the sallow flesh turned to watch, stepping out of formation just enough to not be noticed.

Bernard grabbed him by the ear and started to shave him, tiny black curls spinning their way to the floor.

"Sig Kincaid," Kincaid said, without being asked.

"What kind of a name is Sig?"

"Sigmund."

Bernard chuckled to himself. The motion made his hand jerk and the razor nicked the edge of Kincaid's ear, only slightly, but enough to draw blood. He pulled Kincaid's face back by the chin to get to the eyebrows, rather than moving the chair around to the front. When he got down, he kicked the chair away and moved on to the next person in line.

Denise looked up from her phone for the first time when the chair hit the back wall, and smirked.

"Forrest Rustum," the next man in line said, as Bernard removed from him all the hair on his head, then handed him a razor.

He moved forward to the last in line. The youth with the jaundice flesh looked back at him with narrow eyes. He had no hair on his head, nor even any eyebrows: not even the stubble where some would soon be or recently had been.

"My name is Jean-Claude Maximus," he said, his mouth small and pursed as he said each word in a well-spoken New England accent. His lips came together as a tiny slit then, a dim line waiting to see what Bernard would do next.

Bernard looked him up and down, then stepped away. "For the next week, it's Pledge."

Maximus's lip twitched, unknown to Bernard.

Bernard came around to the front of the line again, standing in front of his chair and Denise. He holstered his electric razor again and took a handkerchief out of his pocket, wringing it through his hands. "You're all Pledge now. You're all the same, you're all alike, you're all brothers. Over the course of the next few days, you'll discover yourself, your identity, who you are and if you're an Epi Gamma Nu man. But until then..." He looked at the five of them, making eye contact with each. "Until then you're all the same."

Kincaid turned and looked at the dark-haired boy and was surprised to see that he did look a lot like Daniel when stripped of the colour that edged his face. He turned around to face Maximus, who was looking at him from across the room as more members of the fraternity finally were free to filter in, and he realized they were both thinking the same thing: no matter how much hair you stripped away, neither of them would look like the other three.

Kincaid nodded at him, cocking his chin into the air. Maximus nodded back.

CHAPTER 17

Los Angeles, California

Theo stood before a large, circular crater in the skin of Los Angeles: a crackling, organic maw that stood out amidst the tempered steel of the city. It was its own eco-system, seeming to exist merely a few feet below the ground-level of the city but which sank to unfathomable depths in others.

There were pools of melted plastic, long since solidi-fied into oblong masses of green and blue that had ceased to resemble the shades they had once represented. The plastic siding of homes and Astroturf blended until they became one and the same, bits of charred carbon cascad-ing about them like swirls in a marble. In many places they had subtracted enough away that they revealed the area underneath, the facade peeling away to show from where it was birthed.

There was not ground beneath the facade, but a long metal husk pimpled with vents and stairwells filled with melted debris. The metal was scorched and burnt, but still retained a glean that hid just under the surface. It had buckled in places beneath the weight and the heat atop it, having crumbled in an implosion of hollowed metal and dark, gray clouds of dust.

As Theo watched, standing just inside the stone walls that surrounded the crater, men in orange suits made their way cautiously down the slope and onto the metal husk that it revealed. The gravel alongside the slope was uniformly coloured in a way he knew natural deposits would not be, and he found himself wondering if the unnaturalness of it were due to the nature of urban development or a part of the grand illusion that had been at play on the outskirts of Los Angeles.

One of the men trailed a long siphon that stretched out like an accordion behind them, allowing it to reach further and further down toward the metal floor. The man -- a bearded fellow whose torso was exposed enough that he could see a City Workers emblem on his breast -- brought the hose to a hole with grayish purple smoke oozing from it lazily. There had been many hot spots in the days and weeks since the fires had burned, with some speculating that there were chemical fires still raging that they were unable to find.

The metal caught the purple-hued light of the evening sun and shone, a splotched metal disk in the middle of suburbia. It was distressing, the more Theo looked at it. It was like the edge of reality had been found, and it was only a scant few feet beneath the surface. It was like Truman Burbank finding the drywall edges of his reality, just a little beyond the edge of where he'd previously ventured. It occurred to him, standing there, that he had no way to prove that there wasn't a metal shell under all of the world, just below the surface.

He bent down and grabbed a segment of the earth, almost as though to prove to himself that it was real, and not made up of billions of segments of micro-plastics. He let it play between his fingers, feeling the dry, ashen weight of it crumble like soot until there was nothing left and his hands were coarse with it. "What the fuck happened here?" he asked himself, leaning against his own haunches and scanning the perimeter of the crater for any sense of normalcy.

There were a dozen more men in orange, some standing with their hands on their hips as they watched the men below, others holding street signs that were contractually obligated but unnecessary -- the new suburb had yet to be populated, and had been far enough away from a populated area that the fire that had consumed it had been raging by the time it had been noticed.

Second from the last in the line of orange suits, on nearly the opposite side of the embankment, a face that was familiar to him surveyed the destruction. She was a stocky woman in a dark blue suit. Her hair was graying and pulled back in a tight bun so tight that it pulled her face taut. It was Roberta Feinberg.

Standing apart from the group of orange jumpsuits, wearing a white blouse and a tie and a skirt that showed long, thin legs, was a woman with dark blonde hair and lips so crimson he could see them from across the field of nothingness between them. She stood alone, her arms crossed in front of her, making furtive glances both to Theo and the workers in the Orange Suits as she did.

Even though they were far away, their billboards were

clear, concise, and understandable. He didn't need to try any of Victor's new tricks to help: the methods of this madness was apparent. Just as his mind had been absorbed by the crater in front of him, so were the majority of the workers. Their billboards were live feeds, as if their eyes were cameras and the backs of their heads projectors, sending the chaos of the gorge at him from different angles and viewpoints, each with their own filter and context. One was focused on the men on the metal themselves as they tried to navigate a section that had caved in, a foreman concerned with safety and insurances. Most just watched, a screen-within-a-screen at the bottom of their billboards replaying some memory that reminded them of the scene. Footage from disasters, sinkholes, or flooding.

Roberta was the only person along that edge who was not mindfully present during the exchange. Her billboard was open to a mental knockoff of Google Doc, and was already composing her report on the scene to a superior.

Which was odd, because he'd known her as a mental care physician.

He furrowed his brow as he watched her. Slowly she looked up in his general direction, and her billboard went fuzzy. Snow crash started to hide the words she'd been typing -- which he hadn't been able to yet decipher anyway -- and eventually it was gone completely. After a moment, it was replaced by the view of the maw that had been ripped in the skin of the city that they stood around... though curiously, not the maw as it should have been from her perspective.

She touched the shoulder of the worker closest to her, smiled, then turned to leave the grounds. She started the short walk back toward a row of vehicles that had been parked a safe distance from the disturbance. Theo watched her go. When she was out of his view, he turned and exited the area himself, walking back toward Los Angeles proper.

He stepped past the stone walls of the Anemone suburb, never noticing that the woman standing alone along its edge had lacked any billboard at all.

Payson, The Past

"Step," said the man in the blue polo shirt and baseball cap with the large brown mustache, and everyone in the field stepped forward one long, exaggerated pace. They all ducked like herring searching for fish, their heads bobbing down and turning left and right in similar -- but different -- motions. There were dozens of them, and they looked like choreographed dancers who had not yet learned to move in tandem.

Jennifer Swaddle was forty-five and had been a part of the search party for Briana every day since it had begun. She had searched this field three times in that brief tenure, and the wood beyond it twice.

"Step."

She stepped forward, as did everyone around her. A man to her right stepped wide, careful to circumvent a large patch of water. His eyes were rimmed red and sleeplessly bloodshot.

In front of her was a small shed that she had seen before. It was scantily larger than an outhouse. There were several of these on the fields of Payson, small domiciles built by those taking advantage of unclaimed land and using it to squat. Sometimes they were literally used as temporary shelters by the homeless, but most of the time they were used as small storage units for fishing equipment and bunks. Its back was to the forest at the far edge of the field, and it was only now that Jennifer realized her day was almost over.

There was a smell, like sickly sweetness and mold and copper. She'd smelled it before in her life, but could never articulate it after the fact. It was not an easy thing to contextualize.

She stepped forward out of sync with the rest of the searchers. "Stop," she called out, absently. Her face was white and yet still losing colour.

The caller held up his hand, and the entire collection stood erect in unison.

Jennifer stepped forward with flesh as white as paper and pushed the already ajar door open. There was nothing inside but walls of tackle and lure, yet the smell remained. She backed out, the way people back slowly out of the wrong room in a mortuary, then stepped slowly around the small enclosure.

Leaning against the back of the shed, propped up as if sitting in a slouched position, was the body of Briana Redding, her face the ashen gray of soot.

Tears found Jennifer's face. She tried to reach up her hand in a clenched fist to indicate she had found something, but collapsed to the ground instead.

Carla stepped down the winding stairs that led to the main floor, breathing in the sweat and smells of coffee that wafted in from the kitchen. In front of her, in the foyer, all the curtains had been pushed back and their rods taken down, opening up the space and making it homey again. The main floor of the house was vast: the stairwell depositing into the hall, which branched *to the living room on her right and the dining room and kitchen area on her left.*

Three people chased each other across the threshold, giggling and laughing as their hands grasped for purchase against each other. They were young, barely sixteen, and their smiles were bright and honest and shimmering. Carla watched them go with a smile that faded the closer she got to the ground floor and had finally disappeared by the time she hit that hardwood of ground level.

She continued to watch them as she had when she had been smiling, but her expression had changed to neutral, even grim, pulling the corners of her mouth down and changing her face.

The three youths vanished into the crowd of people in the living room. There were three couches, each tiered behind the former to make one large seating area, balanced on milk crates. They were all packed high with people some sharing space on a partner's lap, others teetering on the edge of the chair's arm. There were three girls in the front row who were getting their hair brushed by girls in the middle row, the stroking and preening taking on an odd kind of symmetry: blonde curtains were drawn out, then brushed in long strokes, then drawn out again.

There was only one girl in the front not having her hair brushed, a girl with a shaved head wearing a green top with white letters on it that sat near the edge of her seat, her elbows against her knees. Her eyes were red-rimmed, but she smiled as she looked out through the hustle and bustle of people walking to and fro at Carla. A moment later, someone in the back row offered her a brush and she took it, switching places with them to work her hair.

When she moved, a boy who had been seating in the back row rested his hand on her knee.

Carla frowned, her hand travelling to the bulk of her thigh, just above her own scarred knee.

Four people carrying plates pushed past her. She backed up quickly to get out of the way, her horn-rimmed glasses falling down onto her nose as she did.

"Hot behind!" the front one yelled, warning of danger and proximity as they passed her with steaming trays. They delivered eggs and bacon and toast to those waiting in the living room, and it was only when they entered that she fully grasped just how many there were. They came out from behind pillars and corners, like ants smelling a trail of sugar. They piled around the trays of food, hands grabbing and quickly receding with whatever prize they'd won. She watched a grown man shove an entire hardboiled egg into his mouth, then reach and snag a handful of bacon. It protruded between his fingers like a child pretending they had claws.

"We're out of ketchup," one of the servers said as she came back from the living room with an empty tray. She let the other three continue past her into the kitchen, holding the still-hot tray flat against her stomach and not noticing it.

Carla smiled her best customer-service smile. "I'll send someone out. We'll have more before dinner."

"That doesn't solve the problem of this meal."

Carla furrowed her nose. "It's bacon and eggs. What's there to use ketchup on?"

"Eggs, apparently."

She balked, pantomiming vomiting. "Tell those people they aren't welcome here anymore," she grinned.

The woman smiled back. Her name was Odette, and she'd been living with Carla for nearly three years. She looked old, but wasn't. There were rings under her eyes that were premature and gray at her caps that was as well, but her cheeks retained the elasticity and buoyancy of youth when she smiled.

Three men pushed past them, and Odette squeezed close to Carla to let them past. She laughed, fully and completely, then backed up a pace again once they were gone. She noticed, too late, that Carla had not laughed. She cleared her throat. "You weren't at service this morning."

"I slept in," she answered. She spoke with finality, tugging her shirt down as she did.

Odette nodded. "You were missed, is all. You know how it is. New members, new mansion... new rules. And we're so close to the promised land that I think they can just... feel it. The energy of it, everyone's jazzed up." She turned back toward the living room and watched as people came and went, everyone moving as though they were on a tape that had been set to fast-forward. She smiled, then turned back to Carla, and slowly the smile left again. "Aren't you?"

Carla sighed involuntarily. She fixed the positioning of her glasses, and when she was done, her gaze went past Odette, over her shoulder to the bald girl sitting in the centre row of the couch. She was brushing Christine's hair as though she'd been made to do it. Blonde locks flowed like a river crashing over stone: swept up by the brush and then falling down again, over and over in rapid succession. She was transfixed in the task, and the hand of the man sitting next to her still rested on her thigh.

Carla stared at her, the noise and bustle around her becoming a high-pitched whine that blended together into the background. Although there was noise all around, for a moment she couldn't hear anything, her vision tunneled on the bald girl that was brushing hair.

When she snapped back into focus, Odette was mid-sen-

tence: "--Father'd be proud of you," she said.

Carla forced herself to make and maintain eye contact, smiled, then nodded. "Yes. Yes, I'm excited."

Odette squinted, then nodded. "I'll get you some toast. Jam?"

"Anything but ketchup."

She laughed, touched her arm, then continued past her into the kitchen.

Carla let her smile remain until she was out of sight, then slowly fade. She turned and watched the rhythmic hair brushing a moment longer, then turned and made her way behind the stairs towards the back room before Odette could find her with her toast.

CHAPTER 18

Outside Payson, Present

Chad sat on the picnic table on the back deck, his feet propped flat against its seat. Victor's laptop was balanced on his knees, shifting slightly with the stiff warm breezes that came from the airstrip. The meaty weight of the oblique arches of his thumbs rested on pads to either side of the keyboard, but his fingers hovered over the keys uselessly.

"Nothing?" Abby asked.

He sighed, his head sinking a little. "No."

She nodded. She was wearing large red rimmed sunglasses and sitting in a shielded lounge-swing made for two. Alice was next to her, her legs curled up until her feet were beneath her, absorbed in the book she was reading. It was the journal she'd taken from Madison Williams' bedroom.

Abby's legs were outstretched, escaping the shade of the canopy and warming themselves in the sunlight of the day.

"Wifi's shit out here," Chad grumbled. He flicked his

finger against the top right corner of the screen, as if tapping it where the wireless icon was would make the wireless card perform better.

Abby furrowed her brow, produced her phone, then tabbed it on. She examined the screen then turned it toward him. "Seems fine to me."

He huffed again, started to type a word, then removed the computer from his lap and placed it on the table next to him. He ran his hands through his hay hair, clenched his scalp, then let out a frustrated sound that was somewhere between a sigh and a growl.

Alice looked up from her book in a way only a young person could, only her pupils moving, eyelids fluttering. Her gaze shifted from the neat, handwritten pages to Chad without turning her head. "You act like you've never had an issue finding something you're looking for before," she drawled.

"I haven't."

She rolled her eyes. "And they call my generation privileged."

He raised his head and gave her a long, droll, dead-eyed expression that she did not take note of.

"Maybe we're thinking of this wrong," Abby said, rising to her feet. Her hands were before her and waist height, fingers splayed as though she were trying to calm two small children only she could see. Her sunglasses did a lot to make her expression unknowable, but her eyebrows peaked above them and her lips were pursed and ready.

"You think?" Alice snorted.

"Your powers don't work on probability... right? Like,

it's not a lotto. It's not like you can just pick a winner every time, it's specific to *you*. It's what's best, for *you*, whether you know that or not... right?"

"Just say he has good luck powers," Alice said under her breath, turning the page. "What is your people's aversion to saying things simply?"

Abby ignored her colour commentary.

Chad nodded.

"Okay so... so hear me out: what if you're not able to think of something to search for *because* we're going about this the wrong way? Maybe this *is* your luck kicking in. Not producing a result that will lead you on a wild goose chase *is* the luck."

Chad grimaced slightly and looked down at his hands. They were shaking slightly, and he thought of Victor trying to tear the *free* picture in two while sitting around the kitchen table, even the slight laminate making it difficult to do so. "Maybe."

"Okay, so, I vote we get more creative." Abby stepped to the house and opened the sliding door that led into the kitchen. She disappeared inside for a moment, then returned with a single scrap of paper clutched in her right hand. She was checking it even as she walked, craning her head to see around the folds she'd made to check the calligraphy. She moved to the table and slid in next to Chad, so close their hips touched all the way down to their knees.

This made Alice look up.

"Open up your Facebook," she said, smoothing out the picture.

He raised an eyebrow but did so. When it loaded, she leaned across him, the full scent of her shampoo and product filling his nostrils with the lavender bliss of her, and suddenly his mouth was wet with saliva. She typed 'Payson Search & Find' into the search bar and populated several pages devoted to the location of lost or stolen objects across town.

She clicked the one with the most followers and waited for it to load.

"What're you doing?" he asked, frowning.

"Hopefully? Finding a way to make your luck work for us." She smoothed out the piece of paper across his leg until the words were legible. She left the paper there for him and her hand there for herself. He felt the hairs on the back of his neck rise as he looked down at the paper: it was the description of the car Victor had seen drive away at the mall: light blue, two doors, wood paneling with scrapes.

He paused, then squinted, getting it. Clearing his throat, he brought the keyboard closer along his lap and clicked to make a new post. "Lost/Stolen: baby blue --" he paused, then nodded to himself, "-- Ford Pinto. Scraped wood panel sides, two door. Missing since Tuesday. Please contact if seen."

"How'd you know it's a Pinto?" she asked, her breath close to him.

"Educated guess." He bobbed his head. "The wood paneling went out of style a long ways back, the Pintos were basically the only thing that had them that were built to last this long. Fords, man. Built tough."

She snorted and backed away from him just so that she could look at him. "Don't let Victor hear you say that."

Chad smiled, eyeing Victor's El Dorado parked carefully in the driveway on the other side of the lot. He took a deep breath, then hit post. Abby squeezed his leg by way of thanks. She leaned forward and kissed his neck, lightly, between his ear and the hinge of his jaw.

Alice flipped the page of the journal but did not look at it, instead looking over its page at Abby's very public display of affection. "Is there a reason you're doing that?" she asked, finally.

"Increasing his luck?" Abby smirked. "Or, hopefully turning the odds so that finding the car are in his favor."

Alice rolled her eyes.

Chad straightened, processing what she was saying. "Pardon?" he said, finally.

She smiled at him, then kissed him again before taking the laptop from him.

Payson, The Past

Detective Gordon Melquist looked through the window of Interrogation Room One at the young woman who sat at the table within. The youth's name was Cline, according to her driver's license, Cline Cassidy. The shed that Briana Redding had been found at was also registered under the same name, as had the weapons found within, but even so Melquist had a difficult time thinking of the youth that way. He had a hard time rationalizing why any parent post-1960 would give their child a double-consonant name.

Cline was not making eye contact with Melquist, or with anyone. She was sitting alone in the mostly white room, a pair of cuffs binding her arms to a link in the table. Melquist had seen men stare like this before, lost in the gravity of what they'd done or been accused of doing, left in a room with nothing to stare at but your reflection in a two-way mirror... but Cline wasn't in the room with a two-way mirror. Melquist watched her through glass that was transparent on both sides and had been for the better part of ten minutes, yet Cline had yet to make eye contact or acknowledge his presence in any way.

The numerical digit the accompanied Interrogation Room One was unnecessary, Melquist thought, as it was the only interrogation room. The building was a rental, and two-way mirrors were expensive to install, so they watched arrestees through normal panes. Typically this made for a less adversarial experience, for good or ill... that was less the case with Cline Cassidy.

Cline stared into the void that was the other side of the room, dirty blonde hair falling into her eyes and tickling the edges of a brown leather duster. There was soot along her left cheek that hadn't come off despite the efforts of trace evidence collectors and several offers to let her use the washroom. Her mouth, it seemed, was perpetually open and slack.

"You gonna get it out of her?" Susan Waters said, stepping up behind him suddenly.

Though he hadn't been expecting her, Melquist did not startle or jump. "What do you mean?"

"I mean you're going to get her to say what she did to Briana Redding. Put this to bed."

Melquist shook his head, turning back to the glass. "I was already in with her, ten minutes ago. She admitted to everything. Just came out and said it."

Susan furrowed her brow, then turned back to Cline, who made no attempt to look at either of them. She stared into the dark with cold, dead eyes devoid of animation or emotion.

A shiver ran through Susan's spine.

Outside Payson, The Present

Abby stepped into the living room with force, but the moment she crossed the threshold, her step lost some of its momentum. It became a smaller thing, meeker somehow, as soon as the arches of her feet touched the carpet of that room. She had the laptop underneath her arm, but now drew it up without realizing it and making it into a shield.

Victor sat on the couch with one leg crossed. He was passing through pages of documents on his phone. Standing barely a foot in front of him was his pegboard, with the map of Payson and its surrounding area affixed to it. The circle he'd drawn was still there, the edges of the red sharpie having bled a little, but its shape still stark and firm.

His expression was unknowable, hidden behind the near-constant scruff of blond hay that fell over his upper lip. His smiles and grimaces were so slight that even that scant hair could cover them, rendering them invisible. His eyes betrayed nothing, flitting back and forth in time with his thumb every time he swiped to the next document on his screen. There was a picture of a house on the top of each that his eyeline would briefly address, then move on.

"What're you doing?" she asked, swallowing and taking a step into the room.

He looked up to the circle on the map, squinted, then turned back. "Looking for houses sold inside the circle in the last six months." He paused, clicked his tongue, then amended: "There's no way whoever did this has been here that long without making a move, but I'm just being safe."

She nodded. "Found anything?"

He frowned, and it managed to stretch the sides of his mouth enough that its deep black lines became visible beneath his scruff. He did not respond otherwise.

She nodded, then stepped the rest of the way into the room until she found herself next to the empty space on the couch next to him. She swallowed again.

His gaze flitted toward her without moving his head at the hard sound of her swallow. "You okay? You seem... off."

"Yeah," she nodded, her voice a small thing in the back of her throat. She lifted the laptop, briefly. "We're working on a new angle, hopefully we'll hear something soon."

Victor nodded, his eyes falling back to his phone.

She sat, becoming a part of the void next to him.

They sat in silence for a long moment.

"How were the parents?" he asked, breaking the extended silence. "Parents can be rough."

"Good. They were... as good as can be expected. They really took to Alice."

He pursed his lips and bobbed his head. "Makes sense."

"Does it?"

He nodded curtly.

"She found a journal; she's going through it now. Not sure how much help it'll be."

He raised his eyebrows but did not look up from his

phone screen.

She let her gaze wander, following the edges of Victor's red pen along the map of Payson. She watched the street and place names that the line obliterated, blocked out by the felt tip of the marker. Williams' Convenience had been erased from existence under the red tyranny, as had the Cornwall Youth Center. She frowned, leaned the laptop forward, and looked at the area between the both of them. "The Police were there when we were there."

"That makes sense. There will likely be someone there for the next few days at least. Days after a kidnapping, there's a lot of things that can happen that you'll want a cop around for."

She licked dry lips, nodding. "One of them... they mentioned something about this having happened before. That there were kidnappings in Payson, before now."

Victor stopped swiping the documents on his screen forward. His gaze found its way to her, and he laid the phone screen-down onto his leg. He did not respond to her statement, instead looked at her expectantly but without pressure... as if knowing that there was more to what she had to say.

She paused, then leaned the laptop forward again. She reached into the space between her chest and the laptop, and withdrew it with a crumpled, creased picture. It was a picture of Victor and Tash, standing in front of a plane with the word *free* stenciled across it in bright letters. She held it out to him, holding it pinched along its white border as though it were somehow hazardous. "They said the last kidnapping happened... around the same time this picture was taken."

He sighed and took the picture from her gingerly, clasping it and looking at it as if for the first time in a long time. His brow furrowed and his mouth tensed, but she thought -- briefly -- that she almost saw the beginnings of a smile before the frown had taken over. "Chad showed you this," he said under his breath.

"If you want to get technical, I found it first," she equivocated. "But yes. Yes, he gave it to me today."

Victor flapped the rough laminate between his hands. "I don't know what I have to do to convince the lot of you that there's nothing to this." He clasped it and held it in the space between their faces, obscuring her view of him. "It's just a picture."

She nodded. "Maybe stop protesting... quite so much."

He huffed, handed her back the picture unharmed, then turned and stepped toward a side table. He opened a drawer on its front and withdrew a faux-leather book from it. He flopped it down onto the couch beside Abby, where he had been a moment before. "You want pictures? There are pictures. Tons of them."

She opened to a random page in the album's middle, finding a photograph of Tash standing before what must have been a window of a high-rise. There was a long cityscape behind her, but not one she'd ever seen before. There were tall buildings with spires and black domes that didn't match architecture she'd seen in real life, movies, or television. On another page was a shot of Victor and Tash alone on a park bench. They were sitting apart and looking in opposite directions, as if posed, the only thing between them the glimmering memorial plaque in the bench's centre.

On the page after was a yearbook photo of a young girl Abby had never seen before. Its edges were frayed and boxed, as though it had been removed from its perch many times. Abby lingered on that one: the girl had a face shape not unlike her own.

Victor took the album back. "There are hundreds of pictures. Thousands, if you want to check my Google Drive. I don't know why you're fixated on *one* you *happened* to find, one time, but I've no time for it. Not where there's more important things --"

The laptop chimed.

They both stopped and stared down at it.

"What's that?" he asked, his voice different suddenly. Softer.

"The notification on the lead," she said, opening the laptop with haste. "We put out feelers for the car you saw drive off. We said it was ours, stolen. Asked for help."

Victor's eyebrows rose slightly, and he moved around to sit next to her on the couch again and see the screen.

She opened Facebook and clicked on the notification menu, then clicked the highlighted portion. She could already tell it was a picture from the thumbnail. Duke Kriensler commented on Chad's post in Payson Lost & Found: "Is this it, gassing up at Tycho's Gas and Go?" Attached was a picture of the blue Ford Pinto with wood paneling, sitting lazily under a canopy. There were a series of lens flares that cascaded off the windshield, making it look like a picture taken from a 70s scrapbook.

"Tell him that's not it," Victor said in a hushed tone, his hands together at his lips making an inverted V-shape with his forefingers. "Before he goes out and starts trouble with the driver, tell him that's not it."

Abby turned to him, so fast her hair whipped her cheeks, then turned back and typed as he'd said. "But it is it, isn't it?" she asked as she pressed enter.

He nodded slowly. "It is."

He turned back to the map he'd posted to the cork-board. Tycho's Gas and Go sat almost perfectly in the cen-tre of the encircled red region, a few miles into a long road that led out of Payson and into the offshoots of trails and cabins beyond.

CHAPTER 19

Outside Payson, Arizona

Alice lay on her bed in fleece pajamas, her head propped up against multiple pillows so that she could sit comfortably. Madison's journal was next to her, closed and weighty against her mattress. Her place had been marked with a felt bookmark that stuck out of its middle now like a tongue.

Her phone was propped against her knees, facing her and spotlighting her with its bright screen. On it, Cliven and Lindsay Williams huddled together on their couch to stay on screen together.

"Something changed; she started writing differently. You'd have to be looking for it to see it, but it's there," Alice said, finishing her thought.

Lindsay looked pleadingly at the screen, but not at the camera, making eye contact a difficult thing to accomplish. "What do you mean? Different, how?"

Alice's mouth warbled. "It's subtle. I might be reading too much in. She stops using contractions, suddenly. Like, really all of a sudden." She flipped the pages of the book without picking it up, as if to illustrate. "Like, for seventy-plus pages she's speaking teen-speak, and then all of a sudden one day it's like she's writing a formal essay. It's like a switch went off."

"Anything else?" Cliven asked. He was trying to be firm, but his tone was hollow.

"She stops talking about boys around the same time." She looked from Lindsay to Cliven. "Not that she gushed about them or anything."

He waved her concern away.

"No... really. But she talked about them. Like they were people. Then when the formal writing starts, she just... stops."

"Thank you," he nodded. "Thank you for trying. It's good to hear... something. The police, they... they haven't told us anything. I know there might be nothing to tell, but it's... you can't imagine. Waiting by the phone."

Alice frowned, looked at the journal, then at the closed door to her bedroom. She sighed. "If I tell you something, will you keep it to yourselves?"

Lindsay made a gulp of excitement, and they both nodded vigorously.

She sighed again. "We've got a lead. We tried a trick on social media to... it doesn't matter. We have a lead."

"Should you tell the police."

She shook her head. "Nothing that concrete. More like a hunch... but an educated hunch. Police have to act within the law, they have to see what police are allowed to see... we look at the whole picture; it lets us..." she trailed off for a second, then smiled. "It lets us do the math."

Cliven nodded.

"We got a tip from just outside town, out around the

Gas and Go."

"I know the place," he said.

"We're heading out there in the morning. First thing. I'll keep you informed, I promise."

"Thank you," Cliven said, respectfully.

"Be *careful*," Lindsay stressed. She touched her hand to her mouth and then to the camera.

Alice wasn't sure why, but this sent shivers through her. She nodded. "We *will* find her."

She closed the call and placed her phone on her dresser and set about the task of trying to sleep.

After an hour of trying, she turned on her light and picked up Madison's diary and started to read again.

Payson, The Past

Cline Cassidy sat in the only interrogation room in the Payson District Police Department, staring into the null space along the side of the window as if it were a mirror, but it wasn't.

"Fucker's been like this two days," Melquist said, tapping on the glass as if to illustrate his point.

Cline didn't move or make any twitch toward the sound.

"See?"

"You've had this woman in there for two days?" Tash asked, stepping closer to the glass. Victor stepped up to it alongside her, his nose almost to it.

Melquist turned and balked at her and at the accusation. "Of course not. We move her from containment to here a few times a day. Containment's more social... we're trying both, trying to get her to talk."

"Is she social in containment?" Victor asked.

"Fuck no."

"I thought not." Victor leaned forward, as close as he dared to the glass, and squinted. He watched the wispy, stray hairs that puffed out on either side of Cline's head as if he expected them to do something. He did this for a moment so long that Melquist started to shift from foot to foot uncomfortably, then turned to Tash and looked at her in much the same way. He watched her for a moment, nodded, then turned and looked at Melquist, then nodded, then turned back to Cline again... and sighed.

Melquist raised an irritated eyebrow, turning to Tash.

She shrugged. "He has his methods."

"The damage done to the child that the paper reported... was all that true?" Victor asked. He placed a palm against the glass.

Melquist stiffened, then nodded. "What was there was true."

"You leave anything out?"

"You gotta leave something out. Only way to weed out some idiot barging in and knowing all the details of the case."

Victor nodded. "The worst of it, then... the worst of it got left out?"

Tash turned to Melquist, who nodded.

"This isn't right," Victor said, motioning to the woman behind the glass. "To do the kind of violence that the paper talked about... that takes passion. Hate. Emotion.*" He cocked his head toward the interrogation room. "You getting any of that from this... mannequin?"*

Melquist's mouth twisted. "The weight of it, what she done. It broke her, I guess."

"People don't break like that. People do break, just... not like that. *It's slower, it's a process of dehumanization. PTSD, in the way you're describing... it's not a lack of emotion, it's an abun-*

dance of one particular type of emotion. She doesn't have that; she doesn't have anything."

"She's scared then. She knows she's going away and she's just clamming up, shutting down."

"She's not scared, she's nothing. Look at her."

"Anger then. Pissed she got caught. That sort of paralyzing anger, the type your momma used to get at you when you did something really --"

"Follow the trend here. Do the math. Look at her: does any part of this read as anger to you?"

"Can I talk to her?" Tash interrupted, suddenly.

Melquist's head snapped around. "You must be joking."

"You can come in with me. I just... I've dealt with people like this, before. I work with troubled teens." She shot Victor a look. "I think I might be able to help get through to her."

Melquist turned and looked over Victor's head at Susan, who was waiting by the bullpen with her arms crossed. He turned back around, shaking his head. "Unless you've got a law degree in this state and are, in actuality, his lawyer: no. And if you are her lawyer... I'd like to retroactively make what I said off the record." He smirked.

She smiled back.

In the room, Cline Cassidy scratched at her midsection. It was the first deliberate motion she'd made in nearly an hour.

Victor shook his head. "Nothing."

Los Angeles, California

Theo stared into the mirror, the crack alongside it bisecting him in a jagged thunderbolt down his middle. The left half of the mirror was tilted off of its moorings, bending its reflection slightly and making two halves of himself: the right half that was straight, and the left half -- distorted and strange.

"London Waltz" played on a speaker in a room adjacent to him, its volume muffled by the walls until it was barely audible.

He reached up and brought his hand down across the left half of his face, smudging it with his cloth and distorting it further. A streak of dark brown was left behind and began to blend it in, the distinction between the two halves growing. Shaping, contouring, he began to ease and erase the slight shadows under his cheeks, hiding his high cheekbones until they were barely visible at all.

He laid his brush down, his fingers finding a strip of black felt affixed to a thin piece of wax paper. He raised them both, then peeled one from the other -- only glancing away from himself briefly -- then pressed and flattened the black felt to his upper lip.

When he took his hand away, the two halves of the mirror held the images of vastly different men. The one on the right was clean-shaven, toned, and well-kept. The man on the left had had all of the tone of his cheeks masked. There were splotches of distorted flesh and pockmarks along his nose and the beds of his eyes and he had a firm, well-groomed mustache with just a touch of gray in it.

Theo sighed as his gaze went from one man to the other, then back again. His brush found more makeup, and he began to apply it to the right side of his face.

CHAPTER 20

Outside Payson, Arizona

Victor's El Dorado pulled into Tycho's Gas and Go, its chassis bouncing off the steep incline of the driveway like a low-rider. A sharp squeak came from the wheel well, and Abby winced as she felt it connect with the thick rubber of the tire itself.

He pulled into the lot and parked on a diagonal angle across the entrance to the pumps without pulling up to them, blocking them from one side. When he shoved the car into park position, it had two wheels in the parking space nearest the door, and two under the gas-up canopy.

Abby got out of the car, surveyed its situation, and spread her arms wide. She was trying to encompass the entire vehicle in her expanse, but from a distance instead appeared to be pantomiming crucifixion.

Victor got out of the driver's side and slammed the door behind him, producing another hazardous squeal. He looked up at the Gas and Go with his hands on his hips, his knuckles a stark white contrast to his black cor-

duroy tee. He turned and looked at Abby and her extended arms, then raised one eyebrow. "What?"

"And what if someone else needs to get gas?"

Victor shrugged, even as Alice got out of the backseat.
She was clutching the lost girl's diary tightly in her right
hand, where it had scarcely left since she'd found it. He
looked from her to the parking job. "Old military positioning. It's a subtle, subconscious message to people who
would just drop in."

"And that message is?"

"Fuck off."

She rolled her eyes, and was about to respond, when
the rut-rum-rum-rum revving of Chad's motorcycle extended around the corner. He pulled it in over a divot,
avoiding the sharp incline and pulling up next to the El
Dorado.

He rode helmetless, his hay-coloured hair flowing behind him. He snapped his kickstand down, regarded the
car, then nodded curtly. "Nice park job."

Abby made a derisive sound deep in her throat, and
the four of them stepped toward the entrance to the Gas
and Go. At this point, a tall, straggly twenty-something
with red hair and a golfer's visor had started to look out at
them and examine the odd congregation of people.

Victor reached out to open the door, paused, then retracted his arm. "You do it," he said, motioning to Chad.

Chad narrowed his eyes, then opened the door and let
the three of them in before entering behind Abby.

"You shouldn't park like that," the straggly youth
behind the counter said. He was strumming his fingers
against his lotto cabinet in uneven, lackadaisical strokes.

His fingers were dirty along their edges, stained black with oil and brown with grit and gas. His leftmost knuckle and matching nailbed were gashed, giving the tapestry of his hand a bright splash of red.

Victor turned to look outside in a wide arch, his whole body turning instead of his head. His mouth chawed, as though he were seeing the haphazard way he'd parked for the first time. "Sorry about that, Guv'ner," he said, and his voice had taken on the rhythm and cadence of a native Arizonian.

Alice paused, turning to him with a cocked eyebrow.

Victor looked around the shop, his motions exaggerated, like someone performing for the cheap seats. He pulled a piece of paper, folded lengthwise, from his back pocket and pointed it at the man behind the counter. "You Duke Kriensler?"

The man stood upright suddenly. "Name's Dave. I'm only Duke online."

Victor nodded, stepped forward, and unfolded the piece of paper onto the lotto cabinet. He smoothed its edges, and Abby watched the motion with great interest from the sidelines... unsure if the repetitive action was real anxiety or a perfect facsimile of it: a part of the show, like the exaggerated accent that mimicked that of the clerk. "This was you, though?"

Duke leaned forward to see the paper. It was a black-and-white print of the social media post, complete with comments. There was a back-and-forth exchange between two teens arguing over if it was a 'nice ride' or not that devolved quickly into name calling and slurs, but after that there was a notice from Duke Kriensler, his name in bold:

"Is this it, gassing up @Tycho's Gas and Go?"

He squinted, raising himself back up to standing. "I thought that wasn't it?"

"Yeah, now it is," Victor replied gruffly, tapping his finger against the picture. "When did you take the picture? Today? Yesterday?"

Duke paused, squinting. His face looked more natural when he squinted, as though that were his default setting, like Clint Eastwood. "Yesterday. Evening." He motioned to a security camera. "And it wasn't me, I saw the post and went back on the feed for a screenshot. You don't see the wood paneling a lot anymore."

Victor watched him as he spoke, his eyes hovering between looking at the man and somewhere just aside him, then nodded. He thanked Duke, then picked the paper back up and stepped back toward the team. In a hushed voice that was devoid of the regional accent he'd put on, he said, "There's no reason for the car to be out this far unless this is where home base is. This is it -- we go down this road, we find the car, we got this. It's ours."

"No reason," Chad nodded with pursed lips. "Except to dump a body."

Alice turned on him, mouth open and angry as if he'd just said a racial slur. Her cheeks went bright red and she looked as though she might hit him with the journal.

Victor's gaze snapped to his like a magnet. "She's *not* dead."

"It's a possibility." He waved his finger around to indicate the entire setting. "Look around, you couldn't dream of a better place. Woods to hide what you've done, lots of scavengers to aid with decomposition... I'd be hard up to think of a better place, honestly."

Alice clenched her teeth, then turned away from him.

Abby didn't say anything. She turned and looked out toward the forest when he brought their attention to it, the sea of stretched pine faces staring back at them with a myriad of different designs. Her nostrils raised and stretched, her tongue wedging itself against the roof of her mouth, in the way it did when she was deep in thought.

"The girl. Is not. Dead," Victor reiterated, taking the time to annunciate each syllable.

"You get that me saying it doesn't make it happen, right?" Chad replied sarcastically. "I'm just saying, it's a possibility."

"I mean, it might. Is that how your powers work?" Alice shrugged.

"Voice down, please."

Abby looked out at the El Dorado. From the angle it was parked at she could see its gas gauge, lying limp now that the car was off, but finding her focus all the same. Her eyes narrowed and she flitted her fingers back and forth. Suddenly, she turned from the group and back to Duke. "Is that the only time you've seen that car, you think?"

He paused, taking a moment to realize that she was not talking about the El Dorado. "Nah. Nah, I seen it before, for sure. At least twice."

She nodded, leaning forward on the counter, her hands lingering near his. "You the only person who works here, Duke?"

"Naw, me and my three brothers. Equal shifts, Dad owns the place."

She smiled. "You got the image from the security feed...

any chance we can take a look at it?" She made eye contact with him as she asked, looking up at him with a few scant strands of auburn hair falling in front of her face.

He hesitated briefly, then nodded.

She stepped back to the group and snatched the print-out from Victor. She took out a pen and made a mark along its backside, then kept both.

"What're you doing?" Victor asked, looking from Abby to Duke and then back again.

"*Real* math," she said, before following Duke towards the back of the Gas and Go.

Abby sat at a computer that was almost as old as she was, controlling the speed at which the security feed played on the television wired to it with the A, S, and D keys. She was a week back now, and the sheet of paper she'd stolen from Victor had three sets of dates and time on them: each set had a mark under two columns: North, and South.

Victor and Chad were in the doorway to the small, cramped office. They would have been able to have sat inside had the room been only used to house the computer, but there were also empty beer bottles stacked to teetering heights, awaiting recycling.

She hit the spacebar and paused the video yet again, just as the Pinto with wood-panel sides pulled up to the pumps. She nodded, wrote down the timestamp, then let the video resume at normal speed. A blonde woman filled the car, keeping her head down as she did so. When she was done, Abby paused the video again, making an additional scribble before snapping the pen shut. "I think that's enough," she said, rising to her feet. She walked past the boys, and they moved as one to avoid her, like human saloon doors.

She stepped out to the station proper, where Alice was making small talk with Duke, the diary pressed open to her chest as though they had started to talk while she was mid-chapter.

"What're you doing?" Victor asked, following a few feet behind her. His eyes were trained on her in a way that a passerby might have mistaken for annoyance but wasn't. He'd let his fake accent fall away in the time since Duke had brought her to the back room, and although he'd noticed, Duke hadn't said anything.

Abby didn't respond. She brought the sheet of paper to Duke and smoothed it out over the lotto cabinet, just as Victor had. The act of smoothing it smudged the ink, but not so much that it couldn't be seen. "Can you get me the receipts for these times? I think I read the amounts off the meter right, but I want to be sure."

Duke nodded, picking up the paper and heading to the computer alongside the register.

Abby started typing something into her phone even as she turned back to Victor and Chad. "It's not a body dump, they come back too often."

Duke looked over his shoulder at the mention of the words 'body dump,' but said nothing.

"They don't come every day, but when they do, they come twice: once in the morning, and once in the evening."

Duke pressed a button on the screen, and suddenly

the cash register started printing a receipt. It had the word DUPLICATE in bold, black letters across the top.

"What's that mean?" Alice asked, furrowing her brow. "I mean, I know what it means. But why's it important?"

Duke snatched off the receipt when it was done printing and handed it to Abby. She took it, clicked her pen on, then checked down through the numbers she'd marked next to each set of timestamps. She adjusted three of them, checked her phone again, then wrote a quick formula underneath it all: $(\$) \div COG \div 2 \div MPG = (x)$.

"So, real math time. Solve for X," she started, turning the paper around. "Every time they come here, they come here twice a day, once in the morning and once in the evening. Let's assume when they fill up in the morning they're coming from home, and when they come in the evening they're heading back home from the city."

Victor nodded, seeing already where she was heading but letting her finish.

"So when they fill up in the morning, they're filling up the amount of gas it takes for them to get home from the gas station, and back again."

"Unless they're running around in the days between," Chad added.

Abby shook her head, pointing to the numbers in the left column. "It's consistent, within margin for error. It wouldn't be if that was the case."

He tilted his head, then nodded.

"Okay, so we take the average amount they pay when they gas up in the morning, and we divide that by the cost of gas, per gallon. Then we divide that by two, and we get the amount of gallons they burn between here and wherever they live." She nodded at them. Each of them nodded back. "Okay, so then we divide that by the average miles per gallon of a Ford Pinto." She held up her phone. It was open to an auto-trader website, there were statistics from over forty Pinto owners, aggregated. "Ten miles," she finished, showing her work. "They're within ten miles of this spot."

Victor smirked. He reached out and took the paper, gently, as though it were precious parchment.

"How'd you do that?" Alice asked, smiling.

Abby shrugged. "I did the math."

CHAPTER 21

Madison Williams sat in the dark of the closet wearing only her soccer jersey and shorts, the former wrapped all the way around the knees she had brought to her chest. She was shivering, her knees pulled so taut that the scab along her left one had ripped itself open, oxygenating the viscus fluid that came from it. The dull hum of the rest of the house seeped through the walls at her from all direction. Vibrations, she felt, were like water: when they decided they were against you they surrounded you, enveloped you, drowned you. The vibrations from the bass music pulsated its way into the wall around the speaker. That wall shook the walls adjacent to it, which shook the cabinets and the glass within them, and the ceiling, and the floating floor... until it reached the dark corner Madison had found for herself, and it seemed like the entire closet was vibrating.

She laced her fingers together at the base of her skull, clasping them like people in airplane pamphlets: in case of emergency, tuck your head between your legs and secure your head with both hands. She couldn't articulate why she was in this position... she'd flown enough as a child, seen that flip-book comic enough, that it was second nature. Emergency: hands behind the head. Danger: hands behind the head. Stop. Drop. Roll.

She wasn't sure why this was an emergency, only that it was. That feeling came from deep in the well of her gut, no matter how much she tried to fight it. It brought with it hot tears that she hated, curling her lip every time she felt a new one form. Big girls don't cry, she scolded herself. Although it was from within her head, she heard it as clearly as she would a voice. That voice -- that aspect of her -- was so pronounced that it was almost a separate entity altogether.

"You okay?" came a voice from outside the closet. It came the same time as a knock at it and made her flinch. Her leg hit the edge of the door, and when her head rose, she could see the shadow of the person under the door.

Madison sniffed back hard, took a deep breath, then nodded. After a moment she realized that the speaker could not see her nod and responded, "Yes." Her voice was shaky and didn't sound right... it was an odd thing, having a muscle one used every day be so outside one's control.

The shadow beneath the door moved, and there was a sliding sound head over the bass music. There were two shadows under the door suddenly -- both from the same person, Madison thought -- as the speaker slid down next to the door and cocked their legs at an odd angle.

"I know it's scary at first, but that's only at first," the speaker said, their voice calm and cajoling. "I promise, all the weird stuff... after a little while, it seems normal."

Madison felt another tear form and pushed it away, with such force that she hurt her own cheek. It was red from heavy breathing and misuse.

There was a sudden, new light from under the door and the sudden flicker of a lighter. The speaker took a deep breath, and when they exhaled plumes of blue smoke made it through the door and onto Madison. She coughed, the smoke wet and salty.

"Come on out, now," the voice said again. It sounded suddenly less pleasant. Not commanding, but it was clear somehow from the inflection that it was asking less than telling. "Only way to get used to things is to get back on the horse."

Madison swallowed. She wrapped her jersey completely around herself, despite the violent protestations of her knee. The bass of the music surrounded her until she thought it would compress her into a tiny ball.

Los Angeles, California

Theo sat in a rental car across from the glass entrance to Black Springs mental hospital, his flesh the perfect sun-kissed tan of someone who had lived in the Los Angeles heat, without the effort of having done so. His upper lip twitched, still disused to the discomfort of the mole-hair and wax that weighed down his upper lip.

 The building was different than the way he recalled it in his youth in almost every way. Those days were so fogged in turmoil and mystery and doubt that nothing seemed real anymore, least of all his time in Black Springs. In his mind's eye it had been a square, ominous building in the middle of a desperate desert. The building he looked up at shone and sparkled and was surrounded on all sides by stories-tall buildings of a similar sort. There were large glass doors in its front: the sort of doors a marketing specialist would have told them gave the impression of 'transparency' and 'sincerity.'

The last time he'd seen those doors, Victor's El Dorado had been coming through them, turning the glass into beads of shatterproof marbles that fell to the ground with a splash. It had regenerated since and was now exactly as it had been: shimmering, clean, and monolithic. He wondered, and not for the first time, if anything was allowed to change here. If he checked through the halls and found the wing with the Closers in it, would he find himself at fourteen; struggling to paint a straight line in a common room?

He frowned at the thought, the glue of the mustache pulling at the edges of his lips and pinching them.

Three young people approached the building, one with hair so long that she could have been dropped into the city straight from 1960's Woodstock. She was wearing what, for a person of her age and upbringing, would be considered business casual clothing. Black blouse that buttoned down and similarly coloured slacks, but the blouse was untucked and splayed out like a cape at the ends, and the slacks ballooned into bellbottoms at their ankles. Theo watched as she departed from her friends, touching one on the shoulder as she went before breaking from the group and disappearing through the shimmering glass portal into Black Springs.

He watched the spot where she'd vanished for a long

moment, his mind again stretching back to his time at Black Springs, and what a reprieve someone like her would have been, all hair and teeth and cheeks. He tried to guess at her function, too kind to be an aid, too healthy to be a patient. Without trying, his mind conjured the image of a sick man, blue at the lips with many IVs and grayed eyes. He squinted... had his mind created that on its own, or had he gotten it from her as she walked by, gleaning her reason for being here without even the decency of waiting for her billboard to be scrolled in behind her?

He shook his head forcefully, as if pushing the thought out through his ears. He pressed the button on the steering wheel that made the dash cam record, waited for the chime to indicate that it was working, then reached for the spiral notebook next to him. He scribbled the time after checking it, then: 'dirty blond, young, visiting sick man.' He eyed that for a moment as though it were somehow suspicious, then struck-through the word 'sick' and replaced it with 'dying.'

He turned back to the door, took a deep breath, and watched as the billboards of the crowd lit up in his mind's eye.

There was a man exiting Black Springs wearing a nice suit and a leather cap that did not suit the rest of his ensemble. It looked like the sort of thing a chimneysweep would have worn but lacked the soot and grime that came with that profession. He had leather pads sewn onto the elbows of his blazer and walked as though he were in a hurry, his briefcase jutting out in front of him like a blade before swinging back to the other arc of its pendulum. Following alongside him and keeping pace was his billboard, which had a badly animated bee on it bouncing from flower to flower in a lush field, as a non-pictured representation of The Beatles sang, 'Here Comes the Sun.'

Theo made a note about the man on his sheet, and the time he'd exited. He checked his dash cam again.

A woman in gray stepped down the street, sauntering past Black Springs without acknowledging it. Her hair was short-cropped and styled to match the contours of her skull and she wore makeup that sleeked her eyes back until they appeared to touch her hairline. She had on her thoughts, and billboard, a memory from the night before -- a kiss that had happened at a club with a stark green glow to it. She was in the footage -- the billboard was in third person, not in first person -- the memory having already gone through that first, important step to becoming fiction.

One of these days, Theo thought, he would have to watch that happen. Have to watch a memory go from clear, first-person objective into third person and already partly fictional. He'd wanted to see the process since he'd recognized it... which, he thought, was something that had happened the day after he'd met Abby. They'd met in the mess hall at the Port Haven Institute, and later that day he'd caught her thinking about it: but she herself was in the memory, the thought already transferred to third person. It had fascinated him, seeing how she portrayed her own movements and gestures, so different from the way he'd perceived them.

It was then, while peeking into her memories, that he'd first seen the fire come from her.

He shook off the thought, feeling as though the hairs

along his arm had been singed, and returned his attention to the street. Dozens of billboards walked past, some more prominent than other, passing through each other and influencing each other in subtle ways. One large man passed by a woman with dark blonde hair, and for a moment his billboard was solely of her.

The woman had no billboard. She'd been leaning against the far wall of Black Springs while picking a stick of gum out of a cigarette tin, had moved off it, then started down the street, all while the space above and behind her was devoid of imagery. There was no snow crash or colour-bars like when some people were devoid of thought: there was no image, not even the frame of where the image would have been.

Theo's thumb hovered over the record button on his steering wheel as he watched her go. She was wearing a white blouse and tie and a skirt that showed off long, thin legs. Her lips were bright red and distracted the eye with their splash of colour.

It wasn't the first time he'd seen someone without a billboard, but it was the exception rather than the rule. Victor had lacked a billboard... at least, until recently. He recalled the flash behind Victor's head suddenly then, the man standing in the centre of the room with light playing off the greasy heads of children standing away from him in the distance. He shuddered again, as he had remembering the first memory he'd seen of Abby using her power.

When he came back to reality, the woman was gone, but a second had come out of Black Springs: a stocky woman in a dark blue suit. Her hair was graying and pulled back in a tight bun so tight that it pulled her face taut. It was Roberta Feinberg, one of the only nurses who had been kind to him during his entire stay at the Black Springs hospital. Here she was still at Black Springs, when only yesterday he'd seen her at the Anemone site.

As if to illustrate his point, her billboard displayed the massive crater in the Los Angeles suburb that he'd seen her at. It played on her mind, looping like a meme with only twelve frames, watching the men in orange jump-suits as they made their way down toward its uncertain foundation.

Still at the Black Springs hospital, yet somehow also at the site of suburb collapse, with men all around treating her as though she were the one in charge.

Theo hit record on his dash cam, then picked up his phone and scrolled through his messages until he found Victor. He watched her melt into the crowd.

CHAPTER 22

Outside Payson, Arizona

Victor and Alice drove down Needlebridge Road, a thin stretch of pavement that wound between dunes and patches of trees off the main highway. It hadn't actually had a place-marker that they'd seen, but the map named it Needlebridge. Less than a mile in they'd seen why, encountering a bridge over a shallow gorge that was so thin there was only a hair's width between the rails and the El Dorado's mirrors on either side as Victor passed through it.

"Like a camel," he said under his breath, gripping the steering wheel so hard that all his knuckles were strained white.

Alice shot him a look. "What?"

"Nothing," he murmured, his back wheels touching pavement again. He allowed himself a small burst of speed to put the bridge firmly behind him but had to slow again almost immediately for another twist in the road.

Alice sat with Madison's notebook on her knee, her thumb stuck between its pages as a bookmark. Her head swiveled from her side window to the front, scanning each available section of the wilderness that surrounded them. "We're going to find her," she said, her grip on the diary tightening.

Victor raised an eyebrow in her direction, then forced his gaze forward as the El Dorado's engine revved to life.

Abby gripped hard around Chad's midsection as he sped into a turn, hearing nothing but the roar of his engine and the whistle of wind past her. She pressed her head as close to him as she could, her helmet creating a barrier between them, as the world zipped by.

His hair billowed around her, whipping with the wind. He had no helmet, had given her his and his jacket, and was now coursing through the back roads of Arizona with a flapping tee and little between the evening sun and the sun-kissed muscles of his upper arms. Despite the cacophony of sights and sounds pressing in on her, when she squeezed in it was like being in a sensory deprivation tank: all she could hear was the white noise of the wind and the engine, all she could smell was the crisp leather of her jacket, and all she could feel was his warmth.

She felt the bike drop a gear and brought her head up, moving her hands to his legs. Around her, the bustle and blur of movement slowed, becoming whole, tangible things again. The road they were on wound between mounds of compacted dirt and around corners, interspersed with patches of green-gray trees that sprung up like chia pets: contained by some invisible force, limited in their ability for growth by their ability to gain water.

They were at a low point, a valley in the vast dunes of nothing around them. She'd been amazed by the fact of it the first time she'd driven through here, and had not stopped since; the way it could seem to go on forever, the dunes of the foreground blurring with the dunes of the background in one's eye until it looked like a straight shot from where one stood to the horizon... only to be shocked when one came around a turn and found a patch of trees, or a trailer park, or a gas station that had previously been invisible.

Chad let the bike roll to a stop, putting down one booted foot. The road spawned off in four directions from where they stood, slinking and winding around the rises in the countryside so that they couldn't tell one from another. It split around a large section of trees, denser and thicker than nature had any right to be in this climate. They rose high, and the road split in two directions on either side of them. Chad eyed it and chewed a stick of gum he'd been working on since the gas station, but said nothing.

Abby got off the bike without a word, took off her helmet, and walked up the road until she was dead centre in the middle of the fork.

His gaze shifted from the gaggle of trees to her, and the way she walked with determination and agency. She walked as though there were a mark on the ground that some unseen director had planted there in tape, as if she knew exactly where she was going at all times. She reached her mark in the centre of the fork and turned to face each of the four directions at once, her auburn hair blowing around her.

"Which way do we go?" she said finally, turning around to face him. Her foot stomped when she did, as though she were turning about-face to meet a drill instructor.

Chad squinted, his eyes moving from the two paths on the left to the two on the right, then back to Abby in the centre. He snapped out the kickstand on the bike, glanced at the road behind him to make sure there was nothing on it, then got off and stepped towards Abby. When he was within two feet of her, he tried to take a step to the right, paused, and retracted.

He tried again to the left, and again, he hesitated. He frowned, then stepped forward until they were nose to nose, then leaned in and kissed her. She closed her eyes. His hands rose up to cup her cheeks and he moved with her as they embraced, until finally she pulled back.

When she opened her eyes again, he was staring past her, at the gaggle of trees and brush behind her.

They were dry and gray, clinging to life but still closer to death in the middle of the desert. Their trunks looked like flesh made callused with eczema... but their leaves were showing signs of greening, as though recently coming to life.

She pulled back from him and turned toward the tree line, as if expecting it to do something now that their attention was on it. "What is it?" she asked, softly.

He stepped around her, inching closer to the brush. When he was close enough, he picked up one of the leaves and pressed it between his thumb and forefinger until its green moisture was yielded. A little came, but not a lot. "Not many trees grow in the desert," he said matter-of-factly. "It's not like home."

"Payson has trees," she reminded him.

"Beautification efforts. And a consequence of settlement. Think about it: you're looking for a place to settle in the dessert, what do you look for? Trees."

"The mansion has them," she added.

He nodded, pulling his arm away and looking at the residual green smear sink into the pads of his fingers. He reached up and applied slight pressure to the branch, pulling it down. "Call Victor," he said.

She stepped forward to him, taking out her phone and dialing as she did.

In the distance, behind several layers of trees and foliage, a dark rectangle blotted out the light. From this distance it looked like a maw in reality, a hole that was slowly swallowing the zombified forest around it.

In the middle top of the rectangular maw, floating like breaks in reality, were two windows.

CHAPTER 23

The four of them -- Victor, Abby, Alice, and Chad -- stood before the large manor secluded by the trees. There had been an access road, hidden and hard to get into with anything except Chad's bike without causing damage. The El Dorado was parked alongside it, blocking anything coming in or out. Chad had walked his bike alongside the other three as they'd stepped through the winding quarter mile of dirt road. It wasn't even really a dirt road; it was tamped-down foliage beaten by repeated drive-overs.

The building towered before them. It had looked small when viewed between the trees and the branches had obscured its perspective, but it grew up from the crazed desert ground and patches of dried grass like a lumbering giant. It was the sort of bluish gray that was often mistaken for being just gray, the windowsills an even darker shade of the same. The sparsely tiled roof was tar black, based on the small accents of it above the main door and below windows. There were many windows, and though none of them had anyone in them, there was a pervasive feeling of being watched while one was in their glow.

Next to the house was a blue Ford Pinto with faux wood-panel siding. There were scrapes in the wood -- long, winding, continuous marks from the branches on either side of the trail. Chad had one similar scrape, albeit much smaller, on the right side of his bike from the same.

"Is that the car?" Alice asked, keeping it in her peripheral vision as if expecting it to attack. It stayed where it was, a gargoyle overseeing the exchange, its headlights the only eyes they could see on them.

Victor nodded without looking at it again.

Chad stepped over to it, peering in through the back window without touching it. "There's a tarp along the backseat, one of those black ones with the steel rings along the sides. There's a box with canned goods in it wedged into the footrest of the back passenger side... Chef Boyardee, mostly. Some tin milk. Nothing... sinister." He paused before the last word, his eyes flittering over the assessed items one last time. When he turned back, he addressed Abby, not Victor. "What's our play?"

"We knock," Victor said, as Abby was opening her mouth.

She turned to him, as did the others. "We think there's a child in there."

"We have no reason to think that."

Abby looked at him, her mouth agape. "You have been *insisting* for the better part of a *week* that --"

"We have no *legal* reason to think that," he amended, cutting her off as her voice was rising. "If we call the police, what do we have? The fact that there exists a house. A house outside of Payson township jurisdiction, I might add."

"We have the car," Chad reminded, jabbing his thumb towards it.

"We have a car, which matches a car I've seen, but that has not been seen near or in any way linked to Madison Williams. Or anyone, for that matter. We have the existence of a house and the existence of a car. That does not a compelling argument make."

Chad stopped short.

Victor narrowed his eyes at him. "I know you've been thinking it, that you have doubts about... about this."

"I don't," Chad interrupted, looking from The Manor to the car and then back again.

"About *me*. The doubts are valid, but this... this is real. This is happening. I've seen it before."

Abby and Alice both looked at him as he said this, then to each other.

"So," Victor said, then stepped around until he was facing the front walkup of the house. He planted his army boots down on each of the rickety, decaying steps with great emphasis until there was nothing between him and the front door except the air, thick with tension. He took out his cell phone, checked it once, then put it into his breast pocket. He looked back once to see if his team was behind him, saw that they were, raised his clenched-white knuckle, and rapped three times.

At first there was nothing but silence.

"Maybe there's nobody home?" Abby ventured, leaning forward slightly.

"There are over two dozen people in there," Victor said with confidence.

Abby straightened back up at the abruptness of his

comment, then looked down at his hands. They appeared to be limp at his sides, but the muscles were in fact tense, frozen, and flexed. His hands were opening and closing together once per heartbeat, tightening into fists and then becoming claws, then back again -- never relaxed, never calm. Eyes wide, she was turning back to address Chad when the door opened.

Carla answered and opened the door in a way that Chad had previously only thought possible by suburban mother's: cautious yet welcoming and friendly. Her free hand was rested on the door, making a barrier across it with her arm. The door was only open enough for her head and shoulder to stick out, but her smile spread across the entire gap. "Hello," she said, in that sing-song way that people did when trying to be pleasant to strangers. She made eye contact with Victor, and when she did her perfect smile faltered for just a moment, then she moved on to each member of the team in turn. "Is there something I can do to help you?"

"We're looking for Madison Williams," Victor said, his tone gruff and barely restrained. "She's a --"

"I know who she is," she said, pushing a lock of her hair back out of her face. She managed the trick of interrupting without snapping, keeping her tone that perfect customer-service pleasant. Her gaze lingered on Chad even as she addressed Victor, turning back to him only a beat after she'd spoken. "I saw her on the news."

Victor squinted. "I'm sure you did. If it's alright with you though, we'd like to come inside?"

Carla's smile wavered a little. Somewhere behind her, a shadow moved from one side of the door to the other.

When her smile returned it was broad, showing off just how white her teeth were. "You're not the police." Her voice was still musical.

"That wasn't a question."

"No, it wasn't." She opened the door and stepped back, revealing the hall behind her for the first time. There were two people deep in the bowels of The Manor -- they looked far back from Carla but couldn't have been. They had sunken eyes and hair so blond it was almost white, and they waited like statues. "Everyone's welcome here." She extended her hand. It shook slightly. "I'm Carla."

Victor took a deep breath, held it, and exhaled as he passed the threshold into The Manor. His boots were heavy against the floor, each step coming with a firm, weighty sound. He stepped past Carla, turning his head to keep her dangled in his peripheral vision as he found his way to the centre of the hall. He turned slowly as his team entered behind him, taking in the stairwell that wound its way up to the second floor, the hall that went all the way back to the depths of the house, and the living room with its tiered couches, filled with people. They were quiet now, where before they had been loud and rambunctious. The changes in the light on them showed that there was a television on that was just out of sight, but it was muted and nobody was watching it: they were watching *him*. A dozen pairs of blue eyes, each sunken and tired, each staring directly at him in stony silence.

He stared at them for a long moment, interrupting his motion around the room, like a Ferris wheel that had sputtered mid-turn. Colour drained from his cheeks, and when he turned back to Carla, he had to force his gaze away from them.

Carla was smiling at him from beneath those large horn-rimmed glasses that hid her eyes, a knowing smile. It was no longer welcoming and pleasant. Although it would have been difficult to have explained what was different about it, there was malice in it now that hadn't been there before. It was something in the intensity of her gaze once Victor had stepped into the centre of that hallway... and her gaze did not travel from him to Chad, Abby or Alice anymore. They stayed buried in him, burrowing into his face like a rabid dog. "Sorry, it's movie night," she said, motioning to the living room and the people within it. "We were just watching --"

"Cut the crap," Victor spat, turning quickly to make sure there was nobody on the stairs behind him. There remained no one there. He turned back to Abby, snapping into eye contacted with her. "Stay in the door, try not to let it close."

She furrowed her brow, but nodded. She remained in the doorway as Chad and Alice passed her, entering the main hall.

Alice turned toward the living room that had taken so much of Victor's attention and felt her breath catch in her throat. There were children there on the couch: not all of them were children, not even a high percentage of them, but enough that they were the dominant thing that caught her cye. They stared back at her with the same tired eyes as the adults, blank stares and smiles that stretched between blond curtains but contained no humor. Even many of those that were not children were young -- two looked about sixteen, but with the one in green it was hard to tell, baldness obscuring an exact read on her age. She didn't smile, nor did her face reveal sadness. It was a neutral tone, but there was an urgency behind her eyes that wasn't there with anyone else. Twenty, she guessed the median age to be, with the oldest on the couch a man and a woman in their early thirties that dressed in clothes too small for them.

"We're watching Zodiac, have you seen it? One of Fincher's best, I think?" Carla continued after a long pause. "We get DVDs from the dollar stores, the ones in bins. We get some signal up here, but not enough. The hills, you know how it is."

"Chad, you getting anything?" Victor asked, ignoring her.

Chad stepped close to him, turning around the room the same way he had, finally landing back at the living room. Alice obscured a small part of his view of it, the back of her head turned to him as she gaped at them. "Nothing popping out."

Victor squinted. "Your Spidey-Sense not tingling?

Carla shifted, her smile evaporating for only a moment as she swished saliva back and forth in her mouth.

Chad squinted, narrowing in on the two oldest couch residents. Their gazes were less blank than the others, their eyebrows crunched and creases forming slowly in their foreheads. As Chad watched them, one stepped over the back of the couch and allowed himself to drop to the floor, disappearing into the depths of the house. "The older ones aren't looking at Alice like the rest," Chad said finally, his voice barely a whisper. "They only got eyes for you."

"Can I ask what you're doing here?" Carla chimed. Her politeness was wearing thin, but her smile had returned without anyone but Abby having noticed that had been gone.

Victor maintained eye contact with Chad for a moment, again taking a deep breath in through his nose. He exhaled from his mouth in a way that was meant to be calming as he turned back to Carla. He forced a smile, but like the eldest on the couch, his brow had begun to furrow and his jaw clenched. "I'm looking for missing children."

Carla smirked, and struggled not to laugh. "We'll be sure to check the traps." She looked past him to those gathered in the living room, and then up toward the second floor. She spread her arms wide, forming a letter T and enveloping the entirety of the hall with them. "Look, I know it's crowded, but there's nobody here against their--"

"Have we met before?" he asked, his tone less menacing than it had been only a moment before.

It was the first question he'd asked that he hadn't known her answer to before asking it, Alice realized, tearing her gaze away from the living rooms and the gazes that met her own.

Carla stiffened. "I don't think so."

Victor cocked his head. He looked her up and down, from head to toe: from glasses to checkered shirt to rolled-cuff jean shorts and battered knee to flip flops. "I saw you in the mall the other day, I think."

"Perhaps. I get into town a lot. For groceries."

"And before that. I didn't realize before, but there's something familiar about you." He paused, then nodded. "Definitely. Something familiar."

She forced a smile with pursed lips. "I don't think so."

Chad looked up, his head cocking to one side the same way Victor's had when she'd said that the first time. Near the doorway, Abby noticed the reciprocated movement, both Chad and Victor's hay-coloured hair falling onto the shoulder they leaned towards.

Carla ran her tongue along the space between her gums and her lips. She glanced toward the stairwell again. When Victor's gaze followed he discovered that three people had appeared there since he'd last looked: a woman who looked old but wasn't, a young woman with golden hair that came down to her lower back, and a man of roughly twenty-five, with baby-smooth skin and yet gray hairs gathering at the peaks of his ears. When he turned back to Carla, her smile was back to being genuine.

"It's about the media, really. About the way the American media changed. How America changed," Carla said.

Victor furrowed his brow. "Pardon?"

"The movie, sorry. Zodiac. I mean it's about the Zodiac killer, obviously, but that's not really what it's *about*, you know? Like they teach you in English, there's the plot and then there's what it's *about*. The plot is what happens, and what it's about are what those things *mean*."

Victor nodded. "You get into a lot of film theory?"

She grinned out the side of her mouth. "Only on YouTube. I was never one for college, but I've spent a lot of time on campus."

The woman at the top of the stairs laughed, and it drew Victor's attention. It was an unnerving laugh, not divorced from what Carla had said but directly influenced by it. He wasn't sure what she'd said that had triggered it and was already replaying the exchange over in his mind.

"What it's about -- well, what I think it's about, anyway -- is the end of a certain era of law enforcement, and of American life. It's about the end of safety, you know? The cops, they're after the Zodiac killer, and they can't find him. They don't work together; they aren't organized at all... and the investigation goes on forever. It goes on too long, way too long, and people -- us -- we need closure. So, the media steps in and they start giving it. They make movies, movies like Dirty Harry and that, where they catch the Zodiac after the ninety-minute runtime."

"It was Scorpio, then," Victor said under his breath.

"They can call it what they want, it was Zodiac. It was scratching that itch for people that needed justice. It might have scratched it too well, because eventually people stopped caring. The police were still looking for Zodiac, but the media had told them it was all done and over, so people lost interest."

Victor paused. "So it's about, you figure, society learning to trust the media more than the institutions of old?"

Carla's smile slipped. "It's about people in over their heads not recognizing a change even when it's upon them, you ask me."

Victor nodded. He turned back to the cadre of teens that were watching the movie on mute, blue hues coming from the screen and making them look like they were bathed in moonlight despite the sun still being up outside. When he turned back, there were two broad-chested men of about twenty standing in the archway behind Carla. They had similar noses -- thin shafts leading down to small bulbs -- and the same pronounced upper lip. One had his arms crossed in front of him in a way that Victor was sure was meant to be quietly intimidating.

"Vic --" Chad started, touching Victor's arm.

"Mind if we take a look upstairs?" Victor asked, returning his gaze to Carla.

Victor and Chad made their way up the stairs behind Carla, leaving Abby and Alice in the main hall. When they passed by the trio of blondes that stood on the small landing between the main floor and the second, Chad felt a wave of gooseflesh ripple over his skin, starting at the side closest to them. He'd shuddered.

"Keep it together," Victor had said under his breath, low enough that no one but Chad could have heard.

The hall at the top of the stairs was long and stretched out in either direction, one wing above the living room and the other the kitchen. The walls were white and gray, but not all the same shade of each. Doors were askew like funhouse mirrors, hiding small trails of sawdust and debris at their bases.

There were pictures along the walls at every interval where one would fit. Portraits in the posed style of family photos but of groups that grew too swiftly to be familiar. Chad eyed one of a twenty-something girl who looked much like the rest -- blonde with blue eyes. She had a well-defined jaw that was as plump as her spare-tire waist, and a nose that started slender before becoming thick at the nostril. She stared out of the photo at him with unblinking poise, her eyes following as he stepped through the house. He shuddered again.

Victor took three steps down the hall to the right, to the area over the living room. He could hear the sound of the recently unmuted movie coming from below, faint and muffled. As the hallway continued, the doors stopped being of uniform size and started being closer together; the result was disorientation, as though the hallway itself were twisting. Towards the end of the hall, he noticed, there was no paint on the walls at all, just uncovered gyprock. Doors cramped together until their borders touched, in a fashion that did not look structurally sound.

"We're in the middle of renovations," Carla smiled, following his line of sight. "Can never have too many rooms."

Victor narrowed his gaze, then turned and looked down the hall to the left, which was more of the same. There was a window at the far end of that hall, which looked out upon open air and the decaying trees not far behind. He nodded.

From above, the sound of an electric saw buzzed to life, along with the winding squeal as it made its way through something. There was a hard sound of wood striking wood, followed by another immediately after, both of which made Chad jump.

"They're doing them now on the next floor?" Victor asked, still looking up at the dust falling from the ceiling.

Carla nodded. "Can't have too many."

There was a smell of musk in the air, along with a scent not unlike friend chicken that Victor recognized as dried sweat. At the end of the hall, one of the doors nearest the window opened. He tensed and so did Carla, and a moment later a young girl of no more than ten appeared in the doorway. She wore a white nightgown and no expression on her face as she turned towards the three of them, her cheeks chubby and full.

Victor took a step forward.

"Victor," Chad said with a hushed voice.

The girl had a slender nose that expanded only at the bulb of the nostrils. Her eyes were big and blue, and her hair golden and looked long enough that it had perhaps never been cut in any great length. She stared at them for a long moment, then turned to Carla, then receded into the room behind her without a word.

Payson, The Past

Tash poured tea into Victor's cup, keeping one hand on the pot's lid and her eyes on him. The steam from the tea wafted up away from the china, forking when it reached his lips and cascading around him like a wreath. "You need to relax," she said, nudging the cup closer to him.

There was fresh lemon in it, and the citrus pulled at his nostrils. He turned from her laptop and eyed it a moment, then turned back. "I'll have it later."

"It'll be cold later."

"Then I'll have it cold."

She frowned, nudged the cup closer to him again, then sat cross-legged on the bed beside him. She watched him switch tabs between news sites and hit refresh time and again, scrolling long enough to check for new stories or updates to old stories, then moved along. His hand was shaking on the mouse pad, she noticed, but did not comment on.

The hotel room television was on to local news again, but was on mute, the soft blue of the screen bathing them in light and making everything tepid and calm despite Victor's nerves.

"You haven't been following your schedule," she said, matter-of-factly and without judgment.

He let out a breath but did not stop changing tabs. "No, I have not."

"You haven't been using any of your coping strategies, either."

He hit the edges of her laptop, where there were no keys. "You know what I'm dealing with here. Unless you think me resting will --"

"Unless you think killing yourself will bring the girl back, there's no need of this, Victor," she said, her voice gaining a firmness to it that it rarely did.

He stopped short.

"The child is dead, Victor. That is the point where, by definition, there is nothing more that can be done. The child is dead, a suspect is in custody... is there a reason we're not moving on from this... horror?"

His nostrils twitched, his upper lip arching for an instant. He clenched and unclenched his hands, wincing as his left shot spasms of pain up from its damaged flesh at him.

"You can't win them all."

"I know that," he said finally. He reached out without looking and took hold of his teacup. He brought it to his lips, and instantly she could see his facade loosen. His shoulders fell slightly into a more relaxed haunch. "I do, it's just that --"

The computer made a sound, a sharp series of chimes. In the bottom right hand corner of the screen, a white box of text appeared above the time. Below it, the rainbow-coloured flower icon had sprung to life, spinning. In the box were two words in bold, black font from Spoiler: "Got it."

Victor stared at it a moment, then clicked and opened the chat. No sooner had the window been full-sized then a second message came through, a wall of text detailing one person: Cline Cassidy, currently the only suspect in the murder of ten-year-old Briana Redding.

There were links to sources that Victor did not click; he scrolled through the wall of text that only got bigger as more was posted. Tash read over his shoulder. One fact stood out among all the rest: "He was kidnapped as a child," Tash read, when she reached it.

"And returned. Safely returned, a little over a year later. They never found the kidnapper."

Tash leaned in until her cheek was touching his and read the section he'd pointed to, confirming for herself that he had not misrepresented it. She heard him swallow as he looked at her, watching her eyes flutter back and forth over the words

"We're staying," she said without prompting, shifted the laptop away from herself, and opened a new tab.

Outside Payson, The Present

Chad slammed a fist down on the hood of the El Dorado, then raised the same hand to point at Victor. "That was single handedly the most fucked up thing I have ever seen," he spat, angry at no one in particular but angry all the same.

Alice looked from Abby to Victor and then back again, waiting for one of them to say something.

The walk back to the El Dorado had occurred mostly

in silence. Several times they had started to talk and Victor had held up a hand to silence them. Twice this had been accompanied by rustling in the sparse, dead forest around them... forest which should have been thin enough that it had no secrets to conceal, and yet somehow still possessed brushes that could rustle and shake when one's eyes were not trained on them precisely.

"It's bad, yes," Victor nodded, his voice a small thing in the back of his throat instead of the loud, booming thunder they were used to. He turned and looked back towards The Manor, as if expecting it to have crept up on him while he'd had his back turned. It remained a black void in space, a square shadow hidden behind the trees unless you were determined to see it.

"Bad?" Chad almost laughed, leaning forward as he emphasized the word. "Bad doesn't even start it. That was *scary*. Creepy stuff, I'm --" he turned and motioned to Abby, "-- I'm not crazy, right, hun? That was --"

"It was bad," she agreed. "It was *really* bad."

Chad clenched his fists with frustration, laying them both flat against the hood of the car. He sighed, long and loud, through his nostrils. He was used to being argued with when he got this indignant, and the lack of an opponent to vent his frustration at was causing it to mount. He took a deep breath, but it came out just as haggard and stressed as the last. "That house was like Gavin's."

All four of them were silent for a long moment, each of them giving furtive glances back at The Manor. Neither of them made any move to get back into the car.

After a tense moment, Alice broke the silence between them: "Who's Gavin?"

Abby, Chad and Victor exchanged an overwrought look between them.

"Before you came to stay with us, we dealt with... something like this," Abby said, stepping closer to Alice. "There was a man down in Georgia named Gavin. He was... well. He was tricking young people into living with him, on this... like a commune, out in the middle of nowhere."

Alice looked back at The Manor. "Yeah, yeah like this."

"He was... it was fucked up, is all. It got fucked up. People died, one of Tash's students. We, ah... we found out he'd been doing it before. A lot of times before."

Alice straightened. "So... what? He was like, taking advantage of them? Left a lot of broken hearts along the interstate?"

Abby passed a silent look from Chad to Victor, and then back to Alice. "He left *bodies* along the interstate."

Colour drained from Alice's cheeks.

"He went from place to place, looking for this perfect... thing. But he was insane, and every time he'd end up snapping and just... it was bad, Alice. Things got... bad."

Alice looked from Abby to Victor, who was now leaning against the trunk of the El Dorado with his hands covering his mouth. There was sweat lining the creases in his forehead and cheeks. It was distressing, seeing someone with his heft and manner on the verge of breaking. It was like watching Zeus fall. "What..." she stammered, turning from him to Chad. "What are you saying, that people are going to die in there?"

Victor looked at something far off in the distance, focusing intently on it and not meeting either of their eyes. "I'm sorry," he said finally, his voice husky and hoarse. "I never should have gotten any of you involved in this."

Chad hit the El Dorado again, then pushed back from it with his jaw set and made his way to the trunk.

"What're you doing?" Abby asked, as he popped the latch and ducked down within it.

"I don't want to discuss this," he said, pointing a determined finger in her direction but refusing to meet her eye. He slammed the trunk, revealing a tire iron clenched in his opposite hand.

Victor backed up from the car and got between Chad and the trail back to The Manor. "What're you doing?"

"I'm putting a stop to this," he snarled, his cheeks livid and hot. He jabbed the same finger he'd used on Abby at Victor, but this time met his gaze head-on. "This has gone on far enough. There're kids back in that house, man. *Kids.*"

"We don't have anything probative."

"This," Chad said, hefting the iron. "This doesn't care. This does not give a fuck. There are *kids* in that house, Victor. That house that is set up *just* like Gavin's was. Like it smells the same. Like a fucking frat house, like beer and pot and goddamn lube."

"I know," Victor said sternly.

"And there are *kids*. Some of those kids aren't much older than Koy."

"I know," he barked.

"So get the fuck out of my way."

"Chad!" Abby hissed. She hit the roof of the car with her palm, so hard that it split the flesh. She did not wince or take note of it. "Stop it. That won't work and you know it."

Chad wiped his nose with his sleeve. He'd become so angry that his sinuses were starting to drain. "Yeah well, we've pushed my luck before. Maybe it's time we gave it a go again, right?"

"Stop," Alice yelled, holding up both her hands. "This is stupid. You're just... you fought someone like this before, right? This Gavin bastard. So you don't need violence, just take these guys down however you took down him."

The three of them looked at each other. Chad let out a long, hot breath through his nostrils, then rested the tire iron on the roof of his car and stepped away from them to the edge of the shrub.

"Oh," Alice said softly, nodding to herself.

Abby turned and walked back to the edge of the brush that faced The Manor and took a long, haggard breath that shook her lungs. It was the sort of breath that usually came at the end of a breakdown, that sort of breath your body took when it was trying to right itself. It was all that Abby needed. She took her breath, steadied herself, then turned back to the car and the men. She pointed at Chad, who was still faced away from her. It didn't matter. When she spoke, her voice was pointed at him. "You find that girl," she said, saliva arching from clenched teeth. "*That's* what's different here. The police weren't looking for anyone, before. There's a girl *missing*. She's underage. You find the girl, we call the police, this whole thing stops before it goes nuts."

He turned back to her and met her eye.

Victor firmed his frown. "It's not that --"

"Tell me what you know," she said, turning her pointer finger to him.

"Pardon?"

"You know more than you're saying you do about this," she laughed, without humor. "It's not just the shit that went down with Gavin. It was before that. You acted like you'd seen it all before with Gavin too, so just... out with it. Whatever it is: out with it."

He looked at her, and for a moment looked as though he might actually have answered. He let out a held breath that was somewhere between a sigh and a gasp, then fell back onto the El Dorado.

"I'll go," Alice said finally. Her voice came like a snap, surprising even herself. They all turned to her. She shrugged. "I'll go in, I'll find the girl."

"Alice," Chad started, his voice losing its edge and becoming one of pleading.

"No, it makes sense," she said, holding up a hand to him. She walked to the car and opened the door, bent over inside for a moment, and returned with Madison's diary. She turned to Chad, then to Abby. "You have your luck powers, and that's all well and good. And you, your... thing. That won't help. Like, at all. But me," she put her hands out in front of her. "I can't *die*. That's my only power. That makes me useless in a fight, and fucking awesome at recon. You're worried about sending someone into danger? I'm in no danger. It works. I find the girl, I figure out what's going on, I get out."

Victor squinted, then looked away, as if deep in thought.

Chad picked up the tire iron from the hood of the car.

"Hey," Alice coaxed.

Chad nodded. "Wasn't much of a plan," he said, lumbering back to the trunk and popping it again. He stashed the iron back on its hitch along the side. He slammed the trunk again, dug deep into his jeans pocket, and produced a jangly set of keys.

She raised an eyebrow at him, then looked past him to the motorcycle stood at the far end of the trail. She smiled.

"She makes for a quick getaway, if you need one. Keep the keys on you, don't let them out of your sight."

Alice took the keys and smirked. "I'll take good care of the bike."

"Fuck the bike. Get out of there as fast as you can."

She nodded, then turned to Abby. "You got anything to say about this?"

Abby winced, then wished her luck. Victor made sure she had his cell, and then the three of them watched as Alice Loveless revved Chad's bike to life and disappeared down into a dead oasis of rotten trees in the middle of the Arizona desert.

CHAPTER 24

Carla was sitting on the front stoop with two others -- and boy of about twenty and a blonde woman who looked old, but wasn't -- when Alice pulled the chugging, rumbling motorcycle up alongside the blue Ford Pinto with the scratched wood paneling. She'd rode without a helmet, her hair baying behind her. She kicked the stand down and paused over the bike for a moment as it cooled, then turned and faced the three of them.

"Something I can help you with?" Carla called across the lot, her eyes squinting from the sun over the trees.

"Chad said you had a lot of rooms. I was hoping I could steal one." She had her hip against the bike, making it a part of her stance without leaning on it. The diary was held lazily at her side.

Carla looked at the woman next to her -- Odette -- then at the boy -- Marcus. They laughed, then she turned back to Alice. "See, you say you came from that other one, Chad... but you smell more like you came from Victor."

Marcus gave Alice a sidelong look, one that she hadn't seen before. It was interest, but blatant and unashamed.

His head was tilted to one side, as if trying to get her from a different angle than the rest, and he was smirking. He turned after a moment and said something inaudible to Carla, who frowned.

"Victor didn't ask me to come," Alice said, as if saying it would make them believe it was true.

Carla squinted and looked her up and down. "Fresh faces are always welcome," she said, with a smile with no sincerity behind it. She took a toothpick from her breast pocket and pressed it between her teeth, then retreated back into the house. Odette followed her.

Marcus waited on the porch, leaned against it, and continued to eye her.

Alice's back remained straight, despite the chill that ran up it. The Manor had two lights illuminated on its upper floor, and they looked down on her from the gaping shadow that was the building like eyes. She made sure the bike was stood securely, then made her way across the short tuft of dead grass between them. She stepped up the porch steps toward the front door without turning to look at him.

When she was close to him, he said, "Name's Marcus."

She stopped, nodded, then made her way forward into the house. Marcus remained outside, staring out into the tree line.

Alice turned back just as the door was closing and thought that she could see the taillights of the El Dorado as it left and went back down the road towards town.

CHAPTER 25

Los Angeles, California

"Tell me what you're looking for."

Theo startled, shaking his paper as though the woman in front of him had appeared out of nowhere, because from his point of view, she had. He'd been waiting for contact for over ninety minutes on the outside deck of a Bistro and Coffee Bar on 7th Street, so long that he'd begun to get worried that he was going to burn in the sun. In those ninety minutes he'd ordered a bagel, three coffees, and -- eventually -- a newspaper and had been skimming the business section for the last ten.

The woman in front of him seemed tall from his vantage point on the chair but wasn't. She had dirty-blonde hair with highlights in and wore thick sunglasses beneath a broad-brimmed hat that gave her pale complexion some shade from the sun. She had the face of someone who hadn't been in Los Angeles long -- pale and unpeeled, yet without the smudges and stains of product that protected from the rays in sun valley.

She was facing him with one hand on her hip, and

with her glasses obscuring her eyes it made her look as though she was staring directly at him. She likely was. She was looking at him as if she still wanted him to answer her request, despite how she'd taken him off balance.

"I'm sorry?" he asked, sitting up a little straighter than he had been.

She sighed and put her briefcase on the table between them and then sat across from him, as if resigning herself to the fact that this was going to take longer than a moment. She winced, and then -- as abruptly as she'd spoken -- her billboard came online. It was a full screen of an adult film -- not a memory projected as a film, but a memory *of* an adult film. It flickered several times when it started, as though it were a VHS with the tracking needing adjustment, and a second image flipped in: a head-and-shoulders shot of a fully clothed man.

The film on display was of the scripted type that were less and less prevalent since the outset of streaming media: well-lit with people that made no eye contact and said their lines poorly. The camera was just starting to zoom in when Theo tore his eyes away and looked back into her glasses, stammering, "I-I don't understand."

"Victor sent me, he said you needed help," she said, in the same robotic cadence of the woman on the screen behind her.

He winced. "Do you, like, have some kind of identification, or...?"

"Fuck off, I don't have all day. He says he sent you to look into the Anemone incident?"

Theo paused a moment, then nodded. He tried to keep his eyes on her and not on the billboard behind her, though it seemed as though it were growing in size and becoming omnipresent. "There was a woman there that I recognized. From my... from Black Springs."

She nodded.

"I'm sorry. Who are you?"

"Maggie."

"Maggie. You're not what I expected, Maggie."

She smiled thinly. "What you're asking about is very complicated and very above your pay grade."

"Pay grade?" he scoffed, balking.

"Yeah. Your level. It's need to know, and you don't." She paused, then folded her fingers together atop her briefcase. It didn't suit the rest of her; it was large and bulky in a getup that was otherwise trim and stylish. "But you're here now, you're involved. No more blinders."

On the screen behind her, the redheaded star of the film was bent over a kitchen counter roughly yet seemed happy about it. Despite himself his eyes flicked up to it, and when they did, the tracking on the tape slipped again, showing the shadowed silhouette of a man.

"What do you want to know?" she asked, dragging his attention back down.

He paused. "Roberta Feinberg. She worked for Black Springs when..."

"When you were there. Late teens, early twenties."

He stood up straighter. "Yeah. She was there then. She was one of the only nice people that worked there. She *still* works there, I saw her leaving work... and yet she was there at Anemone, too."

"And your question is?"

"What's a mental care nurse doing at a collapsed suburb, and looking like she's in charge there?"

She smiled patronizingly. "Why's an artist and a fencer doing corporate espionage? Or are you the only one allowed outside of your little box?"

He sighed.

She drummed her fingers along the edge of the box, tilting her head to the left for a moment as the tracking on the tape behind her adjusted itself again. Her hair bounced abruptly, and she straightened and pointed those obsidian-black glasses back at him. "Sometimes big companies, they'll set up shell companies. Imprints. Tiny, other, smaller companies to perform specific tasks once those tasks get needy enough. It's like... you ever go to a Circuit City, and the manager's there? Then you go to Best Buy, and the same guy's managing? He didn't switch jobs that quick; both those places are owned by the same company."

"So Black Springs is a subsidiary? A part of a bigger whole?"

She nodded. "Now you're getting it, champ. Yes. And Roberta Feinberg, she's not the manager, but she doesn't work for the subsidiary and she knows it. She might be one of the few who knows it, if we're being honest with ourselves. There's a few we've got our eyes on there... one or two more at Port Haven Institute. Cogs, greasers, that--"

"Whoa whoa, PHI? Port Haven Institute is owned by Black Springs?"

Maggie laughed and shook her head. "No, no... no. Sorry, it goes higher up. They're both imprints. They're tools, made to get the job done. They each perform a specific function. Your subject has a few marbles rattling around upstairs, you send them to Black Springs. They need some training, need some refinement? Direction? You figure out a way to get them into this weird school upstate where they teach weird shit."

Theo looked away from her for a moment, his facade crumbling.

"What? You think normal schools teach fencing? Grow up. They all perform a function. They get your brain ready, get your body ready, get *you* ready. And when you have that kind of cross-pollination, you can't just trust each subsidiary to do their part. There has to be at least one person who sees the whole picture. All of it. You need someone to make nice to the people in the hospital? There they are. You need someone to step in and pretend to be superintendent? There they are."

"You need someone to check out why your fancy new subdivision imploded in on itself?" Theo asked, rhetorically.

"There they are," Maggie nodded. "It's a bit more complicated than that in the case of Anemone. Something I've been looking into for the better part of a year now... but yeah, you've got it. You've got the gist."

"So, who's the parent company?" Theo asked.

Maggie stopped. Her expression was vacant for a moment, even more so that her eyes were covered. The porno on behind her flickered again, and briefly -- as if by subliminal message -- there was a man on the screen. It was almost too brief to have seen, but some part of his mind had seen it. After a moment, she softened. "There's a point you know, when you can't back up from this. There's a point where you learn what it's all about, and you can't get out then. Even if you want to." Her tone changed from what it had been, no longer robotic and recital. "That's what happened to me. You can't go back."

Theo thought for a moment, then nodded. The screen flickered, then changed scenes, as if two disparate parts of the film had been cut together haphazardly. The part it cut to was harder, a zoom-in of penetration as it was happening. It was graphic, and he winced. "Are you... are you trying to block me out?"

She smiled. "First rule of telepaths: get something stuck in your head. Something primal. Baby Shark, the Macarena... something. Adult films work best, they tend to override any other thought process. Anything that occupies the reptile brain is golden, really."

He shook his head in disbelief. "No one's ever blocked me out before. How are you carrying on a --" he paused, noticing again how her head tilted to her left. The glasses were thick, he noticed... thicker than most. Down the earpiece of the left side ran a thin, red wire. "Are you... are you just puppeting what someone else says into an earpiece?"

She smiled, then shrugged. "I've had worse jobs."

He shook his head in disbelief. "This is... this is nuts. This is not what I was expecting."

She nodded, then laid her hand down on the briefcase that sat between them and pushed it forward. "Trust issues."

He shook, startled again. "Pardon?"

"That's what it says in here. Trust issues, and that you're easily manipulated, especially by women."

Theo straightened, even pushed himself back from the table slightly. "Who the hell are you? Are you... is that about me?"

"Abby, Blackheart, Roberta... Alice. It seems like there's always a woman at the centre of your misery, doesn't it? And yet, here you are, and here I am." She pushed her hair back out of her face and behind her ears, much in the same way Abby had when they were dorm-mates. "When do you think it stems back to? Because me... I think it's a loss of family early on."

"What're you...?"

"I think some people would look at you and just see a puppy chasing cars, but I see more... it's the home that it represents, right? The unit of it. The idea that this is how it's supposed to be, and that it's something different than what you had. See, I think when someone bats their eyelashes at you and calls you sweetie... I think it turns off all those other natural defenses you'd be so good at."

Theo straightened, making eye contact with Maggie, and bringing both hands to rest flat on the table in front of him. "Is that... is that why *you're* here?" he asked, suddenly aware of what was happening.

She smiled. "It was as good a time as any to test the theory." She extended her open palm across the table. The screen behind her jolted in an extended flicker. "Simon Monk, at your service."

Theo hesitated, then shook the hand with two strong pumps. "Talking about trust while being a literal facade... a little bit hypocritical, isn't it?"

Maggie smiled, and it wasn't immediately obvious if the smile was genuinely her own or if it was done on instruction from Simon. "This business is where hypocrisy was born, kid. This is the garden that it grows from, watered with lies but tended with love."

He squinted, eyes flickering back to the still-present image on the screen behind her, where bad actors tried their best to provide the facsimile of a complex, intimate moment. It was flickering more now, and other thoughts were bleeding through. He saw himself for an instant, an image of himself sitting across the table from her, as though her eyes were cameras and the billboard lit from a projector produced from the back of her head. He nodded.

"You're doing good work. We've suspected Feinberg was one of the floaters for a while, but it's always good to get visual confirmation. There must be something really interesting going on out at the Anemone site, if they're risking sending out a mole on official business." She paused, her brow furrowing in a way it hadn't at any other point in the conversation. She stared out through her glasses at him, frowned, then shook her head as if dispelling an idea. "Yeah... yeah, good work. But now you can --"

"Wait," Theo said, raising to a half stand and extending an arm to her.

She stopped sharply and reached for something inside her jacket at his sudden movement.

He moved back slightly. "Who's the parent company?"

Maggie pursed her lips until they were a thin slit along the lower half of her face. Her shoulders fell a little, then she reached up and removed her sunglasses for the first time since they'd sat down. She made eye contact with him for a long moment as the screen behind her devolved from video into complete static snow-crash. She folded the glasses together and slid them into the front pocket of her coat, and Theo thought he could hear a slight electric whine as she did so. She picked up her briefcase then, all the while maintaining the eye contact she'd denied him during their meeting.

At the very last moment before she turned, her eyes flickered upward to something behind him and her billboard, briefly, came back online.

He turned to follow her gaze.

Several blocks back, yet still omnipresent and hovering because of its size, was a large office building with shimmering, sun-catching windows all the way from its ground floor to the pinnacle of its peak. In broad letters across its front read the word: Shane.

He turned back to Maggie, only to get a scant glimpse of her as she crossed the street.

CHAPTER 26

Outside Payson, Arizona

The motel was a long, one floor building that snaked this way and that, forming an S along the grounds. The connective tissue between the three sections of the building were a metal awning, but the affect was still there. All the rooms had a doorway on either side: one that led out to the parking lot, and another that connected to a long, shared highway filled with vending machines and ice makers.

Chad hit the switch to the right of the door as he entered and produced no effect. The room was dark. He sighed and looked up, realizing that there were no overhead lights in the room proper: only bedside lamps. He flipped the switch again and again, scanning the room to try and see what change it was eliciting. His gaze finally landed on the tiny red standby light on the front of the TV, which disappeared or returned depending on the position of the switch. "Genius."

Victor pushed past him, his face staring at his phone as he rushed to the bedside desk with his charger and plugged it in. As soon as the battery indicator in the up-per-right corner of his screen switched from red to yellow, he opened up his messenger app and started to compose a text.

"This is a bad idea," Chad said under his breath, stomping across the room to the lamp opposite Victor and turning it on. The room was bathed in bright orange, lamplights that were perpetually the colour of twilight.

"It's not," Abby said, in a voice that revealed it was not for the first time. "It's not a good idea, but there are worse. Your idea was worse."

"She's in danger. I don't care how close we are... it's not close enough if something starts to go sideways. That's the rub. If shit goes sideways, by the time we get our little texty-text, it's too damn late. Especially the way service is out here."

"I'm on the wifi," Victor said, absently.

Chad turned to him. "You didn't get a password." He paused. "Have you been here before?"

Victor ignored him, continuing to type.

Abby put her bookbag down on the floor next to the dresser. "She's fine. She's a big girl, and they can't hurt her."

"They can't *kill* her," Chad amended, turning to her quickly. "There's more than one way you can hurt some-one. When Koy got taken, we weren't worried about mur-der. That wasn't at the top of the list at least."

Abby stopped short, looked as though she wanted to respond, then turned toward Victor. He was standing be-tween the two beds, his buttocks resting against the mat-tress of the one closest to the wall. He was looking down at his phone, which was huddled close to his body secretively. "What're you doing?" she asked, after a moment of watching this behavior without explanation.

"Updating Tash," he said under his breath, still looking toward the ground. He pressed the send button with animation and then turned the screen off and slid the phone onto the dresser. He wiped his palms onto his jeans, then looked up as if addressing them for the first time. "Sending her video, it'll take a minute."

Chad shook his head, then turned away with his fingers in his hair. He faced the wall for a moment, then turned back and yelled, thrusting his hand forward will all fingers pointed at Victor, "How can you be handling this with such... with such kid gloves? These are lives, these are... do you not get that? Do you not get that these are real lives, real risks? Not numbers on a screen or something?"

"Chad --" Abby coaxed.

"Stop taking his side!" Chad stressed, turning back to her. "You always do this, and he's wrong this time. He's wrong and... and it's going to get people killed."

Victor winced but said nothing.

"Is this your thing? Is this what it is? Whatever made you the way you are?"

"Chad, you didn't even believe this was a thing until earlier --"

"Well, I do now," he snapped, his eyes burning when they vaulted back to hers. "Now it's in front of me and I can't ignore it, I've got to do something and... and I can't just sit here."

"They have an ideology," Victor breathed, steadily.

"You can't fight ideas with fists, it just makes them stronger. Even if you beat them, they become surer. Because you're the one who turned to violence, so you must be wrong." He paused, as if choosing his words carefully.

Chad's nostrils flared. "I need to *do* something."

"You can't judge the needs of a situation based on your own," he said, firmly. His mouth was back to moving so scantly that any motion was obscured by his facial hair, as though he'd spent his time since putting down the phone centreing himself.

Chad shook his head disbelievingly. "Are you... do you have ties with them or something? I don't get it, I --"

"Get out," Victor said with authority, his mouth suddenly wide and dark against his face again, like a black hole. It receded quickly, returning to its original size and shape, though a fire had grown behind his eyes that remained, smoldering.

Chad nodded. "Yeah," he said under his breath, as he made his way back out the door that led to the parking lot of Motel 83.

∞

The Main Office of the Motel 83 was a deep mauve, all of it. The roll-out carpet that protected the floor from whatever transients tracked in was mauve, the walls were mauve save for a gold patterned trim the went all the way around it at waist-height, and the ceiling was mauve. Stepping into it was like stepping from one reality into another. It reminded Chad of The Champagne Room of far, far too many men's entertainment establishments, and the association made his skin shiver the moment he stepped inside despite the heat of the evening.

"It's a night out there, isn't it?" said a large man with jelly bracelets hanging loosely from each of his wrists. He was smoking a menthol cigarette from a theatre-length black holder. It expelled more smoke than he inhaled, sending it wafting toward the ceiling in swirling ovals.

Chad looked back out into the parking lot. He could see clearly across its gravel and dust to the straight shot of road and beyond, to the gaggle of dried brush that had lined the gutter on the opposite side, searching for moisture like scavengers search for a corpse. The stars were visible above the straight line of the horizon, twinkling and shimmering. There was no sign of a storm or bad weather or, from here, even a breeze. Chad turned back to the man, whose name plate introduced him as 'Shirley -- Manager,' and assumed that he didn't know what the phrase had meant. "It is night. Earlier, it was day, and I hear we'll get more tomorrow."

Shirley smiled, showing off huge, crooked chicklet teeth that still somehow managed to have the appearance of a gap between each one, the sort of corn kernel effect that many, many years of smoking can bring. The smile was tiny but clearly all he had, the muscles of his mouth not strong enough to push his large, shaking cheeks up any further. "And then night again," he replied. He wheezed when he spoke, and Chad realized that he'd been laughing, soundlessly.

Smoke fell from his mouth in the perfect circles that the type of person who showed off at parties took years to perfect. Shirley did it without thought or intention, laughing up smoke circles towards the desk as though they were vomit, more smoke swirling from the tip of his cigarette.

Chad looked back to the outside again, turning his whole torso at the waist. He looked in lieu of having someone to share the experience of Shirley with, wishing for the sort surreal look between friends that he and Jaycee might have shared in months past. The sort of *are we both seeing this?* look.

There were three wedding bands hanging from a chain around Shirley's neck. The chain disappeared into the folds of loose skin on either side of Shirley's neck, but the shimmering edge of one of the rings caught Chad's eye briefly. They were dull for the most part, made gray with sweat and the grime of dead flesh. All were men's bands, and all were a different size, clumped together near his ample cleavage.

Shirley's mouth went slack, losing the slight upturn of the laugh he'd had a moment before. His eyes were sunken and bloodshot, and stared back at him with a pronounced lack of fervor now. After a tense moment, he showed those yellowed fangs again, clacking them together. "More night on the way I reckon. About eight hours."

Chad swallowed hard, then nodded. "I need a room."

Shirley nodded, then turned to the pegboard behind him. It was mauve like everything else in the room but didn't look to have been painted that way. The pattern on it was that same light then brown then dark hodge-podge of corkboards, only tinted. Chad didn't think he'd ever seen a corkboard that colour before.

Shirley reached for a key next to a blank space on the board, and suddenly Chad's eyebrows went up and his arm jolted forward. "Not that one."

Shirley raised an eyebrow, shooting him a sidelong wry look.

"Not the one next to the one I was in."

Shirley nodded, then let out a grunt of air that smelled like Doritos as he reached higher. The keys were arranged in a vague letter S just like the rooms were, with the front of the building at the bottom. He picked a key at random from the top row by flicking its edge until it fell off its nail, then threw it onto the table between them. "I'll need a credit card on file," he said, all humor gone from his voice.

Chad nodded, reached for his wallet, and produced one. After looking from the card to Chad and back again for a moment, Shirley opened the register and placed it under the cash tray without also asking for ID. Chad nodded in thanks and turned to leave, just as Shirley was disposing of the smoldering butt in his theatre-length holder and lighting a replacement.

The evening air was hot. The sun had spent its day heating the ground beneath his feet, and now in the first moments of night it expelled that heat into the cooling air, catching Chad in the crossfire. He took the long way around to his room, avoiding Victor's and crossing near the barren wilderness on either side of the motel.

There was a gray jay standing at the edge of the property, pecking at the compacted dirt of the dessert with futility. Chad smiled and watched it. "You don't belong there," he heard himself say. The jay looked up and tilted its head as if asking what he'd meant by that, then flapped its wings and disappeared into the night.

There was a shadow under the awning in front of his

room, a deep black with folded arms and a tense stance that could only have been one person. He sighed as he made his way over, his eyes adjusting to the low light of no streetlights until Abby finally materialized into view. "The way we're handling this is messed up, and I don't want to argue about that," he said definitively as he neared her.

She raised an eyebrow. "I'm here to fuck you, idiot."

Chad stopped short at her phrasing. He didn't think she'd ever used that phraseology before in their time together and it took his physiology only a second to discover that yes, he liked it. He stepped to the door and put the key inside.

∞

Abby lay with her bare back glistening in the moonlight, her hair falling wetly along her neck and one shoulder. The pillow that had been fluffed and positioned neatly when Chad had unlocked the door was wedged roughly between her body and the mattress. It somehow still contained pockets of cool material, and she left it there as she collapsed, allowing it to rest the warmth that radiated from her.

Chad watched the way the bluish light from the window played off her shoulders. He'd been with other people, but there were certain things only Abby could do, he realized, as his finger glided over her ribs, following the line where the light ended. Only Abby could turn light into something solid, and she did it without realizing it. The light that came from the night air found her flesh and she made it something real, tangible. When his fingers found their way along the subtle ripples of her ribs, he wasn't touching skin -- he was touching moonlight. She turned away from the window to him, still catching her breath. He moved his hand to cup her cheek, leaned forward, and kissed her hungrily.

"Should we close it?" she asked, her voice humming and sing-song.

His gaze shifted toward the open window, and the light flowing from it. "I will before I sleep. Nobody's coming around."

She nodded, then turned around. Her breasts caught the glimmer of blue along their edge, prickled with goose-flesh. They fell to either side of her, plump and devoid of the pockmarks and scarring that littered his own. She reached out, long nails finding the flesh of his chest and dancing along the patches of white discolouration the light found.

He winced. She brought her gaze to him, checking wordlessly, then continued. There were four long, thick scrapes stretching from his upper ribs to the nipple of his left breast, distorting its areola. She'd discovered it before, the first night they'd spent together, but had never allowed herself to trace it as she did now. The nails of her four fingers found each line, each following one down until they touched the sensitive flesh and his skin pulled back.

"What happened there?" she asked, starting the motion again. Her eyes fell over him, finding more flecks of discolouration. They clustered around that left side and cascaded out, becoming sparser and disappearing completely by the time they reached his right shoulder. Her eyes found each one with calm interest, studying.

"It was The Accident." His mouth strained around the words, as though they were difficult to maneuver around his tongue.

She nodded. In his youth, Chad had been in a car accident that had killed his parents. He'd been in the back seat with his infant sister and had, by instinct, shielded her with his body. It was Victor's theory that his powers had saved them both. Since then, the rare times he spoke of it, she noticed that it was always The Accident, never merely the accident.

"The glass from the window ripped through my shirt. Some metal too, bits of it." He placed his hand over hers, and it disappeared within it. He guided it over his chest and across to the opposite shoulder as he spoke. "It went up and across, all the way over. Like this."

Her deft, light fingers found their way to his abdomen once he'd brought her to all his markings, and he felt himself rise to her touch. She noticed but did not make mention or alter her position. He knew she noticed only by the change in her breath, a quirk of her nature that he had found more and more intoxicating as their time together increased.

"I wish you wouldn't fight him so much," she said, her voice small and wet.

He frowned, knowing without asking that they were talking about Victor and losing some of his vigor with the reminder. Her hands continued to dance along his chest and the contours of his waist, as though her limbs had not registered the change in conversation her mouth had initiated. "He's *wrong*, Abby. He's wrong and he's hiding something."

"You're suspicious by nature. Don't let it make you get in your own way so much."

He shuffled, increasing the distance on the bed between them unconsciously. "I have luck powers, Abby. I can't always justify where I'm going or why I think something, but they're pointing me this way for a reason."

"They pointed you towards him for a reason, too," she said, edging closer. She cradled the curve of his chest in her fingers and stoked with her thumbs, gazing at the area of flesh she was manipulating and how it moved under the slightest pressure. "And to me."

He swallowed but said nothing. He did not nod nor shake his head, and when it became apparent that she expected a response he leaned forward and kissed her, gently, on the forehead.

She waited a long moment. The air conditioner in the room snapped off, and the room became instantly hot, dry from the outside air. It was like someone had flipped a switch on the air, on the atmosphere itself. The pace of her breathing increased, and her chest moved to its rhythm, the smooth circles in their centres tracking their motion. "I trust him," she said finally, with definiteness.

Chad frowned. "I trust him to a point."

"I believe him," she stressed, as if clarifying her point.

His mouth warbled. He opened it, then closed it again, reevaluating what he had been about to say.

"What?" she asked, her nails finding his scars again and pressing lightly. "Don't do that. Say what you were going to say. Don't hold back on me."

"I don't want to ruin the moment. The mood."

She looked directly at him. When he tried to look away, she brought up a hand and took him by the face, gently, so that he couldn't. "You won't. We're not like that."

He frowned, sighed, then spoke. "The people in that house? *They* believe. The people who followed Gavin, to their death? They believed. *Cults* believe, Abby. What's so good about believing in him? In anything?"

She sighed, eyes upturned at his answer. They didn't water -- they never did -- but held the shape of eyes that on someone less strong might have. She nodded, then let her gaze fall away from him.

He shifted. "See? Ruined it."

She narrowed her eyes at him, shook her head slightly, then let go of his face and let her hand glide down his torso until it found the root of him. Their shift in conversation had caused it to lose its tension, but with one deft motion of her small, gentle hand it rose and returned, so suddenly that his breath caught in his throat.

She kissed him with force, pressing her lips into his as her hand found the cluster of scars on his side again and used it like a handle, guiding him onto his back and following his motion until her legs straddled him.

Her hands found his hair and grasped it, and for a brief shimmering moment, he believed.

Victor sat with his legs crisscrossed before him on his bed, his laptop in front of him. He'd run an HDMI cord from the back of it along the wall to the back of the television, which was now on and awaiting input. The blue haze from it was harsh and got everywhere, in every crevice of flesh.

He sighed, then reached forward and pressed two buttons on the laptop. Its screen went dead, and what had been on it jumped to the television, which now displayed a grid of photographs of children. They were packed tight and even without much white space in between. It looked like a page torn from a yearbook, except none of the children were smiling. None were smiling and they all wore the same plain white shirt that was too big for them, staring past the camera with dead eyes.

Victor's gaze fell over each of them in turn, the similarity between them. Each one blond with dark-gold strands near the roots. Each one with blue eyes. Each one with the round cheeks of youth pockmarked. He twitched his nose, stifled a sniff, then took his phone out of his pocket.

He opened the list of photos and videos, scrolled down to the latest -- a video nearly thirty minutes long -- and pressed play. It started with a view of nothing but a white door. The screen shook, stabilized itself, then shook again, and the room filled with muffled distortion as something ran itself directly over the microphone again and again.

"Maybe there's nobody home?" came Abby's muffled voice. The mic did not pick up all of her high-pitched range, and the result was that she sounded squeaky and mousy. "There are over two dozen people in there," the video said next. It was his own voice he knew, but he didn't recognize it. You never sound like you think you do on record.

The edge of his pocket peeked out over the edge of the frame, but not by a lot. As he watched, Carla again opened the door and greeted them into the house. The camera followed her, bobbing back and forth with each step it took, into that large main hall and -- after a moment -- turned to the living room packed with kids.

Victor paused. The picture he landed on was blurred, and he ran his finger along the video's progress bar to scrub and find a frame that was clearer, eventually landing on one where a large portion of those that had been in attendance were turned towards him. Some sneered. He'd noticed it at the time, but it was even more apparent when paused. The lip of the oldest sneering man was like an optical illusion, seeming to rise toward his nostril even though the video was paused.

They were blond except for two that had their hair removed. Each one of them with hair the same colour of wheat, shimmering and shining back at him. He stared at the frame for a long moment, sniffed again, then glanced up at the rows of faces on the TV screen.

The faces on the screen were young. They were all under twenty, but most were under fourteen. Their names were printed -- all in the same not-quite-centred Times New Roman font -- beneath each photo: last name, then first. The last names were a historical map of Arizona, the first names a time capsule from days gone by. Christopher. Ashley. Matthew. Emily. Joshua. Sarah. Jason. Samantha. Jacob.

Victor stared at them for a long moment, then uncrossed his legs and made his way to the area under the television. He paused a moment, took a deep breath, then opened the faux drawer and revealed it to be a mini fridge.

He paused for deliberation, his mouth suddenly dry,

then reached out and plucked out a tiny bottle of vodka from the crowd of other bottles. He withdrew a bottle of Coke and unscrewed the cap with his thumb, then tipped it back until he'd drank the neck of it. He gasped when he stopped, then unscrewed the vodka as well and poured it into the space he'd made in the Coke bottle for it. It filled the bottle well and he took another swing of his new mixture before it had a chance to mix properly, hissing as the alcohol burned his gums.

He reached back into the fridge and took out three more small bottles, laying them on top of the TV stand before turning back to the bed with his drink.

Victor stopped short, then picked up his phone and drew it close to the TV screen. The older boy sneering at him had a long nose that came to a firm point and high cheekbones. He slid it across his vision so that it appeared next to each photo on the screen, looking from one to the other, eventually stopping at Joshua. The nose was shorter on the screen, but still thin and still coming down to a point. The cheekbones were identical.

Squinting, Victor took a sip of his drink then put it down. Using both fingers, he zoomed in on one of the other older kids from the video, then repeated the process, holding it up one at a time to each profile picture until he found one that looked similar.

By the end of the hour, he'd matched every child on the screen with someone plausibly similar on the video save one, the girl in the bottom-right profile picture of the television. She was small for her age and young, her cheeks plump. The name attached to the bottom of the screen read Samantha. Victor stared at her.

By the end of the hour he had also finished the drinks he had laid out atop the TV stand and had gone back to the fridge for more.

CHAPTER 27

Payson, The Past

Victor pulled the El Dorado up alongside the Payson Police Station. He left the engine running and the car growled as it calmed. Although he and Tash were in plain sight, they were unnoticed. The traffic outside the building had an off quality, an implication that movement was constant but sparse: there was always exactly one person coming or going, but never more. Like a director who wanted a New York level of bustle, but didn't have a budget for a large cast of extras.

Tash leaned forward to look past him, up the long row of steps and into the glass doors. There was one uniformed officer sitting behind the desk -- barely visible as a bluish shape that moved from the side of the desk with the phone to the opposing side and back again often -- and another figure, a tall woman trying and failing to sit comfortably on the front steps. She was looking down the road in front of the El Dorado as if waiting for a ride. Her arms were clenched around her as if she were cold, but with the dry heat that wafted through the street that was almost impossible. It was a form of nonverbal communication, Tash decided: people having seen others left outside waiting for a ride holding themselves and looking cold so many times that they assumed that position even when the heat was on.

"This isn't going to work," Tash said, maintaining her gaze at the building in front of her.

Victor looked back and forth between the building, Tash, and the laptop she had balanced precariously on her calves since they'd pulled out of the Motel 83 parking lot. "I'm not sure what you mean. Just go in there and…" He pantomimed typing on a keyboard, wiggling all ten of his fingers an inch below his chin in a way that no one had ever typed, ever. "Do your thing."

She lowered her eyes at him. "That's not how that works. That's not how anything works."

He frowned, deep enough that it was visible beyond the shield of his facial hair. He'd gone several days without trimming now, and the hair nearest the edges of his lower lip poked out straight and white, like a porcupine's quills. His hands gripped the steering wheel and he let out a deep sigh that shook his chest when he let it out.

Tash exhaled, then shoved the laptop under her arm and opened the car door without another word.

Cline Cassidy sat in almost the same position she had before: shoulders slumped, both leaned forward while she was leaned back. She had a vacant stare aimed at nothing in particular, her eyes flittering every now and again from motion they caught.

Victor flapped the manila folder he'd carried in down on the table between them. It was thin, a scant few sheets of paper in them, but those that were inside were so fresh from the printers that they still radiated heat into his fingertips up until the instant he let them go. There was a receipt from Kinkos stapled to the front of the folder, and it flapped and tried to escape in the billowing breeze from the air conditioner.

Cassidy's chair had uneven legs. This was a common, subtle tactic of interrogation rooms disguised as poor funding: give the suspect a chair they can never properly relax or get comfortable in. Cassidy just rocked in it, swaying back and forth slightly at the bob of her heel.

"You feel tense?" Victor asked, his voice lacking the calm demeanor it usually possessed. He paced back and forth along the side of the table opposite Cassidy, bringing his hand to his chest and clenching at it to mime anxiety as he spoke. He never broke eye contact with Cassidy, although he never returned it.

On the other side of the observation glass, Detective Melquist flipped Victor's military ID back and forth along his left hand. Tash stood next to him, her eyes darting from Victor to Melquist and back again. She moved from foot to foot, as though she were the one manufactured uneasily and unable to rest comfortably.

"What's he doing?" Melquist whispered, cognoscente of the poor soundproofing.

"Finding his footing," Tash replied in her best reassuring voice. "Watch." Her eyes flitted toward the door that separated them from Victor and Cassidy just to her left. She forced her gaze forward, on the action.

"I'd feel tense if I were you. Afraid," Victor continued. He leaned forward and craned his neck, trying to force himself to meet Cassidy's eyeline. He gave up after only a moment, then continued pacing. His gait was faux-anxiety, practiced abruptness. "Because if I were you, I'd be going out-of-my-skull terrified. This corner of the world is not well known for treating its monsters well, and ma'am, you are it."

Melquist's mouth warbled, but he said nothing.

"You ever see what they used to do their monsters back in my daddy's time? Whole town would get together with pitchforks and torches if you believe the movies. And I do, but even they cleaned it up some. My father told me once he saw someone in a lynch mob cut the tendons in a man's legs so that he couldn't run." He winced. *"Can you imagine that? They talk about pitchforks; they don't talk about knives. But they all had 'em, and they came out like claws."* He paused and waited for Cassidy to react. She did not. *"They weren't monsters though, not then. People thought they were, but they weren't. It's a sad chapter... but my point being, what're those same people going to do when they come up against you: an actual, legit motherfucking* monster?" He leaned in on his legs at the end for emphasis.

Cassidy's eyes flicked forward at the motion and almost met Victor's by accident, then receded.

Victor watched, moving his tongue from side to side in his mouth. He watched the way Cassidy's hands did not move or clench or change position in any way. She didn't rub her knuckles or crack them. Her eyes -- though avoiding -- remained locked unless Victor tried to get between them and the blank field they were looking into. She moved as little as possible, and her breaths were even too short for her chest to rise fully.

"If this is some kind of ploy to avoid the chair, like Ed Norton in Primal Fear or something, I need you to know that that will not work," Victor said. Without looking, he lay his palm flat against the folder beside him and slid it across the table until it was between him and Cassidy. *"They might have softened on killing the mentally delayed here, but they'll do everything in their power to prove you're smart enough to be strapped in. You can have as strong a poker face as you want, they'll hook you up*

to an MRI and if your brain lights up when they ask you stuff, they'll hook you up to something else and it won't anymore."

"That's not true," Melquist said softly. He crossed his arms. "Not remotely."

"He's gearing up," Tash said, matching his tone.

Melquist looked at her side-on but said nothing.

Cassidy stared forward at the nothingness in the corner of the room, eyes not flitting or faltering in the ways Victor had seen when men hallucinated.

Victor opened the folder with one smooth motion of his wrist. There was a glossy white rectangle on the top, the back of a photo. It had a printer's stamp on it. He sat with his arms at ninety-degree angles on either side of the photo, like a cardsharp sizing up his opponent before choosing to reveal his cards or not. He stared at Cassidy, waited for a moment that from the outside looked the same as any other, then flipped the picture.

The photo was of Briana Redding, as she'd been found behind the shed in Slatery Field. There was blood on and around her, and her young eyes were turned upward to a place just past the camera. The photo was eerie and grotesque, the kind of shot that was taken but then retaken, and never used for media or for main files. No crime scene photos were ever deleted from a main drive, not even ones that were retaken. It looked haunting, like a still from the shock-horror of the late 90's.

Victor slid the photo across to Cassidy, making sure that it interrupted her field of vision. She would either have to look at it or look away. "What's this like, hnn? When you see this, what's happening in there? What do you think a jury will feel when they see this, because me I don't think it'll be great. Just... thinking out loud here."

Cassidy did not look away. Her pupils did not flutter in the *slightest and no colour rose to her cheeks.*

Victor flipped over a second photo, laying it next to the first with a flip of his thumb. This one was of Redding on a table. The dried blood was gone, and her lower half was covered by a cloth, but somehow this photo was worse. The child was pale and bruising from blood pooling had begun to take place. It showed the bruising that had been hidden before, ten dots around the neck and clavicle. "How about this one? This one's different right? The other one," he tapped it, "you'd seen her like this but this one, this one is new. So there's..." he narrowed his eyes, studying Cassidy.

"What's he doing?" Melquist hissed, stepping toward the door.

Tash grabbed him by the arm. "He's pressing her."

Melquist shook her off.

Victor flipped a third photo as if he were laying out a flop in Texas Hold'em. This one was a closeup of Briana Redding's scalp, the hair shaved back to reveal a contusion that the coroner had stated had penetrated her skull. "What about this one? You probably don't get this up close after the fact, right? This is new. This one... I can almost smell it." He squinted.

Cassidy did not move, she stayed with her eyes fixed forward, almost in a fugue state.

Melquist opened the door and looked as though he were about to yell something, then composed himself. He thumbed back toward the hall and said "out" in a way that made it clear it was not a request. When his eyes fell to the pictures in front of Cassidy, he collected them quickly, then exited the room. Victor followed, leaving the manila folder and any other photos he'd printed behind.

When the door closed behind them Melquist turned, his face

red and hot. "What the hell do you think you were doing in there?" He held up the photos and shook them at Victor. In doing this, he saw what was on them; he balked and urged slightly, then pushed them onto a chair facedown. "And where did you get those?"

"It was a test," Victor said, carefully choosing to answer the first question and not the second. He stepped around to watch Cassidy again through the glass, running his fingers through his facial hair. Cassidy sat, unmoving and unwavering. She'd shifted slightly now that there was no one in the room with her but had made no indication that the contents of the folder were of any interest to her at all.

"To see how far you could push me before I bring you in, because boy-howdy --"

"He was trying to get an emotional reaction out of her," Tash clarified.

"And yet look at that," Victor said, cocking his head forward. He was talking only to Tash now, his tone of voice one that was resigned only for her. "Not a twitch, not a gesture, not one feeling anywhere in there. Dead behind the eyes and when you crack her open, she's like a Russian nesting doll: just more dead-eyed, hollow shells all the way down." He clacked his tongue against the roof of his mouth.

"You didn't get anything?" Tash asked.

"Not a damn thing. Nothing. Like nothing I've ever seen... or never seen, take your pick." He paused, lingering on Cassidy for a moment, then turned back to Melquist. "That woman is... hollow. She feels nothing, not a damn thing."

Melquist squinted and looked as though he were about to question the relevance of that statement.

Victor picked up the pictures off the chair and waved them

between the two of them. "This? This kind of thing? This takes passion. This takes hate or lust or fear. It can be a lot of things -- profilers spend their lives narrowing down one from the other... but the thing they all have in common is emotion. This takes emotion." He pointed back at Cassidy without turning. "And she has none."

Melquist moved his mouth back and forth. He looked at Cassidy over Victor's shoulder, then averted his gaze from the sallow, slack-jawed face within.

"She didn't do this," Victor said finally, making sure he could not be misinterpreted. "She's a broken person, she may even be a monster, but she did not do this."

CHAPTER 28

Far Outside Payson, The Present

Alice sat in the dining room of The Manor, watching through an archway as the people watching the television paired off into cliques, each peeling away until there were few left sitting.

A large man with gauges in his earlobes got the attention of two young women as they braided each other's hair, and each rose to their feet without question and followed him out of the room. They left their brushes behind.

A girl with hair that came almost to the small of her back got up suddenly as if an alarm had gone off, then turned and coaxed another two to follow her. They met an older boy at the doorway who had seemed to appear there while Alice's attention had been divided.

There was a bald girl on the middle tier of the couch who watched all of this just as Alice did. When enough people had peeled away, she rose to her feet as well. She straightened her jersey with one pull, then limped out of the room back out into the main foyer.

"It must seem strange, looking at it like this," Carla said, suddenly.

Alice turned abruptly. She hadn't seen Carla come in from the adjacent hallway, but now she was leaned over the back of a wooden chair with her hair dangling lazily between them. In the corner of her eye, Alice saw two more people get up and leave. The sounds of heavy footfalls came from the stairs from the last pair. She opened her mouth to say something, found no words, then closed it.

Carla nodded knowingly as though she had spoken. "I can't remember a time when this wasn't... normal. But I see new people come in and I see the look on their faces as they take it all in -- every time -- and I think: what it must be like to see this through their eyes." She paused, her eyes falling to the last of the people on the couch to pair off as they did so. "I'm envious, really."

"I want to know what's happening here," Alice said finally, watching that last pair -- each of them barely seventeen -- as they walked hand-in-hand out of the room.

Carla nodded, then reached out and gently took Alice by the hand, in a manner not unlike the people of the couch had done. "Come, I'll show you." Alice got out of her seat and followed her into the main hall, just in time to see the last couple make their way up the stairs. "Sister," Carla said, smiling.

Without breaking stride, the young girl nodded as she went up the stairs and repeated, "Sister."

Alice squinted.

Carla spread her arms wide and made her way out into the now empty foyer. "Have you ever wanted to be free, Alice?" she asked. She spoke as though she were addressing her, but her head had turned up slightly. She was staring at a spot, high up on the raised ceiling, where there were portraits hung. "Just... completely free. Like a bird, free."

Alice stepped from the hall into the foyer with caution, turning as she rounded the corner as though she'd expected someone to jump out from behind it. She found nothing but shadowy, darkened hallways as The Manor prepared itself for sleep. "I am free," she said, forcing her gaze back to the woman in the centre of the room.

Carla smiled, bringing her arms back in and holding herself. "Mmmmm. Not really. You're only free until you step out, do something free people can't do. Then you're not free anymore; they take you and put you in a little cage. Or worse." She turned to Alice. "You ever think something as a child and have your father correct it? Not something factual, like one plus one equals two... something theological. A thought pattern, a belief."

Alice narrowed her eyes again. Despite herself, she thought of a moment -- she couldn't have been more than five -- when her father had done just that. She had come home from school with a grand unifying theory, a way to combine her Sunday school teachings with the different religions she'd encountered in public school, and was immediately rebuffed and corrected.

Carla nodded, as if the pause was enough to confirm what she'd been thinking. "Then you're not *really* free, are you? You're not free to believe what you want, not so long as there's someone behind you, saying -- no no, not this, *that*."

Alice looked around, up the winding staircase, but couldn't see past the first turn. "So, is that what this place is then? Some kind of... promised place? A place where you can be free?"

Carla winced. "No, not this place. But we'll get there... soon." She watched as Alice nodded, still looking all around the room without any sign of subterfuge.

Alice lingered on an aged family photo that hung on the wall near its peak, showing a family of five in front of a brick home. The children were young, but it was easy to tell they were a family: all but the father had the same blond hair, and the three young girls each had their father's strong, well-defined chin and squat nose. The children were a mishmash of the parents behind them, their features cobbled together from each.

Smiling, Carla laughed at her. For a reason she couldn't articulate, she liked Alice, despite where she'd come from and how she'd gotten here. "I feel like you get it," she said, closing the distance between them. "I can see something behind the eyes there... you get it. But you don't *believe* it. That's why we let new people in, that's why we're open. Ideas need new ideas to keep going, or they get stale."

Alice nodded. "I spent a few years being poked and prodded by men who told me what to do... So yeah, yeah, I get it. I see what you're saying." The last of it was a lie.

Carla's smile faltered, as though she heard the falseness at the tail end of the truth. She sighed, then motioned to the stairwell. "Let me show you to your room."

Past the first turn of the stairs there were more family portrait-style pictures. The first was of a large group, the photo old. She recognized some of the actors from the photo in the main hall, but the woman -- she presumed, the mother -- was gone now, and there were many more youths. Some had dark eyes and one had a prominent upper lip. It was extended family, Alice reasoned, as none shared the strong chin that the remaining family had.

There was a girl sitting on the stairs with her hands clasped before her and her eyes dazed in that faraway, rolled-back way that people only got during the best of highs or the troughs of passion. There was a man sitting on the stairs behind her with his legs to either side of her, their feet next to each other on the third stair from the bottom. He had pulled her hair back and was mouthing the nape of her neck, leaving a glistening trail of saliva in his wake.

Alice felt a pain in the side of her face as her teeth ground and she tried to retain her composure. The hairs on her neck stood up on end as she stepped past, angling herself away from the pair. When the man caught her movement, he stopped a moment and looked up, dark eyes following Alice.

"Sister," he said, cocking his prominent chin at Carla.

She nodded and continued up the stairs as he gripped the girl and pulled them closer together.

The hall at the top of the stairs was long and stretched out in either direction, one wing above the living room and the other above the kitchen. The walls were white and gray, but not all the same shade of each. Doors were askew like funhouse mirrors, hiding small trails of sawdust and debris at their bases.

There was a photo on the wall across from the mouth of the stairs. In this one, the father was gone and a woman had taken his place -- not the mother, not nearly old enough to be -- and the number of children in the extended family had grown. There were still dark eyes and strong, squared chins, but there were freckles now, often. There were some different shades of hair in the mix as well, but by and large they were blond. They lined up for the photo, nearly twenty of them by Alice's estimate, and seventeen at least were blond. It was like a sea of hay and corn with faces attached. The predominance of it made the few outliers stand out even more, beacons of red and brown.

Alice followed down the hall to the right, to the area over the living room.

"We're adding new rooms," Carla said, her voice humming. "You can never have too many. Yours isn't new though, if you're worried about dust."

As the hallway continued, the doors stopped being of uniform size and started being closer together. They entered an area where there was no paint on the walls at all, just uncovered gyprock. Doors cramped together until their borders touched, many with names on them with the same sort of plating that offices used, names that could be slid out and easily replaced. She passed one with Carla's name.

Alice nodded. There were three people sat against the wall in the middle of the hall passing a cigarette between them. They were huddled next to an open door that she would have thought was their own by their general manner, but when she passed the room there was nothing but a blacklight inside and there were already two people on the bed, only their outlines visible, as though they had been airbrushed onto paper made of shadow. Alice only glimpsed them but could see they were scarcely dressed.

"What's going on here?" she asked, stepping up to catch up with Carla. She turned back and saw that the three waiting outside the room had followed her with their gazes. When the one in the middle passed his cigarette to the last in line, he turned and kissed the first open-mouthed on the lips. Alice held her arms tight instinctively, making herself as small as she could. "What do you expect?"

Carla turned; her eyebrows raised empathetically. "Expect?" she said, speaking as though the word felt foreign on her tongue. She frowned. "You haven't been listening at all, have you? Nothing's expected. That's the *point*." She opened a door at the end of the hall.

Alice steeled herself, half expecting it to already be occupied and ready to defend herself.

There was nobody in the room and, as promised, the room was not new. It had been shortened and renovated, that much was clear, but the walls themselves had the glean of old paint, and the shelves held the weight of things that had been where they were for some time. There was a bed that there was barely enough room for and at its foot, a window to the glowing moonlit night outside. The bed was freshly made and the pillows firm and inviting.

"Nothing's expected," Carla reiterated, cupping Alice's arm in a fashion that was supposed to be reassuring, but which made her skin crawl with gooseflesh. She frowned, feeling the change, and then stepped out of Alice's way to let her into her room. "If you need anything, I'm just down the hall. My name is on the door."

Alice nodded, turning back from inside the room.

Carla stood in the doorway, framed in light. On the wall behind her was another family photo, this one taken from far back to get the totality of the people in the frame. Despite referring to it as a family portrait in her mind, Alice knew that it was too large a collection of people to be. It looked more like a class photo of a large school, of the sort that farmed in schools from small towns all around.

Everyone was smaller in the frame than they had been in previous iterations of the photo as a consequence, but there was still that woman standing in the back behind the rest, with a smile that every grade school teacher had mastered: the "just for the camera" smile. She was older now by several years, but it was her all the same. And now, with Carla standing next to it, it was unmistakably her. Younger, yes, and somehow happier... but Carla all the same.

"Is there anything you need before I go?" Carla asked, snapping Alice out of her trance-like state. "Water? Tea? You know where the bathroom is?"

Alice swallowed, then shook her head once and nodded it, once for each response.

Carla smiled. "Goodnight, Sister." She closed the door behind her, leaving the only light in the room the pale blue of the moon as the sounds of Carla walking away faded, and the sounds of the other rooms of the house crept in.

CHAPTER 29

Payson, The Past

Victor sat with his head in his hands, feeling the scant breeze that penetrated the hallway at Police Plaza. He was sitting on the last of a long row of chairs that were all welded together at their legs, forcing the minimalization of personal space when the row was full. It was currently empty.

Across the hall from him, he saw Tash's shadow on the wall of Gordon Melquist's office. He couldn't hear what she was saying, but her shadow alternated between the extremes of gesticulating with excitement and calm pensiveness.

He watched it for a moment, eyes dancing over what little he could see of her, then returned his face to his hands. His thumbs glided into the corners of his eyes and pressed there, relieving tension but making colours dance across the back of his eyelids. When he removed them, the whites of his eyes were bloodshot.

At the far end of the hall, he heard the familiar sound of children engaging in play. It was faraway and distorted by echoes, giving it a temporal quality as though it had shunted in from a distant past. He tilted his head toward the sound and, much like Tash, thought he could see the shadows of them from just around the corner at the end of the hall.

"Well he's pissed, but you're not being charged with anything," Tash said. Her voice had an acid edge to it, of the type she reserved only for when she had had to go out of her way for him in a way she deemed unnecessary.

Victor's head snapped forward. He hadn't noticed her emerge from Melquist's office. The sound of the children down the hall had stopped suddenly, and he was left to wonder if they'd ever been there at all. He sighed, deep from his diaphragm, then nodded. "Thank you, Tasha."

She paused, her mouth warbling, then laid a gentle hand on his head. Her fingers, though coarse from use and hard work, felt soft as they worked their way through his hair, stroking it and arranging it until its part was neatened. "Why are we still here, Victor?"

He raised his head, squinting from his cheeks. "We need to find --"

"The child. Yes, I understand that. Absolutely... but the child has been found, Victor. Dead, yes, but found. There's no win in this anymore, no innocent to save... just guilt to mete out. That's never been your forte."

Victor looked past her, through the mesh wire that protected Melquist's office window.

"Why is this affecting you so much, suddenly?" She paused, her fingers continuing to run through his hair. "I hate to remind you, but you've seen dead children before."

Victor twitched. The sound of the playing children returned, but he hesitated to ask Tash if she heard it as well, for fear of what her answer would be. He kept his eyes trained on Melquist's office, avoiding glancing down the hallway.

"I've seen your inbox. Simon's been sending you information out of Eastern Europe, there's something there." She paused. "To reiterate: there's something there, and nothing here. Nothing but a dead child, which is very sad, but leaves nothing to be done."

Victor winced, his vision shifting from the mesh wire that protected the glass pane of the door to the contents of the office behind, the file folders and the map beyond, filled with red marks and circles not unlike the ones he himself had presented to Melquist.

Tash frowned, letting her hand slide out of his hair and backing up to where he couldn't avoid her gaze. "Is this because of --"

"Why are the patterns wrong?" he asked, cutting her off by cocking his head toward the office.

She paused, squinted, then turned.

He arose from his chair and stepped up alongside her until they were shoulder to shoulder, staring at the map on the wall inside Melquist's office. There were hastily drawn circles drawn in red marker delineating search patterns. There were three patterns, and where they overlapped was shaded with crosshatching.

"It's pulled from stats," Tash said, motioning along with the circles. "Usually a kidnapping lives so far from a victim's home, so far from a primary location, so far from a school, etcetera." She traced the three circles with her finger. "The whole area is hot, but that crosshatched area where all three overlap? That's the most hot."

"I get that," Victor nodded. He extended his arm. "But that's not where Redding lived, she was ten blocks north and at least three blocks east." He motioned to the scant pinprick in the centre of the leftmost circle, where a compass had punctured to *draw the circle surrounding it.*

Tash squinted, seeing the discrepancy.

"The school's in the right place, but the primary site isn't quite right either. Not as far off as the home, but enough." He clicked his tongue against the back of his teeth. In his mind's eye the red circles shifted, moving upward on the map to adjust to their new starting position. "Do you see what that does to the search area?"

Tash nodded. In her own mind's eye, the crosshatched area that intersected the three circles shifted up, away from the field where Redding had been found and up, up into the vacant, wasteland wooded area that surrounded Payson to its north. "I see it." Her voice had lost its edge. "But the child was found in the initial search area. The field."

Victor nodded. "Yeah. Yeah, she was."

CHAPTER 30

Far Outside Payson, The Present

Alice's room was as black as pitch, so dark that the moonlight outside seemed bright by comparison. Somehow the window and the light outside it existed separate from the rest of the room, the light from the moon existing as a contained rectangle that could not escape its wooden frame. The room absorbed light, as though it were itself a part of the shadow. It made the window into a screen, a window into another world as different from the room she occupied as day was from it.

Despite the dark, sleep would not find her. From everywhere in the house, there were sounds that cked and squirmed their way into the separated boards of her walls like tantric slime. They started slow, with plenty of room between them: squeaks, like old springs being forced into active duty. They came in long, slow screams that cut through the night like a blade, and Alice thought she could hear the rust on them, threatening to pop up and require an emergency room visit. The squeaks came from all directions, finding their way in through gaps in the mold-ing and from between floorboards.

Then came the hushed voices. Long shushes that stretched over the entire length of encounters in the night, leaving little to the imagination. Frantic giggles followed by the clapping of firm flesh. Chides and misgivings, pleas for more or less. Whispers in the dark and hushed requests for silence.

The sounds came from everywhere.

There was a pale green light seeping in from under the door to her room. She didn't know where it could have been coming from and did not investigate it. She swallowed, the tightness in her chest building and her hand rising to clench at it.

The room felt lived in, with scratches on all the furniture and dust in the corners of their shelves... and yet somehow, she felt exactly the way she had felt while living in the cold, sterile world of Black Springs.

Slowly, she rose to sit with her legs over the side of the mattress, pale against the blue light of the outside. She arose and walked to the window, a breeze coming from around its edges and moving her clothes subtly.

Outside the forest beckoned, the branches catching the moonlight and making deep shadows of it. The trees looked back at her with faces kissed by the moon, outlining only the edges of everything with white.

Far below was a patch of loose ground, pale light smoothing the edges of every rock and crevice and making every gap and hole a deep, solid black. Most of the ground was level but in the centre of the gap between trees was a small mound of dirt, only visible now as the moonlight caught its edge and brought it into the third dimension.

Alice stared at it for a long moment, working her tongue around her mouth. She reached into her pants pocket and produced her phone, then turned it on and scrolled through her contacts. She clicked on Williams, Cliven and opened it to text: 'I've got a lead. Will keep you up to date.'

She turned off the phone without waiting for a response, then stared out at the mound of moonlight in The Manor's backyard.

In her room, Carla sat at her desk. There was a yellow legal pad in front of her and she was sketching a vague outline of a house. It was mostly symmetrical shapes -- a rectangle here, a cone there -- but it took on a life of its own as she started to fill in the details.

Under her pen, it began to transform itself from merely lines into a house. And then from merely a house into a home.

"Was letting that girl in a good idea?" came a voice from the dark.

She turned over her shoulder and smiled. "Even in early days, you needed new stock."

Madison Williams lay in her bed that night, hearing the squeaks and hushed whispered seeping in through the walls around her. Her eyes were wide and unblinking, but she could see nothing. There was no light in her room, and no window. The only thing that existed was the pitch of black.

She felt the wall against her knees, rough and unpaint-ed drywall. It was coarse against her flesh in a way she wasn't used to; nothing from her world before had been coarse or hard. She had lived in a world of soft plushness, and now... she was here. Here where there were nails stick-ing out from everywhere and hallways were left askew. Here where every surface was rough and un-sanded.

An arm that was not her own extended around her, squeezing her warmly and tightly, the motion making her own mattress make the sounds she was desperately trying not to hear from the room next door. She felt lips warm against her neck.

Her eyes were wide and unblinking, but she could see nothing.

CHAPTER 31

Maximus sat on his bed next to Mary. Her fingers grazed the tense muscles of his bare chest, tracing the familiar scars and stretch marks of his well-worn flesh. His thick fingers ran through her hair in gentle, rhythmic patterns, tenderly finding each knot and working them out until what draped over her milky shoulders looked like spun gold in the lamp light.

She watched her fingers move as if they were foreign to her will, entranced by the way their slightest pressure caused his skin to buckle and dent ever so minutely. "Where do you think we'll live when we're older?" she asked, her voice sing-song and far away.

He looked around his cabin: at the bent wood stove that provided heat against the winter chill, at the pelts on the wall that kept that heat in, at the rough, rudimentary figures he'd whittled from driftwood on his workbench. "I always thought we'd live here," he grinned.

She snorted, then slapped his chest playfully. He could feel her smile against his chest, the way her cheeks curled and rose into the pit of his arm, and loved it. "I'm serious.

If we could move together, right now, where would you want to go?"

Maximus paused, his fingers dangling near her, moving from the nape of her neck to where her bare back glistened with a sheen of sweat still from ravenous lovemaking. "Maybe Banff."

"Bamf?"

"Banff."

"Why?" she grinned, tickling his ribs. "Because you're a badass motherfucker?"

He laughed. "B – A – N – F – F. It's in Canada. I saw pictures of it once. It's a resort town, one of those places where the population quadruples every tourist season. There are these great glacial lakes – massive crystal-clear pools made from the runoff from glaciers, and it's so clear you can see hundreds of feet to the bottom. And there are these mountains that just stretch on forever... it looks so peaceful."

She smiled. "Banff. Sounds nice."

He was quiet for a moment. "It was the AIDS capital of Canada for a while there too, so the people are friendly."

Mary smacked him again. He laughed.

"What about you?" he asked after a calm moment when his laughter faded.

"Hnn?" She raised her head and may have been in the middle of drifting off to sleep.

"Where would you live, if you could?"

He felt her mouth squish from side to side as she thought, mulling the answers. "Alaska, I think."

He raised an eyebrow, then kissed the top of her head. "Alaska?"

"Yeah. It's—" Maximus was jolted awake by the brilliant flashing of a strobe light and an impossibly loud sound like a zipper being caught and pulled until the metal strained, amplified until he thought his eardrums would burst. His jaundiced sclera shrank back as his pupils expanded to twice their normal size. He sat up quickly and hit his forehead against the bunk above him. "Fuck," he cursed, bringing the heel of his hand to the throbbing pain.

He was grabbed by the side of his head by a firm, clammy grip, his head violently turned to the side, coming face to face with a man wearing thick, black swimming goggles and a red felt glove held to his chin with a strap.

"Ah-ah-Eh-ah-Roooo!" the man crowed, thrusting his pointed nose forward with every syllable and poking it against Maximus's cheek.

Maximus sneered and pulled away; the man dressed as a chicken held two pots up and began clanging them together over and over again. A taller man behind him blew a kazoo into a megaphone and produced the ear-splitting squeal that had shattered his dream and thrust him awake. The taller male was wearing a hastily produced chicken costume as well, with the remnants of three condoms on his head to facilitate a rough approximation of a rooster's comb. There was a yellow smudge on the tip of his perched nose to form a beak. Three similarly costumed men ran past, grabbing at the other bunk occupants. A small man with a rubber chicken mask grabbed Kincaid and shook him awake, in Maximus's peripheral vision.

Bernard stood amongst the chaos as frats ran around him, each coming close to striking him but ignoring him. His arms were folded in front of his chest and he was looking down at Maximus as Maximus rubbed his head and surveyed the room. His expression was vacant for a long moment, then a smirk found its way to one corner of his lips, as secret as a sacrament.

The man with the two pots slammed one each into two pledge's backsides, hard, the fat of their buttocks reverberating with the force. He laughed with great force, as though the pleasure he found from the act were not genuine but manufactured, created from the moment of ritual violence. Three other men were doing the same but with different implements. One had a yellow rubber chicken and was whipping it about with such force that when the red rubber comb of the rooster struck the cheek of one boy it left marks like bright pink streaks.

Bernard made a sound deep in throat, barely audible. Despite that, all the crowing, stamping frats in the room stopped and made a line, four to a side on either side of him. They stood at mock attention, their ill-fitted costumes and drunken states making their angles Dali-esque and obtuse, their musculature melting over their skeletons like clocks.

"Pledges," Bernard said, addressing them all. His eyes made his way from one to the other, lingering too long on Kincaid and Maximus. Kincaid had sat up in his bunk and his feet were now dangling over the edge, nearly touching the floor. "I hope you've enjoyed your first night's sleep."

There were mumbles from the pledges, as they slowly

rose to their feet. The boy who had been whipped with the rubber rooster was now nursing a thin gash from the corner of his mouth up to his cheek, a thin driblet of blood smearing down to form a gallows smile over one side of his face.

The smile that had been on Bernard's face faded slightly, becoming sterner and serious. "It's time to crow."

The frats on either side of him stomped their boots in unison, no longer melting men but suddenly acting as one as if on cue. They shot their chins skyward and bleated out a cacophony of loud staccato rooster caws. The sound was so loud it seemed to shake the paper thin duvet that had covered Maximus through his dream of Mary.

He hadn't noticed the boots until that moment. They were heavy, black jack-boots that had been polished to mirror shines, a stark contrast to the disheveled arrangements the rest of them wore. The boots had been what made had made the racket as they'd come in, the firm soles on the floating floor like thunder in the night sky.

"In EGN you get up early and you work hard. Pledges rise like a cock and pledges prove they're men, not fucking little pussies like you." Bernard again looked from one to the other. "It's time for your first test: this is the Rooster Crow. It's time to crow –" Again, all the men cawed. "Show us your best cock."

Some of the pledges had begun to form a line opposite the frats, as though their mirror opposites. Bernard stepped to the first to his left and held out his chin to him expectedly.

The pledge tilted his head back and cleared his throat. The second he took in breath to caw, Bernard pushed his elbow forward into the pledge's stomach, forcing the wind out of him. He halved immediately, bending at the waist and letting out a pained sound before falling to one knee.

Maximus got to his feet.

Bernard kept him in his peripheral vision but remained facing the fallen pledge. "I didn't say to crow." Behind him, the men stamped their jackboots and cawed at the ceiling in unison. "I said to show us your best cock."

The pledge looked up at him for a moment, understanding dawning on him. He stood to his feet, his bruised midsection threatening to give way as he did.

Maximus found his lip curling slightly, as it dawned on him as well. He turned to Kincaid and saw the knowledge spark in him as well. He swallowed.

"Well," Bernard said, nodding at the pledge. "Get on with it."

The pledge sighed, then reached down and pushed the front of his pajamas down and scooped up his genitals, cradling their lumpy mass in a tuft of curly black hair and presenting them. His uncircumcised manhood protruded from the cup of his palm, the wrinkled foreskin the consistency of packing peanuts around the pink eye of its head, hidden beneath.

Bernard held the pledge's gaze for a long, uncomfortable minute, as the pledge held his cock out in the cradle of his own rough flesh. The longer he held the youth's gaze, the more shaken the youth seemed. Finally, when the tension seemed to be at its apex, Bernard looked down at the pledge's presented genitals.

"Pathetic," he said, his voice thick with contempt. He pretended to stifle a laugh. As if on cue, several frats echoed his snicker. "Sick, really. Are you sure you shouldn't be in the Delt Sorority? That's not even a dick, just a clit that's been stretched out with pliers."

There was genuine laughter at that from the frats, and at least two of the pledges.

Bernard moved to the second pledge in the line, and the first began to tuck himself away. He turned on a dime, again bringing his elbow into the pledge's ribs, hard. The youth fell to the floor again, finally letting go of his penis. It smacked against the floating floor and bounced, making a sharp slapping sound that made Kincaid cringe.

"Keep it out," Bernard said by way of explanation, stepping to the next in line. He raised his chin politely again, as though the second pledge wouldn't have just seen all that had transpired. The second youth pulled himself out, leaving his testicles nestled in the crotch of his pajamas. It was wider than the first had been, and circumcised, the head protruding from the taught tan flesh like a pink Christmas bulb. "You see?" he said indigently, turning back to the first pledge again, who was in the process of rising to his feet. "That's not even a real cock and that's more than you have. Do you have any idea how small a dick is going to have to be for you not to lose this challenge? I've sucked clits bigger than your fucking dick."

Despite his discomfort, the second pledge caught himself snickering at the first's humiliation.

Bernard's head snapped forward. "What the fuck are you laughing at, Pledge?"

He forced his lips tight, the barest hint of a smirk still tickling their edge.

Bernard looked him up and down dismissively. "Wash

yourself more, you filthy fuck. You still smell like your mother's cunt."

The third pledge was a short young man whose cock was proportionately off kilter with the rest of him. His five and a half feet should have yielded roughly as many inches, but when he pulled himself out, he was well over eight on the verge of nine. It was plump and its flesh translucent, like a sausage packed into a sleeve too small for it.

The fourth was markedly smaller, almost as small as the first. It required minutes of inspection to decide if the first was still in last place or not, until under close scrutiny it was decided that its girth was enough to let it pass. "It's like a Coke bottle that's been flattened out," Bernard remarked to himself, as he moved on.

Maximus stood before him with his shoulders squared, his daffodil-tinted sclera narrowed into slits.

Bernard smirked at him. "You know we wondered if we'd even want to see the cock of an ugly fuck like you," he laughed. He licked his lip and thumbed his nose before getting in close. He would have been nose to nose with him, had Maximus's nose not been stubbed short. When he spoke again, his voice was a harsh whisper, like a lover with ill intent. "Do you even have a dick? I'd believe it if you said you reproduced asexually. That way I wouldn't have to think of someone fucking a mother as dirty as yours would have had to have been to squeeze out a little shit like you."

Maximus's lips parted as if to speak, but he held his tongue.

Bernard smirked, waiting, hoping Maximus would rise to the bait. When he didn't, he scoffed. "Let's get this freakshow over with then."

Tentatively, Maximus plunged his gnarled fingers into the front of his pants. He returned with a long penis that was thick at the base but came to a slender, uncircumcised tip. The foreskin was loose and jaundiced, hovering over the edge of the flaccid cock and giving it the appearance of a sickly elephant trunk. It was yellowed throughout, the veins a blue so deep it was black and spiderwebbing their way across it. It was dried and cracked like the skin under his eyes sometimes got, producing large segments of skin the size of corn flakes. The head was unpronounced and difficult to determine the location of, while his scrotum was overly long, dangling far lower than his manhood would have had it been left to dangle.

Bernard laughed, bringing both his hands to his face and cupping them there. Several other frats laughed as well, and the pledges prior to him, who still held their genitals in their hands for comparison, turned to see.

"That looks like something you'd see on National Geographic, holy mother of fuck," he laughed, slapping his knee. "I can't even make you keep that thing out, I feel bad. Really bro, I feel for you. Put that thing away, I can't look at it anymore."

Maximus started to move, then saw the others out of the corner of his eye and stopped.

The smile faded from Bernard's lip. He had been half a step on his way to the sixth pledge and now stepped back, clearing his throat sternly. "Are you deaf, Pledge? I told you, you could put it away."

Maximus remained, shoulders squared, with both cock and balls cupped in each arid, three-fingered hand.

"I said, put it the fuck away. It's disgusting and I don't

want to look at it anymore. It looks like a tapir's dick if it had been left out in the sun to long."

Maximus remained.

Bernard held his gaze for a long moment, then moved on to the sixth in line, whose penis was already in hand. He was pulled back and withdrawn, knowing what was coming.

Bernard smirked, his humor renewed. He turned back to the first pledge and grinned. "You're off the hook, I don't think I've ever seen a cock this small that wasn't a tranny's. You a chick with a dick, you fucking Mic?"

The sixth pledge's lip quivered, but he stood his ground.

"You best hope someone else here is less a man than you, you tiny-dicked motherfucker. We only take real men in Epsilon Gamma Nu."

The next pledge in line was Kincaid.

Bernard looked up at him, then smirked. "Do we even need to bother? Statistically, I mean."

Kincaid took a deep breath, then reached into his pants.

"Stand back, boys, ten bucks says he has a hard on for us." He turned back to Maximus. "Twenty if it's pointed at you, freak."

Kincaid paused, then continued.

"We don't want any n--" Bernard swallowed, catching himself. "Keep it in your pants, Pledge."

He made Kincaid stand there the entire time, fully clothed, as he made his way through the pledges to find the person with the smallest manhood, to be outed from the fraternity. He held his hands clasped before him, ready, as every other man in turn was judged.

CHAPTER 32

Motel 83, The Present

The chill night air kissed Abby's flesh as she stepped onto the porch outside Chad's motel room. The air was crisp and clean in a way it only was in the desert. People expected it to be hot at night, but it never was; the ground expelled any heat it took in during the day almost immediately, leaving only frigid cold in its wake.

Abby liked the cold. Behind her inside the room, Chad was still asleep with all the cheap, papery covers from the bed curled around him. She'd been there only a moment ago, but the night had called to her. She remembered long nights at Port Haven when the night would call to her, when she would stand on her balcony and look out at the waves crashing and feel a solemn connection to them.

There were no waves to see here, just moonlight sketching out the siding of an old backwoods' motel. There was no lovely, rhythmic sound of waves crashing either... just the slow, familiar rumble of an engine that had been taxed to its breaking point and yet still showed no signs of stopping.

She raised an eyebrow, looked back at Chad to make sure he was still asleep, then stepped off the balcony onto the gravel driveway. She walked along the S-shaped group of buildings, feeling the heat come off the chrome panels of each, until she came around to the front of the entire complex.

Sitting in the parking lot with the engine running was Victor's El Dorado.

"Fuck," she huffed, wrapping her shawl around herself tighter and marching over to it. Dirt and dust kicked up in her wake as she stepped with determination now, no longer hesitantly looking around corners as when she'd first been exploring the sound. She strode up to the driver's side door and pulled it. It refused to budge. She bent down and looked into the window, cursed again, then stepped back. She walked around to the passenger's side door, opened it, and got in.

She turned to Victor, her expression somewhere between surprise and concern. "What are you doing?"

Victor sighed. His head was against the steering wheel, pressed into his forehead in such a way that it had left a red streak across his brow. He reached out and turned off the radio, which Abby only then realized had been playing a soft, melodic tune. It had been playing so lowly that she hadn't heard it above the El Dorado's troubled engine.

He clacked his mouth together sleepily, then turned to her.

She balked. "Have you been drinking?" she asked, waving her hand in front of her face to dissipate the stench of whiskey. She reached out and took the keys from the ignition on impulse and the engine died. "You never drink."

He nodded, one eye closed further than the other. "Around you, yes. That's true." He worked his mouth as though he were uncomfortable with how it sat atop his bone structure. "I wasn't driving. I just wanted to listen to some music."

She winced, unsure -- possibly for the first time -- if he was telling her the truth. That fact wedged in her mind like a shunt, and she hoped she would be able to get it out. She looked down at the keyring in her hand, the keys splayed out like fingers and matching her own. She narrowed her eyes. "Will you tell me why this has you so... unearthed? Unsettled?"

He clacked his mouth, then brought his hands up and rubbed his face. For a moment she thought he was crying, but when his hands fell away he was Victor again; as though he'd rubbed his sagging, disjointed face back into something that resembled the Victor she knew: the one with high cheekbones and eyes full of knowledge.

There wasn't knowledge now though, only sadness.

"I know this is affecting you." She reached out and touched his shoulder, gingerly. After a moment, she pushed his blond hair away from his face and back behind his ears where it belonged. "It's affecting you more than anything I've ever seen... please just tell me so I can help."

He paused and looked out through the grease-stained front windshield, his eyes focusing on the nothingness surrounding the buzzing Motel 83 sign. He sniffed, as though trying to compose himself, but did not turn to meet her gaze.

"I need to --"

"I met them before, these people," Victor said, finally. He stared out the front window still, speaking as though entranced. "I met them before they were like this. Before they were so... organized. But it was still them. I met them when I first came to Payson and..." he paused, maneuvering his mouth again. She heard his jawbone pop. "I'd never seen anything like them before. Most people... most people I can read. Like when I play poker with Chad. I can look at them and I can just *know* what they're feeling. There are these little hints and tweaks that nobody knows they're doing... nobody else can see it... but I can. But these people... they don't feel anything. You look at them, it's like looking at a wall." He stopped, blinked, then turned and met Abby's eye for the first time since she'd gotten into the car. "And it is the scariest thing I've ever not seen in my life."

Abby shifted, uncomfortably. "So, you..." she paused. "The woman you saw in the mall, she was like that? Nothing... nothing behind the eyes?" She thought back to the way Carla had smiled at them in the foyer of her home, and how dark her expression had been. She shuddered near the base of her spine.

He nodded. "I saw the same in Gavin, the first time I met him," he said in a hushed voice. "It's how I knew to call the rest of you down to deal with them. It's *cults*, Abby. That's the only thing I've ever been able to find that makes you feel like that, that will drain everything from you." He paused. When he spoke again his voice had gained gravitas. "It's cults."

She nodded, hearing the fear in his voice.

"I think... I think I fucked up the first time I dealt with them."

"I'm sure you didn--"

"No. No, I fucked it up. I did. They're bigger than they were then, so much bigger." He swallowed. "Have you looked at them?"

Abby squinted, then shook her head.

"Look at them. Look at the pictures of who have been taken... look at how similar they all look. Did you see the photos on the walls at their base?"

She nodded, recalling them. All filled with children, all blond-haired, all blue-eyed... she sucked in air sharply as her brain made a connection it wouldn't have, before. "Oh my God."

"I don't think they're kidnapping... I think they're re-cruiting, and the kids run away. When I first came across them, years ago, it was just one fucker... he'd had children with some of them. Now, I think it's the lot of them. All those kids in those pictures, they didn't take all of them into their cult. Some of them --"

"Some of them were born into it," she finished, hating the sound of the words in her own mouth.

He nodded, winced, then lay his head back down against the steering wheel. She reached out and placed her hand along his back, tentatively at first, then with growing ease.

CHAPTER 33

Los Angeles, California

Roberta opened the door to her apartment, almost dropping the heavy ring of keys as she extracted them from the door. She was juggling big, reusable bags of groceries, packed to the point that they stood erect. The tuffets of carrots and celery stuck out from their tops.

The depths of the apartment were as black as pitch, even the light from the hallway barely penetrating its thickness. Despite this, she navigated the dark with a practice and balance typically reserved for the blind and the luckiest of children. She only stumbled once, her foot finding a boot in the hall and fumbling over the obstruction before finding itself again. Her hall was mercifully short, passing only one brief tributary into the living room and past the love seats that stood there before turning into the kitchen. She could see their silhouettes as she passed, round and plump like oranges, as her eyes adjusted to the low light.

"Home, lights on," she said with a huff as she let down the first of the grocery bags. They were premade versions, each with a different pattern on it. The one she laid down had ducks; although in the darkness, they were all swirling masses of gray.

The lights remained out; the apartment shaded in black. There was very little -- almost no -- natural light. She had made every effort to cover all the windows, but some light always got through. That was one thing she'd learned as a light sleeper in the middle of one of the largest cities on the planet: some light always got in, and some sound always got in. No matter how smart you thought you were, there were cracks and crevices where things could get in.

One of the bags Roberta was still juggling fell onto its side on the counter, a can of baby corn falling out and striking the countertop with a loud, startling thwomp. She felt it again an instant later very near her foot. She let out a loud curse, then a frustrated sigh. "House, lights on," she said again. She waited in the dark a moment, trying to arrange her cans so that they were upright and balanced without seeing what they were. Again, there was only the dark.

"House, play voicemail," she said, clearly and calmly. There was an electronic chime that followed, and somewhere in the dark of the living room four multi-coloured dots lit up in response to her request.

"There are no new messages," the electronic, focus-grouped media-marketed voice intoned, before its row of lights went dead again. "Playing first saved message --"

"Stop," Roberta said, her voice strained from frustration. The voice stopped. She cleared her throat, swallowed, then spoke crisply and clearly: "House, lights on."

Again, nothing happened. She cursed, pushed the still-full bag into the wall, then marched out of the kitchen and into the living room, where the Smart-Home system's lights were only now fading from hearing her last command. "House, lig--"

"It's frustrating when things don't work like they're supposed to," came a gruff voice from the darkness.

Roberta's breath caught in her throat, save for a high-pitched instant of a yelp as she jumped, coming to a stop in the dark halfway into her living room. The lights finally came on, and suddenly Theo Flaherty was in her living room. One leg was crossed at the ankle over the knee of the other, and his hand was still on the manual switch of the lamp he sat next to. Though the light was on, his eyes were dark, sunken beads in the centre of his head almost devoid of light except for a small flicker, trained on her.

"I get that," he finished, lowering his hand and placing it with his other one, dangling loosely across his legs. He had no weapon but still managed to look menacing, his shoulders hunched forward and his mouth a tiny, confined thing surrounded by two days of scruff.

"Theo --" Roberta started, her voice startled. She coughed and pressed the folds out of her shirt as if by reflex, then continued in a slightly different accent than she had started in: less Sun Valley and more Boston, if not second-generation English. "Theo. What are you doing her--"

"Was any of it real?" he cut her off, letting his eyes drift around the room now that it was lit. "Any of it? At all?" He frowned, staring at a mocha-coloured wall with only one frame hanging from it, and that frame holding a degree. In Psychology, of all things. His eyes wandered to her bedroom door, which was blackened still. "I get some of it, I do. But was any of it real?"

"I don't know what you mea--"

"Shane Industries," he said, cutting her off mid-sentence again.

She arched her back again, then before his eyes, he watched all of her loosen. Tension, and a posture that was not her own, worked its way out of her shoulders. When she spoke again it was with the slightly accented, too-rehearsed voice of a Sun Valley resident again, as it had started out. It was also deeper, and sterner. Her eyes narrowed and became focused. "What do you want here?"

His cheek twitched, and he looked away toward the bedroom again. "Were the kids real?"

"Pardon?"

"The kids. You said you had kids, we used to chat about them on your lunch breaks... David did this, Amelia did that. Did you have kids? If I went into that room right now, would it be a kids' room, or just some adult's bed?"

"There are no kids."

He paused, nodding. "And the pictures, would there be pictures of kids on the wall in there? Smiling faces in family portraits... fake smiles, but smiles? Would there be any of those, or just... walls?"

"There are no kids," she reiterated.

He frowned, making deep ditches along either side of his mouth that caught the shadow that remained in the room. "See here's my thing: why lie about the kids? That wasn't... that wasn't needed. It's not like I had kids and you were using them to get close to me, arranging play-dates or whatnot… There was no reason to make up kids. And yet here we are, and here you are, and the walls are bare and there are no kids."

Her jaw tightened, and her fists slowly tensed. When he looked away at her bedroom door again, she took one swift step back toward the kitchen. There were knives there; she knew exactly where they were even now.

He stood up quickly and raised his hand to her but made no step toward her. Still, she stopped, freezing again as though she'd been caught in a children's game of spotlight. He worked his tongue around his mouth between his gums and lips. He squinted at the door, then turned back to her. "I find myself mourning children that never existed. They were, literally, never alive. Is that… normal? Is that a normal reaction to that?"

Roberta's shoulders fell slightly. "They were real," she said, her voice softer now. "Their memory is sometimes the only things that --"

"Don't bother, I can see your thoughts behind you. That, and you didn't even register that your children's names were not, in fact, David and Amelia." He shook his head. "So, stop fucking around, right now, because I've had enough of it for one life."

Roberta stopped, her mouth pursing again.

Theo squinted. "It must have been hard, keeping your thoughts shielded. Easier when I was younger, for sure… but still, not easy."

She straightened. "It was the job."

He nodded, then ran his finger along the edge of her framed degree. "Is this real? The degree? Or is this like the kids?"

"It's as real as any degree is. I wrote my Master's Thesis on manipulating thought. It helped... with you. Making myself think a certain way, act a certain way... like getting into character."

The billboard behind her flickered, like static. For a moment an image of the knives in the kitchen flashed, but otherwise the stress of the situation kept his mind focused on the man intruding in her home: her eyes were cameras, the projector-beam coming from the back of her head and shining the reality back onto the board.

"I moved them," he said, without elaborating as to what he meant. "So you can drop that."

She pursed her lips. "What are you doing here?" she asked. She edged toward the kitchen even though he'd told her the knives were gone. Her thoughts didn't change, and he wasn't even completely sure she was conscious of her motion.

"Anemone," he said, stepping back from the wall and shoving his hands into his pockets. "You were there, and I want to know why. I want to know... how all this links together."

On her billboard, a syringe flashed onto the screen, followed by a closeup of an unknown Caucasian arm as it was injected with something deep and black, like tar. "There's a project I'm working on that's been in the pilot stages for... some time. It didn't start with me. Anemone was a small part of a small part of that."

Theo squinted, watching as a hand with blue gloves on pinched off the injection point on the screen behind her to halt its bleeding. There was more blood than what usually accompanied an injection, and the arm was jerking back. It was only becoming clear now that the feed was from the first-person point-of-view of the blue-gloved person. After a moment, the camera started to pan back, but when it did it faded back to the live feed of Theo in her living room. He nodded and watched himself nod a moment later on the screen.

"That's not what you really wanted," Roberta asked. For a moment, her voice was back to the soft, soothing way it had been when they would share meals together. "You could have found that out from anyone."

He nodded. "I want to know how it all links together. I want to know... I can see the links now. The links to the chain that bind everything together... Anemone, Black Springs, Shane... all of it. I can see the links, but not the chain itself. The big picture. I want to know what *that* is."

"No, you don't," she smirked. She smirked the same way he smirked at people, as though she could see a screen behind his head as well. Even though he knew she couldn't, he finally appreciated how unnerving the experience was. "You don't care about that in the slightest. In the *slightest*. So why don't you ask me what you came here to find out?"

His lips curled, involuntarily, and he forced his expression back to as neutral as it could be. He sniffed, composing himself. "Was any of it real? Any part of it? Black Springs... Port Haven... meeting Abby. Was any part of it not thought out and planned?"

She laughed but brought it back to a smirk when his fist clenched again. She thought, clicking her tongue against the roof of her mouth, then nodded. "Yes. Yes, some of it was real. A lot of it, I assume. It's easier to control broad strokes than minor things."

"What was real? What specifically was real?"

She squinted. "I told you about that fishing trip with my father? The one where we sat in the boat and had the beer, about a week before he passed? That was real."

The billboard behind her showed her getting a text message about the death of her father while she was alone in an office. She picked up the phone, glanced at it, then went back to her report. There was a calendar behind her computer of a man and girl fishing together, a bucket of beer between them. It was a painting, in the style of Norman Rockwell.

"At least that was real," he said through a forced smile.

He walked past her and out her door. He was out of the building by the time she found her phone to call for help.

CHAPTER 34

Far Outside Payson

Alice's arms ached from fitful, broken sleep. She stretched them until the calcium deposits in her elbows popped on her way down the stairs, stopping at each family photo along the way as she did. Other residents of The Manor -- some she had seen before and some she somehow had not -- passed her in either direction as she lingered by each photo. She looked at each one in turn out of the corner of her eye to compare them to her mental image of Madison Williams, but neither measured up.

The smell of bacon and maple syrup was thick in the air on all floors, and made her mouth wet with saliva. She hadn't realized she had been hungry -- indeed, would have said that she had had no appetite at all -- until that smell was on her and in her.

The photos on the wall were different in the unflinching light of day. In the night she had only seen Carla, and how she had changed... all the other youth present had formed together into a semi-solid mass of white people. Now she took note of them all. In the photo next to her

bedroom there was a tall boy with blond hair and the barest skimps of facial hair. His eyes were sunken, and he
looked sad.

With each picture she passed she searched the boy out,
winding back the clock on him a little more each time. In
the photo near the mouth of the stairs he had scars, while
in the photo at the top of the stairs he had fresh cuts. In the
middle of the stairwell he looked sad but not yet harmed.

In the photo on the plateau that connected the two
stairwells he looked almost happy... but even then, there
was something behind the eyes she couldn't easily place.
A sadness that was fleeting and may only have been able
to be properly captured in a photograph.

She was sure she could trace back any person in the
photos in this way: from the moment they were broken, to
the moment they first arrived.

At the bottom of the stairs, she looked away into the
living room, and saw the same tall blond boy sitting on
the second rung of the couch, near the bald girl and Carla.
They were eating French toast and passing syrup back and
forth, the bottle always seeming to be in motion: as soon
as one was finished, another needed more. She squinted,
her stomach rumbling, then turned and stepped away toward the back of the house.

Unseen by her, Carla's eyes flicked up from her meal
and watched her walk away.

Getting to the back of the house was like navigating a
maze, with walls that were built and changed to suit the
changing needs of the expanding population of the house.

It was the same way she had felt about Victor's house for the first month or so after she'd moved in, until she'd gotten used to its strange layout.

Turning a corner, she found herself in a hallway under the stairs that was bathed in natural light. There was a greenhouse beyond one glass door and many bay windows, none of which had been visible from the driveway; each wing of the house guarded it from view. The wall opposing all the windows was long and blank and unbroken -- the only one she'd seen of its kind thus far in her exploration of the house. The only thing on that wall at all was a single door that looked to open to the area underneath the stairs. It was directly across from the backdoor to the house as a whole and looked like both doors wouldn't have had the space to be swung open at the same time.

Alice approached both doors, remaining between them. The door that led deeper under the stairs was white and bland, save for a single name plate across its upper middle, of the type that could be ordered from any office supply store. The name wasn't one she recognized. She pondered it for a moment, tried the knob, and found it to be locked.

She turned back to the glass door. Beyond the billowing edges of the greenhouse, sitting just near the cusp of what she could see, was the mound. There was a mound of dirt that sat above the curve of the horizon like a plump tummy, pregnant with possibility and interest.

She turned and reached for the handle for the outside door and yanked it open, feeling the heat from the greenhouse waft past her.

"Can I help you?" came a smooth voice from behind

her.

She turned and saw the tall boy who had been sitting on the couch next to Carla -- the one whom she had noticed from the pictures -- leaning against the wall at its corner. He was looking at her with those smoldering, hypnotic blue eyes... which might have been more affecting if they weren't the same as every other person's in the house. "I was just getting some air," she said, not closing the door.

"You'll find the air in the greenhouse quite hot." He threw her a wink. "Though some like it like that."

His smile sent a shiver through her. Not because it was malicious, but because it was mechanical. It was flirtation as modeled by someone who had learned the roles of flirtation but who had no interest in it -- or its outcome -- themselves. Come-on's from a bot recording. "I was going past the greenhouse," she said.

He reached out his hand as he stepped toward her, closing the door with a gentle push.

She looked past it, the mound of dirt re-framed in the window of the door, like in all of the pictures she'd passed on the way up.

"You don't want to go out there. There's a lot out there that's just... a placeholder."

"Placeholder?"

"Until we can get back to Our Land."

Alice squinted, noting the way he'd said those last two words. They were nouns, not adjectives, she noted. She could almost hear the capital letters on the way he enunciated them. "I just needed a walk."

"You should eat first." He smiled that same tinned, manufactured smile at her. "I'm Marcus, by the way."

He extended a hand to her and she shook it. His hand was cold to the touch and sent a wave of unease through her, but he smiled and held it until it warmed slightly. He pumped slowly with three firm, meaningful motions.

She tried to get her hand back and turn towards the door, but his gaze and grip were both unflinching. Eventually she relented, allowing him to pull her -- slightly -- toward him, and away from the door. Though there was still an arm's length distance between them, she could smell the sickly sweetness of his breath. As he smiled, she couldn't help but see all the previous versions of him that had led to this one: from the small boy with the sadness behind the eyes, to the scarred boy, to this man, whose scars were faint and covered by patches of facial hair -- but still lingered beneath the surface.

It occurred to her, and not for the first time, that supposed immortality would not protect her from everything.

"Come. There are sausages being put on." He kept her hand and started to lead her out of the hall, hand in hand. She turned back as if seeing if anyone else would appear in the hallway that might surprise Marcus the way he'd surprised her, but the only sign of life she saw was the same name engraved on the door below the stairs.

She wondered, briefly, who Gordon Melquist was, and why he deserved to have his own room in The Manor anyway.

CHAPTER 35

Outside Payson, The Past

There were very few houses in the area where the search circles, when properly drawn on the maps, lined up. The area outside Payson was barren save for spots of forest that seems to have been planted by some hand, then abandoned; spots of greenery that marked where a refuge or oasis had once been, but was no longer.

They'd searched local and state records at first, but far enough outside a town limit that people just built. On the official record there were no buildings outside Payson until the limit of the next township. Reality had proven different. There were 217 miles of road in total within the encircled area outside Payson. Driving the speed limit, Victor had calculated that they could search every square inch of it within thirty hours. It had taken them less than eight, all said.

The property was large. It stretched on for what seemed like forever, with green grassy fields that disobeyed the desert that lay just past the tree line like rebellious youth. A mansion of a house sprung up from the middle of those knolls, its brick face absorbing the light from the day and radiating warmth. It had large windows that rose up, showing at least three stories not including an attic.

There were young people walking around the property, without purpose, enjoying the sun. A half dozen of them in total, but they walked in and out with such freedom that there could have been another half dozen inside.

Victor got out of his car and squinted against the sunlight that reflected off the roof of the El Dorado. Three blond children ran past, laughing and taking no notice of him or the car in their game.

Tash got out of the car a moment later, shielding her eyes with her hand. "Victor," she said simply, cocking her head toward the driveway.

There was a police cruiser parked in plain sight, empty.

He sighed, nodded, then let his gaze fall over the children that walked around. They all smiled, warmly and brightly... but they were cold smiles, smiles pulled from family photos. They smiled with their mouths and only their mouths, their eyes sunken and gray.

"There's too many kids," he said in a hushed tone.

She nodded.

"The math doesn't add up. No way can this many kids go missing and everyone stay mum." He licked parched lips. "Does not happen."

The three children ran by again. This time the smallest one -- no more than four -- brought up the rear. She slipped at the end of the driveway, fell, and bashed her knee against the sharp stone at the pavement's edge. She didn't cry or even react much, simply got up and pumped her legs to try and catch up to the other two girls, who looked too similar to her not to be siblings, leaving a red smear in her wake.

Tash stepped over the red-rimmed rock and looked down at it.

"Do it," Victor said, watching her.

She reached into her jacket pocket and produced a clear Ziplock sandwich bag. She turned it inside out around her hand, used it to pick up the blood-smeared stone, then unfolded the bag again so that it was right-side out with the rock inside it. She sealed it, clicked her tongue, then tossed the stone onto her seat.

She turned her gaze toward the squad car and narrowed it. "Watch my back," she said with finality, then started the brief march to the vehicle.

He almost called out to her not to, but by the time the urge reached his larynx, it would have drawn too much attention to them to be heard.

Tash stepped up to the cruiser and stood alongside it, turning a full three-hundred and sixty degrees around. There was grass, a beautiful building, and kids. The oldest person she saw was perhaps eighteen, but even that was generous, and they seemed to be paying her no attention.

She lifted up on the driver's side handle tentatively, expecting an alarm. When there was none, she pulled it open and ducked down into the car, producing a kerchief from her pocket. She rubbed it along the steering wheel and leather seat, and along the visor where Melquist's identification hung. She frowned, then stopped and looked down in the cupholder.

There was a half-filled water bottle there, with a spout stop that was meant to stop water from spilling but, she knew, mostly prevented germs and backwash from escaping more than anything.

She bit her lip, looked out the front of the cruiser briefly, then snapped the bottle up out of its holder.

A small blond child with a skinned knee watched her as she closed the door to the cruiser and walked down the driveway to the El Dorado.

CHAPTER 36

Motel 83, The Present

Chad looked over the photos and files still strewn over the whiskey-stained sheets of the spare bed in Victor's room. Young faces stared back at him, each with their name off-centre below it in Times New Roman font. Christopher. Ashley. Matthew. Emily. Joshua. Sarah. Jason. Samantha. Jacob. Common names. Names that came out of a place and time when Middle America was less stressed than it was now. He picked up one, of a young girl with high cheekbones, and squinted at it until its lines went blurry.

"If it's him again, we aren't going to get him on kidnapping," Abby said, pacing the room with her finger strumming her upper lip. She walked back and forth in front of Victor, who sat on the bed opposite Chad with both of his heavy-booted feet on the floor. "If you're right, it's not kidnapping."

"It's not him," Victor said, his voice far away. "It can't be."

"You sound very sure." She paused. "Same MO. Same

location type. Same victim type. For all that, you sound *very* sure."

"As sure as a man can be about a thing."

She stopped pacing long enough to try and meet his eye. When he wouldn't meet hers, she continued.

Chad looked up from the photos and narrowed his gaze at the both of them, then spun the laptop to face himself and started to move through the open tabs, one by one.

"He's recruiting," Abby continued.

"It's not him," Victor insisted.

"*They're* recruiting. That's what we know. That's why they took in Alice... any word from Alice?"

Chad looked up.

"She sent her morning call-in code, nothing else," Victor said.

Abby nodded. "They're recruiting. People don't recruit for nothing, without purpose."

"Religions do. Cults, they do. Recruiting is an end onto itself."

She knelt down so that they were at eyelevel, her hands in the space between them, almost pleading. "Not like this, though. Not out of nowhere. This is pushing *hard*. This is a push. There's a goal in mind. You've been watching for them... right?" She paused, leaning in and coaxing a response. She waited for his nod, got it, then nodded herself enthusiastically. "Right, you have. That's why you went down to see Gavin. Eyes wide, I get it now. So, you've been watching. And you haven't seen any sign of them... so that means they're only recently back. It's a push. A hard push. A push means a goal, something attainable. We figure that out, we can do an end around."

Victor nodded, slowly.

Chad looked up from the laptop, closing it as he stood. He turned to Victor, stepped away from the bed, and glowered. "You fucking idiot."

Abby's head snapped around to meet him.

Far Outside Payson

Alice stepped around the corner at the back of The Manor again, touching the wall next to the door tentatively. She paused, bit her lip, then turned back to check that she wasn't followed.

The screen door that led out to the greenhouse, and the world beyond, loomed a scant few feet from her. It billowed and shook in some unfelt breeze, not even closed taut. It teased her, beckoning.

She swallowed hard, then stepped forward into it.

Motel 83, The Past

"I don't get it," Victor huffed, flipping through photographs on his bed. "None of the missing kids look like the kids we saw there. Not a one."

Tash strummed her finger against her lips, staring at her laptop screen. Her chat window was full-screened, and she was watching as the spinning icon spun.

Victor held up a picture of a young blonde girl with a ponytail askew to one side. She smiled at the camera the way young teens did in school photos: never quite fully, never quite whole-heartedly. He ground his teeth as he made eye contact with her through the gap of the years, she only meeting his scantly, and off-centred.

The laptop chimed, and a moment later, Victor heard Tash intake a breath sharply.

Motel 83, The Present

"Chad," Abby hissed, standing between the two men even as Victor rose to his feet.

"Stop it, Abby," Chad snapped, then jammed two fingers into the air in Victor's direction. "He's an idiot. He hasn't been straight with us since minute one... since *day* one. He lies and he's a hypocrite and still you stand by him."

"He didn't do anything wrong," she said through clenched teeth.

"Abby," Victor said, starting low.

"I don't believe that!" Chad shouted. "He kept this from us. He kept this from us for a reason. He held things back and now... Alice is there. Alice is there in the middle of this -- this hell." He paused, breathing heavily and hotly. "We are going. *Now*. We're getting Alice and those kids out of there."

"No," Victor stressed, his voice rising to its commanding tone for the first time in what felt like forever. "You're angry, I get that. But we will not storm in like some... some Wild West movie. I don't want the child to be found dead." He paused. "It's happened before."

Chad leaned his head back. He almost smiled, but stopped himself, though Abby saw it. "Hoho, ho. Ho. That's rich, that is rich coming from you. The shit you've pulled, and now you're telling me you've gotten a child killed. That is *rich*."

"Chad," Abby said again, turning from Victor and stepping closer to him.

Far Outside Payson

Alice stepped up to the mound of dirt, the sun low in the eastern sky and giving it low, orange-tinted shadows. It was a small mound, smaller than it had seemed from above: barely two feet across and only four feet in length.

At the head of the mound was a small, smooth stone, barely rising above the apex of the dirt it marked. There was a name on it, etched in the same font and style as had been the name on the door back in The Manor.

She heard the sound of Marcus' footsteps only when he was beside her.

Motel 83

"We need to find that girl," Victor hissed, stepping up behind Abby until she was the only thing that separated him and Chad. "The rest are too far gone, but the girl: we could save the girl. We can stop this before it keeps going. Before it poisons another generation."

Chad laughed, though this time it was not a mocking laugh. It was a genuine, full laugh.

"What?" Victor asked. His eyes were narrowed menacingly at first, but as Chad's laughter continued, they softened. "What is it?"

Abby turned to face Chad.

"You think you're so smart," Chad smirked. He was still laughing, but it was devoid of any humor. "But you're

just like them. So caught up in your own point of view --
in your own zealotry -- that you can't see the forest for
the trees." He turned Victor's laptop toward the three of
them. It was open to the video feed they'd taken during
Carla's tour of The Manor, paused on a still shot of all the
youths sitting on the couch.

Victor squinted. "What? I don't --"

"Come on, army boy. What do you do with a new recruit to take away what makes them *them*? What's the first
thing -- the *first* thing you do? What's the thing you've
been looking for and couldn't see as a result?" He waited
a moment, then plunged his finger toward the screen. It
landed on the girl with no hair, her head shaved cue-ball
bald.

Victor stared at it for a long moment, then swallowed.
"Madison Williams."

Abby stopped dividing them and leaned forward, her
mouth agape.

"If you'd been straight with us, I might have noticed
before now that she was still wearing her team colours."
He let his finger linger down towards her slender frame,
and the remnants of a green soccer jersey that poked out
from under the jacket she wore.

Victor winced, then sighed and nodded.

Chad moved the hand that had pointed out Madison
to be open between them. "Keys."

Far Outside Payson

"We don't leave them here when we leave," Marcus
said. He stood in the stiff desert breeze next to Alice. Despite her willing him not to, he allowed his hand to fall

from the shovel he'd brought with him and clasp to hers. "I've seen places where they do that. Ghosts towns where the dead are just... left. Forever."

She tried to swallow and nod, but it got caught in her throat.

"We love them until we reach our destination. Until they can join us, back on Our Land."

She nodded again, fighting to keep her composure.

Beyond the cleft of the first mound were rows of mounds. They were unevenly spaced, but there were at least five rows back with at least ten mounds in a row, save for that first one. And all of them, one and all, were no more than four feet in length.

They were child's graves.

Motel 83

Chad stepped out of the motel room door and made a beeline for the El Dorado.

"Wait," Victor said, stepping out of the room behind him.

Chad spun around: "No, waiting is what we've done. Waiting is being chicken-shit because you've dealt with these pricks before and got your ass handed to you. Maybe if there'd been a little *less* waiting, we wouldn't be here right now. Right now!"

Victor paused and sighed, reaching Chad and taking the keys back from him. "You're right." He nodded. "Let's go." He stepped around to the driver's side door of the El Dorado, and got in.

∞

Motel 83, The Past

"Tasha?" Victor said, rising off of the bed and staring at her.

Her face was caught in the glow of the computer's glare, as if it held her and she couldn't look away.

"Tasha?" he repeated, placing an arm on her shoulder.

Her gaze snapped to him, as though he'd teleported across the room. "I... he found the match."

"He matched Melquist to someone in the offender registry?" Victor prodded, leaning forward. "Or the child, you matched the child to a missing person?"

"Yes," Tash whispered, then shook her head. "No."

He squinted.

"The girl -- Sample One -- has... half the alleles in common with a... ah... with a teen girl that went missing some three years ago."

Victor winced. "Half? Half alleles doesn't --"

"And the other half in common with Sample Two."

He pulled back. "You can't be saying --"

She nodded. "Gordon Melquist is their father."

CHAPTER 37

Far Outside Payson, The Present

The El Dorado pushed through the trees the led to The Manor, bumping and rocking along divots and mounds that were only meant to be traversed by foot or by bikes. The car bucked so hard as it moved out of the way of a large branch that Victor, sans seatbelt, was thrust up into the plush ceiling of the jar, jamming his neck.

"Push harder!" he yelled.

In the passenger's seat next to him, Chad had both his arms extended, fingers outstretched. "What?"

"Push it! Now!"

"That's... that's not how my powers work!"

"You don't know how your power's work!" he barked, pushing down on the gas and making the car squeal to life. There was a long scraping sound as chunks of branches dug into the paint on either side of the red car.

"Just do it!" Abby screamed from the back. She reached out and clutched Chad's shoulder, half for support and half to brace herself against the rollicking of her seat.

The car screamed to a halt, twisting and jolting to

one side and coming to a stop less than a foot away from Chad's motorcycle.

All three of them stared at it wide-eyed as the dust settled.

"Lucky," Abby said.

Chad opened the door and walked around to his bike. He stepped around it, then placed his whole palm on the side of it. "It's cold," he said, matter-of-factly. "It hasn't been run in hours." He turned toward The Manor.

It stood vacant, a shell of what it had been. All the doors and windows were swinging and open, each one of them showing hollowed, un-shadowed rooms inside. Chad turned, looking around the lot. "I don't get it... What's happened?" He turned to the side of the house. There were several long, winding skids in the otherwise pristine lawn. He stepped closer to them, feeling the freshness and dampness of the mud that made them. "Victor?"

"I'm checking," he answered, digging out his phone. "Her Phone-Finder is still on. She's not here."

Abby winced. She stepped away from the car and walked closer to Chad, her gaze swinging high to the top of The Manor. Smoke was billowing out of its top, from behind. "Victor..." she said, almost to herself.

Chad looked to where she was staring, then followed the trail of dragged mud. He stepped slowly at first, then accelerated into a jog. She followed him.

The greenhouse was burning, the air thick with melting plastic as it flayed in the air, unraveled from its moorings and catching the rest of The Manor alight in patchy, uneven flareups that were just as likely to burn out as to cause damage.

Across from them was a large patch of field with shallow, rectangular holes hastily dug, like gashes torn in the earth by vengeful claws. All of the dragged lines of dirt and grime began at the holes, coming together and forming one gnash like spools of thread.

"Victor," Chad said again, stepping up to the row of holes that -- even with their markers plucked out -- were unmistakably graves -- and turning around. His face was white.

"She's on the move, on the highway," Victor said, stepping around the corner as the blue dot on his phone updated. "I know where they're going."

Alice fell from the car as it rolled to a stop, her face smeared with mud so crimson that it looked like blood. She hit the solid gravel of the driveway, and before the impact was even complete, she vomited, forcing up the bacon and eggs she'd been fed that morning. She gasped for air as the rest of the car opened their doors and stepped out.

She turned to watch them exit, Marcus looking at her with something that resembled pity, but wasn't.

Hanging out of the door she'd fallen out of hung the battered and decomposed remains of a corpse: wrapped in thick, translucent plastic but identifiable as such all the same. She bit back a scream as empty eye sockets stared at her and she stared back, their skull seeming too small to house them properly.

"You're weak," Carla said, stepping out of the driver's seat. She was slathered in crimson mud as well. It covered her and dressed her, making all her clothes uniform. It was smeared across her cheeks like warpaint, cheeks that were turned upward in a broad, genuine smile for the first time in what felt like eons. She didn't address Alice when she spoke, stepping around to her but never taking her eyes off the building in front of them. "You'll never get anywhere being weak, that's what He taught us. You *have* to be strong to survive. Only the strong survive to pass on their strength."

She beamed up at the red brick building in front of her, how it stood strong against the sun and absorbed its strength. The grass around it grew green and lush, as though it empowered the very earth around it. She stepped forward, imagining she could feel the heat of the stone on her upturned face. "Only the strong make it to Our Land."

Alice threw up again, then wiped her mouth with her arm as she composed herself. Through matted, sweat-laden hair, she looked up at the house and found her room, looking out over the driveway. Her jacket was still hung in the window, looking down on her like a spectre.

They were at the Infinity House.

CHAPTER 38

Motel 83, The Past

Victor sat on the edge of his bed in the Motel 83, the blue of the moon filtering in through the curtains and bathing his bare back in light. He took several long, deep breaths as he stared into the darkness, the subtle hint of his shadow on the wall barely distinguishable from the deep black around it. His muscles ached with tension, unease that had started in his jaw and spread downward as he'd attempted sleep. It now rested just under the fascia of his neck and upper back, burning there like hot jelly.

Tasha was asleep next to him, the curve of her shoulder white in the light from the window. She moved in her sleep in a way uncharacteristic for her, shifting and changing uncomfortably.

The police had taken their statement but had been unable to act. So they'd gone higher, to the state police... who had taken their statement but had been unable to act. There were no missing people, they said. There couldn't be a missing person's investigation without a missing person. He'd tried to explain the DNA evidence but had run into trouble attempting to explain where he had gotten it and where he had gotten it processed.

Tash had broken a lamp when they got home. She'd taken it in the palm of her hand and forced it against the wall again and again until her hand met drywall. She hadn't thrown it; she had held it to the last. Miraculously, none of its sharp bits had ended up in her hand: he'd checked. He'd never seen her quite that angry, not even in Turkey. Not even in Country.

She had reached for a second lamp, but he'd stopped her. Not long after that, they'd attempted sleep and she found it right away. She'd always dealt with stress that way: it expended her energy, a depressor rather than an energizer. He envied her that.

He envied her much.

He turned over his shoulder, his dry hair falling over his strong shoulders and ample chest. His scruff scraped against his leathery neck with each breath as he watched her, and how her breath refused to match his. Her breathing was haggard and trialed, the breath of someone fighting adrenaline rushes. He brought his burned left hand up in front of his face, watching the way the moonlight glistened off the slithering lines of aloe as he flexed it.

He sighed, then slowly got to his feet, careful not to disturb the bed and wake her. He got dressed without a sound, in a way he hadn't had to do since he was on guard shifts with the military. He marched when he stepped, stepping in time with a rhythm only he could hear as he got on his coat and stepped out the door toward his car.

Victor started the engine while Tash was between breaths. She didn't stir, even as he pulled out onto the highway that led towards Payson.

∞

Outside Payson, The Present

Chad's motorbike screamed past several cars as he

rode the yellow line between streams of traffic, nearly out-
racing the sound of blaring horns as he flew past. There
were screams and curses -- he heard them coming at him
as people moved from his path -- but his engine kept most
of those at bay as well.

His speedometer passed ninety-five as he rounded
a steep bend, his bike sliding down almost onto its side
with the inertia of it and sending him into oncoming traffic. The tire treads skipped, then caught on the pavement
and he bolted forward again, slipping between a classic
Mustang and the grill of a tractor trailer.

He ground his teeth together until the only sound he
could hear above the strain of his engine was the enamel
snapping.

Alice opened the door to Victor's study, quickly looking over her shoulder.

She forced her way in, pushing past the books he'd
piled up next to his desk until his drawers could open.
She pulled the third one down open, dug both hands in
deep, and pulled out three large books, then a solid wood-
en box.

The box was locked. She huffed, checked over her
shoulder again as someone walked by the room, then
smashed the edge of the box against the edge of his writing desk. Both splintered, sending shards of wood into
her hair. Some slid through the tender flesh of her hand.

On the third strike the box opened, revealing a service
revolver and several bullets displayed in lush red felt.

She bit her lip, loaded the gun, and hid it in the back

of her pants.

Chad twisted his bike to the side as it slowed, bringing it to an abrupt halt alongside the blue Ford Pinto with wood-panel siding that had started all of this. He kicked the stand down and cut the engine in one smooth, quick motion, then got out and looked at it.

The back was piled high with bodies, each in their own sealed plastic bag. The bags were sooty and slathered in mud: they'd been buried that way, he realized. In the bags. Ready for transport. Gaping mouths looked back at him through the mud-splattered windows of the Pinto. He paid them only an instant's pause, then stepped past and up the main driveway he knew so well.

Carla and Marcus were sitting on the back deck, not far from the position that he and Abby had found themselves in mere days before.

"Get the fuck out of my chair," he said, marching up to them with his fists clenched at his sides. He stepped like he wanted to walk through them, like someone who wanted to punctuate their motion with a strike at the end. He stopped himself a few feet from the both of them. "Where's Alice?"

Carla raised an eyebrow to him quizzically. "Inside. Probably in her room, which is still her room."

Chad stopped, narrowing his eyes at her.

"You can see for yourself if you want." She cocked her head towards the sliding doors that led into his home.

He twisted his jaw, then stepped past her into the living room.

Carla turned her gaze to Marcus, cocking her head again. He got up out of Chad's chair and followed him inside.

There were pictures on the wall that never had been, but that looked like they belonged there. Chad swallowed when he saw them, catching a child as he hung a gold frame against the mauve wall where their television used to be. It sat on the floor by the boy's feet, unplugged but undamaged. Three girls worked together to move a couch, from its place on the wall to alongside of a pillar in the centre of the room, using the couch to bisect it.

He shook his head, forced himself to ignore them as they ignored him, moving about their tasks like worker-ants. He made his way to the stairs, passing three teen-age girls as he did. They were carrying boxes and heading down towards the basement.

He leaned his head up toward the top of the stairwell. "Alice?" he called.

There was a sharp pain at the base of his skull and suddenly the stairs were coming towards him.

Marcus stood over him, holding a large plank of wood that had once been a part of their banister. He threw it to the ground even as Chad groaned, starting to rise, then grabbed him by the scruff of the neck and started pulling him up the stairs. "Lucky to be alive," he said under his breath.

CHAPTER 39

Outside Payson, The Past

Victor pulled the El Dorado up to the secluded, foliage-entombed home of Gordon Melquist in the dead of night. He pulled up behind the squad car that was parked in the driveway, blocking it in. The light from the house itself -- every light was seemingly on and looking out through glowing window eyes -- reflected off the slick sheen of both cars, making them shimmer.

Victor gripped the steering wheel with both hands until his knuckles turned white and let out several deep, chest-shaking sighs. He pressed the arch of his nose against the leather of the wheel, turning it into a mask that made his eyelids produce colour on their backs.

He sighed once more, then forced himself to lean back against his headrest, surveying the grounds.

On a white plastic chair just off from two sliding doors toward the back of the house sat the large visage of Gordon Melquist. He was leaned against the chair with his feet up on one another, one arm cocked in the air while the other held a beer so cold that it spewed condensation into the desert night.

In the low light of the evening, Victor could see the light play off the curves in his smile, catching off the folds of his cheeks, fat and happy. His jaw clenched as Melquist raised his glass to him.

He got out of the car without taking his eyes off of Melquist, burrowing deep holes through the hot air and into his fatty cheeks. He slammed the door and tucked his shirt, as black as the night around him. His middle looked invisible from afar, just a wild head of hair and two lumbering, massive arms floating up the field of grass, like the disembodied ghost of a Viking warrior.

The grass sunk under his feet, the soil wet and sponged with moisture. He felt it seep into his boots with every step he took toward that back stoop, the water plentiful but warm from the heat of the earth beneath it: impossible, yet here.

"I hear you've been talking to my friends down at the station," Melquist said, taking a swig from his drink. It was without label, and there were no remnants of peeled glue or paper where one had been.

There were two girls on the chairs next to him, both of them so strikingly blonde that their hair glowed against the tapestry of the night. One was small -- no more than six or seven -- and had a skinned knee that was starting to heal. The other was older, at least sixteen, and sat uncomfortably close to Melquist. She was on the chair across from him, his leg resting alongside her and connecting up the length of her.

Victor watched this, lingering on the stretch of flesh where both forms met, then forced his gaze to the child, then finally to Melquist's eyeline. He nodded slowly. "I did."

Melquist's smile broadened, a thin thing that bisected his face like a knife-stroke. "How'd that go for you?"

"I wouldn't be in the same room as you if it had gone

well."

Melquist clucked, then took a long slug of his drink. "Try the state police next time, don't bother with the local PD when you're pushing against local PD. It gets people's backs up. The Blue Shield, annat."

Victor winced, his lip curling slightly before he could force it back into position.

Melquist smiled, bringing his feet around and away from the young girl across from him. He planted both feet firmly on the patio with a heavy slumping sound. Despite the rest of his attire being relaxed, he kept the large, heavy boots from his work on. They stood across from Victor's military outlet boots, facing off as he rose to his feet. He laughed. "I'm guessing you did that, though. From the look of you."

Again, Victor's mouth twitched.

"Can I get you a beer? We brew at home."

His lip raised, and he shook his head. "No."

Melquist nodded. "You're not from around here, so this is hard for you." He turned, stepped around the chair he'd been on, and toward the centre of the deck. "You see something you think is wrong, and you feel like you got to do something about it. You think you can do something about it, but you never once stopped to think why other people can't. Why other people didn't see it." He pointed the neck of the bottle at Victor to address him.

"Oh no, I see it. I see that all too clearly."

"It's small towns," Melquist continued, as if Victor hadn't spoken. "You get a small group of people together, they want to protect each other. Nobody wants to air out nobody else's dirty laundry because everyone's got laundry of their own. That pup down at the office you probably reported me to? He almost killed his wife last year in a domestic." He took a swig of his beer, then *pointed at the teenage girl sat at his side. "Hell, her father did too before she come here."*

The girl pursed her lips tightly and nodded with solemnity.

Victor turned to her. For a moment he thought he saw something in her, a spark, but it was gone before he had the chance to identify it and she returned to the same dull gray forward stare that all the children in the house maintained. He looked away and back to the house. All the lights were still on, but each window was suddenly now host to a silhouette: solid black shadows that looked down upon the unfolding action on the deck beneath them.

"People, they looked. They went out in their fields." Melquist winked. "But they didn't look too hard."

Victor turned back to the girl, who nodded again. There was a sparkle in the dark of the night that drew his attention, and it was only now that he noticed a solid gold band on her left ring finger. He took in air sharply, then turned back to Melquist. "Cline Cassidy was here, then?"

Melquist nodded. "We'll have her out. Things take time, you know how it is."

Victor nodded with pursed lips, then took two short steps towards Melquist. He backed up a pace on Victor's approach, keeping some distance between them. He tensed, but relaxed when Victor turned on his heel, crouching to approach both the girls. "You two can get out of here."

Melquist laughed, a sputtering thing that brought the foam of beer from his lips.

Each of the girls furrowed their brows and looked at each other, then back at Victor.

"You can leave. Go to my car, go to the main road. I'll catch

up with you before too long and get you home." He turned back to the house and the row of silhouettes, raising his voice. "You can all go home."

The teen girl swallowed, looking behind her to the El Dorado, to Melquist, back to Victor.

His eyes became soft as he searched for something in her, something besides the gray slate nothingness that he'd seen to this point. It did not come. "I can get you out of here safely," he reassured, his voice almost a whisper. "I can get you home."

"We are home," came the small voice behind him.

He turned to see the girl with the scraped knee staring up at him. She spoke with the sort of determination that only a child could, speaking matter-of-factly and with indignation. With pride and with knowledge, with indoctrination.

At the sight of her blue eyes meeting his gaze, Victor felt his shoulders collapse. He let out a deep sigh that he had been holding in since he got out of the El Dorado. A moment later, he felt Melquist's heavy hand patting the nape of his neck.

"Come," he said simply, moving his hand to Victor's shoulder. His grasp was warm and clammy, but avuncular. There was compassion in it, and it made Victor's muscles tense again and coil. Melquist turned to both of the girls. "Come." The girls arose to their feet and Melquist stepped away from Victor, walking back towards the house with the both of them behind him in lockstep. His heavy boots kept time and they followed it.

Victor stared at the supple, moist ground of the grass that surrounded the house. It was dark in the night air, but still seemed to glow a healthy, chloroform green. He forced himself to swallow, his own saliva getting caught in his throat, then turned and followed Melquist's line. Despite himself, his boots kept time.

The sliding doors led into a large living room, bisected by a couch placed next to a solid load-bearing banister. There were family photos on the walls surrounding them, each of Melquist. They weren't arranged in any chronological order, but it was easy to put them in one as Melquist's flock grew. With each photo more smiles were added to the family, but each time only one smile was genuine: all others were masks.

In one, Victor saw the teen girl he'd met outside, clutching a round, full belly. She hugged it with both hands proudly, the glimmering ring on her hand displayed forward.

There was a bell hanging from the far wall, near the hall that would take them through to the rest of the house. When Melquist reached it he rang it, once.

More girls entered the room from all sides, filtering in like water into a sinking ship. They stared at him blankly, not looking at him so much as through him. Many were blonde, and they looked at his blondeness with curiosity: so much like what they were used to, but different at the same time in a way they couldn't quite pin.

There were two boys, both of them younger. One stepped up to Melquist and hugged at his knee, making a long cooing noise as Melquist's hand found his way to his head.

"Do you see it yet?" Melquist asked, smiling.

"I do," Victor replied in a hushed tone.

Melquist's smile grew, spreading to be from ear to ear. "I'm not sure you do. But I can tell that you can... I can tell that you have it in you to see."

Victor raised his gaze to meet Melquist's, fury burning behind it.

"There it is. That's it. That's... the look." He stepped forward slightly, closing the gap between them in a way he hadn't yet. "That's the look of a man who is sure. Of a man who believes in what he's doing." He clucked his tongue, waving his finger in the space between them. "You met someone once who made you see through the mist of the world. Someone who made you believe in something, something that the rest of the world missed. And that belief has brought you here." He tapped his boot against the hard floor. "But it has brought them here, too."

Victor turned, looking out over the amassed blank faces.

"Come," Melquist said again, turning his back on Victor. All of the children began to follow him. They walked slowly so as not to surpass him, lumbering like the dead. Victor followed the line, joining it near its end, where the girl with the skinned knee walked.

For an instant, he debated scooping her into his arms, turning and racing for the door and the El Dorado beyond, and escaping. Escaping with just one, at least.

Instead he followed them to the other side of the house, around the other side of a large staircase. There was a door behind it and Melquist opened it and turned on a light -- one of those bulbs that hung from a long wire to the ceiling, precariously, and started down the long stairwell under the stairs, into the cellar.

Victor watched as each girl braced themselves on the frame of the door before following Melquist down, watching how many of them had rings on similar to the teen girl outside.

It was most of them.

CHAPTER 40

Outside Payson, The Present

The El Dorado pulled up as far into its normal parking space as it could, behind the mud-slathered Ford Pinto with wooden panels and behind the motorcycle, still teetering on the edge of falling over. Victor got out of the driver's side door without even cutting the engine, and Abby got out beside him, her hair billowing in the hot air that was building to the point of storm.

Carla stood on the front lawn, her legs wide and her arms crossed before her. Her people stood behind her, arching back as though she were the cusp of an acute triangle. They glared at them with menace, with a hate that belied the gray nothing that lurked just beyond the sheen of their eyes.

"Where are they, Carla?" Victor called, his voice firm and bellowing and echoing off the stone walls of his home. "Give me back my people and we can talk this out."

"Your people came onto Our Land to try and subvert us. To our Holy Land."

"Just let them out and we'll talk. Let them out and give

me the girl. Madison. Let me get her back to her parents, and we can --"

Carla laughed, finally letting her arms fall from their crossed position and running her nails through her hair. "You still don't get it, do you, Devil? Even after all this time." She smiled from ear to ear, a thin slit along the centre of her face. Her lips were thin -- like his had been. "You can only see it from where you stand. You think you've grown... but I see you. When you came to this very spot to see Gordon Melquist, he was right about you. You were a *follower*. And now you're a *leader*," she bobbed her head toward Abby, "but you still haven't learned anything. Only you, Devil, could do what you've done and not change. Not grow."

"I've grown a fair bit," Victor said, almost under his breath.

"Victor?" Abby hissed, as the crowd gathered around them inched forward.

"Gordon's gone, Carla," he called, his voice definitive. "Stop this."

"We are all Gordon Melquist," Carla said, her voice just as loud and just as definitive. She raised her hands slowly, encompassing them all until they were straight out from her shoulders and the wind caught in her hair. "We all carry a part of him in us."

The hair on Victor's arms and neck stood on end, and Abby noticed.

"Fuck them," Carla said under her breath.

Her forces moved forward with a unified scream.

Motel 83, The Past

Tash woke with a start, shifting back to look at the side of the bed that she knew, somehow, was empty.

She arose quickly, standing next to the bed and surveying the room around her. The motel room was empty, there was no sound of shower or sink running. There were no boots by the door to the lot outside, only oblongs of dried mud where they'd been.

"Fuck," she cursed, grabbing her shirt.

Outside Payson, The Present

-click-

Alice pulled back the hammer on the service revolver and raised it at Marcus. He was pulling Chad along the upstairs hallway between their rooms, his hoodie becoming a noose that was turning his cheeks a bluish hue. Madison Williams was next to him, huddled against the wall, her bald head catching the bright light from above.

"Drop him," Alice sneered, aiming the gun squarely at his middle. "Now."

Marcus released his grip on Chad's cuff, letting him fall to the floor, raising both his hands. He smiled from ear to ear, a thin smile that bisected his face along its middle.

Chad gasped for air, rolling to his side and scuttling to the opposite side of the hall quickly.

"You don't want to do this, Alice," Marcus smiled with a silky-smooth voice, stepping forward. "This isn't the way and you know it."

"Stay where the fuck you are," Alice snapped, bit-ing the air. She waved the gun as though it were a finger, thrusting it at him. "You stay right the fuck there."

Madison looked on with widened eyes.

"I've been talking to your parents," Alice said, addressing her. "They miss you. They want you to come--"

Marcus pushed forward, his shoulders connecting with Alice and forcing them both to the ground. Chad gasped for air then found his footing, piling forward and kicking at Marcus' side until he fell off of her, rolling to his side and bringing the gun up, pointing it at Chad.

Chad backed up to the wall, but there was still less than a meter between the barrel of the gun and his chest.

Madison took a step forward toward the action, hesitantly.

"You're just like him, Devil," Marcus said, sneering with a distorted, monstrously curled lip. "You think you're better, but you're not. You're --"

Alice found her footing and raised to her feet between them, just as the gun went off. Madison screamed. Chad bellowed, his feet in front of him before he could think, his fist colliding with Marcus' cheek. There was a snap of bone and Chad's hand shrieked in pain, his pinky jamming back into the knuckle and breaking, but Marcus' head snapped back and he turned into the doorjamb of Abby's room, coming up solid and then falling to the floor.

The pistol fell away to Madison's feet. She let it stay where it lay.

Chad turned, panicked sweat streaming down his brow, and found Alice on the floor beside him. There was a large hole in her chest and blood expanded into the fabric around it, the burn of the gunpowder blossoming out from the hole like flower pedals.

"Jesus," Chad cursed, pulling back the shirt to unveil Alice's blood-soaked chest. He laid his hands on her flat, trying to find the wound and stop the bleeding. "Call an ambulance," he yelled both at Madison and at no one. At anyone.

His hands fumbled, trying to find the wound but finding little. He brought his hands away, covered in blood, removing most of it from her pale chest. The wound, while still not closed, was mostly so. The bleeding had stopped. "What... wait, what..."

Alice smiled at him, groaning as she rose to a sitting position with great effort. "You forget why I got volunteered for this gig?" she said wryly, wiping some of the blood from her exposed chest. She turned and glared at Marcus, who was still unconscious on the floor, then at Madison and the gun at her feet. "We're just lucky that was me and not you."

Chad nodded, his cheeks slack as he still pieced the events together. He turned to Madison and eyed her wearily, then picked up the gun.

All three of them made their way toward the stairs. They could hear the screams.

A girl spat in Abby's face as she reached for her neck, Abby backing up until she was against the El Dorado. All at once her training took over, and she could see targets on the girl: like targeted pressure points on the dummies that had lined the dojos at Port Haven. She curled her hand into a fist, first three knuckles extended, and jammed them forward into the girl's cervical plexus. She screamed and stepped back, and Abby pushed forward with two more strikes, each to the girl's right cheek. She hit the grass, conscious, but did not get back up, and was quickly replaced by another young woman.

"Stop it!" Victor bellowed, pushing back a large male.

It took Abby a moment to process that he was talking to her, not to the legions that swarmed them. She struck the girl in front of her and pushed forward, turning to Victor quizzically.

At the house, Alice and Chad stepped out of the sliding back doors, with Madison only a step behind. Alice's shirt was bloodied, and she stepped as though it were hard to get air, but her brow was furrowed and resolved.

"You can't hurt them," Victor yelled at her, pushing back against the youths that attacked him and keeping them at bay. "It'll only make things worse."

"Hypocrite," Carla sneered, back behind the masses but stepping forward towards Victor at a slow pace.

Abby was pushed back against the car by a large man who looked like he could have been a football player in another life. She kicked out at him once, twice, three times before he finally backed up and she could get air again. "I don't see how this ends then, Victor!"

He ground his jaw, clenching it as his broad limbs kept his attackers at arm's length.

A shot rang out across the air, echoing off of everything.

All eyes turned to Chad, standing between the chairs on the back deck, with smoke billowing out of the gun he held high into the sky. He lowered slowly, leveling it directly at Carla, who hung back to the rear of the mob closest to him.

"Call them off," he said with authority.

Carla smiled, that thin smile that stretched from ear to ear. Melquist's smile. "Just because you're controlled doesn't mean I control --"

He fired again, erupting a tuft of grass at her feet and sending it in all directions. "Last warning."

She spread her arms into a wide cross again, her smile never wavering. "I know my place in this... do you know yours?"

CHAPTER 41

Chad held the gun barrel flat to his eyeline, staring down it as its crosshairs matched the curvature between Carla Melquist's breasts. She was smiling, her arms wide, while behind her her flock was already resuming their encroachment on Victor and Abby.

He bit his lip, cursed, and put first pressure on the trigger.

Sirens blared through the air as a police car pulled up behind the El Dorado, forcing two followers out of its way and away from Abby. Two more cars followed, their light bathing the trees in red and blue, boxing in people as they started to scatter.

Chad raised his gun to the air instinctively as Carla turned away from him for the first time since he'd come out, her face finally growing pale in the glowing light of the police cars.

Hands were raised from Victor and Abby's throats, finding their way into the air.

Chad knelt, slowly bringing his gun to the grass and then dropped it as the police approached. "What the hell is this?" he mouthed to himself. "Not that I'm complaining."

Alice clicked her tongue, then reached into her pants pocket and produced her phone. It was alive with text alerts, blaring out at her in purple and green from missed calls and missed alerts.

Where are you? -- Lindsay

What's happening? -- Lindsay

Missed Call -- Lindsay

We've called the Police -- Lindsay

They've tracked your phone -- Lindsay

We're coming -- Lindsay

Missed Call -- Lindsay

Be safe - Lindsay

She smiled, then showed the screen to Chad as the police surrounded Carla's followers. Some were already in handcuffs. As if on cue, the squad car to the rear opened both its back doors, and Cliven and Lindsay stepped out into the midmorning sun. "Madison?" Lindsay called, looking over the blond children that looked, at a glance, so much like her own.

"Mom!" Madison yelled, pushing past Alice and Chad. She ran down the grassy knoll that divided them with bare feet, the moisture from the impossible grass seeping into her soles, before finally finding her way into her mother's arms. Her father joined them a moment later, his aged hand cupping her bare scalp gingerly and holding it to his breast.

"Alright then," Chad said with exhausted, exasperated breath. He nodded, stepping forward towards Carla. Alice turned her heard from Madison's reunion with her parents and followed him. "One last loose end."

Carla knelt on the ground, prone before him as he approached, a uniformed officer applying his handcuffs. They were the plastic zip kind; the metal ones had already been run out.

From behind her, Victor approached her as well, followed by Abby. The two fractured halves stepped towards Carla at their middle, like an original approaching its reflection in a funhouse mirror. They met just as Carla was being pulled to her feet. She was being read her rights, but she ignored them, her vengeful glare alternating between Victor and Chad.

"I didn't do anything," she snarled, her lip curling. "This is on you, Devil. All of this. All of it! Every last part of this is on you. Hypocrite!" She stepped back towards them, and the officer had to hold her back. "They're locking me away for breaking into my house, but you they let go? You? Murderer?" She spat, even as the officer helped her head into the squad car.

Chad squinted, turning toward Victor, who continued to watch until the car drove Carla away.

Outside Payson, The Past

The cellar was dark, only a single shaded light loomed overhead, dangling on a nerve-like string. It swung back and forth, changing the light and casting deep, changeling shadows on the brick and mortar and dried wood all around.

Melquist stood in its middle, his shadow a tiny thing below him, his arms outstretched to their fullest. The children were circled around him at the edge of the darkness, the light catching in their hair and making them appear to glow. The girl with the skinned knee was there, Victor saw, behind Melquist and to his left. Her hair was so blonde it looked white in the light, the way some children did but never adults.

"Do you see?" Melquist asked, stepping toward Victor.

As if on cue, all of the children knelt at the edge of the light. The older ones crossed themselves, the younger ones tried to in an attempt that would have been comical in a different situation. Victor flinched when they did this, all moving as one in his peripheral vision.

"I see," he said, his voice hushed. "I see quite clearly."

"There's an old saying," Melquist smiled, his voice taking on the affectation of a wizened priest. "Kill one man, you're a murderer --"

"I'm familiar with it," Victor growled.

"-- Kill a million men, you're a king," he continued, as if Victor hadn't spoken. "Kill them all, a God." He stepped, lightly, to the edge of the circle, placing a gentle hand on the blonde girl's head. He addressed her only briefly, his attention remaining on Victor. "I've never much cared for that. It seems needlessly... violent."

Victor narrowed his eyes.

"God didn't get to be God by destroying. That vengeful God, he exists -- but he was already God, then. You don't get to be God via destruction: you get to be God by creation." He smiled, spreading his arms wide again.

Victor's lip curled, and he made no effort to hide it.

Melquist spread his arms wide again. With each word he spoke he stepped closer and closer to Victor. "Create a single child, you're a father. A dozen, a king. Create them all --"

Victor snapped his arm out, grabbing Melquist by the throat and catching the remainder of his platitude there. Melquist's eyes bulged with surprise as he tried to back up out of Victor's grip, rendered completely around his throat and already squeezing.

Victor's mouth went taut, becoming a tiny line obscured by his matte of hair. As Melquist's feet tried to push him back, Victor went with the motion, standing along with it until he was standing over Melquist, his back flat against the gravel floor.

The light swung wildly overhead, casting shadows and making the men dance... though they remained exactly where they were.

Melquist brought his hands up to Victor's face, clawing and pawing at it, trying to get his fingers into his eyes and mouth and ears but failing, Victor's reach superior. Victor brought his other hand forward, grasping the neck as well and slowly applying even pressure as the blood vessels in Melquist's eyes began to burst, his lips and chin turning red and purple as oxygen was expended and expelled. His eyes bloodshot, and his attempts at striking out at Victor weakened.

"You. Are not. A God," Victor hissed through clenched teeth, spit flying from them and landing on Melquist's motionless cheek. He squeezed one last time, applying all his might and pressure, until he felt the slender bones of Melquist's neck fracture under his pressure. "You're not a God," he said again, plaintively.

He released his hold on Melquist's neck, feeling the flesh loosen beneath his grip. When his hands came away, there were red and black marks where they had been, scouring his neck like tiger stripes.

He sighed and fell to the floor besides Melquist.

The children remained knelt in a circle around the edge

of the light. Most of the older ones were wide eyed... but the smallest of them looked the same as they had before: dead eyes, calm. Without feeling. They turned their attention to Victor as he looked at each of them, his colour and rage seeping from his cheeks.

"He wasn't a God," he mumbled, then, louder: "He was not a God."

Melquist's victims stared back at him, some blankly, some in horror... and some, with a steely resolve.

Outside Payson, The Present

Chad shoved Victor back towards the El Dorado, drawing the attention of the police who had yet to leave. "Hypocrite," he breathed, then repeated, louder: "Hypocrite."

Abby and Alice both stepped forward, Abby to step between Chad and Victor, Alice to hold Chad back.

Victor winced.

"You did this," Chad barked, pointing his chin at Victor as he tried to step around Abby, hardly seeing her for his rage. "That's what you meant back at the hotel. You created this. You killed a man and turned him into... into some kind of martyr."

Abby paused, her hands on Chad's arms. She turned and looked over her shoulder at Victor. "Is that... is that true?"

Victor pursed his lips and said nothing, his eyes to the ground and not meeting anyone else's.

"But you let Jaycee go, didn't you?" Chad snarled, trying to step forward again. "And Kat. Couldn't let her in, she's a murderer. Killed a cult leader! Can't have that. Can't... can't have that."

"You have to be *better* than me," Victor snapped, looking up at Chad from below a furrowed brow. "If I wanted a team no better than me, I'd... I'd..." he paused, looking over the remains of Melquist's followers as they made their way into police cars. He sighed.

Chad loosened and stopped trying to get past Abby. "Fuck this," he said finally, turning back towards the house. "I'm done."

CHAPTER 42

Payson, The Past

Victor stared at the walls of his cell, the bars dissecting them into fourths. Somewhere out of view a clock kept time, snapping away the seconds one by one. He let out a long sigh, then breathed in and got the scent of steeped tea along with the concrete of the cell.

"They aren't laying charges," Tash said, coming around the corner and leaning against the bars of his cell. "Clear case of self-defense, the District Attorney says."

"It wasn't," Victor breathed, his voice barely above a whisper.

"Shhht," she hissed, kneeling down to be at eyelevel with him. "Keep your goddamn voice down with that shit."

His eyes fell to her without his head moving, his expression still and without emotion.

"We'll have to leave forwarding information, which I've done. Agree to come back if there's a trial, which I've said you'll do." She paused. "There won't be one. I've got us flights booked out. Simon's been in touch, there's been news at the border."

Victor nodded, rolling up into a sitting position, his boots coming to a rest firm against the floor. He looked at them: firm and strong and blackened, laced tight. They looked impeccable, like he'd just stepped out of a drill line, the last part of him that did.

He brought his face down onto his hands, held them there for a moment, then wiped them down. There was still mud and grime in the ridges of his fingerprints, and it now lined the pores of his face. He tried to meet Tash's eye but couldn't, his gaze travelling past her to the concrete wall behind: so much like the look behind the eyes of the children he'd found in the cellar. "What about the kids?" he asked, soberly.

Tash nodded. "The ones that were taken are going to their parents. Most of them are of age now, but there'll be counseling. It'll be a hard road, but --"

"It'll be an impossible road."

She stopped short, then swallowed. "The kids... Melquist's kids... they're being sent into the system. Split up, I'm told. To avoid... well, to avoid the things we'd want to avoid."

He nodded, thinking of that bleached blonde girl with the skinned knee, and the way she'd looked at him at the end.

"The house was on public land," Tash continued, though he hadn't asked. "I'm being told they've raised funds from the parents to demolish it. They're going to get what evidence they can, take what they'll need for their casefiles... then just bring it down. Burn it and salt the earth." She paused. "I say good on 'em."

Victor nodded again, then ran his hands through his hair, feeling the power of his fingers as they gripped his scalp.

CHAPTER 43

The air was filled with the flashing lights on police cherries, which lined the parking lot of Epsilon Gamma Nu in swerving, piecemeal formations that made no sense. Maximus observed this from his seat in the back of the second ambulance that had come, a saline drip in his arm slowly removing the fog of alcohol from him. Kincaid was next to him, enough saltwater falling from his eyes to match the slow drip that his own IV was putting in.

Jona stepped away from Herbert Whineguard and walked over to them both, solemnly. One side of his face was bathed in the red from one set of lights, the other in blue. After a moment they switched, but they remained in sync and he remained split, down his middle. "The idiot has been taken in for questioning," he said matter-of-factly, surveying the cluster of police and media around. "He won't be charged, I'm sure, but I've been assured the Chapter is being shut down."

Neither Maximus nor Kincaid responded, and after a moment Jona turned to them and frowned. He pursed his lips, hesitated, then reached out and put a large, firm hand on Kincaid's shoulder. "You did everything you could."

Kincaid shook his head but didn't even look aware he was doing it.

"I'll speak to the headmaster about your accommodations. You needn't have that to worry about at a time like this... we'll take care of you."

"I can't," he started, then snorted.

"It's the least I can do."

"No, I can't stay here. This isn't... he's right. This isn't my box. I tried to fit in a box that wasn't mine and this... this happened."

Maximus looked as though he were going to respond, but Jona cut in. "Of course. Well, wherever you land, I'm sure I can help. A lot of people have owed me things over the years, and I don't mind calling in each and every thing... I'm very high on the board at U of C, and... well, none of this was your fault, remember that."

Kincaid nodded, as Maximus turned to Jona and nodded thankfully. He turned back to the chapter house and eyed it once again, seeing how sinister it really looked in the dark of evening and the red of multiple light-sources below. "Why do places like this even exist anymore?" he wondered aloud.

Jona raised a scant eyebrow. He hummed for a moment, as if unsure if the question were meant to be rhetorical or not. "... The types of bonds places like this are meant to forge *do* still work. Bonds of community and shared fraternity and solidarity, the whole before the self, these are still things that... well, that make society run. Community first, self second. Those bonds still glue people together, and they're the best in place of better bonds." He paused, then placed a hand on both Maximus and Kincaid's shoulders again. "But they're nothing compared to *these* types of bonds."

Maximus took a moment to process that, then nodded, and allowed himself the briefest of smiles.

Kincaid stared at the EGN House for a long, solemn moment. "Can we get some of my things out of there?" he asked, abruptly.

"Of course," Jona said, stepping aside as Maximus helped Kincaid to his feet. Maximus held the hanger with both their saline drips high above their heads and helped him off the ambulance bumper and back toward Epsilon Gamma Nu for the last time.

Jona stepped aside as Maximus helped Kincaid to his feet, and watched as the pair walked back toward Epsilon Gamma Nu for the last time, the red and blue lights from the police and campus security still bathing him in contrasting colours. As he watched them go, Whineguard broke away from his conversation with a local journalist and joined him.

"Are they going to be okay?" Whineguard asked, patting perspiration from his brow with a handkerchief.

"I believe so," Jona said confidently, without turning to look at the small man. "They have each other, and shared turmoil... well, it can be a remarkable catalyst." He paused. "Thank you for making sure this horrid place is closed, by the by."

"My pleasure," said Whineguard, looking around at the house contemptuously, his nostrils curled. "I've no idea why you had me get them in to begin with. And getting young Mister Kincaid's grant withdrawn... Jona, forgive me, but what was the point of all this?"

Jona smiled, as he watched Maximus and Kincaid disappear into the shadows of Epsilon Gamma Nu, their arms around each other and supporting each other.

"Peer bonding."

CHAPTER 44

Los Angeles, The Present

Theo stood on the outskirts of the large, circular crater in the skin of Los Angeles that was Anemone. He stood just above the pools of melted plastic, long since solidified into oblong masses of green and blue that had ceased to resemble the shades they had once represented. He sighed, staring out across it, his hair billowing in the warm California breeze.

The crater was vacant now, the workers having not started for the day. Their equipment remained, locked down but otherwise left to the elements, like husks of bone jutting from the earth.

Between he and the equipment, along the edge of the crater, a dark blonde woman in a white blouse and skirt walked along the edge towards him. She wore a tie that billowed in the wind in time with his hair and showed long, thin legs.

He squinted, thinking of Roberta. Of Simon and Maggie. Of Shane. But mostly, he thought of Black Springs and Port Haven. He turned back through his memories of those places, wondering how many of the memories that made him *him* were manufactured, and how many were real. He remembered the first time he held a paintbrush, and how different Black Springs was in that memory compared to in others.

He knew, more than anything, that he had to warn Abby.

"Hello," the blonde woman said, finally approaching him along the circle's edge.

He snapped out of the well of his mind, returning to reality. She smiled at him broadly and warmly, with thin lips made thick with crimson.

She extended a hand to him.

"Hello," he nodded, taking it and shaking it.

She smiled, then gestured back to the scar in the skin of Los Angeles behind them.

Outside Payson, The Present

Alice sat in the rec room of her home, hearing men stalk about upstairs. She was standing in front of the pool table, the balls still stuck in their random pattern from the game she'd played earlier. The eight ball was nearest her, and she maneuvered it back and forth between her fingers, feeling its weight.

She took out her phone and pressed the screen on again. The wall of text alerts were still there, none of them yet dismissed.

Where are you? -- Lindsay

What's happening? -- Lindsay

Missed Call -- Lindsay

We've called the Police -- Lindsay

They've tracked your phone -- Lindsay

We're coming -- Lindsay

Missed Call -- Lindsay

Be safe -- Lindsay

Now, there was one more, right at the top: Thank you -- Lindsay.

Her mouth warbled. In her mind's eye she saw the graves: the mounds upon mounds of shallow graves that had been dug out along the back of The Manor, then the holes they'd become as Marcus and his team had exhumed the plastic shrink-wrapped bodies from them.

She shook her head, then pushed the pool balls away from her on the table, forcing them one by one back into their holes. She took out her laptop and laid it against the table, turning on the screen and closing anything she'd left open from its last use.

She opened a Search window and began to look for missing children in Arizona, the images of those poorly dug graves still lingering in the back of her mind.

Arizona State Prison

Carla sat at the edge of the bench press, her forehead laden with sweat. The yard was full of women of all different sizes and shapes, each clothed in the same orange jumpsuit, each moving from one corner of the yard to the other.

There was a guard at the yard's middle who looked back and forth at them all as if her head were on a swivel, rarely stopping to linger at anyone. She lingered on Carla, though. And often.

Carla panted, struggling for breath. She brought a bottle of water to her lips, sucked a healthy portion down, then released it and let it pour over her scalp. When she opened her eyes, the guard was watching her.

The uniform reminded her of when she'd been just eight years old, and a man in a very similar uniform had brought her to her new home. It was a foster home. It had been supposed to have been temporary... but wasn't. It had been on the outskirts of Arizona, one of those foster homes where the children ran wild by the dozens and the parents collected their government checks to gamble and drink with.

They were Evangelicals, she remembered. She remembered their oldest natural boy, Dilbert, bringing her to a room and showing her a large, golden cross they'd had hung there. It was massive and oppressive and had the entire room to itself while she shared one with four others.

She'd still been picking at the scab on her knee when he brought her in there, and explained that they -- as a unit, all of the children -- would go there every Sunday to worship. She remembered him asking, almost conversationally, if she knew about God.

She said the same thing then as she did now, as she walked past the guard and over to the table of women beyond her, playing cards and cursing, laughing at each other. She spoke the same words and, for the first time in a long time, felt as justified and fulfilled in saying them as she had that first day in the foster chapel:

"Let me tell you about *my* God."

EPILOGUE

Abby sat on the back deck of her home, kneeling near the fire pit in its centre. It was lit and simmering, just the start of a full flame.

She would not sit on the lawn chairs, not until she had cleaned them properly.

On her knees before her was Victor's photo album, turned to the recently returned photograph of him and Tash, standing in front of a plane and obscuring its name until only the word *free* remained. They were smiling in the photo... but there was something wrong about those smiles. Something she'd learned to recognize from the photos that had lined the walls of The Manor... several of which were now on the floor of her living room, waiting to be handed over to the police.

They were mannequin smiles, she knew now, and as she flicked past the pages and saw Victor and Tash again and again, each time in a different location, she saw them more and more. Only at the end did she see one different, one she thought might, maybe, be a genuine grin from the both of them. There was a third person in that photo:

a young brunette girl, with a smile equally as bright and real and lovely. They were all holding ice cream, their tongues out.

Abby lingered on the photo for only a moment, then closed the album and placed the whole of it into the fire.

She walked up the walkway into the house as she heard it light, the telltale whoosh of fire catching synthetic fibers, but did not turn around to see it. Instead she stepped into the house and up the stairs, finding her way into the halls that were still stained with the blood of her friends.

She stepped past Chad's room, paused, then entered without knocking. He was standing over a suitcase, packing a bag.

"You don't have to go, you know," she said, her voice even and emotionless.

"I do," he nodded. "I really do." He closed his case, snapped it shut, then turned to her. "I think what you mean is, you don't have to stay."

She winced, looking away from him into the shadows of the emptied room.

"Really? After all this... after what we found out... really?"

She pursed her lips, then nodded. "I think so, yeah. Really."

His eyes became wet, but it passed quickly. "When you figure it out... I'll be--"

"Very lucky," she finished for him, smiling.

He leaned in and kissed her, lightly, on the lips.

Before she could kiss him back, he turned, made his way down the hall, down the stairs, and away from the house.

Payson Airfield, The Past

Victor sat at the end of the airfield, watching as planes took off and landed one after another. He was wearing a checkered red shirt with the collar pulled up, over the top of his black tee. He had an off-brand bag of potato chips in his hand, the kind that overcompensated for a bland product with far, far too much salt.

Tash came around the corner of the bench and looked at him, frowning. He craved salt when he was in a bad place, she knew. "Our flight's coming in," she said, nodding to a dot in the far-off sky. It was a small airfield off of the main terminal, so small that on clear days they had patrons sit on a section of the runway with their luggage to wait.

Victor's rucksack was next to him on the tarmac. He was used to travelling this way. Tash had no luggage, just a bookbag stuffed with clothing.

"We'll be out of here before you know it, and we won't have to come back to this... place... ever again, okay?"

He nodded, then folded his empty bag to its smallest possible variation and then stood up, sliding it into his pocket. "I bought the house."

She blinked at him, her mouth opening slightly despite herself. She started to speak, stopped, then shook her head. "You... I'm sorry, you... what?"

"The house. The one Melquist was in... I bought it." He paused, waiting for her to say something. She didn't, so he continued, "I think we need a home base. A place to be when there's no other place to be."

"Because that happens so often," she said, rolling her eyes.

"Stop it," he said, forcing a humorless laugh. "We'll find time. Besides... those kids going out into the world, spreading out... I want to stay close by."

"Why the fuck for?" she huffed.

"I feel like this isn't over. Not yet."

She frowned. "Victor... that is a house of evil. Melquist kidnapped children. He brainwashed *children and turned his abuse into some kind of... some kind of religion. It. Is. Evil."*

He nodded with a frown that grew only at the end. "But it doesn't have *to be."*

She sighed, bringing up her hand and rubbing the bridge of her nose.

"Come on... we'll put in a pool table for you." He nudged her arm.

She sighed, rolling her eyes and turning them skyward.

He turned around to see their plane incoming, his facade failing and a look of desperation coming over him. "I need to do this." He paused. "It needs to be made right."

She waited, watching him a long moment... then nodded. She opened her arms, pulling him into a hug, which he embraced.

After a long moment, she looked past his shoulder, to the incoming plane. It was close now. There was another on the airfield not far from them, a man standing in front of it, sweeping.

It was a jet, large and modern. It was a sandy beige, its nose a silver tip and its wings splaying out with metal winces that looked like claws every few feet. They looked like talons, but at one point they'd carried payloads. The cockpit was a glass oval that peeked up from the nose of the craft, its window the gray tint of sunglasses.

The word freedom *had been stenciled across it in loopy*

black calligraphy.

She smiled. "Look."

He turned, following her line of sight until he found the plane. "So?"

She took him by the hand and started to walk with him toward it, leading him gingerly. "That's the point of this... why we're doing this, isn't it? To be free?" She smiled at him. It was a full smile, wide and toothy. "Isn't that what He wanted?"

Victor smiled, softly and wanly. Tash led them both to the man with the broom, already fishing her camera out of her bookbag. She led him to a spot roughly ten feet in front of the plane, told him to stay, then turned and got the attention of the man sweeping the tarmac.

She shooed Victor this way and that, guiding his position in the frame with her hand. When he asked why she was doing it, she said that she was getting him to cover up some of the letters, and he almost laughed. Almost.

When he was in position, she showed the custodian the back of the screen and how she wanted the image to be. He smiled and nodded, and she gave him twenty dollars. He smiled and nodded gratefully again, and she left him to take her position next to Victor, ducking under his arm and coming up so that it was around him.

He felt her smile against his chest, the beaming of her cheeks.

"Smile," she said, pinching his ribs.

He pursed his lips. "I don't feel like smiling."

She turned and looked up at him, her expression somber and serious as her lashes batted. "Smile anyway."

He paused, regarding her for a long, silent moment... then nodded.

They took the picture.

Outside Payson, The Present

Victor sat alone at his kitchen table, eating the last of his reheated Peanut Green Stew. He ate in silence, his shoulders hunched, the only sound in the house of his slurping.

Alice came into the kitchen from the eastern hallway. She stopped when she saw him, paused, then walked to the cupboard and began to pour herself of bowl of Frosted Flakes.

Abby came in from the southern hall behind him, touching the tense muscle where his neck met his shoulder. He turned and looked up at her, asking a question without asking it. She nodded, and he nodded back.

She stepped to the fridge and found a leftover omelette, stepped with it over to the countertop next to Alice, and put it in the microwave.

The two women looked at each other, paused, then nodded. Alice made a pot of coffee.

When the omelette was done, they both walked around the island in the middle of the kitchen, pulled out the chairs to either side of Victor, then sat next to him. Abby poured up a coffee for each of them, then a third cup, laying it gingerly in front of Victor.

He turned to her and smiled.

The three of them ate their meal in peace.

ENGEN TIMELINE

With over twenty novels spread over three different series by many different authors, the Engen Universe of titles is growing every day and into genres we couldn't have imagined! From the original ten book *Black Womb* thriller series, its crime novel sequel series *Xander Drew*, our flagship adventure title *Infinity*, or single-novels like *Jacobi Street* or *light|dark*, there's something in the Engen Universe for everyone with more books by more authors on the way soon!

...But how do the events relate to one another, chronologically? While some astute readers have guessed at the potential timeline (some accurately, some not), we're going to finally set the question of the Engen Timeline to rest.

Turn the page for an up-to-date guide of the ever-widening world of Engen, featuring the works of Ali House, Ellen Curtis, Andrea Hackett, Sarah Thompson, Jay Paulin, and Matthew LeDrew!

In the 10 Years Prior Black September

"Reptilia" by Matthew LeDrew
published in *light | dark*.
Danger descends on a small secluded town in the form of a deadly virus with fantastic and terrible side-effects. Can a small group of doctors escape alive?

Compendium by Ellen Curtis
Three short stories forming the basis for the Engen Universe's ties to suspense, genetic engeneering, and the supernatural. Features the stories "The Tourniquet Revival," "Falling into Fire" and "At Midnight, the Dawn."

"The Theogony" by Matthew LeDrew
published in *light | dark*.
A tale of young Theo Flaherty of the *Infinity* series and his time admitted against his will to the Black Springs hospital, where he learns to paint, and seeks out his father.

Black September

"Revving Engen" by Matthew LeDrew
published in *light | dark*.
A direct lead-in to both *Infinity* and *Black Womb*, Tasha travels to Coral Beach, Maine on a hot tip about a recently discovered young man with incredible abilities.

Infinity by Ellen Curtis & Matthew LeDrew
Faced with a destiny he's uncertain of, the enigmatic Victor must bring together four unique people with very special abilities… or face the tasks ahead alone. Guaranteed to excite!

Black Womb by Matthew LeDrew
Fifteen years ago, something happened in Coral Beach, Maine that resulted in the present death of a seventeen-year-old boy. Now four high-school students must try to solve the mystery… before the killer picks them off.

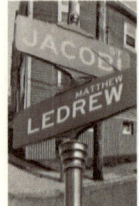

Jacobi Street by Matthew LeDrew
When a mysterious painting shows up at an art gallery he works at, Bob must work with Eddie and Sloan to track down its sinister origins and convince the people living on Jacobi Street of them, before its too late!

Transformations in Pain by Matthew LeDrew
When two girls are assaulted and one is hospitalized, the residents of Coral Beach must put their shared tragedies behind them and stop the man responsible, as well as unlock the secrets behind the true nature of the Womb…

Year One: October

Smoke and Mirrors by Matthew LeDrew
The approaching trial of Genblade brings closure to the people of Coral Beach, until people start showing up dead in the same manner they did when he was at large.

"Scarlett" by Andrea Hackett
published in *light | dark*.
Introducing Scarlett, the slightly damaged hunter on a mission to save others from the monsters from her past.

"The Inevitable" by Ali House
published in *The Lightbulb Forest*
A young woman must contend with the
emergence of a frightening new power alongside
the emotional high of a first date.

The Tourniquet Reprisal by Curtis & LeDrew
A man lives in Atlanta, Georgia that people
don't talk about, but everyone knows he's there.
He arrived a year ago and turned a gaggle
of uneducated youth into something new,
something to fear.

Roulette by Matthew LeDrew
As the teen suicide rate in Coral Beach starts to
climb astronomically fast, Xander travels to Los
Angeles to fight his most terrifying adversary
yet… and learns that the only thing worse than
looking for release… is finding it.

Year One: November

Exodus of Angels by Curtis & LeDrew
Victor's enigmatic past is illuminated when
Jaycee accompanies him to visit a new friend
in the paliative care ward of the Black Springs
hospital, where Theo also happens to be
searching for a cure for Leigh.

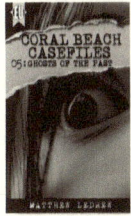

Ghosts of the Past by Matthew LeDrew
Coral Beach faces its most awesome threat when
one of Engen's past mistakes is unleashed upon
the unsuspecting populous. Friends and enemies
unite to fight a common enemy… but will even
that be enough?

Touch Your Nose by Matthew LeDrew
Simon Monk must infiltrate the San Fransico branch of Shane Industries, a massive company with deep ties to the Engen Universe. Where do his true loyalties lie? And can he get out without causing harm?

Ignorance is Bliss by Matthew LeDrew
After being set through the ringer one too many times, Xander decides that his life with Julie needs a little more attention… which is bad news because a new villain has come to town with his sights set on Adam Genblade.

"Gristle While You Work" by Jay Paulin published in *light | dark*.
A short story centering around the rise of a new, and possibly cannibalistic, serial killer in the Engen Universe.

Becoming by Matthew LeDrew
For months Xander Drew has been doing his level best to keep the streets of Coral Beach clean, which means it's time for the forces of darkness to strike back… all at once.

Inner Child by Matthew LeDrew
Julie is hospitalized with life-threatening wounds to both body and soul. But the real threat comes from the hospital walls themselves, as a demonic presence makes itself known to Xander and his friends.

End of Year One

Gang War by Matthew LeDrew
The Tees, a homicidal gang of evil men, has finally been taken down by Xander Drew. But his victory is short lived, as retired Tees are mysteriously killed. With a town of suspects, anyone can be the culprit… including one of their own.

Chains by Matthew LeDrew
Sociopath Derek Smith has been freed from prison and is praying on the weak; and none are weaker than August Styles: a pregnant girl with Down Syndrome who has run away from home.

"Omega" by Ellen Curtis
published in *light|dark*.
A sinister division of Engen begins a series of experiments on pregnant women in a fashion eerily similar to those that created the original Black Womb project.

The Long Road by Matthew LeDrew
Xander meets the American people — and realizes that the world is harsh and wicked, but can also be soft and gentle, even loving. Xander Drew comes of age on the road, and sets his new direction.

Year Two

Cinders by Matthew LeDrew
Detective Horton enters a violent and dangerous world he didn't know existed beneath the veneer of order and structure that he has based his entire deductive method around.

Sinister Intent by Matthew LeDrew
One of the killers Detective Horton could not
catch has resurfaced: a serial killer who flaunts his
sinister intent in front of the Los Angeles Police
Department, making it so that no one is safe.

Faith by Matthew LeDrew
Xander's mysterious and troublesome past returns
to haunt him on the streets of Los Angeles; a place
where even more people can get caught in the
crossfire of the games of death and deceit that
makes up his life.

Flickers in the Night by Matthew LeDrew
Lisa Rowdan is hunted by her haunting -- and
powerful -- ex-boyfriend Ryan through a lonely
city street. Can she escape him?
One of over twenty great sprine-tingling short
stories!

Garden of the 8th Circle by Curtis & LeDrew
Victor brings Chad, Abby, and Alice into a
dangerous conflict a decade in the making,
fighting an out of control cult for the fate of a
young soul. Meanwhile, Theo investigates a
mysterious event in Los Angeles.

Family Values by Matthew LeDrew
Xander and his new friends Crowley, Lisa, and
Tim investigate a series of kidnappings and
murders that stretch back decades, all of which
have the same similar twist: victims being found
after years of being missing.

Fate's Shadow by Matthew LeDrew
When one of Xander's old cases comes up for trial, Megan Greene returns with it. The former friends are led into conflict regarding her client's innocence. However, they put their difference aside when they both become targets of the vigilante known as Shiro Gilbert.

The Future

"Remers" by Sarah Thompson
published in *light | dark*.
In the not-too-distant future of the Engen Universe, young athletes are the targets of a scouting program to create the next stage of super soldier with cybernetic enhancements.

THE XANDER DREW SERIES

COMING SOON FROM ENGEN BOOKS:

FIRST AID

When Xander takes his feud with mob boss Stephen Fields to the streets, his attracts the attention of the *Infinity* team of Tash, Nick, Kelly, and Iseult. Before the arrive, he'll have pushed the mob boss into an all out gang war, the likes of which the city will never recover from.

DARK STORIES FROM ENGEN BOOKS

THE HOWL BECONS

Werewolves and a dark family secret in Northern Labrador! Growing up without his father, Tyler had no way of knowing the horrible secret that has plagued his family for generations. To free himself and find the cure, he will have to look beyond himself and into his dark history.

"The perfect mix of suspense and literary storytelling, Werewolves as metaphor for the original sins of Newfoundland & Labrador make this book the best in its class ,"
— Matthew LeDrew, author of *Infinity* and *Xander Drew*.

WESTON'S WAR

Something evil grows in the heart of Colorado. Bill Weston was a man of the West. He knew it – its land, its people, its stories. It was where he plied his trade, hunting men for money. His life wasn't easy, but it was predictable. That all changed when he captured Faraway Sue and he was led on a trip through the Colorado forests

"Take a little Zane Grey. Add a little Penny Dreadful. Read with Sam Elliot's voice. Discover Jon Dobbin's masterful The Starving." — Darrell Power, Great Big Sea

FANTASY FROM ENGEN BOOKS

HEED THE CALL

After a heated fight at sea between twins Ben and Alex, Ben vanishes from their boat without a sound or even a ripple in the water. Unwavering in his dedication to find his brother, Alex begins the adventure of a lifetime armed only with the help of a local girl named Meg and his own mysterious musical abilities... the key to which, and to the mysteries that surround him, may be tied to the alluring song of the dangerous girl he finds among the ocean's frothing waves.

"A mysterious figure in the ocean, a suspicious loss in the waves, a riveting treasure hunt, and surprise after surprise, how could anyone not want to read this novel?"

~Alice Kuipers
author of Life on the Refrigerator Door

"Loved this book and can't wait for the next one."

~Helen Escott
bestselling author of Operation: Wormwood

"It's been a while since I've read an entire book in one day, but...Whenever I tried to put it down, it would call out to me, luring me back like a siren's song."

~Ali House
author of The Six Elemental & The Fifth Queen

"Call of the Sea seamlessly weaves together the hardships and humour of rural Newfoundland life with a fantastical storyline that will leave you wanting more. This book will not disappoint."

~Lauralana Dunne
author of Ashes

The early years of **Xander Drew** as he struggles with the evils of his small rural hometown of Coral Beach, Maine. Cursed with the heart of the Womb and the gift of seeing the world around him for what it really is, Xander must learn the hard lessons about the nature of humanity to traverse the minefield of criminals, gangs, and abusers that stand between him and ultimate happiness -- but most of all that **sometimes it takes a monster, to catch a monster.**

"THE WRITING OF ITS GENERATION- - VISUAL, TO-THE-POINT AND IN-THE-MOMENT."

- The Northeast Avalon Times

The Coral Beach Casefiles series by Matthew LeDrew:

For more information, please visit

www.engenbooks.com

SUPERHERO FANTASY FROM ENGEN BOOKS!

infinity

The world is changing, and we have to change with it. That was the one thing that Victor was really sure of when he started looking for special people: people who could change the possibilities of the future from something certainly grim... to something *infinitely* positive.

Now four unsuspecting people from different backgrounds and walks of life have been thrown into the mix together, and nothing will ever be the same. But there's a difference between hoping for a better world and actually having one, and there will always be resistance to change.

Written by the superstar team of Ellen Curtis (*Compendium*) and Matthew LeDrew (the *Xander Drew* series).

Destiny doesn't wait for anyone.

about the authors

Ellen Curtis is a writer and web tv personality born and raised in St. Johns, Newfoundland; whose aptitude for the written word began at a young age, when she began writing short stories, poetry, lyrics and novellas.

She was 'discovered' at a Sci-Fi on the Rock writing panel in 2008, and her first collection of stories, *Compendium*, was published just over a year later in October 2009.

She has written three novels for the Infinity series, a book of short stories, and is co-editor and co-creator of the *From the Rock* series.

In her spare time she enjoys reading, art, music and spending time near the ocean.

Matthew LeDrew holds an Honours Degree in English from the Memorial University of Newfoundland with a minor in Anthropology, and studied Journalism at College of the North Atlantic in Stephenville, Newfoundland. He was honoured to be a jury member of the 2018 NLBA awards.

He has written twenty-one other novels for Engen Books: the ten book Coral Beach Casefiles series, *The Long Road, Cinders, Sinister Intent, Faith, Family Values, Fate's Shadow, Jacobi Street, Touch Your Nose, Infinity, The Tourniquet Reprisal,* and *Exodus of Angels* the latter three of which with co-author Ellen Curtis.

He lives in St. Johns, Newfoundland.

www.ingramcontent.com/pod-product-compliance
Lightning Source LLC
Chambersburg PA
CBHW030552020726
47494CB00005B/1586